BLOOD, SW

THE 1992 IAN ST JAMES AWARDS

Judges

BLOOD,
SWEAT AND TEARS

The winners of
the 1992 Ian St James Awards

Fontana
An Imprint of HarperCollinsPublishers

Fontana
An Imprint of HarperCollins*Publishers*
77–85 Fulham Palace Road,
Hammersmith, London W6 8JB

A Fontana Original 1992

1 3 5 7 9 8 6 4 2

Copyright © The Ian St James Trust 1992

ISBN 0 00 647293 1

All royalties from the sale of this book will be paid to
the Ian St James Trust and used for the furtherance and
expansion of the Ian St James Awards

All events and persons represented in these stories are
fictional, and any resemblance to actual events or persons
living or dead is purely coincidental

Set in Linotron Sabon

Printed in Great Britain by
HarperCollins Manufacturing Glasgow

Foreword

Over the past four years, a certain weekend in early
summer has acquired the characteristics of a ritual,
surprisingly perhaps since it is dependent upon the
weather and a fine weekend in early summer must never be
taken for granted. Luckily it is a moveable feast and I have
several from which to choose, since it can be any weekend
from the middle of April to the beginning of June. So from
mid April onwards I sniff the air, cast looks at the sky and
listen to the weather forecast with more than usual interest
– waiting for a spell of good weather likely to last two or
three days, for this special weekend starts early on Friday
evening and finishes late on the Sunday.

The weekend concerned is the one set aside to read the
fifty manuscripts selected by the readers as pick of the crop
for the current year's Awards – and every year those
manuscripts have provided a weekend of sheer enjoyment.
Beneath a tree, deep in the garden beyond earshot of
telephones, sustained by a bottle or two of wine, bread,
cheese and some fruit – I plunge into the carton of stories.
The variety has always been there, for the stories are as
diverse as the authors themselves – but what has surprised
and delighted the judges is a quality which scales new
heights every year – leaving no doubt that some of this
year's Award winners will join those from the past who are
already establishing themselves as professional novelists.

By choice and design I am merely one of the judges and
every year seven or eight distinguished people, all pre-
eminent in their respective fields of endeavour, deliberate
over the top fifty stories and it is the cumulative result of
the votes cast by all of the judges that decides who of the

final fifty become the twelve Award winners for the year. A list of the year's judges appears elsewhere in this book. As with judges in previous years they have all freely donated their time and expertise as their contribution to the work of this small charity. To them, we are greatly indebted – as indeed we are to a very large number of people, to whom I should like to express grateful thanks.

So many people contribute to these Awards that it is difficult to know where to begin, but may I start by conveying the special thanks of my bank manager to HarperCollinsPublishers and Parker Pen who have helped me meet the cost of running these Awards during the past four years. Without their generosity, the Awards might not have come into being, let alone have become the sought-after platform for thousands of aspiring authors throughout these islands. Thanks are also due to booksellers and Parker Pen stockists everywhere for making entry forms to these Awards available on every high street in England, Ireland, Scotland and Wales. In similar fashion *Bookcase* magazine, *Books* magazine, *Writers' Monthly* and *Writers News* all distributed entry forms to their millions of readers – and to them we are equally grateful. May I also thank my many fellow writers who by their attendance at various functions have helped advance the cause of the Awards – and finally Merric Davidson for the unflagging energy, expertise and dedication which he has brought to the administration.

To the authors whose blood, sweat and tears have won them a place in these pages, I offer heartiest congratulations and best wishes for the future. To the readers of this book, may I suggest that you choose a fine weekend, take a chair into the garden, uncork a bottle of wine, open this book ... and enjoy.

IAN ST JAMES
June 1992

Contents

If you would like to enter the Ian St James Awards and would like to receive further information, please contact:

Merric Davidson
c/o Editorial Department
HarperCollinsPublishers
77–85 Fulham Palace Road
Hammersmith
London W6 8JB

A WEEKEND
IN MONTEVIDEO

Belinda Caminada

Belinda Caminada was born in Beirut but grew up in London. After reading English and History at Hull University, she took off on some travels which included crewing a square rigger across the Pacific Ocean.

Following unsuccessful attempts to adjust to an office environment, she went to the Falkland Islands where she ran the local newspaper for two years. She is now back in London, working as a researcher for a small international news agency.

A WEEKEND
IN MONTEVIDEO

A weekend in Montevideo. I said it several times, trying to see if I could make it sound like a weekend in Paris or Manhattan. I couldn't. It didn't. But there was something in the last two syllables, especially if sprawled on an exaggerated Spanish accent, that gave it hope. A weekend in Monty-vee-dayo.

'Dayo' had a religious ring. Perhaps it was less of a sentence and more of an invocation. But religious thoughts, even frivolous ones, were difficult to pursue when I was lying as I was; resting on my head and shoulders on the bed with the rest of my body propped against the wall, feet facing the ceiling.

It is one of two habits I picked up from a cherished schoolfriend at the age of nine or ten. The other was picking noses, usually my own, but that pursuit had soon been broken by my mother. She had less success weaning me off this one which I think came with a let-out clause that I would grow out of it. I didn't or at least I haven't. There is some petty relief in finding that mother isn't always right.

Stephanie had copied the upside-down habit from her aunt. There could be no better source. 'Gravity,' Steph would say in piping mimicry, 'is our foe so upside down we go. It'll stop our tits from drooping.'

'But we haven't got any,' I remonstrated once.

'Can't start too early.'

3

So it was that when we were idle, which I suppose wasn't often, we would prop ourselves against a nearby wall or cupboard (doors were not favoured), whilst we pondered life and its limitations. The answer to any problem or the inspirational cure to the curse of childhood – boredom – could be found by gazing beyond two skinny legs and a pair of scuffed sandals to the vacuum which lies below all ceilings.

Amongst other things, adulthood showed me that gravity was not fooled by the stratagems of Stephanie's aunt. Neither are designer suits as tolerant of such manoeuvres as school dresses. Nevertheless the habit remains, although it now takes a little longer to find the balance – whether because of age or height I suspect I shall have to wait until I am older and shrivelled a little to discover.

This Uruguayan ceiling, my first Uruguayan ceiling, was less bland than those in most hotels. There was an interesting collection of marks to the right of my feet but as one who doubts fortunes being found in tea leaves, I was reluctant to interpret weekend plans into ceiling stains. The upside-down on this occasion felt uncomfortable. It seemed to be requiring effort to stop my legs from falling off the vertical. Perhaps it was something to do with being on the fourteenth floor or just fatigue but it felt wrong and I didn't like the thoughts which had started to seep into my mind.

I crumpled back to the bed, tucked my blouse into my skirt and fumbled for the telephone directory on the bedside table. I thought I was looking for the number of a national newspaper but on the same page as *Diarios*, I found the fate cast in my ceiling. There between *Destructoras de Documentos* and *Detergentes*, was the listing *Detectives*.

There must be few occasions when it's an easy choice

4

to pick one private detective from a directory, but this was one of them. When you're a foreign stranger in an obscure South American country – one whose telephone kiosks, advertisements and notes you don't recognize, let alone understand – fourteen floors above a city whose language you don't speak, hiring a private detective is merely adding one oddity to a stack of them. After two and a half weeks of solo travelling, I was so far through my looking-glass it seemed as natural as calling room service.

'Detective Alvaro Carnelli?'

'*Si*,' he growled.

'Speak English?'

'*No*.'

'Oh. Well, I'm sorry but I don't speak Spanish but I want . . . *investigaciones privadas*. I need your help.'

There was an uneasy pause before the growl barked: 'Wait.'

Investigaciones privadas. I had used his advertisement as a cue sheet. Private investigations lightly done and a bottle of mineral water to room 1412, please.

'Hello,' said a new smooth voice. 'I'm Jorge Carnelli, Alvaro's brother. Can I help?'

After a brief, disjointed three-way conversation in two languages, Jorge and I agreed that the three of us would meet in a nearby café.

'You don't want to come my hotel?'

'Oh no, thank you,' said Jorge politely over Alvaro's Spanish mutterings in the background. 'Alvaro doesn't like your hotel.' I couldn't blame him but still I felt offended.

'And what is Alvaro saying now?'

'Oh, well, he . . . He says perhaps he don't like your investigation. Perhaps we meet, have a drink, have a talk and then he says if he do your investigation. You know,'

5

he added with a kindly laugh, 'my brother is strange. He don't like working for women.'

It was only when I was waiting for the lift that I began to have second thoughts about meeting a misogynist Uruguayan private detective. I had been on my tour of Latin America for two and a half weeks. Rio had been difficult, Lima had been frightening. The work schedule had been fairly frantic until now and it had been difficult to relax on anonymous evenings, isolated in a hotel room. I was tired. Too tired to start digging back over the past. I hadn't thought this thing through. It was merely a whim and a dangerous one at that. Perhaps the weekend would be better spent taking foam baths and eating chocolate in bed.

With a shrill 'ping', the lift landed amongst the chocolates. Alberto, the bell boy, resplendent in a uniform which carried more gold braid than a five-star general, and a South American five-star general at that, welcomed me with an over-stretched grin. It was time to practise his English.

'The weather his cold this hevening. You must ride a taxi or you will be cold.'

'I shall be fine,' I replied. 'I come from England, I'm used to the cold.' I was speaking like Mary Poppins but it was worth the effort. Alberto had had an English conversation and he gurgled with appreciation.

As it was late September, my body was programmed for autumn. Uruguay was in its spring but there was little to distinguish between the two as I walked across the darkened Plaza Independencia, hunched against a stiff, cold wind which raced up from the sea to frolic with the litter and palm trees.

The café was simple, cheerful, warm and welcoming. So was Jorge Carnelli, but not Alvaro. He remained slumped at the table, coldly appraising me over a

6

cigarette whilst Jorge, slim and blithe, leapt to his feet.

'Nina Armstrong?'

'Yes, hello . . .'

'I am Jorge,' he shook my hand, 'and this is Alvaro.'

Alvaro nodded curtly through a heavy breath of smoke, clenched his jaw and narrowed his eyes. The brooding silence looked like being an equally serious performance and I was grateful that negotiations were going to be conducted through the amiable Jorge. I opened my mouth to begin.

'Why are you in Uruguay?' Alvaro broke in flatly.

'I'm on business here.'

'What business?'

'I'm a journalist.'

He grimaced.

'Writing what? For who? Why come to Uruguay? There's no news here. Nothing happens here. Go to Peru, El Salvador, Colombia or Brazil. Why here?' he sneered.

'And why all these questions?' I replied sharply. 'Besides, I thought you couldn't speak English?'

He shrugged and scowled into his drink. 'A little.'

'Here is the waiter!' Jorge broke in cheerfully. 'What will you drink?'

'Red wine, please.'

'As you're interested,' I continued calmly, 'I'm writing for an English magazine, a news magazine. I'm writing a piece about the economic changes in South America and I have been to Brazil, Peru and Argentina but not Colombia or El Salvador. That's my job but as I've called you about a private matter, it's irrelevant.'

'Perhaps,' shrugged Alvaro, fumbling for another cigarette.

Jorge leant across the table and smiled keenly into my face.

'Yes, we understand. But this "irrelevant", what does it mean?'

'It means it doesn't matter. It's not important.'

'I understand,' he said again smoothly.

It was difficult to believe the two were brothers, if they were. Alvaro's heavy, soured features suggested his contempt extended to himself whereas Jorge, with his swept hair and neatly manicured moustache, looked the picture of a Latin ladies' man.

'Ah, your wine. Have some wine.' Jorge poured me a brimming glass.

'I hear you don't like working for women. Is there any point in discussing my . . . idea, if you're not going to do it?'

Alvaro looked darkly expectant at Jorge who translated earnestly. Either he was unaware that his brother was taunting me or, like me, chose to ignore it. With an equally brisk willingness, Jorge translated Alvaro's grumbled response.

'It depends. Perhaps, if it's different from most women's jobs he will do it. You must tell us first.'

'And what are most women's jobs?' I asked.

Jorge smiled apologetically. 'Well, you know, some women . . .'

'All women.' Alvaro broke in in heated English. 'Their moods, their emotions, tell them they have problems. Problems big enough to pay a detective but every time it is the same. They want me to tell them who their husbands sleep with. Or they want me to tell them if their husbands know they sleep with other men. It's dirty, yes,' he spat, 'but also it's so small. A detective to them is just a support for their . . . vain-ity. Buy a new lipstick, buy a new dress, buy a detective for a few weeks, make you feel important.

'Whatever I do is always wrong. I say, yes, their husband sleep with another woman and they cry and scream and . . .' He waved his hands over his head in an exaggerated mime of hysteria.

'I say their husband not have lovers and they say I lie or I am bad at my work. They don't want *the* truth, they want *their* truth. They don't understand things. Their minds and hearts are' – he mashed the air in front of him – 'garbage.

'You know, once this woman comes to me and says "my husband has a young lover. I must know the size of all her clothes, *all* her clothes, especially her, her . . .",' he scowled at the elusive English word, 'her *sostén*', he finished, planting his heavy hands on his broad chest in a parody of breasts.

I smiled.

'Did you take that job?' I asked gently.

For the first time I found myself looking straight into his eyes. For a moment I thought I saw a glint of humour in their depths but then suspicion flared back. He quickly dropped his hands and shrugged. Jorge bent over and remonstrated softly with him in Spanish.

'I say to him, these are not things to say to a woman,' he explained, turning back to me. 'An English lady,' he added glibly.

'It doesn't worry me,' I replied. 'My job's not like that. I'm not hysterical or emotional.' I ignored Alvaro's snort. 'I just want facts.' I finished and waited whilst Alvaro continued glowering in silence at the unlit cigarette in his hand.

'So,' he said softly, stretching for his lighter, 'what is it you want me to find out?'

I sipped at the wine.

'It's quite simple. I have a friend who I used to know in London, who I think is living somewhere in South America. She could be anywhere but I think, well, there's a chance she's in Uruguay . . .'

'Why do you want to find her again?' He scrutinized my face.

'I'm just interested. We lost touch.'

'So what happened? She took your man?'

'No.'

'Took your money?'

'No.'

'You were lovers?'

'No! Look, I said it's nothing like that. There's no scandal, no drama. We grew up together. I just want to know if she's here, if she's okay. We were good friends . . .'

'And if she is in Uruguay and I find her, you will see her?'

'Perhaps. Probably. I'll see.'

'So if she is a good friend why are you not sure you want to meet her again?'

'Look, your job, if you want it, is just to find out if she is here. That's all.' I tried to hold Alvaro's cool dark look but failed.

'What's her name?'

'Stephanie Allen.'

Even here, even now, the words were difficult to say.

'Why do you need a detective for this? Two, three calls will be all it'll take. There are only three million Uruguayans in Uruguay and what, a few hundred English, if that? Call the English Club tomorrow and they'll tell you if she's here.'

I hadn't thought of that.

'She won't be a member of that sort of club. Anyway, I haven't got the time. I only arrived on Friday and went straight into meetings. I've got a lot more on Monday and I leave on Tuesday . . .'

'You go Tuesday?' Jorge seemed sad. Alvaro was scathing.

10

'You give me three days to find your friend?'

'You've just said yourself that there aren't many English people here. It's a small community. If she is here, I suppose someone will know. But if you don't think you can do it then okay, don't do it.'

A wave of fatigue washed over me and I wished I was in a foam bath, fourteen floors above my unease. Alvaro barked at a waiter for another beer.

'Stephanie Allen,' he said slowly, studying my face. 'Why do you think she will be in Uruguay? Most Europeans go to Buenos Aires or Rio. Why Uruguay?'

It was my turn to shrug.

'It's just a hunch.'

Some hunch; blended only from Steph's appetite for the improbable and a distant comment of hers. She had been studying the globe in Tim's study and had been curious about the small state, wedged between the expanse of Brazil and Argentina. She had investigated – a bit – and reported back. Uruguay was the size of England and Wales together and the second largest exporter of wool in the world, she said. It had few people, most of whom were either of Spanish or Italian descent and lots of old cars. The ideal antidote to London, she had suggested: 'A sheep farm, an old Ford with sideboards and a couple of Italians each – what do you think, Nin?'

'Which would she like more – the city or the *campo* . . . the country?' said Alvaro.

'The city. If she's in Uruguay, I'm sure she'd be in Montevideo.' Whatever her fantasies about sheep farming, Montevideo would give her a better audience.

'So describe this Stephanie Allen.'

It was difficult but I gave him the basics. Age twenty-seven, medium height, thin with shoulder-length brown hair – at least it had been that when I last saw her two years ago. She had also been unmarried then. Blue eyes. Bright blue eyes.

'And how does she dress? What does she like to do?' Alvaro was scribbling notes on to a paper napkin.

'It depends. It can change according to her mood. Sometimes she can be very modern, even outrageous, like shocking. But not all the time. She likes going to the cinema and she's musical. She plays the violin and the guitar.'

'Did she work in London?'

'She had lots of different jobs. She was a waitress, a secretary, a busker, a photographer, a musician. Sometimes she made jewellery and sold it in a market. But most of the time she was a waitress.'

That was all I could think of to say. A paltry accounting of a lifetime's friendship. Thinking of her was difficult at the best of times and doing so between the glib charm of Jorge and Alvaro's sour scorn was making it even harder.

'How much will this cost me?' I asked abruptly.

Alvaro smiled darkly and teased the edge of the napkin notes between two thick fingers before he replied in Spanish.

'It depends how long it takes,' Jorge translated, 'and how far Alvaro must travel, most times he charges one hundred and fifty dollars a day . . .'

'Standard charges, travel and expenses on top,' Alvaro added quickly in English.

'One hundred and fifty dollars for what you say will be a few phone calls! Forget it.'

Alvaro shrugged. 'I guess it would be cheaper to do it yourself.'

There was a long silence. The best thing would be to leave but something held me heaped in my seat, sinking

12

through the café's moist warmth and murmur. I kicked back to the initiative.

'If you make some phone calls tomorrow and call me later to tell me what you find out, I'll give you eighty dollars,' I said finally.

Alvaro pouted, his eyes glowering at where his hands toyed with the cigarette packet, turning it on one end and then the other.

'US dollars, not *pesos*. Forty in advance,' he said.

I pulled my purse from a pocket and dropped a few shabby *pesos* notes on the table.

'That's for the drinks, and this' – I added a twenty US-dollar bill – 'is the advance. I'll give you sixty more tomorrow.' I got to my feet.

'Oh stay, please,' cried Jorge, his eyes fidgeting between my face and my wallet. 'Have some food, yes? Dinner?'

'No, thank you.' I smiled reluctantly at his avaricious grin. His eyes flared keenly. I turned to Alvaro.

'Will you call me tomorrow? Have we got a deal?'

'Yeah I'll call you', he gave a twisted smile, 'mañana.' He lifted the twenty-dollar bill, read it and dropped it. 'Women's work,' he jeered softly as I left.

The next morning, the ragged events of the previous evening seemed remote. Reality was a bright morning, willing at the window. Somewhere in the sprawling conurbation below, under one of the cluttered rooftops, was Alvaro and his familiarity. This was mine. Up in the air. Outside peering in. Upside-down fumbling for the right way up.

On the dark landing, I pressed the lift button and thought: you have to be very strong to travel by yourself. Three days here, four days there. Checking in, checking out, check-mating yourself. Most of the numerous,

13

intricate props of your existence are stripped away. They lie back 'home', freeze-framed, along with the expectant post which bears the public password to the personal; the same one snared, in different tones, by the answering machine. Here, isolated, in thick foreignness where even civility, manners and particularly humour are distorted, where only kindness and cruelty can claim to be truly international, here there is no reassurance of you. The identity becomes weak, shifts and sometimes falters. So you look inside for confirmation, just to check that you're still there. But there is so much in there that you'd forgotten that there's foreign too. I thought I was strong enough, experienced enough to know the problems of over-contemplation. I should have known the minute I looked inside, there'd be Stephanie, cluttering up the hallway.

'It's cold today,' said someone. It wasn't me or Stephanie.

The face loomed nearer and the grin cracked wider. It was Alberto, still stabbing lift buttons and still eager to practise his language skills so he didn't have to.

'The sun shines but the wind is cold. No rain, however.'

'Oh good,' I said vaguely.

Alberto's soft brown eyes melted with sudden concern.

'Are you boring?' he asked gently. 'You look boring.'

'Yes, I probably am,' I laughed, waking up to the gold braid and the ground floor.

'We bring you good videos,' he suggested brightly. 'Stop you being boring.'

'No thank you, Alberto, I'm going for a walk.'

I walked briskly down Avenida 18 de Julio – Montevideo's equal to London's Oxford Street in the 1950s perhaps.

'The whole country is stuck in 1952,' a Uruguayan

14

journalist had told me the day before. 'That's the last time anything really worked properly; the economy, the welfare system, perhaps the government, and perhaps even our optimism!' he had added with a laugh.

I was too far off-base to know if he was right or not but the shops, with their exaggerated fittings and slogans, and yesterday's cars motoring smoothly through the taxis and the occasional horse and cart, suggested he might be. I didn't feel disorientated – a 1963 product of Wimbledon, walking through the heart of Uruguay in 1952. I was losing the person who claimed my passport.

I tried to lose myself further by ambling about the side streets, browsing deeply in the cluttered windows of the pawnbrokers. But the jewellery merchants with their fragile street stalls reminded me of Stephanie and when I thought of having lunch and found myself under the cheerful yellow awning of the café opposite the hotel, I remembered Alvaro's dark scowl and turned away. Down a side street, I found a cheap *parrilla* restaurant where the customers looked at me curiously and hushed to hear my clumsy, random recitals from the menu.

Where was Alvaro laughing now, I wondered. I felt sure that he wouldn't call me. Why should he stoop to 'women's work' when he got a couple of free drinks and twenty dollars out of an English woman who was due to leave in three days' time?

'Any messages for me?' I asked the hotel receptionist when I collected my key.

'No, no messages.'

Alberto was off-duty so I returned to my eyrie in silence and settled down to Friday's interview notes and tapes. Here was some confirmation of my existence, at least – in my notes, my tapes, my business cards. I stayed with the professional me for several hours.

It had grown dark outside and I was deep in agricultural matters, weighing a decline in meat exports against a boom in dairy produce, when the telephone jarred my concentration.

'Hello?'

'It's Alvaro. We must meet now, outside the Teatro Solis.'

'Why? I'm busy.'

'You ask me for facts, I have facts, okay.' Alvaro aggravated.

'You've found her?'

'I've found something. Hey, I don't have time for this talk. Come to Teatro Solis, now, okay. No more than ten minutes.' He hung up.

I tipped back on my chair and glowered at the ceiling. No, not okay.

'Alberto, where is the Teatro Solis?'

'Oh very near. Outside, in the Plaza Independencia. Er, *opuesto*, er opposite the hotel. It is a very good place. You go to concert?'

'No, I'm just going for a walk, to have a look.'

'Oh, it's a beautiful place. You will like it. You will not be boring at the Teatro Solis.'

I had a feeling he was going to be right. We reached the ground floor but my stomach carried on into the basement.

Alberto was right. The theatre was close and it was beautiful. The curving colonnades, sleek stone and marble evoked the city's past splendour. From the interior soft lights glowed. Outside, I found Alvaro's thick silhouette hunched against a pillar.

'Good,' he grumbled, grabbing my arm and hustling me inside.

16

'Where are we going?' I hissed.

'To a concert.'

'What!'

'*Rapido*!' urged a doorman, as we ran past into a curving corridor of rich red velvet. Clapping rippled from the auditorium.

'Alvaro . . .'

'Ssshhh.'

The applause faded and the lights dimmed as silence tightened over the audience. Alvaro stopped abruptly by the door of an empty box near the front. The stage lights caught his hard features as he glowered into them, waiting for the conductor to make his move before he made ours. The conductor lifted his arms and, in a warm rush, we were engulfed by Mozart. With mocking chivalry, Alvaro motioned me through the door. We sank on to seats by the low balcony. I looked around for some explanation but he kept his eyes locked on the stage. The orchestra was trilling loudly and I turned back to the earnest musicians.

Stephanie.

In the violin section, close to the front, there was Stephanie. Her face, set in a seraphic pose of flawless innocence; the slim fingers and wrist deftly manipulating the bow. Her hair was longer, darker, thicker and loosely, elegantly swept back in a gold scarf. But it was still Stephanie.

Near the end of the first half I finally turned to Alvaro. I anticipated mockery and triumph but found only cold indifference. It was almost as impressive a performance as Stephanie's.

I sat rigid until, with a flourish, the music died. As the applause erupted, Stephanie slowly lowered the violin, and her eyes, with a gentle smile. Without a word, I rose and left; walking briskly along the claustrophobic corridor, across the marbled lobby, to the darkness outside where the cold wind slapped me.

'Nina.'

Alvaro's voice stopped me on the bottom step. His shadow slithered down the steps to merge with mine.

'You said a few phone calls,' I said quietly. 'Why did you play that trick on me? Why didn't you warn me?'

'It's not a trick,' he replied evenly. 'I made the phone calls. Stephanie Allen was in Montevideo. Someone at the English Club said she was a member of the City Orchestra and they were playing tonight.' He shrugged. 'If I had told you she was here, you wouldn't have come – I don't think. It was better that you came as you did. You can see her. She doesn't see you. Then you can decide.'

'Decide what?'

'If you want to meet her.'

'No,' I snapped. For a minute I feared that Stephanie, never one to miss a cue, would come tripping down the steps. He sighed and shook his heavy head.

'Is this really all you wanted to know? That she is here and plays the violin in an orchestra? Perhaps she is married, has children, is in trouble, is rich or poor? I think perhaps there is something more?'

In my silence, Alvaro lit a cigarette and took a long draw.

'I'm meeting her after the concert. We're having dinner here.' He nodded towards the lights of the Theatre's west wing. 'Join us.'

I gazed at him. 'You know her?'

'No, I don't know her.' He scuffed his shoe against the step. 'I called her before the performance, said I liked her music and would she join me and two friends for supper?'

'And she agreed?'

'Yes.'

18

'Did you tell her about me, my name?'

'No. Nothing.'

'And if I don't join you for dinner?'

He shrugged.

'Then Jorge and I meet Stephanie Allen without Nina Armstrong.'

I stared at the ground. Start running. But I stayed where I was, thrashing against the indecision and shivering in the cold air. Alvaro gently cupped my elbow.

'Come on, let's go inside.'

'No.' I pulled away. 'The first half was enough. Thank you.'

'Okay. The restaurant then.'

Through a large revolving door we found the elegant El Aguila restaurant.

'I'm not dressed for this,' I mumbled.

In my rush to meet Alvaro's ten-minute deadline, I had left the hotel in a pair of old jeans and baggy sweater and felt even more conspicuous here than I had done in the theatre next door.

'It's no big deal,' Alvaro said with a dismissive wave of his hand. 'Anyway, when you're sitting down, who knows, who cares.' I care.

We ordered drinks and sat in silence until they arrived: I was still groping for a decision and Alvaro was preoccupied with his cigarettes. His face was smoother and less scrunched than it had been the night before and I wondered where his thoughts were.

'Why did you invite her for dinner? Are you going to expect me to pay more? Charge me further expenses?' The words came out harder than I had intended and he scowled.

'Where's the sixty dollars you were going to bring today?' he barked.

'I'm sorry I forgot,' I said feebly. 'I was in such a hurry to meet you . . . I can get it for you later' – an escape route opened before me – 'or now if you want.'

He shook his head.

'Later. We can sort it out later. I asked your friend because I think you want to meet her again. You don't want to want to, but you do.'

I could feel his gaze on my face as I toyed with his cigarette packet.

'You leave Montevideo on Tuesday. So if it all goes wrong, who knows it? Stephanie Allen, Nina Armstrong and,' he shrugged, 'a Uruguayan detective who you won't see again. What's the problem? What frightens you?'

'If I tried to explain, you'd laugh.'

'I don't laugh.'

Nothing in his face suggested sarcasm but somewhere behind the prickly machismo, I was sure he was laughing; jeering at the fool who paid him for 'women's work'. He was shrewd; he had found my weakness and wanted to make it pay. I didn't resent him for it. I had invited him into the shambles and he was out to make money from it. At least he didn't pretend otherwise. If I had failed to save myself from Stephanie and seemed unable to do so from Alvaro, why try and save myself from me.

Quietly I agreed to stay. Not for dinner but to meet Stephanie, providing he could think of a convincing story line for how we knew one another. How flattered she would be if she knew I had gone to the effort of hiring a detective. No problem, he said; he would think of something. Deception had been one of Stephanie's greatest talents but this was the first time that I was about to practise her art against her.

As Alvaro stood to leave, Jorge breezed in.

'Nina. It's so good to see you again. You look . . .'

20

Alvaro interrupted.

'I'm going to meet Stephanie. The concert finishes in a few minutes so I'll be ten or fifteen minutes.' He mustered a stiff smile for me. 'Don't run away.'

'I hope my brother has been kinder to you today,' Jorge said after Alvaro had been swallowed by the revolving door. 'He's a good man but he's bad to women. Oh no, he doesn't hit them or anything but you know, he makes them cry.' He assembled an expression of thoughtful concern. 'There are reasons,' he added obliquely.

'Did his wife leave him?'

Jorge looked up sharply. 'Did he tell you?'

'No, he's told me nothing. I just guessed.'

'She is so beautiful and very clever. But she played with him. I shouldn't tell you all this. He doesn't want anyone to know. But I think you are understanding, Nina,' he added earnestly. 'I think you see that he is hurt?'

'Are you married, Jorge?'

He told me of his wife, their home in Paysandú and how the factory where he had been a foreman had been closed down.

'I've come to Montevideo to find a new job, perhaps in a bank. Until then, Alvaro is helping me. But I miss my wife. I'm not like Alvaro. I like women. I understand them. I miss their company.'

He turned the conversation to my life in London. I tried to talk about the red buses, the football and the Royal family but Jorge wanted to know about my relationships. Not married? No boyfriend? How strange English women were. I was still pulling against the drive of his interrogation when the door shifted to disgorge Alvaro, chatting, and Stephanie, smiling.

Next to his bulky and awkward frame she appeared startlingly neat and slender. The black dress was well-cut

21

and flattered her slight figure. One hand clasped a shawl around her shoulders; the other carried her violin case.

I had never seen Alvaro's face so animated as he carried on talking smoothly, guiding her through the tables towards us. When he stopped, Stephanie lifted bright and serene eyes which snagged immediately on mine. Her face froze.

'Do you know each other?' Alvaro asked with a casual surprise. There was a pause.

'Yes, we were at school together,' I said stiffly, watching the fear and cunning struggle on her face. 'And we knew each other in London,' I added tentatively.

She recovered quickly.

'Nina! What a surprise!' The voice was endearing as she stepped forward and kissed me lightly on the cheek. Inside something shivered. 'What an amazing coincidence.'

The soft lilting tone was as unfamiliar as the measured movements of her new identity but the flash of suspicion which stabbed at Alvaro told me the raw Stephanie was still there and very raw.

Alvaro missed the look and offered her a seat.

'How wonderful,' he said smoothly. Wonderful was not a word I suspected Alvaro used often. 'Nina visited our trade union headquarters on Friday for an interview with my boss. And when I knew that Jorge and I would be having dinner with a talented English musician, I thought I'd get another talented English woman along.

'Travelling as you do,' he added politely to me, 'you must get lonely by yourself in hotel rooms.'

'Yes,' I replied lamely. How did Alvaro know I'd been to a trade union on Friday? Where had this immaculate English come from, and was this obsequious charm real or not?

'So you're travelling by yourself?' said Stephanie.

'Yes, I'm on an assignment here.' Alvaro's pomposity appeared to be infectious.

'What, *Parents and Prams* have sent you to Montevideo!' She laughed in the genuine, raucous way that so many people had loved in her. The Carnelli brothers stared in amazement.

'I don't work for them any more, I'm now working for *Global Business*.' I was on the defensive already. Stephanie leant towards Alvaro:

'When we were living in London together, some years ago, it was so funny. Nin was working for this magazine called *Parents and Prams* – you know, for young couples expecting their first child. She didn't know the first thing about babies but there she was, scribbling away about nappy absorbency, pushchair design, bottles versus breasts, etc. She had to be so serious about it all. It was absurd!'

Alvaro's rich laugh embraced hers.

'I had to start somewhere,' I mumbled but my words were lost in the breathy introduction Jorge had been itching to make since Stephanie's entrance. We ordered drinks but I declined to choose a meal.

'I'll have to go back to my hotel in a few minutes. My office is calling me,' I lied.

'On a Saturday night?' queried Alvaro.

'Yes, it's important.'

'It must be for you to miss a meal!'

It was a typical Stephanie comment; one that could have been harmless enough but it wasn't. It was also a familiar ploy. Conversations on food and body sizes never failed to draw her audience's attention to her slender frame. She had been practising her grace well. Sitting between Alvaro and Jorge, she looked like a gazelle who, with big nervous eyes, had been persuaded to come out and graze in public.

'Your English is so good, Alvaro . . .' she purred.

'Yes it is,' I added darkly, recalling our first meeting and the broken presentation I had received. I was sure that this suave and flirtatious Alvaro could prove equally adept at *sosténs* and bras.

'Where did you learn?' she prompted.

Alvaro looked uncomfortable.

'At school,' he said vaguely.

'He's being shy,' Jorge cried. 'He spent a lot of time in Europe. Paris mostly, but sometimes in London as well . . .'

It was obvious that Alvaro didn't want to discuss it, so it was equally obvious that Stephanie would make him.

'Why were you there?'

'There were some years when it was better not to be in Uruguay,' he said darkly, answering my silent question mark over his role during the military rule. Deftly, he swung the conversation around to music, Stephanie's music.

'I saw you in *The Magic Flute* and *La Traviata*. I was impressed,' he said smoothly.

'But I'm just one of many violins. How can you hear my playing?'

Alvaro shrugged and carried on gazing at her. 'I can't but I watch the faces of the musicians when they play and yours, well, it showed something . . .' He looked meekly into his glass and Stephanie blazed with a new thrill.

'You're very flattering.' Was there an edge to her comment? 'But I'm not that good, ask Nina.'

'That's not true. The Piccadilly and Circle lines loved you.'

It was the sort of joke that had once been the essence of our double-act humour, a line which in the old times she would have played on.

She was wounded.

'Oh yes . . . Well, there you are. When I was broke, all I could do was busk in the underground, as Nina says. But when I came to Uruguay, I knew no one, had nothing – and there isn't even a metro system here! I fell deeply in love with this man soon after I arrived. He was a politician. I better not tell you his name because he's still in the Congress. I tried not to but when I fall in love, I fall deeply. I can't help it. Anyway, of course it broke up. He obviously didn't feel the same about me – perhaps I was just a novelty,' she grimaced.

'Anyway, my heart was broken. I felt completely numb and the only thing that gave me any lift was my violin. I played and played and improved I suppose. Anyway, the Montevideo City Orchestra gave me an audition a few months ago, so now I have two jobs – teaching at the British school and playing my violin.'

'And love?' asked Jorge.

She looked down. 'Perhaps, some day . . .'

When their food arrived soon afterwards, it was the obvious time for me to leave but I knew that I had to hold out a little longer. The ache inside was deepening and I had to find a chance to ask her. I watched her accept another glass of wine. My opportunity couldn't be far off. It was Alvaro who led the way.

'So when did you two last see each other?' he asked, waving a casual hand between us.

'Oh, I can't remember,' Stephanie said breezily.

'June 1989.'

'Was it then?'

'Yes, just before the fire.'

Alvaro looked at me. 'A fire?'

'Yeah. There was a fire in the flat where we were living.'

She lifted her eyes and watched me closely.

'How did it start?' asked Jorge.

25

'No one's too sure. I wanted to ask you, Stephanie, do you have ideas?'

'About the fire? No.' Her tone was one of well-modulated concern. 'I told you on the telephone, like I told the police, I went out on the Saturday evening and came back the next day to find . . .' She shuddered.

'Was it a bad fire?' Alvaro asked me gently.

'The flat was completely gutted. Everything literally went up in flames.'

'At least it was insured,' she said.

'I got the money eventually, but it took a long, long time. The police and the fire brigade were very suspicious about how it started.'

'Did they have any ideas? Where did it start?'

'The damage was so bad, it was difficult for them to tell but they said that they were sure it started in my bed, the middle of my bed. I was away at the time.'

'A toddlers' toy fair in Scarborough,' Stephanie laughed dryly.

I continued: 'The neighbour upstairs tried to get in to put it out and got a few burns but fortunately no one was badly hurt. The worst thing was that, although the insurance company paid up, they couldn't replace all the personal belongings I lost. All my photographs and letters. All my mother's letters, her clothes, her furniture and her pictures. It was so upsetting. I lost everything.' I paused. 'Some of it I still miss.'

Her tight face ignored the cue.

'I know it was difficult for you,' she said softly, 'but it was difficult for me too. I knew you'd blame me. That's why I left so quickly.'

'Blame you? Why should I blame you?'

'Well, I was there. I was supposed to be looking after the flat and . . .' She stopped. The blood pounded in my head. And? But there was no 'and'. She kept a mournful,

26

mute vigil over her lemon sole. She was waiting.

'How's Nico?' My voice quivered but held.

'He's fine,' she spoke slowly. 'He's settled down well and loves it here.'

'I'd love to see him.' Despite my efforts it came out as the impassioned plea it was.

'I'm not sure that would be best – for him. For any of us.' At last she lifted those bright eyes. Cold. Defiant. Triumphant.

The telephone rang twice on Sunday. First it was Alvaro who said he wanted to know how I was. He said it was a shame I left when I did. They had had a good evening.

'I owe you some money,' I replied dryly. 'How much?'

A deep sigh crackled down the receiver. 'I think we agreed sixty dollars.'

I was surprised. So surprised that I said, 'You don't want more? What about the concert and the meal in the restaurant?'

'The concert was free,' he growled. 'We agreed sixty so let's stick to sixty. I'm busy today so I'll send Jorge to collect it this evening. Is six convenient?'

'That's fine. Well, thank you for your help,' I added lamely, silently cursing my mother for insisting on good manners at all times.

'You didn't tell me about Nico.'

'What about him?'

'Who is he?'

'It's none of your business. It doesn't matter.'

'I think it does. You started this so you should finish it. I have Stephanie's number. Do you want it?'

'No.' I hung up.

The second call came in the afternoon and was from Stephanie; the warm, exuberant Stephanie.

27

'Nin, it's me. Nico and I are downstairs in the lobby. We're going for a walk. Come down and join us.'

Alberto was in charge of the lift, with his weather reports and video reviews but I didn't hear any of them.

'Ground floor,' he said bitterly.

The doors parted and there they were. Stephanie in a long white raincoat, Nico at her side on a long gold chain.

He'd been a year old when I had last seen him but now he was a full grown shaggy dog. He still had the one drooping ear and the pink tongue peeping from his mouth. When I crouched down to touch him, he bounded into my arms, slapping his tongue against my face with relish.

It was impossible to hope that he remembered me but at least he was still the loving, enthusiastic bundle I had rescued from a sack dumped on a motorway. His four brothers and sisters had died that night but he had survived – with some assistance from Nico, the car mechanic who, when he arrived in his relay van, had proved to be as knowledgeable about dogs as he was about faulty alternators.

'Let's go for a walk,' said Steph, pulling Nico away. We stepped outside into the warm spring sunshine, turned right and headed into the old town. The narrow streets, bathed in a rich light, were deserted.

Nico trotted between us, his tousled snout gulping in the air, his glistening nose challenging every scent. With his mouth open, it looked like he was laughing.

How could I still have so much love for an over-haired dog after two years' absence? It was ridiculous. But he had arrived two weeks after my mother's funeral, fully prepared despite his bleak experience of manunkind, to offer all the love and support required, in return for a bowl of leftovers on the kitchen floor and a daily stroll round the park. To someone who had previously regarded dogs merely as other people's accessories and who had doubted the mawkish claims of panting dog-lovers, his love and fidelity had staggered me. On to Nico's shaggy head I had heaped all my bruised emotions. He became so precious to me that when Stephanie had taken him, my grief had nearly over-whelmed me.

Walking through this slumbering Sunday, two years later, Stephanie and I chatted normally. We talked of her life in Montevideo, my life in London and our friends from the past. We also talked briefly of Alvaro.

'Do you think he's attractive?' she said.

'No, not really.'

'I think there's something about him . . . He's asked me out for dinner again tonight.'

'Did you tell him you were meeting me?'

'No. I told him I was going for a walk and did he want to come but he said he was busy building crates or something.'

I was disappointed to learn that Alvaro's charm the previous night had not been an act but I suppose I couldn't expect too much for eighty dollars.

Finally we reached the sea where a few fishermen sat on the wide wall which jutted out into the slopping water. Stephanie slipped Nico off his lead and he raced off into the stiff tangy breeze, with the bounding gait of a rocking horse.

'Do you still go upside-down?' I said.

She looked at me curiously then laughed. 'God, I'd forgotten that. No, I don't. I think we must be too old for that now.'

'You told me it would stop my tits from drooping,' I teased.

'So I did.' She looked at me. 'Well, perhaps it worked. Ask me again in ten years' time.'

We followed Nico on to the sea wall.

'I thought at first that Nico had died in the fire,' I started bluntly, 'but the fireman said there wasn't the smallest shred of dead dog in the ashes. I made them look twice.'

'I know what I did was wrong, Nin, but you must have known I wouldn't hurt him.'

'And me?'

She turned to face me. This time the eyes' appeal was genuine. The same confused look that every misdemeanour elicited. The look that had persuaded me – on most occasions – that Stephanie was as bewildered by her own cruelty as were others. I'm out of control, she had once sobbed. Nin, help me.

'Why did you take Nico, Stephanie? When you knew how precious he was to me?'

She took a ragged breath. 'I wasn't thinking. I was so angry. The night after you left to go to Scarborough, I went round to see Tim. You and he had just split up . . .'

'Because I found you in bed together!'

'I know. I haven't forgotten either. But I loved him. I really did. You had just given me the week to find somewhere else to live, so I went to see if Tim, to see if he would have me.

'And?'

'He was furious and very spiteful. He said he loved you,' she gave a dry laugh, 'and accused me of seducing him. He said I'd killed off a special relationship. He said lots of things. Some of them were just . . . dreadful.' She blinked hard. 'When I got back to your flat, it suddenly seemed as if you had everything and I had nothing.'

'So you set fire to my bed, took Nico who you knew I doted on and pissed off to South America,' I said coldly. 'If it was anyone else, I'd have said it sounded unlikely, but knowing you . . .'

30

She smiled. 'Yes, I suppose I always have been rather dramatic. But you and I had talked so often about going away and yet it never happened. I was going mad with boredom.'

'My mother had been very ill for two years, I had a mortgage, very little money, a job and I had a dog. I couldn't just upsticks, Steph, I told you that. It had to wait.'

She beamed at me. 'Just like old times!' she laughed. 'Oh Nin, forget the past. I'm thinking of coming back.'

'Back?'

'Yes, back to London. I've been here over two years and I'm bored. I miss London. I miss you. I thought Carlos would marry me and we'd move to Brazil but . . .'

'Carlos?'

'My boyfriend. Didn't I tell you last night? He's administrator of the orchestra.'

'So where was he last night?'

'I told you. He's in Buenos Aires for a week.'

Nico galloped past barking loudly at nothing.

'Anyway, I thought, perhaps I'd come back and we could share a flat again. We could have one hell of a reunion party. I've really missed you.'

The appeal was genuine enough — help me get back under control.

'You slept with my boyfriends, "borrowed" money I never saw again, burnt down my flat and stole the one thing you knew I loved more than anything . . .'

Nothing registered in the blue distress signal.

'Forget it. There's no room for you in my life anymore.'

'There will be! I know it'll take time for you to trust me again but I'll . . .' She trailed off as she recognized my expression. Her face fell and stiffened.

'I'd bring Nico,' she said coolly. 'If you have me back, you get Nico back too.'

31

Nico was peeing against a bollard.

'No, Stephanie. Not even for Nico.' And I left.

Early on Tuesday morning, a taxi sped me along the coast road towards the airport. The city, still asleep, had its blinds and shutters closed against the sun's rich overtures and there were few people about; just the occasional Uruguayan jogger and a man walking his dog on the beach.

My briefcase was replete with notes and tapes. The draft article was well advanced and for now, at least, my assignment was done and I could relax a little. Monday had been a demanding day but I had been grateful for the tight schedule which had kept me preoccupied. I had heard nothing from Alvaro or Stephanie.

If I had decided anything about my weekend in Montevideo, it was that it should stay in Montevideo. The only regret, perhaps, was Nico. It was still there, twisting under my ribs, the pedigree love for a shaggy mongrel.

It was when I was at the airport, standing at the back of the check-in queue, that I looked round to find both of them standing there, watching me. Alvaro and Nico. Alvaro smiled at my shock.

'The English and their dogs,' he said with a laugh and a shrug. He watched me run my hands through Nico's thick coat.

'I saw Stephanie last night,' he said, flatly. 'We went for a drink, for a meal and then, back to her flat. I found out a bit more about Nico, about her and about you. This morning she . . . she didn't want to get out of bed, so I offered to take Nico for his early morning walk. So here we are . . .'

'She knows you're here?'

'No, I said I would just go round the block.'

I straightened up and gazed at him.

'I don't understand . . .'

'So, I've fixed it all at this end. I've built a crate which should suit everyone's specifications, including Nico's, and I've sorted it all out with the cargo authorities here. There's some paperwork still to do,' he waved a sheaf of papers before my nose, 'but they'll let you both on board.'

'But . . .'

'I called the British Embassy to find out what might happen at London – you know what the English are for their rules and discipline. They said they thought it will cost you a lot, in quarantine, and that there would be more paperwork there. But, the most important thing is that Nico can go back where he belongs.'

'I can't take him, Alvaro. He's been here for two years, it'll be too much of an upheaval for him. And Stephanie . . .'

'After what she's done to you?' He shook his head. 'Believe me, Nina, he'd be far better off with you. I've been to Stephanie's flat and seen the mess there. Her life and her problems aren't for him. It's not for Nico.'

He extended the leash towards me. I took it.

'I want a postcard from Nico, to say he's arrived safely,' he added, handing me a business card. *Investigaciones privadas*, it said.

'I got a good deal for eighty dollars.' I laughed.

'Yeah, well, we're just a small-time country . . .'

Finally I plucked up courage to look at him. 'I'm glad you still do "women's work".'

'So am I.' And he grinned, a wide open smile that transformed his face.

BETWEEN ME AND THE STARS

Peter Naylor

Born and educated in Bradford, Peter Naylor won an exhibition to Selwyn College, Cambridge where, after two years of learning Russian in the Army, he read Modern Languages. After a brief period in the wool textile industry he joined the British Council. He has lived and worked in Thailand, Poland, Pakistan, Argentina, Brazil and Greece and took early retirement in 1986.

In the following year he was appointed CBE. Peter now lives with his wife Barbara and family in Saffron Walden where he draws and paints.

BETWEEN ME AND
THE STARS

Julia is less the centre of my story than one of its corners, one of the four fixed stars which form my constellation. If I am the apex, the North Pole, she is the base-point on which all else rests. To one side is Pernel Mortimer; to the other, Killer Black. It is the figure in which I have lived for thirty-five years. Everyone else I have known seems, in comparison, to be no more than a briefly curving trail on my time-exposure of the heavens, existing in other dimensions, on other planes, different in kind from the four burning points of this quadrangle. Such as it is, my peace of mind throughout the years has depended on the constancy of their relative stations.

Now, the two lateral points are visibly closing on the Pole; the base has lost its brilliance, the illusion of stability can no longer be sustained and the consequences frighten me.

Chronologically, Julia comes later, a whole year after I met Pernel. But if I am to stick to the proper order, I knew Killer before either of them. We were in the army together. Killer; an odd name for someone who looked so vulnerable, with his thin knees always pressed tight whether he was sitting or standing. His shoulders bent round his narrow chest, forcing his fair, choirboy head forward. One of life's victims, perhaps, until you saw his eyes. They looked up at you from under pale brows, cold and blue, with tiny pupils whatever the light. During a boot-bulling session, when we were all sitting round the barrack-room stove, one of us said, 'Them eyes, they give me the screaming abdabs.'

Others joined in, relieved that the topic had come up.

'Yeah, right. Piss-holes in the snow . . .'

'It's worse than that. A zombie, more like . . .'

'He's measuring you for a coffin . . .'

'Or deciding whether to have your balls before or after the thumbscrews . . .'

'They're the eyes of a killer.'

So Killer he became. He didn't seem to mind. Now and then a crooked smile would appear on his face. He liked to be on the fringe of things, not an outcast but a man who walked a higher contour-line than the rest of us.

He and I were only together for a few months. He went away to become an officer while I stayed with the lads. My family didn't go in for pips; it was bad enough that I was going to Oxford rather than the local tech.

When that moment arrived, in 1954, when I stood in the golden gateway of St Saviour's with crowds of others, trying to identify my trunk in the mountain deposited by the GWR, the only familiar face I saw was Killer's. We hadn't known each other well enough to have talked about the future. I'd no idea that he had a place at Oxford, let alone at my college. I wasn't pleased to see him. He detracted from the legendary quality of the moment.

A scout was trundling his baggage away on a trolley. Killer looked at me with his hangman's eyes as we shook hands.

'So,' I said, 'here begins the first day of the rest of our lives.'

'A new phase, certainly,' he agreed, after a moment's thought.

Twit.

The day was too special to spoil. When Killer had gone I got another bloke to lend a hand with my trunk and then spent the next few days learning how to break college rules. I used to see Killer around. He was a Scholar. He had to wear a long gown which made him look like a blond vulture. He, like the rest of the world, slipped out of focus when Pernel appeared.

I first saw her in the Ashmolean, alone in one of the Renaissance rooms. She had her back to me. Pale golden hair streamed over the dark red woollen dress she was wearing. Wanting to see her face, I caused a commotion by pretending to trip in the doorway. She turned, startled, and from inside the waterfall of hair came half a smile and a soft grey look.

'Sorry,' I said. 'Careless of me.'

By this time I had stumbled a good way into the room.

'Enters, pursued by a bear,' I said, facetiously.

'It's exit, isn't it?' she said. 'Exit, pursued by a bear. *Winter's Tale*.'

We laughed. Then, as someone else came into that tumultuous room, we shushed each other like a pair of stage conspirators. All around hung blue Annunciations.

It developed from there. Coffee at the Kardomah, foreign films, tea and crumpets toasted over the gas-fire in my rooms, cycle rides and walks through winter fields, the touch of warm lips on cold cheeks. Very ordinary from outside, I dare say, but the secret side was coloured scarlet and ochre, tangerine and indigo, purple and emerald, all in swirls and vortices like the exquisite iridescence of insect wings but with the power of apocalyptic storms; glimpses of Eden through a screen of

39

despair and jubilation, fire and salve, under the silent recitals of the Aurora Borealis.

I exaggerate, of course. It was my first taste of passion and I let it overwhelm me unreservedly. Well, as unreservedly as she would allow. Pernel was an old-fashioned girl who believed that the final step, as she called it, was worth waiting for. I had twinges of regret about that but there were so many things to do to delight one another that it didn't seem to matter, not all that much. We loved each other and the world swelled to accommodate our happiness.

She was at Forster College, in her final year. The History of Art was her subject but she should have been at proper art school because she drew like an angel. She had friends, but I refused to ask her about them or, indeed, about her past, knowing that curiosity could only be satisfied at a price in jealousy that I wasn't prepared to pay. As far as I was concerned, she began in the moment we met.

When her parents came to Oxford they invited me to dine at the Randolph. The Mortimers were so rich that I was hostile from the start. Pa Mortimer liked to be called Brigadier, but he was a civvy now, just like me, so I wouldn't play. Mother was the usual twin-set and pearls type, quite pleasant even though I couldn't understand a lot of what she said. She and Pernel had this in common: they called things by their names. What to me was a tree, a bird, a horse, a weed, was to them an elm, a redwing, a gelding, a sow-thistle. It gave them an intimacy with the things named and therefore an illusion of power over them. Mrs Mortimer went further: she spoke in an impenetrable code which consisted of a multitude of personal names. Pernel, more elusive than ever behind the webs of hair which she continually pulled across her face, listened as her mother described how some names had drawn a covert, some had farrowed, one had been coppiced, one had covered several others, one had big-end trouble, two had married and any number had been slaughtered. Fields had names, bits of the garden had names, rooms had names, and, of course, the house itself had a name. Redwarden. Not House, not Manor, not Palace. Simply Redwarden. The pretentiousness of it made me squirm.

Relations between mother and daughter seemed shuttered: a whispery progression through secret passages where the girl didn't wish to be but was hustled relentlessly on. It was all very different from the way Mum, Dad and I went on at each other.

Pa Mortimer had a lot to tell me about the war. It was clear that he expected some sign of gratitude from the generation for whose sake he and his like had made so many sacrifices. I did try. At one point I even heard myself say, 'I only hope our lot would have done as well, sir.' When he replied, 'I doubt it,' I lost interest.

Instead, the devil rode out. I told him how shocked I had been during a visit to Germany the previous year to see a great city like Darmstadt reduced to a uniform five bricks high. When I went on to tell him how my German friends had suffered as children during the Allied thousand-bomber raids, I saw him drawing breath. Before he could speak, I said, 'We were bombed out of our house in Hull, you know. My baby brother was killed.'

I gave them my level look.

It wasn't true, of course, but it shut him up.

'I didn't know you'd had a baby brother,' said Pernel, so distressed for me that she held her hair away from her face with both hands. 'I thought you were an only child.'

My shrug was designed to convey the untold tragedy of the War at Home.

41

Later, I tried to explain to her why I had lied.

'The war's over,' I said. 'Old soldiers should only tell their tales to each other and leave the rest of us to get on with the future.'

She was surprisingly unforgiving and for a few days she went off me.

'You really shouldn't tell fibs like that,' she scolded.

'An only child has to lie,' I said. 'That's how he makes his privacy.'

Though she was a gentle girl, she was neither weak nor pliant. It was the first time she had found fault with me. I tried to laugh her out of her disapproval, but she went on, 'You have to be careful with words.'

'Not in Yorkshire you don't. Words are weapons. You attack or defend with them. The more you throw and the straighter they are, the more you're left alone.'

'Have it your way,' she shrugged. 'In my world words are deeds.'

Perhaps she was right, because what she said then sticks in my mind whereas it costs me an effort to recall much else that we said to each other all those years ago. Or I might have remembered because her words suggested a chink in her armour.

When she warmed to me again, she brought pictures of Redwarden for me to see. It must have been hard work balancing such large books on her bike. There was a coffee-table book on the English country house, a tome on Humphrey Repton who had improved the grounds, and yet another on Jacobean architecture. Even through my envy I saw what a beautiful place it was, all rosy pink at the top of meadows which tilted into a lake.

'One day,' I joked, 'all this will be yours.'

'It's not something to look forward to, believe me. A house like Redwarden, with all its history ... you can only ever be a tenant. It becomes your turn, like looking after an elderly relative. You're terrified it's going to die on you before you can decently hand it on. It's like a very slow game of pass-the-parcel. And it's going to be up to me. Poor Daddy, he did so want a son.'

I was never invited to Redwarden. Pernel must have asked her family but they wouldn't have me. In contrast, my mother and father responded enthusiastically when I proposed that Pernel should spend a week in York after her finals. The thought of showing her my country buoyed me up during the purdah which she entered as the exams approached.

Killer makes another appearance at this point. As far as I was concerned, he had become a distant planet, moving in his own orbit, surrounded by satellites who were mainly the nobs from the Augustan Society. Now and then I'd felt a chill, though, as his eyes rested on me.

One early summer evening I heard Pernel's footsteps in the quad. I hastily tidied away a few half-clean socks and waited for her. When she still hadn't come three minutes later, I shoved my head out of the window. Right underneath me she was talking to Killer. I couldn't hear what they were saying, but I noticed that the tops of Killer's ears were pillar-box red and that Pernel's hair eddied. She lifted a hand to calm it. Abruptly, Killer made an about-turn and stalked away. Within moments, Pernel was in my arms.

'What did Killer want?' I smoothed the hair out of her eyes with my tongue.

'Killer?'

'It's what we call the bloke you were talking to.'

She twisted away from me and plumped into a chair.

'Nothing, really.'

'Come on. He's like you. He's careful with words. I want to know.'

43

She didn't want to tell me. At last she said,

'He warned me off you.'

To this day I remember that surge of rage. A third of a century later it still has the power to make my face burn.

'He said you're not sound.'

She made a feeble attempt to mimic him. When she realized that I was going to need a lot of quietening, she moved on to my bed and let me go further than ever before. So for that evening, pleasure washed away anger and the knowledge that for the first time in my life I had an enemy gave a strange excitement.

My parents took to Pernel at once and, more surprisingly, she to them. They couldn't believe that she had never before been in the North Countree. I watched them welcome her as if she were their long-lost daughter. Straight away, Dad was out with his heavy humour.

'It was me made up your bed, love,' he said, his eyes flicking towards me out of his poker face.

Because I'd never seen them so open and fulsome with a stranger, I listened for false notes; there weren't any, and in the end I accepted that they genuinely liked each other. It was odd hearing Mum and my girl nattering away. Mum wanted to know all about her and Pernel was happy to oblige. She glanced at me often to make sure I was listening. I learnt a lot that I didn't know.

'You don't talk to me like that,' I teased, in one of the few moments we had to ourselves.

'You never ask the right questions,' she replied. Quite cutting, for her.

Dad, who'd taken to slapping me wordlessly on the back, took a day off from Rowntree's and drove us to Whitby in his beloved Singer. As we crossed the moors, Pernel became more and more preoccupied. We were on the back seat – Dad being arch again – and I felt through the sinews of her hand that something was happening to her. I pushed my nose into her hair to ask her. For a moment, she let me see her huge, moist eyes. Pernel was moved, and it troubled me in a way I couldn't define.

In Whitby she produced a Voigtlander which her father had lent her for the trip. Dad perked up at once. He turned the camera in his hands and subjected the girl to a technical catechism from which she emerged remarkably well. Before long, the two of them had their heads together over Dad's light meter. There was much talk of ASA and DIN numbers, stops and shutter speeds. He pulled out a wallet full of colour filters and adapted a couple to fit her lens. Watching her take photographs of Whitby made me see the town in a new way. In front of her camera, the earwig tail of the harbour piers seemed to twitch with pleasure; the phantoms of Frank Meadow Sutcliffe's naked boys posed again along low-water mark; fishing boats bobbed like women surprised by royalty; a black dredger rattled its chains on the pewter river and fish-scales túrned the quay to silver. Up the shady cliff-side, snakeskin roofs coiled towards the church and in the open fields beyond, St Hilda's Abbey loomed against the sky.

On the way home, Pernel twice asked Dad to stop so that she could take pictures of the old stone crosses which marked the way across the moors.

When we had eaten our fish and chip supper, Dad said to her, 'You finished your film, didn't you? Do you want to see what you've got?'

He led her into the dark-room which he had made in a corner of the garage. They were in there for hours while he mixed his chemicals and initiated her into the mysteries of developing and fixing, printing and enlarging. When she finally emerged, blinking in the sitting-room lights, she was clutching a handful of damp printing paper and smelling of hypo. There was an excited gleam in her one visible eye.

Ten years ago, Pernel had a solo exhibition at the Serpentine Gallery in London. I have the catalogue. The introduction begins: 'Pernel Mortimer was first drawn to North Yorkshire in her early twenties . . .'

Drawn? By her hair? By wild horses? By some hyperborean magnet? Why not come out and say that she was drawn there by me?

In the circumstances, perhaps it is enough that her first book is dedicated to Dad: 'To George Lister who first showed me how.'

It was the high-spot of his life when she gave him an autographed copy. Silly old sod.

In sentimental moments, though, I sometimes think that the best thing I ever did was to broker her affair with the North, when she was in love.

On our last day, victualled with sandwiches and a flask, we set off by bus for Helmsley. I had great plans. We explored for an hour and then walked to Rievaulx. Among the abbey ruins, Pernel walked round as if in a trance. In an area that might once have been a side-chapel she came to a halt. A huge square stone, furry with lichen, was either sinking into the velvet turf or rising out of it. Walls lanced with space towered over us. Even at midday, with many visitors about, it was a numinous place. She took both my hands in hers. A light wind combed back her hair.

'I want to make a vow,' she said.

'Careful,' I joked. 'Words are deeds, remember?'

'Hush, I'm serious.'

She faced me and made me look at her eyes. She began to speak, slowly.

'John Lister, I love you and I know that I shall always

love you. I . . . devote myself to you.' Then she added, at normal speed, 'There, that's what I wanted to vow.'

'All without benefit of clergy,' I said, gazing round. It was easy to tease her about her attachment to the church.

'If ever we marry, what I promise then won't mean more than I've just said.'

'Darling, it was a lovely vow. I'm touched.'

I stooped to kiss her. We stood in silence for a while. I was rehearsing in my mind how to move to stage two of my plan.

'About two miles from here,' I said, choosing my words with care, 'there is a place which belongs to me. It doesn't really. It belongs to the me inside. I pretend I'm the only person in the world who knows about it.'

'I'd like to see it.'

'It's very quiet.' I gave her my level look.

She coloured slightly.

'Let's go, then,' she said.

There is a tight little valley running down from Hawnby Moor into the head of Ryedale. From the road it looks like a crease between buttocks, hairy with trees. Once, when I was orienteering with the Scouts, I got lost, did a bit of trespassing and found myself pushing out of vegetation into a miniature amphitheatre of cropped grass. Grey stones littered the place. Sheep lifted yellow eyes to watch me. What made my heart miss a beat was the waterfall at the top end. A great ledge forced the stream to leap perhaps ten feet into a pool below. Up above, the trees closed in again.

Ever since I'd discovered the Gaelic word taghairm, the art of divination practised while lying enveloped in a bullock-skin behind a waterfall, I'd longed to have a go. That day, I didn't have a bullock-skin, but I unfurled my ex-army waterproof, squelched around the margin of the pool and, having wrapped myself up, plunged through the curtain of water into the little cave behind. There wasn't much room and it wasn't comfortable, but after a bit of wriggling I worked myself into a tenable position. Through the stream, the clearing shone in the sun. Below, the trees made a black wall. Over their heads, far across the valley, the moor-edge above Bilsdale was the colour of cinnamon. I allowed my eyes to slip out of focus. I waited for divination without understanding what it was.

The rush and splash of the water grew louder. When nothing more exciting happened, I squashed my fists into my eye-sockets. The resulting kaleidoscopic show produced the beginnings of a headache so I took my hands away. As the shooting stars faded, a pink-and-gold light shimmered between my lashes. I felt less wet; the rocks poking into my rump became rounder. The falling water reverberated in the cave and it was easy to persuade myself that the sound might have held the whispers of antic voices. Still unsure of what was supposed to happen, I let my mind drift into familiar channels. Instantly, a girl appeared on my inner eye, a girl with long fair hair who paddled up through the beck, her green skirt swagged above her knees . . .

Five years later, I drew Pernel through the edge of the wood into the sunlit clearing. Everything was as it had been. Even the sheep looked the same. The tang of their suint filled the air. Curlew cries floated down from the moor. The waterfall splashed. I didn't tell her about taghairm. If she had laughed, I would have lost control. She accepted that this was my secret and most special place. She spent a long time absorbing its atmosphere.

'It feels right,' she said, at last.

She helped me spread the groundsheet which I happened to have at the bottom of my rucksack. We found a spot which was free of sheep-droppings and in the shelter of a dilapidated lathe. There was no unseemly haste. We imbued the moment with proper ceremony. She knew that it would hurt and stifled her cry in my neck.

When it was done, I looked down on her with immense tenderness. She lay on the ground with her hair radiant, her face naked.

We dabbled in the pool. Then, after we had picnicked, she pulled me down.

'Again,' she ordered, 'before I go off it.'

My skin still crawls when I think, not of her vow, but of my failure to respond in the way she must have hoped for. It wasn't deliberate cruelty on my part; it was much later that I comprehended the sexual war that was fought that day. Before she had taught me the importance of words I might have answered her in kind in the abbey. Why, when I had evaded her trap there, had she gone to the clearing, knowing what was bound to happen? I can only think that she had not then understood that a man does not commit himself by deeds alone. It was the flaw in her argument. Only words commit and an instinct for self-preservation had prevented me from saying them. I maintain to this day that I made her no promises.

One of her most memorable images, one which by now is familiar and admired throughout the world, is her photograph of our little clearing. Unlike much of her work, this piece is in colour. She must have had a ladder or climbed a tree because it is a giant's-eye view. You see the moor-edge under a swollen sky. Below a dark forest, the clearing is innocent green, bathed in the last brilliant sun before a storm. The waterfall streaks mercury across the mouth of the cave where I practised taghairm. Oddly, there are hints of red in the pool, perhaps from submerged objects. A few aimless sheep stand around among scattered stones. The picture evokes mystery, apprehension and loneliness. It includes one almost invisible detail which can mean nothing to anyone but us. Almost off the bottom edge, lost in the lattice of branches which gives the picture its astonishing depth, is the olive-drab corner of a groundsheet.

The picture is entitled 'Sacrificial Site, Hawnby' and a print hangs in the Tate Gallery.

What did she feel when she went back there? Why did she choose that elevated viewpoint? How did she get up there? Did she really go to the trouble of lugging a groundsheet up through the woods? And am I the only person in the world who in consequence sees the picture as a contrivance? Or is even this an oblique comment on my own behaviour that day? As for the title, who or what did she think was sacrificed and in what cause?

If the Italian post office hadn't been on strike that summer, all might have been well, but young love wilts without frequent nourishment. Pernel went off to do a course at the British Institute in Florence. I don't think it was a plot cooked up by her parents to keep us apart – everyone thought that Pernel's increasingly impressive talent would benefit from a dose of the Uffizi – but if there was such a plan, it could hardly have worked better.

We saw her off at Victoria. I stood at a distance wondering at the difference between the way Pernel kissed my mother and her own. When the platform was empty, the Mortimers wished me a perfectly polite goodbye and left. I'd come a long way: they might at least have offered me a cup of tea. Lord, how I resented their ability to buy so casually for their daughter a couple of months in Italy! And what was I supposed to do all summer without her?

In the end, I complicated things. A college friend, who had got himself a holiday job guiding British tourists round Switzerland, had to drop out at the last moment. He recommended me to take his place. The tour company was happy enough and within days I was at Basle airport waiting for my first planeload to arrive.

I wrote to Pernel immediately to tell her what I was doing and to give her the address of the hotel which would be my base. Week after week I reported there, fizzing with impatience for her news, increasingly desperate as week after week there was nothing from her. Only two of her letters ever reached me. Both had been forwarded from York and bore British stamps. Even then, she merely wrote about the beauties of Florence and the people she was meeting. That wasn't what I wanted to read. My own letters to her, scribbled every evening as soon as I had got my party bedded down for the night, were outpourings of love and longing and amazement at the miracle that had befallen us.

After a few weeks with no word from her, my efforts dried up. I tried telephoning her hostel in Florence but my Italian wasn't good enough to penetrate the system.

It was mid September when I returned to York. By then, the thought of Pernel caused me such anguish that when my parents told me that she was now in Leeds and had rung several times I couldn't bring myself to call her. Did I know that she intended to spend a year on a teacher training course? If I did, I'd forgotten. In Leeds, for crying out loud! Filthy, red-brick, jerry-built Leeds. She must have been able to find a college closer to Oxford. Eventually, of course, we spoke. I was stunned when she blamed me for the breakdown in communication. She deserved to be punished for that, so that when she suggested that we meet before I went back, I made an excuse. We tortured each other for the deficiencies of

51

Friar John and vaguely, grumpily, arranged a weekend when she might visit me in Oxford.

In the interval, Julia happened.

Now we are back with Killer, who, a few days after the beginning of term, set the college by the ears when he was seen by two independent and reasonably sober witnesses walking down the Turl with a young woman. Not just any woman, if the reports were to be believed, but a poppet, a cracker. Those of us who were Killer-watchers were amazed. In the absence of evidence to the contrary, we had assumed that he was of the other persuasion.

That year I was in digs. It was while I was visiting a friend in college that one of our cronies came to the door, breathless with excitement.

'She's in with him now. In his rooms.'

'Get the others. We'll meet outside chapel in ten minutes.'

A dozen of us assembled. A volunteer was picked and sent off to beat on Killer's door.

'No sign of flagrante,' he reported on his return. 'Door opened without delay. Jacket on, tie straight.'

'Shoes?'

'On.'

'And the lady?'

'Only caught a glimpse. Decent, as far as I could see. Sorry.'

'What were they doing?'

'Making tea. I saw a cake, cups, saucers . . .'

'Saucers?'

'Saucers. Killer is civilized.'

'And morally unblemished.'

'Silly sod.'

We calculated that a respectable tea would end at five-thirty. At exactly that time, a second volunteer was despatched to knock on Killer's door. He had only just reached the foot of Killer's staircase when he suddenly retreated, signalling frantically. We sprinted to our posts, so that when Killer appeared with his girl, we were standing like a guard of honour all the way to the porter's lodge. Killer stopped and glared death at us. The girl, after a moment's hesitation, lifted her chin, put on a glorious smile and did a Zuleika right through our midst. She bounced, she pranced. She was high-coloured, with a mop of brown curls, shining black eyes with whites like fresh milk, a rounded bust, long striding legs and principal-boy boots. The mettlesome creature turned our jeers into cheers. I think we actually clapped her. There and then the race began to be first to take her away from Killer.

I won.

Julia Appleyard was a student nurse, newly arrived at the Radcliffe.

'David's parents asked him to keep an eye on me,' she said.

We were in my rooms off the Banbury Road, drinking cheap red wine. She had her shoes off and her feet tucked up on my best chair. I sat on the thin carpet, my chin on her knee.

David. I'd forgotten that Killer had a Christian name.

'I'm not his girlfriend or anything.'

'Does he know that?'

'Go on! We've known each other all our lives. All my life, anyway. Dad's the chief clerk in Mr Black's office. It's a big family, really. Christmas parties, outings, that sort of thing. Mr Black takes care of his staff. He's famous for it. So when he heard I was coming here, he told David to look out for me. There's nothing else to it, honestly.'

To make sure that I understood, Julia scrubbed my

head with her fists. She was always a vigorous girl.

She hooted with laughter when I told her what we called her David.

'Killer? I don't believe it. Why? He isn't a bit like that, really, he's not. He's very well brought up and a bit shy.'

'Perhaps you go for shy men.'

'Depends. What sort are you?'

'I'm the domestic kind. I like to come home to a woman who's thigh-deep in golden baking . . .'

'You'll be lucky!'

'Soon as she sees me, it's off with her mop-cap and house-coat . . .'

'Under which . . .?'

'She's plucked and ready. She takes me in her floury arms, we roll on the floor among rare ingredients . . .'

'Mm, pinches of salt?'

'Cloves of garlic, yokes of egg . . .'

'Don't forget the zest of lemons.'

'There's kneading and tenderizing . . .'

'Lightly brushing with ginger syrup . . .'

'Stirring and dissolving . . .'

'Pricking and turning . . .'

'Julia!'

'Piping with whipped cream . . .'

'And laid on a rack to cool. And somewhere there's got to be a row of wholesome children with impeccable manners.'

'Tough luck.'

When we stopped giggling, she said, 'You still haven't answered my question.'

'About the sort of man I am? Unsound.'

'What's that supposed to mean?'

'Search me. Ask Killer.'

'I did ask him about you. He doesn't like you, did you know? He said you're practically engaged to a

54

girl called Nell. True or false? Come on. I want to know.'

She propelled herself out of the chair and bore me down to the ground.

Pernel. She was with me all the time, in my body as well as in my mind, like some sporting injury. I ached with an unspecific guilt. Yet looked at from the brilliance radiated by Julia, Pernel seemed introverted, over-serious, fastidious, lacking in colour and passion. Julia's philosophy was simple.

'You have to take life by the scruff of the neck,' she liked to say, usually grabbing me by the scruff of the neck for emphasis. 'Life is for laughs' was another of her precepts. At first I ridiculed her superficiality but after a time I realized how pleasant it was to see life on her terms. I began to fall in with her easy hedonism. I once tried to make her concentrate on a heavy issue – Suez or Hungary, it was about that period – but she rounded on me.

'Look, John. For the last ten hours I've been on duty among blood and guts and nasty human juices. I've still got a couple of hours' study to do before tomorrow. But I rushed back to the hostel, tarted myself up and pedalled over here like a mad thing so as to spend as long as possible with you. The last thing I want is a session on current affairs, okay?'

She was marvellous, joyous company, carrying round within herself all the elements of a good party. I used to compare her to a Christmas tree, continually lighting up as the blood came and went under her skin; or to the Seven Lady Dwarfs, all rolled into one: Uppity, Bubbly, Earthy, Lusty, Winsome, Blushful and Bountiful. The first time we made love, not long after we'd met, the occasion was the spicier for the knowledge that I'd done her right under Killer's snooty nose. He wanted her, I'd no doubt about that, but I'd had her. So had someone else, I discovered. Surely not him.

She wasn't coy about it.

''Course there've been others. They're nothing to do with you. Now it's me and you. That's enough, isn't it?'

'Killer?'

'You must be joking.'

As I'd thought.

Pernel, I decided, had practically emasculated me with her carefully calibrated emotional climate. What a waste! It wasn't as if our coupling in the clearing had been a riot of pleasure, for all its hieratic ceremony. Julia, by contrast, was all red meat. I had to brighten my ideas just to keep up with her. She, like Pernel, was establishing a culture, but in her case she presented such a challenge and was so sexually imaginative that I felt stretched, fulfilled, always eager for more. If ever I went over the top and encountered the black dog, she would take charge, tell me a string of the most obscene hospital stories and in five minutes have me shouting with laughter.

I told her about Pernel, as honestly as I could.

'She's coming up this weekend,' I said, 'just for old times' sake, really.'

'Damn,' said Julia. 'I've got the weekend off. Ah well. Be kind to her but make it final. I don't like loose ends.'

A note arrived from Killer. On a card bearing the college crest he had written. 'I should like the chance of a private chat with you. Please let me know when and where. It really is important that we talk before things get out of hand.'

It was signed D. Black. I'd no idea what he was on about so I threw it away.

He must have worked himself up into a rare old state. When I went into the college showers a few days later — my landlady charged extra for baths — he must have followed me in. I emerged from the gush and steam to find him waiting for me, fully clad, head forward, legs tight as ninepins. His murderous eyes travelled up and down my body.

'Didn't you get my note?' he asked. The tiled interior gave his voice awesome resonance.

I moved towards him.

'Towel,' I said.

'Not until . . .'

'Shift.' I pushed him out of my way.

'You can't treat Julia like that,' he said, barely under control. 'She's not some toy. Can't you see that? I . . . I have some responsibility for her . . .'

'No you don't.' I roped the towel and sawed it across my back. He couldn't stop his eyes from straying. 'You only think you have because Daddy said so.'

'You . . . you've discussed me?'

I didn't answer. I turned my back on him and reached for my clothes. Something heavy hit me on the back of my head. I lurched forward, wits scattered, and the next I knew, he'd shoved a hockey stick between my legs and hooked it upwards.

'All right,' he hissed. 'If you won't do things the civilized way, I'll have to come down to your level. Don't move. Just listen. You call me Killer. I tell you this. If you harm Julia in any way, Lord help me, Lister, I'll prove you right.'

It was crude, schoolboy stuff but I was in no position to argue. I nodded.

He pulled the stick sharply towards him. I grunted.

'Understand?'

'Yes, Killer, all right. You've made your point.' I affected a bored voice, though by this stage I was longing for someone else to want a shower. 'Now leave it out, will you?'

'I've been watching you, you and that lovely blonde

57

girl. Don't think for one moment that I'll stand by and see you do to Julia what you've done to her.'

I'd no idea what he thought I'd done to Pernel. His imagination must have been overheating. I touched the swelling lump on my head. It was sticky with blood.

'You make me sick,' he said, and gave one more tear-jerking yank. Then he released me. I heard the stick clatter into a corner. When I looked up, he was a silhouette in the tunnel mouth. Several possible shouts came into my pounding head but they were either unworthy or unwise. One of them was 'You're too late', but I kept quiet.

From the moment that she climbed down from the train Pernel made it obvious that her aim was to mend what had gone wrong during the summer. She ran the length of the platform, hair flying, until her arms were round my neck and her fragrance filled my senses. Italy seemed to have brought her on. Despite Julia, I was easily roused.

Lord, how young we are when we begin to spoil each other's lives! My landlady had no bed for Pernel, but, with a sliding look at me, she found her a room with a neighbour across the street. The neighbour seemed to relish the part of bawd. Miming fluster, she tiptoed out of the room with pantomime discretion and softly closed the door behind her. Pernel had come prepared for anything. Her system of rules had simply disappeared. I responded with such enthusiasm that she must have thought she was winning.

'I got your letters,' she whispered. 'They all came at once, in a bundle. The Institute sent them on. Oh, John, I'm so happy.'

I tried to remember what I'd written. It was a different me then.

I should have felt guilty at taking advantage of her, but

Julia's carefree morality had infected me. Even so, once the first flush of passion was over, I began to resent this other girl who believed that she owned me, and who was keeping me away from Julia. Every kiss tasted staler than the last. I stopped forcing myself to be kind. At a certain point, Pernel rolled away from me and lay on her back, staring at the ceiling.

'Something isn't right,' she said.

She didn't interrogate me. She listened to my reassurances and interpreted them for what they were. So we got up and talked like strangers in brown streets where a back-endish wind was blowing. When I took her back to her lodgings, as early in the evening as I could, it was as if I had survived an ordeal.

Next morning, Sunday, there was no time for her to go to church before her train left, so we walked in heavy silence in the Parks, me carrying her holdall so that we didn't have to go back to her room. I noticed how pale she was. Mauve shadows stippled the skin below her eyes. Was she trying to punish me by not speaking? If so, she misread my mood entirely. I looked at my watch. We had come to a place where several paths converged. If I had calculated well, Julia should appear at any moment on her morning run. I made Pernel dawdle. At last, in the distance, between the trees, with dead leaves flying about her feet, Julia came into sight. I stopped and so did Pernel, wonderingly.

But Julia was on the wrong path. That way she would miss us altogether. I shouted to her. She didn't stop. I became desperate to make her hear. I gave another bellow that made the air ring. I could feel Pernel stiffening beside me. Julia waved but ran on.

'Julia! Over here!'

Tousled and flushed, she pulled up and trotted over the grass towards us. She looked cross.

'Julia, I want you to meet Pernel.'

'Hello,' said Julia, shaking hands.

'Pernel, this is Julia. I want to spend the rest of my life with her.'

There was a long silence. Then Pernel's cold fingers took the holdall out of my hand. I can still make myself feel the edge of her nail on my palm. She simply walked away, back the way we had come. I didn't follow. All that mattered to me at that moment was that I was alone again with Julia. I gazed down on her fondly.

'You berk,' she said, eyes blazing. She ran back across the grass to the path which she had been following and for a few minutes I stood watching the retreating backs of the two girls on their diverging tracks. Dimly I began to realize that I hadn't managed things well.

I never saw Pernel again, but in the end Julia married me.

Months before I graduated, the Wilberforce Wiseman Corporation, known on the London Stock Exchange as Wawa, offered me a job. It was in Calcutta and the financial inducements were so good that Julia and I decided to marry immediately.

There was no problem with her Dad. He and I shared a passion for pub games and quizzes. He used to look forward to my going to Sudbury so that we could go round to his local for some rowdy matches. Potentially more difficult was the meeting with Killer's parents. Since the death of Julia's mother, Mrs Black was her senior confidante. I soon discovered that, much as she liked Julia, Mrs Black reckoned that her son could do better for himself. Julia was the childhood sweetheart, the girl next door, the one you practise on, but she was far from being the ideal daughter-in-law. As for Mr Black, he had no independent views on such dangerous subjects. He wished me well, slapped me on the back and counselled moderation in all things. Little solace there for their son who slunk around with red-rimmed eyes in which, for the first time, I read defeat.

My parents would have preferred me to marry Pernel, but they welcomed Julia kindly. Julie, as Dad called her.

'Can't get my tongue round Juliah. Too posh for me, that is.'

Whatever disappointment they might have felt was soon allayed because not long after Julia and I had gone to India, Pernel moved North. How or why she should have done so is a mystery that I have never solved. She simply seems to have turned her back on Redwarden, bought herself a decent little house in Helmsley and settled down as an art teacher serving a number of local schools. She must have devoted her spare time to photography.

Although Mum and Dad had no grasp of the depth of the gulf which had opened between Pernel and me, they sensed enough to make sure that we didn't meet on my visits to York. I noticed from their letters, however, that as soon as I left, Pernel came visiting again. Her peculiar reaction when we crossed the moors offers the best explanation, which is borne out by her pictures. She must have undergone some kind of revelation and decided that she had to live in the North. As the years passed I resented her invasion of my family and my territory more and more. Whenever I was at home I was always aware that she was just up the road and might appear at any moment. There was another explanation: she had settled in Helmsley in order to punish me.

Julia and I threw a party in Oxford before we left. As we were to marry in a Registry Office and spend our honeymoon on the ship, it was our wedding breakfast. The Fellows lent us their garden for the occasion.

Towards the end, when most guests had left, Killer, whom Julia had invited as an old family friend, came up to her and kissed her cheeks with reverence and an air of finality. Then he squared up to me, took my hand and shook it strongly. Through the water in them, his eyes were terrible.

'Remember,' he said.

For a few years afterwards, my firmament contained three stars: myself and Julia in the East, and Pernel, palely malpositioned on the edge of my parental home. Killer wasn't then anything more than a fading, malevolent glow. Then he joined Wilberforce Wiseman.

Julia was the one who saw the announcement in the house journal. A Mr David Black had joined the corporation through our New York branch. The brief write-up had him through Oxford, the Harvard Business School and accountancy training in one sentence. He had then taken charge of an office which his father had opened on the East Coast. As soon as old Mr Black died, Killer had sold up and been taken on by Wawa. He had an American wife and a couple of children.

Lest I be accused of paranoia, it was Julia who said, 'It's a bit odd, isn't it? Of all the organizations in the world, David has to join us. It's more than odd, it's sinister.'

That was twenty-five years ago. There's been no contact between us – not surprising in such a huge, far-flung trading company in which people specialize in one area of the world – but it's an uncomfortable situation. I'm now head of Southeast Asia, he's still involved in the USA. Over the years I've followed his promotions in the journal, three of his to my two so that we are now in the same grade. Whenever I return to headquarters I catch myself looking over my shoulder, just as I do in York. I feel stalked. In mad moments I suspect collusion but I know that is nonsense.

My parents are well into their eighties now. They still write every week. In almost every letter there is some reference to Pernel. As a result, I know that she married a sheep-farmer by whom she had a son, who in turn married and had a child. I have clippings and catalogues which mark her progress as a photographer, and all her books. She has taken over my landscape and made it her own. When I was a boy, those hills gave me strength. Now, her camera has sucked the mana out of them and left them as husks. Her pictures are almost always in black and white: bony, scratchy images which critics praise for their 'intrinsic honesty' and 'naked grandeur'. How she must laugh at them. What she is saying is 'look at these puny hills, so little even in comparison with the great clouds that people the skies, their famous beauty is nothing but dry skin over old bones; you'll find no love there.' I know I'm right about this. Why else would she include so many dry valleys and the skulls of sheep? Lord knows what her sheep-farmer husband makes of it all. He must lose a lot of stock.

Disaster. I can't believe it. I can't stand it. Life does that to you. You think up a worst-case scenario and suddenly you're faced with something that's worse still. Here's the house journal. Bang in the middle of the front page, Killer, head and shoulders, spectacles now, same eyes though, and a twist to his mouth that makes it clear who he was thinking of when the picture was taken. Mr D. Black, newly appointed to the Board. As far as I'm concerned, that gives him the power of life and death.

Troubles never come singly. The very next day Personnel faxed to say that Mum was dead.

63

Singapore to London is the long route. You keep pace with the night and arrive starving. Betty from staff welfare met us at Heathrow to help with Julia's wheelchair and the hire of a car that would take it. I drove us straight to York.

Mum was in the Chapel of Rest. Dad took us to see her, though Julia needed me to hold a mirror for her.

'She'll not be long after,' said Dad, when Julia was out of earshot.

He may be right. She's coped marvellously well all these years, having decided that the advantage of servants outweighed the heat and humidity. But now, with this other thing, she's got no fight left in her.

That evening, when I had put her to bed, Dad and I sat in the firelight, relaxed and warmed by grief and whisky.

'You're well on with the funeral,' I said.

'That's all Pernel's doing. I could never have coped on my own.'

'She'll be there tomorrow, then?'

''Course she will, and her Charlie and his Annie and the little 'un, Carrie.'

'Not her husband?'

'Whose?'

'Pernel's. The sheep-farmer. Mum wrote and told me.'

'Oh, aye, him. I remember. No, he's been gone many a year.'

'I didn't know. Poor woman.'

'Aye.'

'I met her parents a couple of times. What became of them?'

'Long dead, I'd say, and good riddance.'

When Dad had gone to bed, I poured myself a last whisky and opened the letters which Betty had given me at Heathrow. My stomach churned. One of them was from Killer, on Boardroom paper. The usual condolences ended with 'please call on me before you return to Singapore. I want to hear about Julia's accident.'

For the millionth time, a ghostly grey bullock cart trundled across my headlights. It was such bad luck. We'd only been married two months.

In the bedroom I checked that Julia was asleep before drawing back the curtains. Dad's bungalow overlooked fields on the edge of the estate. At this time of night there were no lights anywhere. The blackness suited my mood. A wind strummed the wires outside and moved the branches which I gradually distinguished against the sky. It would have been a fine thing to see the Aurora tonight, a last flourish for Mum, but cloud covered cloud so that even the stars were invisible.

I tried to recall Pernel. I started with her hair but it hid her face. There was a strand caught between her lips; her fringe obscured her eyes the moment I thought I had them. Like clips from an old film, images of her moved for a few frames, then froze, then faded. I saw her arms, like pipe-cleaners in the skinny sweaters she used to wear, lift her hands to shift her hair. For an instant she lay beneath me on the groundsheet but her face was a blank. If we had married, would she have become famous? If I hadn't married Julia, would there have been no accident?

Behind me, she stirred on the bed. Automatically, I felt a pang of guilt. I checked that she had everything to hand in case she woke in the night.

Killer, Killer. You will never understand this, but we have been happy. We have honoured our vows. Despite the accident, I have kept faith.

I watched tears glisten on my black reflected cheeks.

At the cemetery, a young assistant stepped forward to help me with Julia. When she was settled and well wrapped against the late November cold, he pushed her

65

while I supported Dad. I didn't at first see anyone who looked like Pernel.

On my knees, in chapel, uncontrolled thoughts rushed into my head. Lord, save me from the inconvenient people, the ones who have seen me at my worst. Don't let me have to meet them any more. It all happened such a long time ago. I'm not like that now. I've improved. Haven't I been punished enough? Lettest Thou Thy servant escape in peace ...

There were perhaps thirty people near the grave, most of them elderly neighbours whose faces jolted me back into childhood. I stood with Dad, the assistant behind Julia. We were at Mum's feet, the vicar at her head, all together among the leaning stones. The winter wind spilled leaves and rooks out of the bordering trees. Far to the north, touched by pale sunlight, lay the low hills, the ones which for so long have risen up between me and the stars. In their midst, Helmsley, Rievaulx, the sacrificial site. As I lowered my eyes, I encountered hers. Grey. Steady. Moist with grief. Unmistakably hers, and more compassionate than hostile.

Soil rattled on the coffin lid.

We stood in a line on the muddy ground, Dad, me and Julia. He put both sticks in one hand so that he could greet the mourners as they edged past. Each was invited to the house for refreshments. Pernel took his hand. He held it, speechlessly nodding, blinking, unable to let her go. At last she stood in front of me. Her grip was firm. I could not hold her gaze. Worms and serpents writhed inside me. She looked at Julia with sympathy.

'This is Pernel, darling,' I said.

'I know,' came on my wife's breath. 'We met.'

One tortured Sunday morning in the Parks. Oh, yes. I hadn't really forgotten.

As Pernel moved away, Dad got his voice back.

66

'You'll come to the house, love?' he called.

She raised one hand and smiled over her shoulder. Her smile encompassed me. Her hair was shorter and ashier, her figure broader under her dark blue coat, but she was still a slim woman.

The assistant shook Dad's hand. A young mother with a child came last.

The same three were still at the house, along with Pernel, Julia, Dad and me when the others had gone. Then the penny dropped. The young man wasn't an undertaker, he was Pernel's son; the young woman was his wife, and the long-haired little girl must be Carrie, Pernel's grandchild. I looked at them with new interest.

Carrie saw me studying her and burst into tears, overcome by strangers, the severe clothes and by air thick with sadness. She buried her face in her mother's skirt.

'I want my Granny,' she wittered. 'Where's my Granny?'

'Hush, darling. Granny's here, see. It's Great Gran who's gone to the Good Shepherd.'

The woman, stooping over her child, looks up at her husband in sudden confusion. He glances at his mother. She is looking at me. There is a stillness in the room. All eyes seem to be on me. I see embarrassment, contempt, and above all, irony. On the arms of her wheelchair, Julia's hands have clenched. My constellation whirls away in the darkness. There are many stars, in random orbits and of different magnitudes, spiralling upwards in a glittering tower of light.

I look at Dad, who reads in my face a question which my mind has not yet framed. His brown eyes look back at me out of his poker face, but there is a gleam in them, as if of triumph.

Slowly, he nods.

A DARK CIRCLE

Sylvia Baker

Fifteen years ago, Sylvia Baker moved from her native Hertfordshire to Devon to pursue the 'good life'. Unfortunately growing things and breeding dogs didn't work out and she has now concentrated on writing full-time. She has had several articles published in various magazines and writes regular features for a local paper.

A DARK CIRCLE

I was really surprised to see that strip of wallpaper hanging down from the ceiling just above the coroner's head. I thought the court would be like a palace. Mind you, Montgomery Duvall could have been a king sitting high up behind that enormous desk, with his bow tie and suntan. People with suntans at this time of year always look so important. The man they called the clerk bowed to him and I heard one of the policemen call him sir. Every time my stomach tightened with fear, I made myself look up, right over his head, and concentrate on that bit of wallpaper.

Yesterday, when the doctor said I was fit enough to attend the inquest, I was terrified and I couldn't sleep thinking about it. And I was worried about the sight of my legs. They don't hurt so much now but I can't bear people seeing them

The nurse said I should wear trousers, so I did because I was acting like a zombie, hardly able to think anything out for myself. When my mother came to fetch me, she asked what the hell was I doing dressed like that which made me all the more scared, but there wasn't any time to change. And in the end it didn't seem to matter, what with the peeling wallpaper and the state of some of the other witnesses. The man who'd found me in the street was dressed in jeans and a leather jacket. I looked up as he took the oath because I recognized his voice although I couldn't remember his face. The only thing I remembered

71

was how he wrapped his coat round my legs and held me until I stopped screaming. And how I didn't say a word to him.

The smartest witness was a lady doctor. She had a foreign-sounding name and swingy dark hair that kept falling across her face. When I realized what she was there for I kept thinking how could someone so pretty do such a job. Once, at the end of a sentence, she looked straight at me, her lips slightly apart, and I could see the word 'sorry' all over her face. But everybody was sorry; I'm used to those pitying looks. I stared back for a moment, thinking how I'd rather be me than have to do what she did.

After she'd given her evidence, the coroner beckoned the clerk to his desk and said to him: 'I don't think it's necessary for the family to see these.' He lowered his voice but I was in the front row and could hear every word. Even when I was staring at the ceiling I was still listening. He had hold of some photographs and was fanning them out like a pack of cards. Then he leant forward and spoke to my mother.

'Is that all right, Mrs Poole?' His voice was still very quiet and he didn't even look in my direction. That's it, I thought, treat me like all the others. Is that all right, Mrs Poole, I mimicked inside my head. Why didn't he ask *me* if it was all right? My mother nodded and then fumbled about in her handbag which she'd put between us on the bench when we sat down. I could hear her sniffing and realized I'd never heard her cry before.

When they called my name I didn't know who they meant for a moment. I still thought I was Lizzie Poole, and then the clerk came over and tapped me lightly on my shoulder.

'You needn't go into the box, you can stand beside Mr Duvall if you like,' he said. 'But he must ask you some questions about the accident.'

'She won't speak, I know she won't.' My mother had stopped crying but her voice still sounded snuffly. 'She's been like it since she was five – can't get the words out. She shouldn't be here.' I wished she hadn't tried to explain; it only made me worse.

'Perhaps you'd like to take her,' the clerk said to my mother. But I didn't want her to 'take me' so I stood up and went to the witness box on my own.

My mother used to take me to school every day, right into the classroom, otherwise I'd creep back home after she'd gone to work. I couldn't get indoors but I used to sit in the porch and wait for her even though it meant a good hiding when she got back. Sometimes my brother Vince took me to school. He'd grip hold of my wrist so tight and if I struggled he gave me what he called a Chinese puzzle which was like being strangled. I was always crying when he finally pushed me inside the classroom door. But I never told the teacher what was wrong because he said if I told tales I'd get worms like our cat and that they'd eat up all my food and grow huge inside me until I died of starvation. It was his fault about the roundabout.

Before I started school, before my mother went to work, we'd go down to the recreation ground when Vince was on holiday. While us kids were busy swinging and climbing about, our mothers sat on the benches by the cricket pavilion and talked and smoked and took off their tights to get their legs brown. It was the only time my mother seemed happy, laughing and joking with the other women. One day there was a terrible storm. It was the first storm I remember and I'll never, ever forget it. The sky got so dark it was like night-time and some of the kids said the end of the world was coming. I didn't know what that meant and I only got frightened when it started to rain and all the others ran for cover and left me clinging to the roundabout. It was going too fast for me to jump

73

off; I wasn't quite five and very small for my age. Then Vince shouted that I'd be struck by lightning because I was holding on to the metal bars. I called for my mother but she was round the side of the pavilion talking to the man who cut the grass and didn't take any notice. When the first flash of lightning came I leapt off but the bar caught me in the stomach, knocking every bit of air out of me. I couldn't move. I just lay there in the pouring rain struggling to get my breath, every gasp hurting my ribs so much I nearly stopped trying. When my mother finally came to pick me up she kept shouting at me, what was wrong, but I couldn't answer. Then she started shaking me and saying, look at the state of my dress and why was I always such a nuisance. She swung me round until one of the other women stopped her. I can't remember whether Vince got told off; probably not – he had a father who used to come and take him out on Saturdays and that's why my mother liked him best. I only remember the pain and not being able to speak and wishing and wishing that she was not so angry with me.

When I started school I was worried that she might not be there when I got home; that's why I didn't want to go. Well, that was part of the reason, the other thing was the way all the class laughed when I couldn't speak. Sometimes I was all right but just the slightest bit of anxiety and my breath just seemed to grip in my throat and I couldn't say a word.

It was better at the special school, the teacher was really kind and helped me to read aloud, two or three words at a time. Most of the others couldn't read at all. I didn't mind so much if they laughed because they were always laughing at nothing anyway. I was the cleverest in my class and probably the only one who got a job all on their own. I saw the notice in the window of the Burger Bar at Waterloo Station when I went to get my mother's cigarettes from the kiosk. At the interview they didn't seem bothered that most of my sentences consisted of only two words. As long as I was prepared to work late on Saturdays, they said the job was mine.

I was so excited the first time I put on my uniform. I'd ironed it twice, spending ages on those little creases that gather at the edge of a collar as though they've nowhere to go, when everything has to go somewhere. Then I tied up my hair and put on my cap, which took much longer than you'd think because I have such a lot of hair and it's very frizzy and springy. My mother used to plait it for school. That was agony because she brushed so hard and I didn't dare yell or she'd do it harder.

Even when I had secured the cap with all the grips I could find, some hair still hung round my face, so I chopped it off with nail scissors and had just flushed it down the toilet when I heard my mother's key in the front door. I rushed downstairs certain that for once she'd be pleased with me; smile and say how smart I looked the way she had when Vince first appeared in his army gear. But she just looked at me and sighed, her lips pressed together in a crinkly line. Then she said: 'Pop up the station and get me some fags . . . and take that lot off before you go.'

Every week I gave her half my wages and put the rest in the Post Office. Seeing my savings grow gave me more pleasure than spending the money because I couldn't think of anything to buy. I never went anywhere or did anything apart from work.

I liked my job even though I was always the one who had to do things like unblocking the sinks or scraping the fat from behind the fryers. They just asked me and I did it. Nobody bothered me and I kept really busy gathering up the dirty plates, emptying the ashtrays and filling up the cutlery and sugar. Sometimes I slipped some of the

75

packets of sugar into my overall pocket to take home. Lots of customers did it, even well-to-do looking old ladies who should have known better. They'd take half a dozen, put one in their tea and the rest in their bags. I used to wrap them in a serviette and give them to my mother as a present but all she ever said was: 'So that's the kind of thing you're learning at that place, is it?' Once I took home a bag of rolls that the manageress had given me but my mother said they were stale and threw them in the bin. There was no pleasing her. I should have learnt that after trying for nearly seventeen years.

And then Joe came to work at the Burger Bar. On his first day he smiled at me and called me darling and for the first time in my life I felt as though someone really liked me.

Everybody liked Joe; he was always singing and telling jokes. Even when things got dropped and he had to mop the floor or when customers complained, which they did all the time, he was always good tempered. And he never ignored me like most of the others did. Sometimes, when a group of them were gathered round laughing and talking in the break, he'd pull me forward and stand with his arm round my shoulders so I didn't get left out. And he never got impatient when I couldn't speak.

He reminded me of the only friend I'd had at school because his hair was very black and shiny and his face was covered in small holes. Sabina had got the marks on her face from having smallpox when she was a baby in Pakistan; I don't know how Joe got his.

He also had something wrong with his eye. The lid hung down like he was winking but he wore dark glasses most of the time. But now and again when he was standing over the smoky fryers, he took his glasses off to wipe them. When he caught me staring at him, he just winked at me with his good eye.

In a way, I was glad that Joe wasn't perfect; it made me think that perhaps I stood a chance with him. I'd never had a boyfriend and sometimes I wondered if I ever would.

When he began to take out some of the other girls who worked at the Burger Bar, I was quite disappointed and I tried not to think about him, only I just couldn't help it. I'd stand in front of the mirror at night and hate myself for being so skinny. In fact I hated everything about myself. If I had big tits and sleek blonde hair and pale skin that I could dab with powder and blusher, I knew he'd take me out.

Then one day as I was wiping the trays he came up behind me and slipped his arms round my waist and pressed his lips against my ear. I just giggled, it was nothing unusual, he did it to all the girls.

'Well, Lizzie, are you coming out with me tonight?'

I kept on wiping away at the trays and giggling because I thought he was only teasing me.

'Come on, you can answer me, it's only yes or no,' he laughed and tickled me and blew against my neck and then I was sure he meant it and I said yes so loud he put his fingers on my lips. My heart felt as though it were jumping up and down all day and I nearly forgot to collect my pay packet.

My mother was waiting when I came downstairs in the new T-shirt I had bought on the way home from work. It was bright red and very tight. I had tried on so many but only this one had made me look less skinny.

'Where the hell are you going in that?'

'With Joe.'

'Joe from work?' She sounded as though she didn't believe me and I knew she didn't like the T-shirt.

'Where are you going with him?'

I didn't answer. It wasn't the disapproval in her voice

working its old trick of keeping me silent, I didn't know.

'That's it, play dumb. Well, my girl, just make sure you can say the word "no". I've had enough trouble with you already without worrying what you're getting up to with some randy little Eyetie.'

Normally when she got angry I was filled with panic because I couldn't answer her and I was afraid I'd never speak again, but tonight it was different. The excitement I'd been feeling all day was still there, swimming around in my stomach, tickling about deep inside me, freeing me from the anxieties that had chained me down for so long. I just didn't care what she said any longer. The realization spread through me until I couldn't help laughing with the sheer joy of it. She gave one of her disgusted looks and told me to clear off.

Sitting in the pub in Kennington Park Road, I watched Joe laughing and talking at the bar while he got our drinks and I thought, what if he doesn't ask me out again, if he takes someone else out tomorrow? From the back, when you couldn't see his pitted face, he looked so handsome. His hair curved round his neck like the feathers of a sleek dark bird making me want to reach out and stroke it. I was consumed with longing to keep him and gripped with fear that I wouldn't be able to.

Later, back at his flat, when he pulled the red T-shirt over my head, pressing his lips against my neck and saying he loved me, I couldn't believe how easy it was to please him. And once I got the hang of all the things he asked me to do, there was no stopping me.

'You've got hidden talents, you know that?' We were lying naked in front of the gas fire and Joe was trying to light a cigarette from the flame. We couldn't go in the bedroom because Joe's mate and his girlfriend were in there and the flat only had the two rooms. It was quite tidy compared to our house but there wasn't a lot to get untidy; you'd call it bare I suppose, not squalid – it all depends what you're used to, which in my case wasn't much. But that evening I wouldn't have swapped places with anyone. Once, when I was at the special school, we had to draw a picture of our mothers and I was allowed to take mine home because it was so good. My teacher said I was like a dog with two tails. That evening with Joe a thousand tails wouldn't have been enough.

I went to his flat every night that first week and on the Friday, which was his thirtieth birthday, I drew out eighty pounds from the Post Office and bought him a watch.

'Hey, it's wonderful! How much did it cost you?' He looked really pleased.

'A lot.'

He put it on and held his wrist towards me. 'Can you tell the time?'

'Course.' I didn't offer to read the hands because sometimes I got it wrong and I didn't want Joe to think I was stupid.

'It must have cost you a week's wages,' he said.

'My savings,' I replied, despite the fact that my mother had made me promise never to tell anyone about my money.

'Savings?' He looked surprised, then grinned. 'I've never known anyone with savings.'

I showed him my Post Office book. It was wrapped in a brown paper bag as I'd had to smuggle it out of the house. My mother would have gone mad if she'd known I'd bought Joe the watch.

'My God, Lizzie, you've got nearly a thousand pounds!'

'For the future,' I told him. That's what my mother had said when she made me open the account.

*

The future came three months later, the day after I married Joe, when we went and drew out half my money. Part of it went to repay my mother for the wedding expenses: the licence, Joe's suit, my dress from the secondhand shop and the drinks at the pub for our friends – or rather Joe's friends; he didn't have any relations but a lot of friends. The rest went on a video.

Verity, one of the girls at the Burger Bar, was really nasty to me. She was the first one that Joe had taken out and she caught me alone in the cloakroom one day. She said that I was a slag and that my baby would be retarded because I was backward and Joe was diseased. I wanted to say she was a liar or tell her that Joe said she had ice in her knickers – it had sounded really funny when he said it, only I didn't feel like laughing now. But as usual, when anybody was aggressive towards me, the words stuck in my throat. I just stood there holding my breath with the awful feeling that something was tied tight round my neck. Even when she reached out and pulled my cap off I didn't move. Anyone else would have stuck up for themselves, maybe even hit her, but I had never hurt anyone in my life.

Most of the others were kind to me. The manageress even knitted some jackets and bootees for the baby, which was more than my mother did. She also reminded me of the days I was supposed to go to the clinic, although I was soon skipping my appointments because they asked so many questions.

Apart from the antenatal clinic, I loved being pregnant. For the first time in my life I got plump – I had the sort of figure I'd always wanted and I looked healthy. Even my skin seemed to get brighter. When I got ready for work, I spent a long time looking at myself in the mirror, putting on eye-shadow and lipstick and thinking I wasn't so bad after all.

80

Two months before the baby was due I changed to part-time hours. I should have packed up altogether – all that standing – but I was fit and we needed the money. The Post Office book showed a balance of one pound and Joe had been sacked for bad attendance. Once I had to ask my mother for a loan. You'd think I'd asked for one of her kidneys. I decided I'd rather starve than ask her again.

Luckily Joe went back to work two weeks before I had the baby, so we managed to get a few things together. The old man who sorted out the waste food at the Burger Bar died and they offered Joe the job. He was quite pleased at first because they seldom took back people they had sacked, but I didn't think the work would suit him and I was right – he walked out the day I went into hospital. It was a shame because we really ate well that fortnight; six burgers each for dinner and mountains of chips – you'd never believe what makes its way into the waste bins!

Giving birth to Tommy made me feel like a star. Joe visited with armfuls of flowers, took me home in a taxi and made plans for our son to be heavyweight champion of the world. He'd started to decorate the flat – that was like painting the whole street for Joe – and he'd bought the biggest teddy bear he could find. I don't know where he got the money; I didn't give it a second thought. And I didn't care that the fridge was empty, the rent in arrears and we'd received a summons for not having a television licence. The only thing that mattered was that Joe and I had this perfect baby. For the first time in my life I felt special, like I'd performed some sort of miracle. Most of our belongings were either secondhand or rented but Tommy was brand new, darkly beautiful and he was mine. And Joe adored him.

Even my mother was impressed with Joe's devotion to Tommy. She called in each day to help us when I came home from hospital and she and Joe hardly had a cross word. Once I saw her smiling while she watched Joe holding him and she said to me, if only your father had cared so much about you. I wanted her to say more but she just looked at me and said, no use now. I expect she'd noticed that her words had made my eyes fill with tears; she hated people crying.

When Joe went off down the snooker club, he told her he was looking for work, so that pleased her as well. Every day I was happy.

At the end of the week she took the dirty washing to the launderette, cleared up the mess from the takeaways we'd been living on and said she had to get back to work. The same day Joe went off to light a candle for his son in the church and didn't come back until three the next morning. When he did finally come home the first thing he did was lift Tommy out of his cot and hold him so close I thought he would suffocate him. But then he laid him down again as gently as if he were made of glass and I knew he could never do anything to hurt Tommy in a million years. It made my heart hurt to see how much he loved him.

My mother sometimes popped in after work. She made a fuss of Tommy but began to pick fault with me so much that I wished she wouldn't come. She was worse than the health visitor with her nagging. They seemed to think I couldn't manage. But looking after Tommy was easy. At first he slept a lot and so did I, and when he got bigger we spent hours curled on the settee with the comics Joe brought home. If he cried I cuddled him until he stopped. And Joe was with us quite a lot of the time.

When his giro came he went down the snooker club every day, but I didn't mind because when the money ran out he stayed with us.

We'd walk down to the river taking it in turns to carry

Tommy because the wheel of his pram was broken. In the good weather the office workers sat outside with their sandwiches and we fed the ducks with the stuff they threw away. Sometimes on the way home we stopped in the car park at the back of the supermarket and gave Tommy a ride in one of the trolleys. If the coast was clear, we wheeled him right the way home in it then left it in the street for the kids to play their racing games with.

On really hot days we just sat in the park. There was always something going on and it was quite crowded in the school holidays. Tommy loved watching the dogs. They weren't really allowed in there, but someone had scribbled over the notice and no one ever came to turn them out. Tommy squealed at them and reached out his hands but we had to be careful, some of them looked really fierce. Joe said the drug dealers used them for protection and they were trained to kill, but if one of them hurt his son then they'd be dead themselves!

When Tommy learnt to crawl we had to keep a watch out for the mess they made. The health visitor told me it could blind a child if they got it in their mouths and she said I ought not to let him on the grass. Joe said she was talking a load of crap and I couldn't stop laughing because he hadn't meant to say it like that.

Tommy learnt to crawl in the park. He was sitting on the grass, good as gold as usual, when he noticed the flowers in the border. I think it was the colours that caught his eye, he loved anything really bright and there wasn't much like that in our flat. He moved quite fast, his black eyes big and surprised as though he couldn't believe what he was doing. Then he caught his knee on a stone and toppled over. He started to howl but Joe picked him up and covered his little knee with kisses and carried him over to the flowers. He soon stopped crying and pulled the head off one, cramming the petals into his mouth before Joe could stop him. We let him pick a few more but made sure he didn't get them in his mouth this time. Then a posh-looking woman came over and called us vandals. Joe just laughed and broke off the biggest flower he could find and gave it to her with a bow. I giggled about it all the way home, the way her snooty old face had puckered up trying to make us feel ashamed and we just didn't care.

Sometimes we stopped at the Burger Bar hoping our old friends would be on the till. I was getting used to handouts and the feeling that people felt sorry for me, but I wasn't bothered because I'd never been happier.

It was my mother who said I had to take Tommy to the doctors. He'd been sick twice and I knew it was my fault because I'd let him eat a cake that an old lady had given him. She was one of those who beg for money outside the station and I remember her when she used to come in the Burger Bar and get turned out because she was so filthy. But I didn't want to say no, she was only trying to be friendly and anyway Tommy had seen the cake and had his hand out for it.

The doctor said he doubted if the cake had harmed Tommy so that was a relief, but he did keep me quite a while and ask me lots of questions and it was getting dark when I left the surgery. I was a bit scared about walking home because of going through the underpass; so I called in the snooker club for Joe.

I looked through one of the windows but I couldn't see him, so I wedged Tommy's pram against the wall – we'd fixed the wheel but now the brake didn't work – and went inside. Joe was in the bar and didn't see me put my head round the door because he had his face pressed against a woman's neck. She had blonde hair and it was all mingled up with Joe's black hair and looked so beautiful that I just stood there staring at them for a moment. Then I got this bad pain in my stomach and couldn't get my breath. I pressed my lips together and backed out into the passageway because the gasping noises were in my throat. I crouched behind the door with my hands over my mouth until someone stopped to ask if I was all right and was it my baby crying outside. I just nodded and ran out to Tommy and forgot all about being scared even though a man was peeing up against the wall in the underpass.

Joe came home really late. He smelt of beer and cigarettes like he always did, but there was another smell on him. It was thick and sweet like the perfume counters in expensive shops and it reminded me of everything beautiful like flowers and silk – and blonde hair. In the morning he gave me two bars of chocolate but I didn't feel like eating mine and after he'd gone out I gave them both to Tommy.

He was still eating it when the health visitor came. She fetched a flannel and started to clean the chocolate from Tommy's hands and face. Then she told me a social worker would be coming to see us and she said I must take better care of Tommy or he might not be able to stay with us. I thought she was fussing about the mess he was in, but then she started telling me lots of other things, only I couldn't hear what she was saying properly because I had the pain in my stomach again and I kept hearing a noise like a train. It got louder and louder until I had to put my hands over my ears, but when she asked me what was wrong, I just smiled and said, nothing, nothing. When she left all I could remember was that I mustn't give Tommy any more chips.

Joe went to their office that afternoon and when he came home he was swearing and laughing all at once. But it wasn't happy laughter. I thought he'd be able to make everything all right – like he'd made my life all right – then I thought of the woman with the blonde hair.

Tommy had fallen asleep on the floor. The washing-up liquid container that he'd been playing with was squashed beneath him and it let out a sigh as Joe picked him up. He put him gently on the settee and covered him with his cot blanket. Then he picked up a piece of plastic which Tommy had chewed off the top of the container and waved it in my face.

'You incapable dummy!' The words wouldn't have hurt so much if he hadn't pulled that face – just like my mother when I had tried so hard to please her and failed. I felt like hurting Joe back – but I didn't know how.

He threw the bit of plastic at me and then bent and kissed Tommy's forehead. For some reason seeing his lips brush so softly against his son's head made me want to hurt him even more and I was glad when he went out.

I went to the window and listened to the sound of his footsteps until they had faded away up the street and still the desire to hurt him was there, right inside me.

He'd left two cigarettes for me that morning along with the chocolate. He often did that. I didn't smoke much; it was something to do more than anything else. I lit the first, inhaling deeply for a change and trying to blow smoke rings just as Joe used to do when he taught me to smoke. At last I made one. Perfect. It drifted upwards without breaking, hovering over my sleeping baby's head like a tiny halo. He was a beautiful little angel, I thought, the only beautiful thing left in my life. His lashes were thick and dark like Joe's and now and again they fluttered against his cheeks as though he were about to wake, but he didn't.

I finished the cigarette and lit the second one from its glowing end, wanting to keep the fog of warmth that was filling my head. But halfway through it I began to feel sick and my throat was prickly and dry with smoke. I propped the cigarette in the ashtray and went for a drink of water.

When I came back it had fallen on to the arm of the settee and there was a small black hole smouldering away in the vinyl. I stood there sipping my water and watched as the hole grew bigger. It was like a living, growing thing, a dark circle full of life, and I couldn't take my eyes off it. Curls of smoke started to climb out of the middle and for a few seconds it glowed quite brightly. Then it died down, back to that smoking black hole, spreading and spreading like all dark things do.

How long I stood there I don't know. I watched the vinyl curl open, the edges splitting and turning black right down to the cushions. My eyes were stinging and I couldn't help coughing with the smoke even though I kept drinking the water. I watched as the pile of comics beside the settee began to smoulder and then I reached out and pushed them and they burst into flames. I knew exactly what I was doing but I felt nothing except the certainty that Joe would be hurt beyond all the pain he had caused me.

Even when the flames caught the hem of my skirt, I didn't move. I wanted to stay, more than anything I wanted to stay, but then it felt like my legs were on fire and I just lost control and ran outside screaming for help.

And now I had to tell them. As I repeated the oath after the clerk, I was surprised how easy the words came – only two at a time – but easy, sort of mechanical. I looked round the room as I spoke. There were just rows of blurred faces, people I didn't know. Then, as I repeated the last 'truth', I looked at Joe. He was sitting the other side of my mother staring at me and for a moment I thought how ugly he had become, his pitted face stamped with misery, his black eyes dull and sunk in shadow. I tried to think of him laughing and gentle, coaxing me to talk, making me read the comics aloud to give me confidence. I tried to remember his smile of pride in the hospital when I had Tommy and the roses and carnations he'd brought me and all those beautiful flowers in the park. I tried to put them right there at the front of my mind but I couldn't; I had no control over my memories, just like I had no control over my life.

The clerk tapped my shoulder and I realized that the coroner was speaking to me.

'... but I must ask you just a few questions.'

I nodded. The questions were simple. All about Joe and me. All I had to say was yes or no.

'And tell me what happened after you smoked the cigarette.'

I looked down, trying to escape all the eyes that were on me. He beckoned me out of the box and let me stand by his desk. There was a large yellow folder in front of him and I read the name across it – Montgomery Duvall – with a name like that and the suntan, it was certain he'd feel sorry for me, just like all the others. He'd be thinking, she couldn't help it, poor, stupid girl – forgets her words, forgets she's left a cigarette burning ... I'd never said it was an accident, never. The police had filled in the gaps when I couldn't talk and I just let them because I couldn't bear what I'd done and anyway when did I ever decide what I did?

Joe thought it was an accident. He'd visited me in hospital with flowers, just like before. But I wouldn't say anything and after he'd gone I crushed them, scattering the petals all over the floor, and the doctor came and gave me another injection. Standing by Montgomery Duvall's desk, staring at the yellow folder, I wished I'd ripped the flowers to pieces in front of Joe.

'I did it.' The words came out quite loudly and I felt as though I'd torn apart a thousand bouquets.

'What do you mean, Lizzie?' The coroner leant back in his chair and I caught the familiar edge of impatience in his voice.

'I let the cigarette burn – I made the comics burn.' I spoke easily because I was suddenly very sure of what I wanted to say.

'You mean it wasn't an accident?'

'No, no!' I was crying now and he was telling me to stop. Talking or crying I didn't know and I didn't care. I could hear a jumble of voices but mine seemed louder than any of them. 'I'm not stupid – I didn't do it by accident.'

I looked across at Joe. He had his head in his hands. My mother was clutching her bag against her chest, her lips moving silently as though she were trying to speak but couldn't. I felt like I was bigger than them, that no one could use me or laugh at me again. Even Montgomery Duvall had lost that look of pity and his brown forehead was all creased up and shiny with sweat. He called the clerk over and started whispering to him.

They were probably discussing what to do with me. Oh, I knew that I'd be punished but it wasn't important. I'd already paid a terrible price and nothing they could do or say could possibly hurt me anymore. Joe would be hurting for a long time but that didn't seem important either now. I stopped crying and went back to the witness box and sat down. I felt calm and I wasn't frightened anymore because I was completely in control for the first time in my life.

GOOD AT THINGS

Francesca Clementis

Francesca Clementis spent ten years in advertising, following a degree in Philosophy. For the last two years she has been writing full-time for women's magazines and compiling puzzles for puzzle magazines.

Last year, she wrote the English lyrics for the song that narrowly missed being Turkey's entry for the Eurovision Song Contest! She wrote the lyrics for a musical comedy, *Dear Lonely Heart*, which was a finalist in the 1989 Vivian Ellis Prize. Musicals are her first love although her current project is a TV sitcom.

GOOD AT THINGS

CATHERINE: '5 . . . 4 . . . 3 . . . 2 . . . 1 . . . Happy new year!' Party poppers and kisses came at me from all corners of the room as we all sang 'Auld Lang Syne' out of time to the scratched record accompanying us. My husband, Alex, was about four drunks away from me trying not to look down his sister-in-law's dress. The circle of linked arms evolved into a conga line and Alex danced over towards me.

'Happy new year, sweetie.' He kissed me with an exaggerated smacking sound. 'How long do you want to stay?'

I looked at my watch. I don't know why I did this but perhaps time was too abstract a concept to grapple with so late at night, and I needed a clock face to help visualize the possibilities.

'That's funny, my watch has stopped.' I shook my wrist, which had about as much effect as shouting into a dead phone.

'Maybe now you'll get rid of that old thing and let me buy you a proper one.' He hated this watch because I'd bought it for myself when I returned to work after having David. I loved it for the same reason.

I ignored him rather than start 1993 with a row. 'It seems to have stopped dead on midnight. Don't you think that's funny?'

'Hilarious. So how long do you want to stay?'

'You could read all sorts of things into this, couldn't you?'

'All sorts of things. It could mean that the battery has gone, perhaps leaking corrosive acid into the mechanism if we're lucky. It could mean death of old age or perhaps my threats and insults have crushed its will to live.'

'But it could be a sign, couldn't it?' I've liked the idea of signs since getting married on the hottest day in recorded history. I once wrote an article entitled 'Why Portent is Important' but I didn't know what to do with it. Nevertheless, coincidences should always be acknowledged, taken seriously and acted upon for there are few in one's life and they must mean something.

'Hello in there. Is there anyone at home?' Alex was knocking on my head and shouting into my ear. He knew what I was thinking and was getting ready to deliver his particle physics speech on how coincidences can be explained statistically. It was at times like these that I wished my husband was a poet or a footballer and not a research chemist. I resorted to the distraction of a sweet smile and a smoochy dance before he could start his lecture.

We got home at about one o'clock although, according to my watch, it was still midnight. The kids were spending the night with my parents so the house was empty. I called from the kitchen to ask Alex if he wanted some hot chocolate but he was already asleep on the sofa. I sat on the cold radiator and licked the creamy froth from the top of my drink. My kitchen was a haven that I had not allowed to become a family gathering place. Even the Waltons had enough respect for their saintly mother to save their confessions and problems for the dinner table. No wonder Ma Walton was always baking, it was probably the only chance she had to escape from her twenty-seven children. I refused to have seats in the kitchen in case it encouraged people to linger and talk to me.

I looked at my watch again. Because the hands had stopped moving, I felt as if time had also stopped for me. They say that some people can't wear watches, that watches always keep bad time on certain individuals, which suggests to me that a watch is actually responding to some force in the person wearing it. At midnight tonight, that force in me stopped being. I felt different, which was further proof that something had happened to me and I needed to deal with it.

1.30 a.m. is probably not the ideal time to make long-term resolutions. The blue silence can concentrate the mind a little too effectively and change seems simple. You really need the dilution that daytime noise imposes on the background if you want a lifelike setting when picturing new dreams. Still, by the morning, Jenny and David would be back, the television would be switched on for the day and there would be no private moments for a mother.

I thought about my hormones and wondered if I had them. They're supposed to spend their time coursing around my body like suicidal test pilots inducing mood swings and manic cravings. Mine seemed to have treated the whole journey like a vintage car rally, chugging along at a steady twenty miles per hour. I suppose I could have waited for the certain madness of menopause to make life interesting but I was only thirty-seven.

I was actually thirty-six when I started the juggling lessons which could be seen as the start of all this, but I only took up juggling because Callanetics was full. It provoked a gratifying response. My work colleagues were suspicious of any non-vocational activity and casually left leaflets on my desk with details of evening classes in Hospital Administration (Management). My husband thought I might be having an affair, a situation he considered more suitable for people like us than a course in clowning. Jenny was vaguely interested and David thought it was cool. My mother remarked that a tendency to early menopause ran in our family.

After a lifetime of amusing others with my clumsiness, I displayed an unexpected aptitude for juggling and basic acrobatics. Even more surprising was my new-found capacity for fun. Having it, that is, rather than providing it for my kids when children's television ended each afternoon.

My teacher's name was Toto. It was actually Trevor but he liked us to call him Toto in class for reasons of inspiration that I sort of understood. Anyway, Toto always called me out to the front when he'd taught us a new trick because I seemed to pick things up before the others. Once he said to me: 'Catherine, if you carry on improving like this, I'll have to watch out because you could be stealing my audiences!'

I wonder if my watch began to stop working at that moment.

ALEX: Her mother reckons that it's an early menopause. You can get pills for that now apparently. I know I never wanted her to go back to full-time work but I understood that she needed some kind of fulfilment outside of the home. And yes, I have to admit, the money has made our life a lot easier. So now she wants to throw it all in and become a busker. It's obviously all my fault for not paying her enough attention. What am I supposed to do now? I've already taken her to see 'Phantom Of The Opera'. What more does she want?

CATHERINE: 'Have you spoken to the doctor about this?' Alex asked me.

'There's nothing wrong with me. I'm just changing my career before it's too late.'

'Catherine, becoming a secretary would be changing your career. Learning to teach would be changing your career. Becoming a juggler is the act of a crazed, irrational woman who has lost touch with reality.' I thanked him. I'd always wanted to be perceived as crazed and irrational and to achieve this goal without the assistance of oestrogen gave me immense satisfaction.

'What about the money?' he asked reasonably. I was earning almost as much as Alex when I filled in forms for a living. It afforded us two cars, two holidays a year, private education for our two children and about two hours each month to ourselves.

'I'll still be earning, it just won't be so regular, that's all.'

'That's all? How are we supposed to pay school fees with pennies and buttons tossed into a hat by passers-by who pity you?'

'Toto says he can take over £50 a session some days.'

'That's in Covent Garden which is not quite the same as Southend Railway Terminus.'

'Hundreds, if not thousands, of stressed, weary commuters pass through the station every morning and evening. If only a fraction of them give me 50p, I could be generating a good daily income.'

January was a cold dry month. The IRA terror campaign continued with a series of incendiary devices placed at selected railway stations in the South East. Macdonalds launched MacEscargots to celebrate the opening of the Channel Tunnel.

JENNY: Nan says that mum must be having her menopause and she needs hormones. I think she's just gone barmy and it's a bit embarrassing. Tamsin's mum is pregnant and that's bad enough but at least she stays at home so she doesn't show Tamsin up. Everyone will see mum at the station and Stephen Fletcher will never fancy me now.

DAVID: I've got a great new computer game called 'Revenge of the Killer Croissants'. Mum's chucked in her boring job at the hospital and she's going to be a busker. I think it's brilliant. She's really good at juggling. She can do five things at once which is amazingly hard to do. Mum says all mothers learn how to do five things at once but no one else I know has a mum who can juggle like she can.

CATHERINE: You think I'm pathetic, don't you? A ridiculous woman making a fool of herself out of some kind of frustration. Well, there's something you need to know. I'm good. Really good. This is no false arrogance either. I've never been good at anything before now so the discovery of my one talent is all the more rewarding and I'm not going to waste it. Nor am I stupid. I recognize the risk I am taking, not just of failing financially and bringing hardship on to my family, but of facing personal failure, finding that the one thing I am good at, I am not good *enough* at.

I worked my notice in January but started busking on January 31st out of a superstitious feeling that a new year's resolution should be carried out while the year is still just new.

DAVID: Now that mum is home in the day, she's started cooking again. That's a shame because she's not very good at it. We never get Chicken Drummers or oven chips any more.

ALEX: Catherine has always been the one to take care of the money. We both preferred it that way. She liked to

98

think of me as an absent-minded professor, out of step with the material demands of the modern world. The truth is, I let her organize the household because she needed to feel needed. It's hard to say whether she has been any good at it but I've never seen a red bill come through the door. Maybe I was wrong and the pressures were too much.

CATHERINE: On my first day I took £6.27 despite dropping my Indian clubs a few times. It was the greatest achievement of my life, earning money by my own skills, every penny a willing payment for my personal efforts. As it was my first day, I blew the lot in Sainsbury's on steaks and a frozen gâteau. That evening when we sat around the dinner table, I actually felt part of a family instead of a socio-economic unit. The food was earned by me, prepared by me and cooked by me. I was more than a mother, I was a provider and a good one.

David was the most excited by it all. 'Everyone at school was jealous. They've all got really boring mums. And they said you were brilliant and that you should go on *Opportunity Knocks*.' Alex deliberately ignored this suggestion. While limited embarrassment in Essex was a tolerable burden, national network humiliation was unthinkable.

'You don't think your skirt was a bit short?' Jenny asked anxiously. At fifteen, any pride in my unconventional behaviour was tempered by a strong yearning for a mother a little more like Jane Asher.

February was bitterly cold and there was heavy snow across Great Britain during the second half of the month. The Post Office went on strike the day before St Valentine's day. Fifteen passengers were killed by a bomb placed on a busy commuter train in Kent. The Channel Tunnel was closed when the new snow-sweeping trains from British Rail swept 250 tons of snow into Boulogne, knocking down an electric pylon and causing a national power cut.

CATHERINE: Summer will be easier. I'm taking a steady £15 a day but it's hard. It takes me all day to thaw out from the cold morning and, by the time I feel warm again, I have to go back for the evening session. But I'm getting better all the time, not just technically but also in the way I communicate with the audience. Usually I only have their attention for a couple of minutes because their timetable is so strict, so I can't waste any time building up a rapport. It's immediate impact or you've lost them. I'm having to make up the money with my savings but Alex doesn't know about that. He sees bills being paid and believes he has nothing to worry about.

ALEX: I think my rash is stress-related.

JENNY: I've got a new boyfriend. His name is Spunk and mum will hate him but I don't care.

March was cold and dry. The Princess of Wales had a baby girl with red hair. Questions were asked in The House. The public finally took notice of police warnings to be alert and suspicious and became paranoid. While the police were kept busy dealing with the sevenfold increase in reports, crime rose by 23 per cent. The Channel Tunnel reopened.

CATHERINE: March wasn't a bad month to get arrested. It wasn't so cold that the magistrate was short-tempered, and the promise of spring was close enough to make him generous. Of course I knew that I should have sorted out some kind of permit before starting my new career but I'd made this decision to get away from bureaucracy and I resented the pull of paperwork so soon in my bohemian life. I was fined £200. I earned £176.77 this month. Alex hasn't spoken to me for two days. Jenny has a new boyfriend. He seems very nice despite his haircut.

April was dominated by a mini heatwave over Easter and a series of bomb scares that brought the capital to a standstill. The Channel Tunnel closed for three days when English Animal Rights protesters occupied a stretch of tunnel where a family of moles were nesting.

JENNY: I could have died. The headmistress called me to her office and gave me a letter for mum and dad. Then she asked me all kinds of weird questions about home. I opened the letter in the toilets because the stupid old bag hadn't stuck it down. It said that the cheque for my summer term school fees had bounced, 'returned to drawer' it said, and that this was the third reminder that payment was seriously overdue. I could have died. I mean, Jennifer Tinsworth's mum works in the school secretary's office so she'll know about this, she might even have typed it herself, and she's bound to tell Jennifer and then everyone will know we're poor. I hate mum.

DAVID: Only three weeks until my birthday. I'm getting a new computer with colour monitor, digital graphics and CD sound unit. I hope mum buys a cake from Selfridges like last year. She's not very good at making them.

CATHERINE: The April sun felt different to the March sun. The light was more insistent, the temperature more intrusive. The pavements chattered with the click-clack of flimsy sandals and people smiled. Business was not

101

good because the police didn't like me standing on the station concourse. Security, they said. Bloody IRA. I've got no more savings left, not enough money to pay the mortgage and three red bills stuffed in the desk drawer. Oh yes, and David's birthday coming up. There's a boot sale on Sunday. Perhaps I'll see something there for him. You can find amazing bargains at boot sales.

ALEX: I went to the bank to cash a cheque today and was told we were overdrawn. We've never been overdrawn before now. I don't know what to do about this. Every time I mention money, Catherine gets tetchy and accuses me of not trusting her. Trust is one of those loaded words she lobs at me which she feels I am unworthy to return.

May temperatures soared into the eighties. The Channel Tunnel closed when the railway tracks buckled under the heat. The IRA considered taking responsibility for the well-publicized series of disasters befalling the Tunnel but obviously decided to wait until the first trainload of English football fans finished off the task properly.

JENNY: I'll get pregnant. That'll teach them.

ALEX: 'I suppose you're doing this because I refused to fire Sara.' She didn't say anything to this. 'Well, I don't know how many times I have to explain myself. She's the best lab technician we've got and I can't fire her. That would have to be a group decision and I would have to give the group a good reason for firing her.'

'I haven't even thought of Sara in the last few months.' She didn't look up from the mixing bowl, just reached past me for the rolling pin, tutting slightly as if I were in her way.

'She means absolutely nothing to me. It was a stupid mistake . . .'

'Once is a stupid mistake. Eighteen months is a long series of very clever mistakes. Eighteen months is not a stupid mistake.'

'I knew this was what it was all about. You're trying to get back at me by ruining all our lives. Well, what about the children? What happens to their education when all the money has gone? What about the house? Is it worth losing our home just to punish me?'

'Believe it or not, Alex, there are whole parts of my life that have nothing to do with you or anyone in this family. You've just got on and done whatever you wanted to while I have watched my life being shaped by everyone else's needs. Now it's my turn. I'm still your wife and the kids' mother but, first and foremost, I'm a thirty-seven-year-old woman who has not lived for herself since she got married.'

DAVID: Sometimes my Dad is stupid. He had a row with Mum in the kitchen today. It was bound to end in a row in there. Mum hates us going in the kitchen when she's cooking. Once she dropped a leg of lamb on the floor and I went in while she was rinsing it under the tap and sticking bits of parsley into the holes. I think that sort of thing happens quite a lot and she naturally doesn't want us to see what she's doing to the food. Frankly I'm happier not knowing. I'll have a word with Dad if he doesn't work it out for himself. My birthday tomorrow!

CATHERINE: Today I was happy just to be out in the open, under the sun, doing what I'm good at, making people smile, earning a living. I never noticed the reluctant handover of spring to summer before. Just when you get used to the heat of the day, a prickly breeze blows in with the evening to remind you that it is only May. In my former life it was either hot or cold, Christmas or Easter, Monday or Friday. There were no wriggly intangibles to guide me firmly from one faceless day to another.

My earnings are increasing all the time. I've just about made enough to begin paying off some of the mortgage arrears. I don't know what to do about the other bills yet. I'm going on a talentsearch night next week at the Ritzy. Top prize is £1000 and a regular spot. I really need to win that. I really need to.

The weather turned in June. The heaviest rainfall was in the South where residents welcomed the end of the hosepipe bans after five years. Twenty-three people were killed after an explosion in a West End theatre. Madonna got married for the third time. The Channel Tunnel was open for the entire month but only 673 cars and 342 rail passengers used it because nobody else realized it was open.

JENNY: I'd rather be pregnant than just fat. The doctor gave me a diet sheet. I ate four Mars bars while I read it.

ALEX: Christ, that woman doesn't care who she hurts. She didn't tell me that David was expecting a new computer. His face when he opened that box of secondhand children's encyclopaedias . . . I could have killed her. Why didn't she tell me? Not that I could have done anything since my salary appears to be doing little more than nibbling away at our spiralling overdraft. But I think she might have told me what *my* son wanted for his birthday. Or even told me that it was his birthday at all. Christ.

DAVID: I'm going to sell my old computer then wash cars and do errands until I have enough money to get a new one. I felt really sorry for mum. I know she's got money problems but she's getting really good at juggling. She should have won that contest. That other woman only won because her dress didn't fit properly. Anyway, after the first shock that it wasn't the computer, I was quite pleased. I'd always said that I'd like a set of encyclopaedias of my own and these were brilliant. I'm doing a project on natural and unnatural disasters and I've found loads of great examples. Dad was late home as usual and lost his temper when he realized that he'd missed the birthday dinner. We did save him a piece of cake but Jenny ate it.

CATHERINE: There are talent contests all over the place if you know where to look. I buy *The Stage* every week and there are pages filled with announcements of Starsearch nights. There's big money involved too. I only need to win one and we'd be on our way to solving the money problems. Not that it's my fault it rained all month. I'm self-employed in a job where the elements have a major impact on my turnover and earning potential. I pawned my engagement ring to pay for groceries. David's birthday was a success even if Alex forgot about it and turned up smelling of toothpaste and talc at half past nine. I made a birthday cake decorated like a computer to compensate for not being able to afford a real one. I think David was pleased. A homemade cake is always more appreciated than a shop-bought one. Jenny had four slices. It's nice to see her eating so well.

It was a glorious July day for the marriage of HRH Prince Edward to Kylie Smith. The former Page Three girl looked elegant in a catsuit. The Abbey was

not as full as expected since most of the European
guests were stuck on the royal train which broke
down in the Channel Tunnel. The terror campaign
ceased for two weeks while IRA masterminds were
on holiday in Camber Sands.

CATHERINE: I came second! £250 and a rosette! Mind you I deserved it. It was the best performance of my life. I finally found my gimmick. I decided to learn from the success of female alternative comedians who have played up their femininity instead of competing with men on men's terms. I juggled a doll, a foodmixer, a bra, a copy of *Delia Smith's Cookery Course* and a tampon with 'I Will Survive' playing in the background and the audience loved me. Now that I have my niche, I should be able to supplement my income from busking with prize money and get the phone switched back on again.

ALEX: I don't care what she thinks of me. Seven months is more than enough to stretch the tolerance of a reasonable man. I opened a new bank account and had my salary paid directly into it. I'm being more than fair. I give her £200 a month which pays for all the groceries and I pay the bills when I find them screwed up in a drawer somewhere. I told the building society that my wife had had a nervous breakdown, hence the neglect of our monthly commitments to them. They seemed to understand and were happy to accept my offer to pay instalments until the arrears were cleared then increased payments for the remaining fifteen years on the mortgage. And I told Catherine that if she didn't get a job within the next month I would leave her.

JENNY: I don't think mum even noticed that I'd shaved my head. Anyway she'll notice when I lose weight. I'll get anorexia and then she'll be sorry.

DAVID: Mum won £250 last night. She was fantastic! She juggled all sorts of weird things and people laughed. Anyway, she came second and won all that money. We'll be rich again now and dad will probably come home more. I wish he could have seen mum last night. He said he'd try and get there but he didn't try very hard. Still I don't think mum minded too much. At least she had me there.

'Phew, what a scorcher!' The traditional August headline of The Sun *made its appearance on the day England lost the Ashes. The Ashes were being sent by train to France to be exhibited as part of an Anglo-French Cultural Exchange. British Rail blew them up thinking the box to be a bomb planted by the IRA in a fiendish plot to destabilize the Channel Tunnel which had just completed three weeks' unbroken service.*

DAVID: I think mum and dad are going to get a divorce. Dad sometimes doesn't come home all night. And now that we've had the phone reconnected, there's no excuse for not ringing to let mum know. When he is home, they argue all the time. I had a word with dad about not trying to talk to mum in the kitchen but he ignored me. But that's nothing new. Anyway when dad's not around, mum's really happy. She's won three more of those contests. I didn't get to see them because they were in Manchester or somewhere. She gave me £25 to go towards my new computer. That was really nice of her. Only another £173 and I'll have enough. We're going to Butlins for our holiday. I can't wait! Free funfair and a fantastic waterslide and go-karts and activities all day and night. It's all free. We've always had to go to France before. Boring.

CATHERINE: I'm going to make it. I've started telling jokes during my act and suddenly I'm a star. Well, not exactly a star but a Starsearch winner. And they're not even jokes, just stories about Alex's and my marriage, the kids, that sort of thing. It's just like talking to a friend and audiences seem to love it. I won the big £1000 prize last week, plus the £600 from the beginning of the month. I paid all the bills and had enough to put away for new clothes for Jenny and David. Apparently they can wear what they like at Southend Comprehensive but I'd like them to have some new things to make them feel better about their new school.

I still do a bit of busking but only to try out new routines. I've also applied for a pitch in Covent Garden. I'm taking the kids to Butlins for a week. They have a weekly talent contest with an overall prize of £2000. I've booked a chalet for four but I don't know if Alex will be coming. He says he has a course that week.

JENNY: Southend Comprehensive. I'm going to Southend Comprehensive. They'll all be drug addicts and have tattoos. I'll never see any of my friends again and I won't make any new friends. Who's going to talk about Sylvia Plath and Virginia Woolf with me? And I'll probably be the fattest girl in the class. I'm not doing very well on the anorexia front. And Butlins. I'm too embarrassed to tell anyone where I'm going. It will be the worst holiday of my life. I wish I could go away with dad wherever he's going. I wish I could just talk to dad.

ALEX: All right, so she's had some luck. At least we've still got a house, a phone and electricity. But what sort of life have we got? We've had to take the children out of private school and abandon them to the public sector. My children at a comprehensive. I hope no one here finds out. It's competitive enough in the research establishment without having to include family status in the equation. Christ, it all comes down to money. And of course I can't discuss money with Saint Catherine. Ever since she found out about the flat I got for Sara, she's carried her superiority with her like a halo. Well it was *my* money, *my* trust fund. And I said I was sorry about Sara, didn't I? And it's all over now. As good as.

The leaves decided not to fall in September this year. Since British Rail had already attached new untested leaf sweepers to their trains, the absence of leaves was ignored and the sweepers promptly scraped most of the coating from the rails causing wheels to stick and jam on the surface. The Channel Tunnel was closed while French and English engineers redefined the seasons.

CATHERINE: I could easily live in a hot country where it was sunny all the year round. Even though I now have a regular cabaret spot at the Circus Tavern and don't need any extra income, I still enjoy my mornings outside the station. I look forward to recognizing the pale faces that started the year gradually turning biscuity as the year relaxes its hold on them. I'll never know the role I play in their life. Do they talk about me to their friends and families? Do they laugh at me? Or envy me? Do they care about me? I suppose an eyes-down smile and a coin is as much acknowledgement as I can expect from a stranger.

I saw Alex at the station today. I suppose he lost the company car when he got fired. I should feel sorry for him but it's a long time since I've found naivety a sympathetic quality. Actually naivety is too kind a word. Stupidity is closer to the truth. Did he really think Sara wanted him back after he dumped her so coldly last year?

'You just can't believe that anyone could want me when you so clearly have no interest in me yourself. Sara never stopped loving me. I should have left you when she first asked me. But no, I let you talk me into the famous "one last chance". Fat chance, more like. I give up the promise of a new life with a beautiful, young, intelligent ... young ...'

'You've said "young" already,' I pointed out reasonably.

' ... successful young woman who loves me. And for what?'

'A successful eighteen-year marriage and two surprisingly nice kids who would rather have two parents than one?'

'You see, you're doing it again, making me out to be the villain. Well, I did my duty, stayed with my family, carried on providing so that you could all continue to do exactly what you wanted. And none of you ever thought about what I wanted.'

It was like arguing with Jenny so I didn't bother. He moved into Sara's flat and a week later she stole all the papers from his briefcase documenting his confidential work and sold them to a rival company for the price of a new job. Alex was fired the next day. Apparently Sara had written to his boss but Alex doesn't know what she wrote. Still it did the trick. The woman in me admired the effectiveness of her revenge and the wife in me hated her.

JENNY: It was the most wonderful holiday ever. I met a gorgeous boy called Steve and he lives in Basildon so I get to see him at weekends. We spent every minute of the holiday together, swimming, dancing, playing crazy golf, going on the funfair, everything. It was just so wonderful. And mum won her competition which was a bit embarrassing but it means we all get a free week's holiday

110

at Butlins Skegness in December for the Grand Final. And Mum said Steve can come if I still want him to in December. Of course I will. Dad's living in a grotty bedsit on the seafront. His girlfriend got him fired and then chucked him out. Serves him right.

DAVID: I won a computer for taking part in the most activities over the week. I did everything, entered all the contests, played all the sports, joined all the clubs. As soon as I saw that there was a computer to win, I just set out to win it. Mum cheered really loudly when I went up to get the prize. She cried a bit which was really silly because it was the happiest day of my life and not a bit sad. I cheered when she won her contest too. I can't wait to come back here another year. Dad didn't come which was great because it meant we could have chips every night. I think they're definitely going to get a divorce because he doesn't live at home any more.

ALEX: I thought it would be a good idea to move into a flat by myself for a while to think things through. This time last year I had it all – house, career, girlfriend, wife, kids, pension plan, six numbers in the Readers Digest Prize Draw. Sorry, that's the drink talking. I'll try and be serious. After all this is serious, isn't it? I'm forty-one years old. I've got no home, no job, the girlfriend turned out to be a bitch, the wife turned out to be Miss Juggling England 1993, the kids will probably become juvenile delinquents, I can't touch the pension until I'm fifty . . . and it's all Catherine's fault. She couldn't let things be. We were fine, just fine, until she decided to change all our lives. And look at her now. Making a fool of herself all over the country. Making money too, I agree, but if it was money she wanted she could have got her old job back just like that. Or even a better one if she insisted on being ambitious.

111

Well, she's not the only one with ambitions. Does she think I'm living out my deepest dreams? Does she never think that perhaps I might have liked to be a tap dancer? Or a bus conductor? Or anything but a chemist? It's easy for a woman. Ultimately she knows that the man will always provide the financial safety net so that she can go off and fulfil herself whenever and however she chooses. Want a baby? No problem. Just take five years off work and let your husband work out how you'll manage. Want to become a juggler? Easy. Just become a juggler and let your husband renegotiate the mortgage. Becoming a husband was the most poorly thought out career move I ever made.

DAVID: I forgot to mention that Jen and I started a new school. It's got a computer club every lunchtime.

Terrorist attacks fought for front-page supremacy throughout October. There was so much death that the weather wasn't even mentioned until page three in most of the tabloids. It was hot, really hot, not just 'warm for the time of year' but 80° hot at any time hot. If there had been nothing better to write about, a journalist would have checked the records and come up with some dull statistics about this being the hottest summer on record. British Rail ignored the temperature since they had officially redefined the seasons and it was now winter. The Channel Tunnel closed when British Rail staff went on strike in protest against the compulsory wearing of woollen balaclavas and donkey jackets from October 1st.

CATHERINE: Have you ever smelled October? Or watched it? October was the only month when my eyes were so dazzled by the intensity of the sunlight that I preferred to work in the shade. It's strange to think of sunshine as disabling but I am beginning to prefer the more consistent atmosphere of the gaudy clubs where I make my living. The Covent Garden crowds are great though, a patchwork quilt of ages and nationalities enjoying the language-free entertainment that a good street performer delivers. I sometimes take a couple of hundred pounds in a day but I think I'll stop when my TV contract comes through.

I'm very worried about Jenny. She hasn't settled into her new school at all. I try to talk to her about it but she just clams up.

I wonder if this heat is a sign.

DAVID: Mum's going to be on the Paul Daniels show every week. And she says that I can go along and meet him and get his autograph and that he might even let me take part in one of his tricks. So I might be on telly. Mum's won millions of competitions since Butlins and she bought me a computer table. We had an unbirthday party like Alice in Wonderland with a cake from Selfridges and Chicken Drummers. It was the best party ever. Even Jenny enjoyed it now that she's not on a stupid diet any more and she's not going out with that stupid Spunk. Mum invited dad and he bought me a game for the new computer. It was a really good laugh and dad didn't go into the kitchen and have a row with mum so that was even better. I reckon they might get back together.

JENNY: Mum's going to be famous. I expect David and me will have to go on 'Whose Baby?' and 'This is Your Life' and mum'll have to give us a hug even though no one has hugged anyone in this family since David was a toddler. I think mum and dad are going to get a divorce. Rebecca Potts says you can tell when they start buying you presents. Well, mum hasn't stopped buying presents since she got rich and dad bought us presents for the first time ever. They had this unbirthday party for David because he didn't have much of a real birthday party this year. I thought it was going to be boring but it was quite good fun really.

The new school is fantastic, much better than my old one. But I'm not going to tell mum that after all the fuss I made about leaving St Saviour's. When I got to Southend Comp, everyone had heard of me. They all thought it was really cool to have a mother like mine. I've got loads of friends and they all want to come home with me and meet my mum. They obviously haven't tasted her cooking.

ALEX: I know I should be gracious about this and congratulate her on her success but it's all so unfair. How lucky can you get? Just when the world of entertainment decides that the one fish missing from its vast ocean of mediocrity is an alternative juggling feminist, along comes my wife, *my* wife, who casually dips her toe into the water and drowns in celebrity. But look at what it's done to the children. David is a computer junkie, so miserable that he's cut himself off from us all and lives in a blinking, beeping world where mutant turnips do battle with avenging matchboxes. As for Jenny, she could be on drugs for all we know. She won't talk to either of us. At least she's eating normally and has got rid of that ghastly freak she was hanging around with. I can't say I approve of this new one though. She met him at Butlins and you can just imagine the sort of boy that goes there. Catherine has asked me if I want to go with them to the grand final of the talent contest in December. Pretty ridiculous when she has a TV contract and fame oozing from her pores right now, but she has this obsession with seeing things through. I suppose it wouldn't do any harm to go. We're getting on quite well at the moment. The good thing about being self-employed is that you can take holidays whenever you like.

November crept up on the British just when they were becoming complacent about the warmth. A winter curfew descended as doors closed firmly during the evenings to be opened only reluctantly the following day. Stewing beef was in demand and diets joyfully abandoned as three layers of thick clothes provided perfect excuses for getting fat. Heating on the Channel Tunnel trains was so efficient that fifteen people were taken to hospital suffering from heat exhaustion. Prince Edward's wife gave birth to a baby boy. Buckingham Palace confirmed that the baby was five months premature but at 9 lbs 6 ozs was doing fine. The baby, who appears to be very dark skinned, will be named Prince Rasta George Edward Ziggy. Her Majesty The Queen has just begun a six-month tour of the Australian Outback. She is unavailable for comment.

ALEX: I went to Mafco Pharmaceuticals today to tie up a sponsorship contract and they told me that my old team had all been made redundant. They can't all have been sleeping with Sara so obviously firing me was just a strategic move towards breaking the whole team up. I'm not really interested any more. Mafco are setting me up in my own lab and giving me a free hand in choosing a project from their wide range of research commitments.

'I'll be hiring a couple of assistants,' I told Catherine as she sat in the bath. I've learned my lesson about the kitchen.

115

'You could always give Sara a call. Just joking.' Sometimes I feel that my wife's sense of humour is more highly evolved than my own.

We talk every night while she's in the bath. Sometimes I get in with her. I only do that when Jenny and David are both out because I'm sure they'd be horrified to learn that their parents still fancied each other.

She took the disappointment really well, better than I did actually. I was furious with them for treating her like that, leading her to believe that a TV contract was practically hers when really they couldn't even guarantee her an audition. She doesn't seem to mind. She's back busking outside the station again as well as playing at the Circus Tavern and travelling all over England for talent contests. She's still making more money than me. She's still my wife.

JENNY: Yuk, it's so grotesque. They're all over each other. I hope this is just a temporary phase, a second honeymoon like Philippa Sanderson said, and they stop all the kissing soon. And they've started kissing me too and asking me caring questions around the dinner table. And that's another thing. We all have dinner together every night. If one of us is going out, we eat earlier or later, but always together. It's like *Little House on the Prairie* only with Marks & Spencer food. That's the good part about mum's money, the Marks & Spencer food.

CATHERINE: Working for himself has changed him. I knew it would because I've been through the process myself this year. I don't think he resents my earning more than he does because he knows how shaky my earning potential can be. I may have made a lot of money in the last few months but juggling feminists could be replaced in fashion by plate-spinning Croats next week.

Our marriage is a new place. He's stopped provoking me in the kitchen and switched to seducing me in the bath. He's never been like that, not even when we were first married and a relationship only really changes when both the people involved change. I know I've changed but although Alex is behaving differently, I don't see any real transformation in his character. Perhaps if I did, I wouldn't trust it. One thing that did surprise me was his attitude to the audition fiasco. He hadn't shown much enthusiasm for the idea in the beginning but when it fell through he became an avenging knight seething with indignation on my behalf. I didn't like to show how disappointed I was about being let down in case Alex was incensed enough to do more than write to *The Times*.

JENNY: Steve came to stay this weekend. Although he's the most good-looking boy I've ever seen, he doesn't wash very often.

ALEX: 'Have you spoken to Jenny about . . . things?' I couldn't say the word.
'They learn all about that in school. There's nothing left for a modern mother to say.'
I've never thought of Catherine as a modern mother. Juggling apart she has always been the most conformist of women.

CATHERINE: Alex thinks Jenny is getting up to 'things' with Steve. Why do men know so little about the women around them?

DAVID: I'm president of Southend Comp Computer Club. It means I get to try out new games first and print newsletters from the new desktop publishing programme. I'm going to be a publisher when I grow up.

117

*A bomb went off on Platform 3 at Southend Central
Railway Station at 8.17 on Tuesday December 7th
killing nineteen people. One of those killed was a
wanted IRA terrorist who is believed to be responsible for the spate of bombings on the mainland over
the last eighteen months. Flann O'Gerraghty had
reserved a seat on the 11.45 Dover/Paris train giving
rise to suspicions that the bomb was aimed at the
Channel Tunnel just when tabloid coverage of its
inefficiency was at a tolerable low.*

ALEX: Butlins was a revelation. It was the best holiday I
can remember and I think the whole family would agree
with me. Thank God Jenny decided not to invite that
yobbish boyfriend at the last moment although I was
quite prepared to be civil to the lad. Catherine was busy
with rehearsals and photo sessions for the first couple of
days before the first heats began. Jenny got in with a nice
enough gang from London and we only saw her at
breakfast and when she ran out of money in the evening. I
spent the time getting to know my son. I don't know how
he ever turned out so well adjusted but it certainly wasn't
my doing. He showed me some of the computer games in
the amusement arcade and I was soon hooked. It's a bit
irksome to be humiliated so conclusively by one's son in
competition but I like to think that I taught him
something about gracious defeat.

'Why did we go to France?' I asked Catherine in the
shower on our third night.

'Because you wanted to.'

'I thought you wanted to.'

'Well, the kids certainly never wanted to, they were
always bored by the third day. What do you think of this
new concept of having fun with your family?'

'I wish someone could have shown me that life could be

118

like this fifteen years ago. Is there room in the shower for two?'

JENNY: I've met this really lush boy called Philip. He's from London and he looks just like Marty Pellow from Wet Wet Wet. His sister won them this holiday. She's in the junior talent section singing 'Honeybun'. She's revolting, all highlights and eyeshadow which looks gross on a seven-year-old. I'm praying she gets through to the final on Friday night otherwise the whole family is going back early so that Honeybun doesn't have to suffer the indignity of early public failure. The family all talk like that. I think they watch *LA Law* too much.

DAVID: Dad's rubbish on the games but he's trying really hard and he pays for all the turns. Every morning we play crazy golf then we go to the amusements. Dad gets £10 worth of 10 and 20 pence pieces which last us the rest of the morning. He keeps on with the same game – Dirtsmackers – and he says he's not going to give up until he gets his name on the High Score board. I like playing all the games and if I don't get a high score after five turns I give up. It's just a waste of time to keep on if you know you're not ever going to be very good at something.

CATHERINE: I thought I'd get through the preliminary heats at the very least. I lost to a teenager singing 'What I Did For Love'. Alex, David and Jenny were all in the audience cheering me on and I felt guilty for letting them down.

'Sweetheart, perhaps feminism hasn't reached Butlins yet.' Alex was more upset than I was. He was too kind to mention that I'd stumbled at least three times raising laughs where there were supposed to be gasps. The truth was that I hadn't been able to concentrate since hearing of the bomb on Tuesday. 8.17. I knew exactly who'd be there at that time. There would be the man who never smiled but gave me 50p every Thursday, the woman who always wore mini skirts even though her legs begged to be covered, the weary woman who cleaned the station, the paperseller who knew which paper all his regulars preferred, the girls going to St Saviour's in Laindon where Jenny used to go. I wrote down the telephone number you could call for details of friends and relatives you suspected could be involved but I couldn't phone because I didn't know the names of any of the faces. The papers printed the names the next day but none were familiar.

JENNY: No one I know was in the bomb blast. It could have been me. This made me feel a bit funny but Philip was very understanding. His sister's through to the Grand Final so he's staying. Mum got knocked out but we're staying anyway because this is the best holiday of all time.

DAVID: I cried when mum lost. She dropped things and people laughed. I hated them and hoped everyone laughed at them the next time they dropped anything. I think we made her feel better. Now she's got the rest of the week free to play with me and dad.

CATHERINE: Alex was dragged into a Lambada competition by one of the redcoats and won first prize. I've never seen him less inhibited or more pleased with himself.
   'She said I was a natural dancer. I just picked up the steps and then added something personal. That's what made me stand out to the judges apparently. I was always good at dancing if you remember.' He was good at everything and it had brought him the rewards a man in

120

his position craved. The recent setbacks only served to reinforce his skill at survival and made his achievement more substantial. I was a good juggler and it had brought me to a holiday camp in Skegness in December.

ALEX: Catherine has signed up for a hospital management course starting in January. She has come to regard the whole year as a sort of madness. Her mother was probably right all along, it was probably something female that a gynaecologist could have sorted out. Still it's over now and we've paid off all the debts she accrued in those first seven months so nothing's been lost. Since she's decided to take a more positive, productive approach to the coming new year, I'm going to do the same. There are no commercial skills I need to acquire so I'm going to pay attention to making myself a more well-rounded person. On January 2nd I begin tap dancing lessons.

WATER

Adrian Williams

Adrian Williams is an actuary and a management consultant who, until recently, has written
only on business topics. He neither reads nor
writes novels, preferring short stories as an art
form. His favourite author is Elizabeth Taylor.
Adrian plays the guitar and sings a little. He lives
in Oxford and sometimes in Malta.

WATER

The place to buy books in Istanbul is a small courtyard behind the Beyazit Mosque. It's an unexpected find, but it's not *hard* to find if you're expecting it – off to the left as you come down the university steps, under the half-dozen plane trees that shade that corner of the Beyazit Square, and there it is: 'Sahaflar Çarşísí' in a plaque over a little archway that gives on to a wall fountain that doesn't work, and then the book market. Several dozen kiosks with the usual eclectic assortment of the world's learning from every age including our own – you can find out how to run MS-DOS for IBM PC Compatibles in Turkish if you want to.

I should explain that it wasn't the purchase of books that took me to Istanbul. It's true that I run a small specialist bookshop in Highgate in North London. You may know it. You certainly do know it if you are interested in Islamic calligraphy, because that's my particular speciality, and most years I take myself off to the Middle East to replenish my stock. It was the search for Turkish miniatures that took me to Istanbul and, at the time this particular sequence of events began, I had just completed an especially successful day of a very successful tour, that had started in Morocco and had taken me right the way round the Mediterranean. Today, after three hours of careful negotiation, I had acquired a set of eight beautifully detailed hunting scenes with the very last of the money that I had set myself to spend. So,

125

with the virtuous feeling of a job well done, I resolved to drop down the hill to Eminönü for an extended dinner at one of the fish restaurants under Galata Bridge and then back up the Tünel to the not very smart hotel that I patronize when I'm in Istanbul, in a sidestreet just up the hill from the Pera Palas.

It was the middle of May, and the evening of the last day of Ramazan. A few elderly shopkeepers were minutely dusting away the sprinkling of blossom that had drifted down from the chestnut candles overhead to lie on the courtyard in front of their kiosks. Others were putting up shutters, although it was only five o'clock – for tonight was the end of fasting, and even an Istanbuli bazaar trader wants to get away for the Bayram holiday. Here and there you could find a male child or an old man with a set of bathroom scales who would weigh the pious for TL 50 and, though I hadn't been stinting on my own diet in the last three weeks, I hopped on to one of the squeaky bits of apparatus to let its infant custodian drive through a final deal at today's close of business.

Though my route to Galata didn't need to take in the Grand Bazaar, I can never resist the diversion. What an astonishing place it is! If all the racks of gold bangles were stretched end to end, I reckon they would cross the Bosphorus five times over. I came into the enormous covered market through the leather-sellers' quarter – which was a mistake because I had to run the usual gauntlet of bomber-jacket salesmen and attendant Lacoste rip-off merchants – but I was soon out of that and into one of the main avenues, which even at this evening hour were still glittering like Aladdin's cave with a hundred million useless gewgaws, and the crowds were milling about and through the market, tourists looking at carpets and offering $20 for a $2,000 silk Hereke, always haggling, never buying – how do the traders make ends

126

meet, I was wondering, how often do they turn over their stock? – when I came surprisingly upon a shop in that dazzling array of beautiful nonsense that did indeed seem to have foundered; for, alone in the blazing lights of this oriental Vanity Fair, its glass shop-front was dusty, there was no stock in the window, and there was just one dim light burning somewhere inside that showed no movement of an attentive owner waiting for trade. It had the look of a dead, black tooth in a row of sparkling dentures. Its contrast with the scintillating parade, stretching on either side as far as you could see, was so striking that I paused in my stride to peer in at the door. That's always a mistake, and so it seemed to be now, for immediately at my ear I heard, '*Effendi*? You are perhaps interested in books? In Islamic writing? I have some interesting examples that I think you might like to see . . .'

And, before I had time to protest that my day had finished, I was in through the door and sitting on one of those absurd low benches that can just about accommodate a husband and wife seated side-by-side while a salesman beats them into submission by showing them 239 carpets.

'You don't look as if apple tea is your tipple,' pronounced my host, producing this phrase with much the same pride he evinced in sweeping a cup of coffee on to the low table that sat in front of me. 'Please . . . *Effendi* . . .' He motioned towards the cup.

What can I say about him? Below average height. Slight of build. Self-effacing. Wearing one of those dull greyish-grey Turkish suits that are the same colour as the exhaust fumes in Taksim Square. Only his eyes were at all remarkable – greyish too, but of a hard, dark, luminous grey-black colour quite unlike the usual grey of a man's eyes. All this I could see in the feeble light offered by what

127

turned out to be a mosque lamp hanging by chains from the ceiling.

'What do you have?' I asked. Thoughts of my fish supper and a bottle of Doluce took precedence for a second.

With an elaborate flourish he laid a sheet in front of me, then another. I grunted, in a display of polite interest. He unfolded a larger sheet and laid it out, stood back to await my comment. He came forward again, and laid down other items.

His stock was pathetic. I use the epithet in its literal sense. It brought a feeling of pity and shame to my mind, that anyone could be trading in the dazzling company of Kapalí Çarşi, the Grand Bazaar, the world's largest covered market, in which you could buy anything which foolish man's heart could desire – and could offer nothing more enticing than this tattered garbage. A few apprentice pages by an aspiring calligrapher who didn't look, to my mind, as if he would have completed his term. Several letters of a very mundane character that had been penned no earlier than 1920. A mawkish miniature. His best item was a *firman* under the *tuğra* of Sultan Mahmut II concerning a rather unexciting land tax in the Canakkale region – which might have been worth something if a more recent authority hadn't rested a wet wineglass on the lower edge.

'Well,' I said. He stood back, so that I couldn't see him too clearly in the guttering light. 'Well. I don't really think that I see anything I want at the moment.'

'My prices are very reasonable.'

'Yes . . . well . . .' I was floundering a bit. 'I have, just, well . . . actually, completed all the, er, you know, things I was . . . you know . . . going to buy on this particular trip . . .'

He appeared rather unexpectedly from a part of the

128

gloom that I hadn't seen him move into. 'Look at this Qur'an, *Effendi*.'

Now, I don't normally deal in Korans. It's not that I'm superstitious or anything, but I feel that it could offend some of my customers, several of whom drive up to Highgate in very smart cars with CD plates accredited to embassies that I should prefer not to upset. However, it's quite a good idea to have two or three Korans around in the shop to encourage the European trade – not to sell, but to entice the punter into calligraphy, so to speak, by showing him what he can aspire to if his collection really gets going. And I had been induced to sell a couple of Korans recently to my richer and rapidly enthusiastic European tyros, so I was a bit short of stock in that department.

'Yes . . . please do show me.' I was at the stage of wondering whether it was a 1991 printed job that he had lifted from the Beyazit Mosque up the road. How wrong I was.

I ought to explain at this point that Islamic calligraphy isn't just one style, but several – and that calligraphy is used much more widely as an art-form in Islamic countries than we are used to in Europe. A sultan's signature, or *tuğra*, is a case in point: it's not a casual scribble, but a highly elaborate series of flourishes arranged to produce a harmonious and impressive effect, with each part of the pattern having a meaning within the entire composition. The style of a *tuğra* would be one of the secular scripts such as Divani. Sacred writings like the Koran wouldn't use Divani, but one or perhaps more than one of the six canonical scripts such as Naskhi or Muhaqqaq established by the Baghdad calligrapher Yaqut al-Mustacsimi in the (Christian) thirteenth century.

I say 'one or perhaps more than one'; that's where the

Koran that I was holding stood apart from any others that had ever passed through my hands. What I was looking at was executed in no less than the full set of six scripts. More than that – the calligrapher seemed to be fluent and expert in all of them, drawing on the full range of expressive arabesques and using them as he liked, at will, to their best advantage in text and headers. It was an uncanny expression of virtuosity – an apprentice work by an unsurpassed master, a very pattern book of calligraphy. Was it unique, even? It must have been worth thousands. Even the illumination on the title page, though not particularly outstanding, was of a quality that would fetch £300 for that sheet alone. I leafed through the pages, thinking furiously.

'That's very . . .' I said, 'very . . . er . . . unusual. Yes. That's certainly very unusual.'

I glanced up. The vendor was hard to find in the gloom. I wondered if he had slipped out for a moment, or into the back of the shop. Another deft cup of coffee appeared on the low table at my elbow.

'You know it for what it is, then?' he asked. He was invisible in the dimness except for his bright little stone-like greyish eyes.

'Yes. Yes, I do.' We held each other's gaze for several seconds. In the covered arena outside, people were banging up shutters and chucking jokes across from shop to shop as they prepared to close up for the holiday.

'Look, I'm at the end of my tour,' I told him. 'I really don't have a lot of money left. It's an amazing piece of work, it truly is, but . . .' All this was true, I thought, as I made the exaggerated shrugging sign that says 'It is out of my power to pay your price' – all this was true, it was the most astonishing Koran that I would ever see in my life, and I was virtually skint. I could have sold it thirty times round London for a five-figure sum within a week of getting home, and without worrying about scruples in the embassies, either.

'It is for sale at 500,000 lira, *Effendi*,' he murmured. I gawped. He was asking little more than £200 for possibly the finest example of calligraphic expertise that I would ever handle. I heard him whisper, 'It is a genuine bargain.'

He had now completely vanished. There was an utter silence in the tiny shop, made all the more palpable by the raucous happenings in the street outside. But even that noise was beginning to die down, I began to notice, and lights were being extinguished.

Into the gloom, I croaked, 'What's wrong with it?'

For ten seconds or so, nothing happened. Then at my ear suddenly he whispered, '*Effendi*, it is mutilated.' He paused. He had something else to say, I could feel it. 'No, it is defaced. See, *Effendi*. It is defaced!'

He seemed now to be urging me to find fault with it. I leafed through it again, searching . . . until I found what I was looking for, on the very last page – which is the first page you come to in a book written in Arabic. There it was, and had been staring at me all the time, a message written in the crudest of scripts:

I Have Sinned

I Am Judged

I Shall Suffer

'This is poorer workmanship.' It was all I could think of to say. I wasn't in bargaining mode – it's just that I couldn't think of anything else. And anyway I was broke. 'Do you take American Express?'

And I promise you, as he fished around under the dusty

131

folds of a table-covering for the little machine, he said, 'American Express? That will do nicely, sir.'

We completed our transaction like any two business-men wrapping up a deal. I got a receipt, and the blue Amex counterfoil, and my purchase conveyed to me in a supermarket-type plastic bag. There's really nothing more to say, except that, as I made to go, he suddenly gripped my arm and said – no, he hissed, with an intensity that was chilling in the clammy bazaar heat: 'Deal honourably with this book, *Effendi*.'

His grey-dark stone eyes glowed at me – and he was away again, into the depths of the shop, leaving me blinking outside in the Grand Avenue, clutching my little collection of parcels acquired in the day's work and wondering what the hell was going on. So, anyway, off I went down to the Galata Bridge and had my fish supper and went back to my hotel as planned and went to bed.

There's not much to say about the trip home, except that I was unfortunate enough at London Heathrow HM Customs & Excise to cop one of the Keen Types. I mention the episode because it turned out to have significance later, although everything seemed perfectly normal at the time. I'm always one for the Red Channel at Customs, and more often than not I pay my whack and get on my way with the minimum of fuss and formalities. But today had to be the day when I was battened on by one of those tough, weatherbeaten thirty-five-year-olds who look as if they're taking temporary leave from the Special Boat Service.

'So that's all, is it, sir?' he said, clearly not believing me.

'Yes, absolutely, officer.' What a fatuous addition that 'absolutely' was. If ever there was an admission of guilt, that was it. 'Absolutely the whole bang show, nothing else whatever. Zilch. Nix. Niente.'

'Are you sure, sir?' This is the point at which the citizen commits himself irrevocably or – in an alternative scenario – breaks down, sobs, and rips open the concealed panel of his briefcase to reveal the real contraband, which the customs man has known to be there all along.

'Yes, that's it, officer.' I tried to add an air of clipped impatience at this point, as of a serious businessman who came and went through Customs most days of the week and wasn't used to having his word questioned. What did this fellow know about Islamic calligraphy, anyway? If he had any expertise at all, it looked to me more likely to do with winning at squash rackets at some sort of fierce sports club near Portsmouth.

'Right. Take this Qur'an now. This receipt. How did you pay for it? Amex? Could I please see the counterfoil.' You've got to hand it to them – they don't mess about. 'Are you seriously telling me, sir, that you paid no more than the amount on this receipt for this article? Do you have any other Amex counterfoil relating to the transaction? Or any other credit card? What can you tell me about' – he read off the receipt with exaggerated precision – 'Kahveci Antiquities? You do understand, sir, that I have powers to call for and search all credit card accounts held by you or in your name to verify the truth of what you're telling me now? Would you like to change your statement, sir?'

No, no, I mumbled, it was a perfectly straightforward sale, and this was the amount I had paid, and I had frequently dealt with Dr Kahveci, and I had never had my bona fide questioned before, and I was quite prepared to sign the necessary form, which I knew he had, that would commit me to the truth of every statement I had made.

'Right, very good, sir. In a few minutes, I'll make out a receipt for the duty you owe on the items you've

133

declared.' His aerodynamic SBS beard faced me down; he looked me straight in the eyes for about four seconds and began the most thorough search of my baggage that I have ever sustained. He took about twenty minutes over it. He took everything down, and even squeezed out my toothpaste tube into a small plastic bag that he had ready for the occasion. But I wasn't bothered, having been suddenly overcome by a stabbing attack of Ataturk's Declaration that sent me off to the gents without too much concern for the likelihood even of his following me in to do an orifice-job. Probably the effect of last night's fish supper, I thought, as I wrote out my cheque on my return. Or dehydration on the flight, perhaps – my mouth was as dry as the desert. Pride sustained me as I hauled myself upright and, pain notwithstanding, began to claw my dirty underclothes back into the suitcase.

'Find anything, officer?'

'Just remember, sir. False declarations to Customs & Excise can get you into' – through gritted teeth – 'very serious trouble.'

And with this injunction, I piled into the Underground and would have gone straight home to Highgate had there not been a pressing necessity to tip out at Acton Town to relieve the pain in my gut.

I was in good health again by next day. Being back in the shop after a hard stint in the Med is always such a pleasure. It's so calm, for one thing. And the customers don't bargain. Well, they bargain a bit sometimes – think they're very daring if they propose a ten per cent volume discount for two books bought together. But they don't haggle, not as a general rule. So my first morning was spoiled when the door banged open at coffee-time to announce the entry of my least favourite client.

'Professor Damant!' I cried, simulating as much pleasure as I could summon up. '*Ahlan Wassahlan*,' and I made the traditional gesture of greeting.

'Stop that bloody nonsense, Pickering,' he grunted. He was casting around for the new stuff, I could tell from the way he sniffed the air. It crossed my mind once again that, for all he was one of the country's foremost Arabic scholars, he hadn't actually understood what I had said. 'How you hope to run a business, I'll never know. You're *never* here to open the shop. Don't you understand the rudiments of service to y'customers?'

It was always the same: he knew I loathed him and, as for him, he loathed everybody – but he knew I was likely to have something he wanted, and I knew I wanted his money. We sparred for a few minutes; I sent him the long way round, starting with some leaves from Cairo that I hadn't thought much of except as collection-starters. At last I got him on to a series of sixteenth-century letters that I had found in Alexandria. A killing here, I thought. But I was disappointed.

'Bloody useless,' was his opinion. 'Especially at that price.' He turned away and crashed around the shop disconsolately, at one point knocking over a pile of books that he came upon. He was up and down the library steps every now and then – he was a short man, but would have died before asking me to help him by getting something off the higher shelves. After five minutes or so, he hauled out one of the folios from the Persian nineteenth-century section and settled down to browse through it, laying it flat on one of the low glass-topped display cabinets and sneering audibly at it every now and then. I got on with some correspondence, sold a postcard of Waterlow Park, phoned my ex-wife to say I was back, made some coffee, took a call from my accountant . . . and suddenly Professor Damant asked, 'What's that?'

Well . . . he'd seen it pretty well as soon as he came in, I surmised, although I hadn't got it on display. In fact, it was still lying on my work-table, half-hidden by a stock-list.

'I picked it up in Istanbul. Have a look.' I hadn't shown it to him before, because I wasn't going to sell it. Not to him, anyway. But I was so pleased with my Qur'an that I was quite prepared to like anyone who admired it – even Professor Damant. And he was certainly someone who would know the value of what he was looking at. I fished it out from the stock sheets and stood watching him as he leafed through it.

I've got to hand it to Professor Damant: he didn't show, by even the slightest tremor of an eyelid, that he had anything in his hands that was more than run-of-the-mill. He turned at a constant pace – page by page to begin with, and then sampling through the rest of it, making the short, dismissive exhalations through his nostrils that constituted his habitual expression of disdain. At last he reached the mutilated page. He brought the book an inch or two nearer to his gold-rimmed half-glasses, and painstakingly translated aloud to himself for my benefit.

'I have sinned . . . der der . . . judged . . . der der . . . suffer . . .' He set the Qur'an down on the table, the better to gesture his contempt. 'Well, there you are, Pickering. Typical of the tat I expect to find in this place. Can't you ever think of giving a decent service to the world of scholarship? How much did you pay for this rubbish?'

'About two hundred pounds.'

It was worth telling him, to see his expression. And I wasn't going to sell it to him anyway, so I was losing nothing by declaring my good fortune. I watched the emotions chase across his face: envy, fury, followed closely by cupidity. For a horrible second I thought I saw a hint of conspiratorial mateyness, as if the Robinsonian Professor of Oriental Languages were about to suck up to a humble bookseller. But the moment passed.

'And I don't suppose you'll stick at your customary five hundred per cent mark-up either,' he snarled. 'Some poor devil's going to have to shell out about two thousand quid for your shop-soiled crap, I *don't* doubt.' Then he bowled one that I wasn't expecting. 'There'll be some people in Ankara that would be *very interested* in what you're up to, Pickering. I doubt that you'll be welcome in Istanbul again if news of *this* shoddy day's work gets about.'

'No problem,' I had pleasure in telling him. 'In point of fact, I haven't even begun to put a price on it. It's not for sale. It's for my own collection. Shall I help you to put that folio back on its rather high shelf?'

He was still snorting when he left the shop. But the last I had seen peeking over the top of the half-glasses was a piggy gleam of avarice. I wasn't surprised when, back in my flat that evening, I took a telephone call from him.

'Is that Pickering?' He knew it was. He knew that I lived alone; and he had telephoned at a point in the evening when, as he probably knew too, I had been back long enough from The Flask to be past the end of a bottle of wine with my supper, and possibly on to another one. 'Is that Pickering?' He came on strong then, man to man. 'Look, Pickering, I'm willing to give you £7,300 for that book of yours, and we'll say no more about it.'

'*Il' hamdullilaah!*' was all I could think of to say to that. As usual, Professor Damant was unable to interpret this basic phrase of Arabic, probably the commonest utterance of thanksgiving in the language. There was a splutter at the other end of the line, and a throat-clearing.

'Look here, Pickering. I'm not prepared to mess about when there's an important question of literary custodianship at stake.' He half-covered the mouthpiece, I think, and pretended to speak to someone in the room with him. Then aloud, but not to me, 'All right? But absolutely no

137

further in any circumstances.' Then directly to me again, 'I can go as far as £8,250, and that is absolutely my top limit. I'd advise you to take it, Pickering. It's a fair price – and I'm sure you don't want there to be any trouble with the authorities.'

What a nasty little man, I thought. 'Professor Damant,' I cried. I waved my glass in the air to him down the telephone, and took a quick swig. 'Professor Damant! For you ... for you ...' I had had something very clever to say here, but it slipped my mind for a second.

'Good God, man, are you ...?'

'For you, Professor Damant, my famoused ... my ... my fav-ou-rite customer ... for *you* I am prepared to sell this notable object for your opening offer of ... what did you say? ... £7,300!'

There was a silence. Finally, 'Now look, there's nothing wrong with it, I hope? We don't want a repetition of that unfortunate incident of 1986.' The Professor was referring to an occasion when I sold him something that, he later alleged, was a modern copy and not the eighteenth-century original that I knew it to be.

This was the time for hauling myself together. I focused carefully on the door-knob at the far side of the room.

'Professor Damant,' I enunciated carefully. 'You will recall that, in our conversation this morning, I made no statement that could be interpreted as an attribution of date, authorship, or even country of origin. I said only that I had picked it up in Istanbul, for about £200. Now, you and I both believe that it is worth very much more than that. Probably between twenty and thirty thousand pounds, perhaps even more to a keen buyer.'

The strain was telling. I refocused, and set off again.

'But, if you care to present yourself in my shop tomorrow with a banker's draft for £7,300, I shall sell you the article – with an attribution on the receipt that

138

will be guaranteed by me myself personally. And I should just like you to know that I think your friend in the room there with you is a nasty little prat.'

Pause. 'I'll forget you said that, Pickering.' Down crashed the phone, and I was left to my reveries.

Why had I done it? Because my accountant had telephoned me again that afternoon, with some to-the-point comments about my cash flow. Quite simply, I needed the money and I needed it that month. It's no good aiming to be profitable next year if you go down the tubes on the way. It would take months to find a private buyer who was willing to pay the full value; and the only auction likely to draw the right interest wasn't to be until September.

But why drop near on a thousand quid? Had the Wirra Wirra Cabernet Sauvignon taken the edge off Pickering's customary negotiating skills? Well, to be absolutely honest – yes, it had, a fraction. If I hadn't had a bottle or so, I might have throttled back to just £7,800 and still have got the satisfaction I was looking for – which was quite simply the joy of having something with which I could belabour Professor Damant in all of our trans-actions to come. What joy, what bliss unconfined! I swerved and dodged away to bed that night a happy man.

Of course I began to think better of my charity next day, especially when Professor Damant turned up after lunch with his banker's draft.

'I've had the cheque made out for the full amount, as you'll see.' He patronized me with an offhand gaze round my shelves. 'But I've been thinking – I've been a bit lenient with you on the price, really. I think what I'll do is take that French commentary on Isfahan that I was looking at yesterday, to make up the balance. Just put that on the receipt too, if you will.'

I had written out the receipt that morning: 'To: one

book, probably not of European origin, end-paper defaced. £8,250 less allowance of £950 for vendor's goodwill: £7,300.' I was particularly pleased with the inclusion of 'allowance'. I handed it to him without comment and took his cheque over to the window, where I held it up to the light and ostentatiously examined it. It amused me to observe that you can hear a person fuming as well as seeing him; Professor Damant fumed in short snorts inhaled through the nose and exhaled through the mouth. I wrapped the Qur'an and handed it to him as I ushered him to the door. A sharp memory of the little kiosk in Istanbul pricked my mind.

'Deal honourably with this book, Professor,' I enjoined him. He turned as if to strike me, but made a sound instead, that could even have been 'Pshaw' or 'Bah'. I wished him good-day, as any tradesman might.

The next time I saw the book was about three weeks later, when a young man called at the shop and introduced himself as Professor Damant's stepson. He was carrying the Qur'an in a Harrods plastic bag. The shop was empty, so I got him a chair out of the back and sat him down.

'I was very sorry to hear about your stepfather,' I told him. 'It must have been very sudden. He was here only a few days ago . . . I saw the obituary in *The Times* . . . I could hardly believe it. Had there been . . .? He was a very valued customer here.' You know how people prattle on in times of bereavement. I'd almost begun to persuade myself that I liked the man.

'No,' he said. 'No, it hit him quite suddenly. He'd been abroad, you know – in Damascus, we think. So it might have been something . . .'

We contemplated mortality and the perils of foreign travel.

'Or something he picked up on his return, perhaps,' the

140

young man said – Stephen Pomeroy, his name was. 'The doctors just don't know at all. It was very swift, whatever it was. All over in a night. Mother's very cut up, naturally.'

Personally, if I had been the widow of Professor Damant, I should have been on my knees thanking God for deliverance. 'The obituaries were full of praise for his contribution to Islamic scholarship,' I offered.

'Rather too full, perhaps,' he murmured, in a wistful vein that made me feel quite warm towards him for a moment. So I wasn't inimical when he loosened the plastic drawstrings of the Harrods bag and pulled out the Qur'an. 'I'm terribly sorry to be embarrassing, but do you think there's any chance of your taking this back? The thing is, what with the funeral and all that . . . Mother's not finding it terribly easy at the moment. He'd had to borrow the money to buy it, you see. I know it might seem the most frightful cheek. Of course, we wouldn't expect anything like what Bunjy gave for it.'

Bunjy? That was a new one. I was circumspect.

'If you'll take my advice, you'll hang on to that particular item. It's worth a lot more than what I sold it for. But I'd be happy to visit Mrs Damant and value the other items in the professor's collection – I'd want to buy some of them, I'm sure.'

He looked puzzled. 'Collection? There's no collection. Not of this sort of thing, anyway. You don't mean his library, do you?'

So much for the professions of a duty to scholarship – the crafty old bastard had been in business on the side. I can't say that I was surprised. Anyway: my cash flow had improved, I could afford to do a good turn to someone I felt mild sympathy for – and I didn't mind giving myself the option of selling the thing at a proper price, either.

'I'll give you what he paid for it,' I said. 'No, that's no

trouble, no problem at all. I've already told you, it's worth more than that. It's the least I can do. If you could just sign something for me . . . and I'm afraid I'll have to date the cheque for Monday, I hope that's okay?'

I was writing out a receipt for him to sign, not paying him much attention, when he shifted in his chair and made a curious bleating sound. 'Maaa. Maaa. What could he have been thinking of?'

'I'm sorry?'

He made the sound again. 'Maaa . . . maaa.' He picked at some fluff on his sleeve for a second or two. 'He was calling it out. The night he died. All night, it was horrible.' He winced at the recollection. 'He died in great pain, you know.'

'I think he may have been asking for water,' I said gently. 'The Arabic for "water" is something like that. Maa'. Would that be it?'

He was aghast, and stopped halfway through signing my receipt. 'Do you mean we could have done something? None of us had any idea. We all thought it was some sort of reversion to childhood. They thought so at the hospital, too – thought he was delirious, anyway. Didn't we do all we could?'

'I don't suppose it would have made a difference to the outcome,' I said, trying to reassure him. There was something not quite right. 'It's odd that he would have been saying that. I don't actually recall Professor Damant speaking Arabic. As opposed to reading it.'

'No, that's right, he didn't,' Stephen said. He sat there, remembering. Then he stood up smartly, folded my cheque into his wallet, and stuck out his hand. 'Well, I mustn't keep you any longer, Dr Pickering. You've been awfully decent. Mother will be very touched and grateful. Thanks.'

And off he went, leaving me with the satisfaction of

having done a good deed in a naughty world. And the renewed prospect of clearing thirty thousand notes as well.

Or so I had hoped, until the shop was broken into. It was a couple of days later, and I hadn't even started putting out feelers, so there was no question of anyone who had heard about the Qur'an targeting it in a theft. No, it had all the signs of an amateur break-in: what little there was in the money-box had gone, and a bottle of Scotch, and some of my business cards. He had made a thirty-minute call to Australia (as I learned when the next phone bill came in). He had messed some of the files up. And he had taken the contents from one of my display cabinets, having smashed the glass to get in. Part of his prize was the Qur'an.

Less than a week later, I was telephoned by a police officer attached to one of the Central London police stations. They had reason to believe that I was the owner of stolen property that had recently come into their possession. Would I be able to come in and identify it? Yes, sir, this evening if you wouldn't mind, since we are hoping to charge someone within a very short time and it would be helpful to that endeavour if the ownership of certain articles could be established before tomorrow morning. So, at the end of the day, I hopped on to the Tube and took myself into town.

It was one of the old-fashioned sorts of police station, in which the linoleum is still brown, and the walls are still painted a dullish shiny green. A lugubrious sign on one of the doors off the reception vestibule showed the way to Female Cells. I was taken through to a small office, where Detective Constable Jefferson sat with a cardboard box, out of which he produced the four articles that had gone missing from my display cabinet.

'No Scotch, then?' I asked, but it didn't seem worth

waiting for a reply. 'Yes, they're all mine. Smart work, getting on to me so fast.'

'He took your calling-card, didn't he?' He shrugged morosely at the callow lack of imagination that had been the undoing of this particular felon. 'What would he hope to clear on this sort of stuff, d'you suppose?' He scrabbled around in the box and came out with four or five of my business cards.

'Oh, nothing. He wouldn't have had the least idea where to begin. How did you . . .?' Catch him, had been my question, but it sounded so *Boys' Own Paper* that I was embarrassed to finish it. We were interrupted by a uniformed constable, who put his head round the door and did one of those elaborate mime shows that would have achieved better results if he had simply said, 'There is a panic out here. Can I talk to you immediately?'

The DC excused himself. I could hear them outside the door, shouting at each other in tiny whispered shouts. '. . . been like it for more than an hour . . . what d'you expect *me* to do about it . . . getting worse by the minute . . .'

'Well, get someone in to see him, then,' I heard the DC say. 'Yes, double quick. Go on, move move move.'

He mooched back into the office and, seeing me there, braced himself suddenly into action.

'Here, I need you, Dr Pickering. Come with me, would you?' And he was off into a warren of corridors, upstairs once and then down again, with me pounding along behind him and beginning to pant a bit. In reply to my gasped question, he hardly slowed down to say 'I'm taking you to see your mate, aren't I? The pillock who's done your place over.'

We arrived at what I took to be the cell-block. He stopped at one of the doors and squinted through the judas-hole for a good twenty seconds.

144

'There you are, Doctor. What d'you make of that?'

He ushered me forward. I'm bound to say that, brought up as a lad on jurisprudential notions of innocence until proven guilty, I was embarrassed to be offered the chance of peering in at someone who, as far as I understood, hadn't even been charged yet. I cleared my throat and, moving close to the door, cocked my eye to the judas-hole.

The person inside was standing in the centre of the floor, moaning slightly and clutching his lower abdomen. He was a youngish man – twenty-four or so – with lank black hair that was pulled back into a short pony-tail. His clothes were designer-scruff, with distressed jeans that showed two parts of a very hairy thigh. Just about exactly the type who would go raking around in other people's property, I thought, letting my natural instincts get the better of middle-class squeamishness about justice. He was clearly in great pain. My unfamiliarity with the use of spyholes was tiring my sight; I began to experience the illusion that he was suspended a few inches off the ground. We were interrupted by the arrival of a couple of uniformed constables – one of them the mime-artist from downstairs.

'How's he going on, Jeff?'

'Dr Pickering's just clocking him now,' my DC said. 'What d'you think, Doctor?'

At that moment I heard a cry from inside the cell. He had seen my eye on the other side of the spyhole, and was now seemingly lurching towards the door, holding out his arms in piteous supplication but without in fact moving a step from the spot where he seemed to be both standing and dangling.

'Maa'. Maa'.'

It was a cry that would come back to me in the darkness of the night for years to come, no matter where I

145

buried my head beneath the pillow. 'God Almighty,' muttered the DC. We had all heard the cry, but only I could see what was going on. 'Better open up, Frank. Took his shoelaces off him, did you?' There was a jangle of keys at my elbow; I stood aside while the mime-artist fiddled and rattled, and pulled the door back to let the three of us in. Seeing us, the prisoner threw his head back and roared in pain.

'Maaaaaaaaaa'.'

There was no doubting it. 'He wants water,' I said. 'He's asking for water. Look, I think we ought to get him to lie down until the doctor gets here.'

'I thought you *were* the doctor,' the second uniformed man grumbled, made nervous by this outturn of events – and also by the astonishing difficulty that the four of us were having in moving the one man, sick as he was, from his standing position to the pallet-bed at the back of the cell. 'What about this water, then? Do I go and get some, or what?'

'Better had, Trevor.' DC Jefferson seemed to be the one who had most command of what was going on. Right at this moment he was having some trouble commanding anything, since all his efforts were going into holding the prisoner's shoulders down on to the pallet, while Frank sat on his feet. The shrieks of pain were hardly abating. 'You still here, sir? Well, thanks very much for helping us out, but I really don't think there's anything else you can do . . .'

'I wouldn't give him any water, officer. I really wouldn't. I've no medical expertise at all, but I believe I've read that Nil by Mouth is the best thing if there's any doubt about causes . . .'

'Just as you say, sir.' He flashed me one of those pitying, contemptuous looks that true professionals reserve for the people who bottle out when the going gets tough. 'If you could just find your way back to my office, Dr Pickering, I'll attend to you as soon as I can.'

As it turned out, I didn't see him again that night. After I had been waiting for an hour or so, the desk sergeant advised me to go home. DC Jefferson telephoned me next day at the shop.

'I'm sorry about that business last night, sir.' He coughed. 'The fact is, sir, there'll be no charges. The young man died in the early hours, I'm afraid. Nothing to be done, apparently.'

I murmured something that I hoped would sound both sympathetic and non-committal.

'Nice of you to put it like that, sir. We'll do what we can to get the formalities out of the way so that you can retrieve your property. And . . . I'm afraid it's quite possible that you'll be asked to attend the inquest.'

And I was. It came as a surprise to me to realize that I hadn't known the name of the deceased until then: Jasper Goodlaison. All of a piece with the pony-tail, I thought. The cause of death was quickly established as peritonitis, but the proceedings seemed to me to be drawn out beyond what it should take to reach a verdict of natural causes. I gradually twigged that Jasper was the scion of a house – well, if not noble, then at any rate monied; and that, while it was clear to everyone who knew him that being in possession of stolen property was not all that outrageous a possibility, the Goodlaison family had got the scent of righteousness in their nostrils – a scent bearing the label 'Police Brutality'. There were several of the family there, and a very smart lawyer acting on their behalf. I felt a distinct *frisson* of disapproval from the family group as I went up to give my evidence – for it was fairly clear that I was there, as the police might put it, to give their side of the story from an unbiased viewpoint. I

147

explained what I had seen and heard, the coroner dandled his silver pen.

'You saw no marks on Mr Goodlaison's body? No . . . And no actions on anyone's part that might have led to the severe bruising and the condition of the upper and lower abdominal region of which we have been told in the medical evidence? No.'

He paused to think. 'Dr Pickering, you are not a doctor of medicine, are you? A PhD in the fluid dynamics of gases. Quite. Quite.' He made a minute note, waiting for the respectful titter of amusement that he had conjured up to play itself out through the courtroom. 'Two questions, then: how did you come to let yourself get caught up into the scene that you have described? And how was it that, having no medical knowledge, you nevertheless ventured an opinion on the inadvisability of giving the deceased a glass of water? When, by your own account and yours only, he was so clearly desperate to have some?'

My being there was simply how it happened, I told him; the pace was all so fast that no one stopped to let me explain. The other was just . . . a layman's best guess.

'Yes, I see, Dr Pickering.' He was a kindly man, and hadn't been angling to catch me out, I believe. He smiled across at me encouragingly. 'Well, as it seems from the medical evidence, your layman's best guess seems to have been spot on. It's just a sadness that the beneficial effects could do no more than prolong this unfortunate young man's life for a few hours. Now: is there anything else you have to tell us?'

He waited for a few seconds – waiting for something, I thought – and then discharged me. Afterwards, in the hall outside, the station superintendent touched me on the shoulder and let me know that he and his colleagues were grateful to me for taking the trouble to come along and give a straight account. Nothing more was said; but I think I can say that there's a patch of London within a mile of Hyde Park Corner where I'm welcome to park on a double-yellow, at any time.

Of course, there *was* more to be said. The coroner knew it; but he didn't know what it was, and he didn't know how to get me to tell him. What's to be told? I was reading the relevant passage over a bottle of wine on the night before the inquest; it says it all. It's an extract from an account, by the English traveller and adventurer Thomas Potts, of his journey in Egypt and the Middle East in the early 1800s. He's writing about a particular person, but the same could be said of thousands of poor wretches in the hundred years that had gone before:

The criminal Suliman al-Halabi had been convicted of the assassination of General Kléber, in his garden near Ezbekiah on June the Fourteenth 1800. He was condemned to have his right arm struck off at the wrist, and then to be put to death by that means which the Egyptians call *al-khazuq*. His mutilated forearm was first seared in pitch, so that he might not bleed to death; and he was then taken to a public square in Cairo where we saw him to be impaled on an iron spike, about the height of a man's shoulder. After some forty-five minutes of agony and torment, he began to cry for water, and we made to go to him so that we might help to relieve his suffering. But the executioner came forward and, in the most officious language, forbade us to minister to him, saying that the drinking of water would immediately bring about his death, whereas the withholding of it could prolong the agony of the condemned man for many hours.

I got the Qur'an back from the police, eventually. But I didn't feel like keeping it. Not after hearing that cry. And I was naturally unwilling to trade it – for who knows what little foible of negotiating tactics might be judged as less than honourable?

So I gave it to the British Museum, from which it cannot be removed except by Act of Parliament. And I hope that the Trustees of that venerable institution may never be tempted to act with regard to it in any way other than the way of total rectitude.

DIVIDED LOYALTIES

Ellen Eugene

Ellen Eugene has had a 'you-name-it-I've-done-it' life – art teacher, barmaid, civil servant, antique dealer and she once ran a pub in the back-end of Donegal. At present she works as a freelance journalist and writes a regular page for a newspaper.

This year she went back to school to do her 'A' levels in Art and Business Studies.

DIVIDED LOYALTIES

I'm not really mad, I know I'm not. Of course they say the madder you are the more you profess not to be. But I'm not! I know why I'm in this god-forsaken place with its sanitary walls heavily disguised in pathetic, gaudy murals. I know why I succumb to the ministrations of starched nobodies who hush and tut and treat me like a two-year-old having tantrums. Gently humouring or mock-severe. But always wary, like soldiers watching for snipers. How appropriate! For that is why I'm here. I'm a sniper, a threat, a wild, evil woman whose mind became so abused by the violence of it all that she will finish her days finishing that one long scream started so long ago.

I know they fear me for I see my own fear reflected in their eyes. They switch on concern when they realize I'm watching. Watching them watching me. Me! All five foot three of me armed with a toothbrush, sinister in my combat gear of blue towelling robe and padding slippers.

Stewart bought the robe for me when he put me here. 'Keep you nice and warm until you're better,' he said, smiling with his mouth, avoiding my stare. My accusations. Silent accusations now, with no hope of a trial. For I was the one to be tried – and found guilty. Guilty of suffering, of knowing yet not knowing what to do. Now, I do nothing.

'It takes time,' they tell him, when he asks how long? 'Time will heal the wounds, eventually. Time heals all.'

Some past presence smiles within me at those words –

153

Stewart's own words thrown back at him – and I wonder if he remembers as I do.

I had had it all. I had proved pessimistic friends and troubled family wrong. I had gained and guarded a settled, cosy little world of coffee mornings and garden centres and candlelit dinners. A world walled in by happy trivialities and financial security. Personal security was something else, but then even the most beautiful roses had a thorn or two. And the thorn of worry and resentment that accompanied the marriage of a Catholic girl to a Protestant policeman had, over the years, become blunted. I had proved to all that their insular, tight little fears were groundless. That they were blinded by time and events and had accepted divisions that were unacceptable to intelligent people.

Oh, I had known of the tragedies and the heartbreak. I had mourned with other wives and checked the car before getting into it. I had grown angry with the bigotry and petty jealousies. Stewart wasn't an alien being whose only aim in life was to annihilate every man, woman and child who looked to the Church of Rome for guidance. He was kind and funny and allowed me to want for nothing. A good husband, a loving father.

For eight years I had lived a serene, comfortable life, only occasionally touched on the outskirts by bombs and bullets. What if I had learned to pull the curtains as soon as darkness fell, and what if my heart had stopped momentarily every time the newscaster's doleful voice rhymed off the casualties in another blast? Minor inconveniences. Other people's major disasters. Only slight hiccups for me, just part of the pattern. A tightly woven pattern that curved and coiled and intertwined like a protective netting. Until, on a whispery, white snow-covered morning, hatred and greed and stupidity,

154

in the guise of fighting for life and liberty, had blasted through the illusions. Within seconds my rosy world had become bleached of warmth.

I was washing the breakfast dishes, pearly pieces of delicate china, as fragile and as easily smashable as life. A silver rain fell on my hands, tiny shattering fragments of glass turning into rosy ribbons of blood as I stared, mesmerized. I felt rather than heard the blast. Stomach clenching in cramps of fear I ran to the front door. Through the cloud of dust and smoke and screaming chaos I remember the relief as Stewart's angular figure appeared through the nightmare curtain – then I saw his face.

'Mark?' I whispered, then screamed, 'Maaaark!'

They took me to the hospital. In the haze of sedation separate, ordinary details flashed like stills in negative. My fluffy slipper lying forlornly on the slush-turning pathway. The snow-covered hedges, like the criss-cross tracks of a child's puzzle. A maze of black and white. Dazzling, sun-white, blue-shadowed. And the gaping black hole and tangled mess of metal and wire and stones – and my seven-year-old Mark.

They apologized afterwards. They had only meant to kill the father, a policeman like Stewart. Mark had taken a lift with our neighbour and his son, his friend. They were sorry about the two boys. So was I. So was Barbara, who wrapped herself in widows' weeds and turned her sorrow into manageable hatred, then turned that hatred on me. I tried to understand. I grappled with Stewart's reasoning that Barbara was unhinged by her loss and looking for some near-at-hand recipient for torture. I wanted that too, but there was no face I could spit in, not as Barbara did in mine.

'I hope your lot are satisfied now, Ciara Williams! I hope it does them a lot of good to know my husband is in bits all over the fucking road. And my wee Geordie – ahhh!'

After the first rage of interest and inquiry died down I was left alone to my own sorrow. It was as if Mark had never existed. Stewart took away all his pictures, his toys, clothes, everything, before I had even come home from the hospital the next day. That part of our lives was over. You have passed Go, collect £200, and carry on. And I carried on, even though I noticed Barbara wasn't the only one who was treating me like a leper. A contagious disease to be avoided, to be disinfected and purged from the small, Protestant community that had been my home for eight years. And when a stone shattered the living-room window I knew it was no threat to Stewart or anything to do with terrorists. Not the kind we were used to, anyway.

And the fear for Stewart that had always lain under the surface now turned inwards. A new fear became my constant companion, the lonely fear of ostracism. And with the fear grew anger. Anger at the faceless men who had so wantonly killed two little boys, innocent of any crime or shame or hatred. Then anger at Stewart's friends, for they were no longer mine, if they ever really had been. Anger at their suspicion and innuendo and the pity and false concern that said, 'We told you so,' from my own people. My own! How laughable the situation was, the irony of it all and the sick comedy.

When I married Stewart I turned my back on my own religion, never going to Mass or involving myself in any of the rituals. I was part of my husband's life, a life that caused me to be spurned by my Catholic friends. And, there I was, neither fish nor fowl. The irony of it was that the 'man' who had so casually destroyed three lives, not only three, was probably a better Catholic than I was. I

156

retched with disgust when I contemplated the whole, filthy picture of abuse.

But worse than the outside glares and avoidance and threatening behaviour was the acceptance. Stewart's acceptance. 'It's over now. We have to pick up the pieces. Things will soon calm down. Don't worry, forget about it!'

Sweep it under the carpet, flush it down the lavatory, but don't keep on about it. He humoured me by moving house, then I discovered the move had been an order from on high. And I still lived in fear. Watching the faces of strangers in the street for signs of hate, or suspicion. Locking doors behind me until life itself took on the smell and odour of a prison. Until almost a year later I could take no more.

Stewart was leaving for night duty. He presented me with his usual, dutiful peck and, 'See you in the morning, love.' It was then that something snapped. A year of guarded looks and quizzical glances. 'Are you all right, love?' Without wanting an answer. A year of repeating, 'I'm fine,' yet wanting to scream and yell and draw blood. To shout to the world, 'No, I'm not all right, I'm angry and sick and totally screwed up. My life is a sickening hell of fear and nightmare with a great gaping hole where my son used to be and my loving husband doesn't give a damn!' Don't rock the boat! Time heals! A long year of trite, useless, surface nonsense culminating in that last Judas kiss that sent my insides writhing and splattered the last of my control, bloody, against the cream walls of a suburban bungalow. It was then I packed. Calmly, methodically, I packed the sum total of my needs into two suitcases and left. I ran away.

Cats' eyes hurtled through the tunnel of night like myriad blazing bullets from a machine-gun. Silent though, but continuously streaming from the inky cavern of darkness. To snuff out under the body of the engine-purring car. The even slick-slack of the wipers changed to high screeching and I switched them off. The rain had stopped. Only the occasional swish of wheels through puddles was an indication of the torrential rain which had recently speared from the heavens. The silvery veil that had enveloped the little car and made me feel isolated, yet safe in the private darkness of the interior. Safe! A year ago I had thought I would never get into a car again, let alone drive. Yet here I was, on a bleak, January night, in the middle of nowhere, alone, behind the wheel of a car. But then alone was safe. Alone I had only to fear the direction of my thoughts and the agonizing jolt of heart as memories taunted.

But the memories could be kept at bay by concentration on the road. The blue, wet road that ribboned endlessly ahead. Hypnotized by the intermittent flashing lights of passing cars. The clashing dazzling. Then quietened by the darkness. Mindless. Stiff-jointed, robotic. I concentrated on turning the cold wheel and flicking switches. Bright lights subdued. Dipped. Dipping and bowing like royal nods, acknowledging my existence, approving almost my passing, then shrugging off the reality. I slipped comatose into the dreamlike quality of the black-hemmed road, the actions involved in steering, braking, accelerating seemed a panacea, a balm to the ache that teased at my heart. And I gave myself up to the long-ago familiarity of the road.

This was childhood terrain. Without being visible I knew the order of green-quilted fields had changed to marsh and bogland and haphazard stone ditches. The raw surfaces of road twisting and turning, taking me back to that haven of peace and carefree holidays with my cousins on the west coast. I could almost smell the tangy aroma of burning turf and feel white sand, tickling and trickling through bared toes. The welcome of my aunt's pub was a reality ahead of me, her aproned body, stooped and bony, dour in the rigours of her life yet with a humour that bubbled like an underground well. And Finbar, Finn to all but his father, with his black curls gypsy-like framing the robust flush of tanned cheeks and sparkling eyes.

But that was a long time ago. The reality was a witch-like figure who half-opened the peeling door, allowing lemon light to slide eerily on to cracked tiles and escape from the steamy, grubby bar.

'What d'ye want?' Aunt Maggie's voice rasped. 'Quare time of night to be on the road – don't ye know we're closed?'

'Would you close the door, Ma, ye'll have every guard in the place down on us. Come on in, missus, don't mind the mother.'

Tall, heavy-jowled, a man separated himself from a silent cluster of men hugging the wooden counter and came towards us. Red-rimmed eyes slitted as he stared at me, then, flaccid lips smiling wetly, his forehead wrinkled in recognition.

'Ciara? Ma, d'ye not know her, sure it's Ciara from Belfast!'

Stools grated on rough flags. Smokefilled, silent stares passed between the three men at the bar as they glanced from me to Finn then down at the wizened figure of my aunt. Her yellow eyes were uncertain, her smile water-weak, but she pressed my hand gently and ushered me around the bar to the kitchen behind.

'It's been a long time. The oul eyesight's not the same and you've changed an awful lot. Skinnier than I remember – and the long brown ringlets. Ach, you were a lovely wee girl.'

There was apology in her tone, and censure. I realized it must be almost fifteen years since I had been there. A rounded, awkward schoolgirl with the white line of convent, grey socks still around my ankles as I eagerly ran barefooted with Finn to the rocky beach below the pub.

'It's not the time of year for a holiday.' The statement asked all the questions written in the glances she threw towards me as I sat at the scrubbed kitchen table, wondering where to begin. How much did my aunt know?

'It was a pity about the wee lad. I read it in the papers.' She bustled around the black range pouring water from a bubbling kettle, brewing tea, clattering mugs across the plastic covered table. Her movements were old, her voice crackling with criticism, not the sympathy I had expected.

'I'm sorry,' I apologized, hardly knowing what it was I was sorry about. 'I should have written. But – ' I remembered why I hadn't. They had never been in touch with me since I had married Stewart. But surely they wouldn't hold that against me now.

'Aye, well, when you turn your back on family you're on your own. You made your bed – '

Hostility sat like a familiar ghost on her papery cheeks as she glared at me across the table. I felt stupid, embarrassed by my own crime, like a child caught playing 'doctors and nurses', guiltily innocent of the seriousness of the crime.

Finn's noisy entrance at that point cleared the air. 'I got rid of that lot and closed the bar, Ma. It's not every day me favourite cousin comes to town.'

Roughly pulling a chair across to the table, he grinned from his mother to me, a white moustache of Guinness giving his ruddy face a clown-like appearance. His neck muscles bulged like a wrestler's around the grubby collar

160

of striped shirt but the black eyes still held the boyish twinkle of mischief that had made him my hero in days past.

'You've been having a bit of a bad time.'

An understatement, certainly, but the small hint of sympathy in his voice washed over me like a warming blanket and opened the battened-down hatches. I cried as if I had been saving it all up. Words flowed with the tears as I relived the whole, rotten nightmare of my life for the past year. Then I went to bed.

Grey light streaked hazy around the room as I opened my eyes and lay for a second, grappling for my bearings. Memory swelled through sleepy confusion, like old photographs, browned and withered bringing the past to life. A past when a grazed knee had warranted a kiss on the injury and a slice of Aunt Maggie's steaming soda bread, the butter melting, swirling warmly down fingers to be licked off contentedly. That was what I had wanted Stewart to do. Kiss it and make it better. To squeeze inside my heart and head somehow and wipe away the pain and fear, cleanse and purify and exorcize. Not coat it all with a layer of whitewash, out of sight out of mind. Time will heal, you'll forget in time! Damn him! Time had stopped. Geordie and Bill and Mark hadn't been the only victims.

Wide awake now, I scrambled from the stiff sheets as if pushing myself out from this unwanted, hidden train of thought. Distant voices wafted upwards from outside. Finn's voice recognizable. Another man's gruff, argumentative. I slid across to the window and watched as Finn waved his arms dismissively then turned from his companion and disappeared into the bar. 'I'll handle it,' he had said. 'She's nothing to worry about.'

Why did I feel they were talking about me? Washing in the deep porcelain sink with its pattern of hairline cracks, the icy water refreshed and cleared my addled brain. Exhaustion and fear had confused my mind to such a pitch that my imagination had taken flight. I was developing a persecution complex. Twisting thoughts had, for so long, become poisoned darts aimed at my own heart and I was becoming twisted too. Finn had probably been referring to Aunt Maggie. No doubt he had something planned which needed her permission and he would twist her round his little finger with a sly grin and an 'Ach, Ma, go on.'

Breakfast was fresh wheaten bread with salty butter and a mug of tea that reminded me of my mother's laughing criticism of Maggie's brew. 'Sure you could stand a spoon in her tea, she stews it thick.' While I ate I became aware of discomfort. Finn fiddled with his spoon, stirring then thoughtfully licking, talking about the old days of the fishing and the crack there'd been in the pub when we were young.

'But times have changed,' he sighed, 'The fishin's finished, the young 'uns have all gone to Dublin or London or emigrated. There's no money around any more, other than the dole.'

'Why do you sta?' I asked him, conscious of Maggie's sudden glare as she turned from the range, kettle in hand.

'Where would he go? Hasn't he a business to see to – Pat was never interested.'

I realized then that Finn's older brother, Pat, hadn't been in evidence since I arrived. He had been the clever one. I remembered plans for university when Finn and I had been playing cops and robbers around the rocks, only dreaming of endless summers and the coming circus which was the highlight of our fourteen-year-old lives.

'Where is Pat?' Another sullen glare from Maggie, then, shoulders hunched, she continued to stir whatever was cooking on the black range. Finn fidgeted. Where had all this uneasiness come from?

'As a matter of fact, he'll be here the day sometime. He's been in England – coming over for a few days. Which reminds me, Ciara – were you thinkin' of stayin'?' His eyes slid away from my questioning gaze as he continued, 'It's just that he'll need the room you were in last night and what with nobody stayin' for years the other rooms are kinda rough.'

I was about to protest that they'd be fine, I wasn't fussy, but the air of discomfort began to choke, to smother the memories of hospitality and I realized that 'blood is thicker than water' was a saying of the past. It held no meaning nowadays, not for me.

'Oh, don't worry. I hadn't planned on staying, I knew you wouldn't be prepared for "visitors".' A rising sense of rejection made me stress the word. 'I thought I might find a bed and breakfast somewhere around – just for a few days. I just need some peace for a while, to be on my own –'

My words trailed off as Finn rose, relief and guilt apparent in his wet smile.

'There's a woman up the hill might put you up. She's a bit odd, keeps herself to herself, but she does a bit of B and B during the summer. I'll take a race up and see how she's fixed.'

And with that he grabbed a jacket from behind the door, which was slammed on departure with seeming eagerness for escape.

Stunned, I sat motionless, lost in the lonely anguish of my own thoughts. What had I expected? I hadn't been a part of their lives for years. Why had I expected them to welcome me with open arms? Maggie came towards me, her work-reddened hands clutching and clasping like claws at her apron.

163

'It's not that we don't want you, Ciara. It's just – well, it's a bit awkward, you being married to an RUC man and all. There's ones round here might think you were spying –'

My sudden burst of sound – it was meant to be laughter – took her unawares and she stopped, staring warily at my strange amusement.

'Spying?' I spluttered, 'Oh God, that's a good one! Now I know how a double agent must feel – I'm the enemy in every camp!'

My anger saw me through Finn's return to say that Mrs Jackson could keep me for a while, through sullen farewells and the rocky drive up the hillside. Bitter laughter still churned within me as I approached the whitewashed house. Sometimes veiled in grey mist then glowing starkly like modern art, all shapes and angles and chiaroscuro. It was a house that had been added to at different times. I remembered a big cottage, now it looked as though it spilled and sprawled awkwardly until bits would start to slide down the hillside at odd angles. Windows of different sized rectangles stared from the walls at varying heights. Part of the building seemed to be a separate house until, nearing the front door I realized it was joined to the rest like a siamese twin.

Before I had a chance to lift the gnarled knocker, incongruously decorative on the plain, slatted door, a figure rounded the corner of the house. At first glance, a country woman in her trailing overcoat and man-sized wellies. A tweed hat pulled a fringe of grey-black hair across heavy eyebrows, dark eyes squinting through the misty rain making black smudges in the weathered face. But the voice belied her appearance. Deep but distinctly female.

'Hello, dearie, you must be Ciara.' Her English accent took me by surprise, I had expected a local woman. 'I'm

Naomi Jackson, your landlady, for lack of a better description at the moment.'

She ushered me into the house where coat and boots were shed in an untidy pile beside the door, displaying the full splendour beneath. A gypsy blouse cloaked in a shawl of shimmering purple riveted my attention before my eyes followed the folds downwards to a multicoloured skirt, its uneven hem drooping floorwards. The term, 'ageing hippy' slid smirkily to my mind.

'I'm afraid you must take me as you find me, I'm not ready for tourists just yet.' She waved a casual hand to indicate the disarray of the room before us. Though long and large the room gave off a cosy aroma. Book-littered, rug-thrown, it held worn, body-shaped furniture and the carefree air of haphazard housekeeping.

'Leave your luggage for the moment while we get acquainted over a cuppa.' Naomi urged me towards an armchair in front of a stone fireplace which occupied the full length of the wall, ruling its domain with a welcoming heat. Gratefully I sank into its comfort.

'I hope I'm not putting you out, Mrs Jackson.' I felt I owed apologies for my sudden appearance although I had no ready explanation for my precipitate arrival.

'Finn told me you're a relation of his – wasn't expecting you. I suppose they're not geared to visitors these days. They lead very busy lives – But do call me Naomi, and don't worry, I'm rather glad of the company at the moment.'

With that she disappeared through a curtained doorway leaving me staring into the glowing turf, my thoughts wandering through my brain like lost souls. Had she been sarcastic when she said Finn's life was busy? Busy with what? Maggie's words danced in front of the flames – spying. I wasn't to be trusted. Because of Stewart I was the enemy – Stewart, where would he be now? I hadn't left him a note, would he be worried – or perhaps relieved? I needed to phone. I owed him that much, at least to let him know I was alive – if he cared.

Naomi reappeared carrying a tray laden with cups, coffee pot and a plate of biscuits which she deposited on a small table beside my chair.

'I'll see to this fire, then we can have a chat.'

Tall, masculine-square, she bent from the waist over a big creel beside the untidy hearth and carelessly flicked sod after sod into the now smoking heap. Straightening then she pushed her heavy drapery of grey-streaked ebony hair behind her shoulder, the folds of the mad skirt flaring like the fire around her bare ankles. Silence settled comfortably as she stared into the flames, giving me the opportunity to study her. There was something almost regal about her stance. The strong, straight lines spoke of solidity, dependability, without being detracted from by the frivolous lines of her clothes. Square fingers clasped a cigarette and played a light tattoo on the mahogany mantle, square like her hands. Reliable hands, not beautiful but sure, certain, weatherbeaten like her face. Only the eyes above the patrician nose held sign of softness, and I realized with a guilty jolt that they were staring, laughingly, into mine. Black as jet and deep-set they sent out jags of light sparkling with veins of blue and violet and causing me to smile sheepishly into their dancing depths.

'Not your idea of a guest-house landlady, eh?' Naomi chuckled as she took a deep drag from the cigarette and sank gracefully into the depths of a large sofa.

'I'm sorry for staring, but you have taken me a bit by surprise.'

'Well, at least you're smiling, I had begun to wonder if you could.'

'I'm sorry –'

166

'That's the third time you've apologized since you arrived. What did he do to you? Make you feel you owed the world a reason for your existence?'

Straight as an arrow, Naomi's insight hit me right between the eyes. I gasped, speechless. Floundering in an attempt to rescue conversation and put this strange woman where she belonged – outside.

'What has Finn told you?' I demanded, my voice hoarse, tears choking my throat. Indignation vying with the need to unburden.

'Nothing,' replied Naomi, concern now evident in her dark glance, 'I use my own eyes, my own intuition. Sometimes I'm wrong, sometimes I make a stab in the dark and hit rock, other times I draw blood. Looks like I opened a wound this time. Or has it had time to close?'

I thought I had cried a year's worth the previous night but once again the dam broke. I just buried my head in my hands and sobbed, suddenly mindless of the woman's presence, only conscious of a great vortex of sadness which swirled around me and sucked me into its depths.

That night I lay awake staring at the night shadows of the strange room. Naomi's guest rooms were not as comforting as her living room, nor her own warm presence. Heavy pieces of furniture, rectangular shapes like the house itself, seemed to advance on me like a lumbering army until I was forced to close swollen eyes to dispel their seeming attack. Stewart's face swam through my thoughts. A drowning vision not wanting rescue.

Something in Naomi's navy eyes had inspired confidence within me and I had found myself telling her my whole, sordid life story. After listening gently to my hiccuping outpourings, the unabridged edition of my trauma, she had plied me with brandy, sympathizing, questioning, understanding. It was as if I had found a substitute for the mother who had died four years

167

previously, still broken-hearted at my treason. Naomi seemed to wrap herself around my wounds just as she wrapped her muscular arms around my shoulders and hugged and hushed and comforted. Afterwards, drained, I nevertheless felt refreshed, energized. So much so that I squared my shoulders and asked if I could use her telephone.

'Won't that defeat the whole purpose of the expedition?' Naomi asked, head cocked, eyeing me knowingly. I was dismayed by her misinterpretation of my actions.

'I didn't leave for that reason –'

'I know, dearie.' She soothed my ruffled feathers and led me up a long hallway to where a telephone sat on an elegant if dusty table. 'But it probably wouldn't do him any harm to worry for a while. A little anxiety works wonders on the male ego, shows them they can care about someone other than themselves. I have had my own experiences with the male sex,' she added as she sailed off down the hall again, after explaining the intricacies of the old-fashioned telephone system.

It was some minutes before the local exchange connected me to Belfast, and Stewart. My throat constricted and tears welled again as his familiar voice rattled in my ear, sharp, suspicious.

'Stewart, it's me, Ciara –'

'Ciara! Where the hell are you?'

'I'm – at Aunt Maggie's, I had to get away –'

'What the hell are you playing at? Have you any idea what I've been going through?'

Have you any idea what I've been going through, I thought, then, 'So you've left me, is that it? I can calm everyone and tell them you've only run away from me?'

'It's not like that, Stewart – Tell who? Who would notice I had gone?' His words suddenly made sense.

168

There wasn't anyone, apart from Stewart who might notice I was missing, not yet anyway.

'My boss for one, I had to report it, you know, for all I knew you might have been kidnapped – or gone over.'

'What do you mean – gone over?' There was a scream beginning at the back of my head.

'Well, that's what they're going to think now, isn't it? You can take the woman out of the Falls but you can't take the Falls out of the woman!'

It was the first and only bigoted statement I had ever heard from Stewart and I felt a gaping hole open at my feet. A crater of doubt and suspicion.

'You don't understand, Stewart – I just needed – '

'No, Ciara, I don't understand. But you understand this, I want a divorce!'

'A divorce! Stewart, I don't want – I can't – '

'Don't give me that damn Catholic bit. If your bloody church can condone what's going on here, they can damn well turn a blind eye to a petty little divorce. When you send me an address I'll start proceedings!'

'Stewart, you don't mean – ' But the line had gone dead. Stewart was no longer listening. Though someone else was.

'I'm afraid you've been disconnected, missus. D'ye want me to try it again?' The operator's voice sang in my ear as I sat in stunned, disbelieving stupor, then slowly replaced the receiver without replying.

The rest of the day passed in a blur of heartache. Guilt fought with resentment, sadness with anger. I must have raved incoherently. One minute screeching my remorse at having brought things to this pitch, the next banging my frustration at the unfairness of it all into the padded arm of Naomi's armchair. And still she soothed. Until at last my energy flagged and, emptied of all emotion, I allowed her to lead me to bed.

169

I lost count of the days. I wandered through time, carried along in a momentum that was not of my own making. I was caught in a slipstream of memory and pain and nightmare. Like a twig being rushed along by a flooding river, battered and beaten, flung against rocks, sucked under by the current to surface again and become snagged on overlying branches.

It was Naomi who caught me. Rescued me. She saturated me with sympathy, then cajoled and coaxed and humoured until she had cushioned me from the outside world, then, ruthlessly, it seemed, dragged me by the hair back into it again.

As if to put my own troubles in perspective she told me about herself. How the child she had prayed for during fifteen years of marriage had been born mentally and physically handicapped and had died shortly afterwards. How her husband, Sam, had brought her here to Ireland when London had become unbearable and the noise of people and traffic had grated on her and she had become a whirling dervish in her frustration. When he retired they had moved here permanently, to the tranquil murmur of the countryside and the dead-slow-and-stop pace of the west coast. Then, when they had become a somewhat wary part of the tiny community, Sam had 'up and left, disappeared'.

'I went berserk! Then numbness set in and then the anger. I decided I would survive without them, without him. Now I have another child.'

I had a moment of panic when she said that, thinking she meant me, but she carried on, 'I write. My stories are my family. Husband, child, friend, all wrapped up together.'

'Have you had any published?' I asked. She answered with a strange, knowing look which I couldn't interpret then continued as if I hadn't spoken.

'No one here knows about my writing and that's how I want it.' She threw me a warning look and I nodded as if to assure her that her secret was safe with me, though at a loss to understand why. 'The villagers have accepted me now. They treat me like a shabby eccentric. An old oddity who keeps herself to herself. That suits them, you see, they don't like strangers poking their noses into their business. I've become invisible.' The last part was said with an air of satisfaction, as if she had succeeded in attaining some exalted position.

We spent our evenings trading confidences before a roaring turf fire. Then, in bed, I would listen to the tapping of her typewriter, a noise I had been previously half conscious of, attributing it to the tapping of branches outside in the wind. It became for me a comforting lullaby, like the soothing hum of parents' voices as sleep wafted, dulling the troubles of the day.

For a time I wallowed in peace and friendship. Naomi's friendship was like a raft, solid, riding the swell of my torment. She saw to my physical needs as if it was her duty, a service she was bound to through love, like a mother. And I accepted willingly my own dependency on her.

My peace became a guilty peace, though. Roaming the hillside, the wind pulling and pushing, I revelled in my aloneness. The horizon a purple line in the distance I gazed across the endless stretch of the ocean, its very emptiness a comfort to a mind that had been imprisoned behind fear-erected bars. My grandmother's words rustled on the wind. 'My bounty is as boundless as the sea, my love as deep; the more I give to thee the more I have, for both are infinite.' She had been quoting Shakespeare to an empty-headed sixteen-year-old, explaining the value and the lack of limit on love. And I saw how little value I had placed on my own love. I had put limits on my love for Stewart, the boundaries of behaviour, his behaviour and that of his friends. And to satisfy my own selfish need for solace and peace and space I had run away, never considering the effects my behaviour might have on Stewart.

'I think I should go home, Naomi. I haven't had any word from Stewart so maybe he's changed his mind about the divorce. It might only have been an empty threat –'

'You can't go home!' Her words startled me, spat as they were from rouged lips which seemed to gash her face like hardened blood. Then softened once more as she handed me a mug of coffee laced with brandy. A nightcap, a routine built up over the past two weeks, when we would talk before the dying embers of the fire, swopping information and warming ourselves on confidences.

'It's only been a few weeks, Ciara. You're not ready. Give yourself some time to build up your resources, your strength.'

'But I feel fine, physically, thanks to all the looking after I've had. You've been marvellous, Naomi, I'll always be grateful.'

It was as if a dark cloud passed across her eyes, shutting out the sparkle. She gazed into the fire then turned her black glance towards me, studying for a second, then, as if a switch had been pulled, the lights twinkled again. Hypnotized, I listened as her voice took on a little-girl-lost pleading.

'Stay for a while, Ciara. I need your company. Since Sam left I've been lonely, with no one to turn to. I can't trust the locals, they wouldn't understand my writing. Please stay, just for a while.'

I felt I owed her. The least I could do was give her my company, such as it was. I ignored the niggling voice in my ear that said it was emotional blackmail, and I blocked out the half-sensed notion that her pleading lacked honesty. I stayed.

I tried to phone Stewart, to try again to reason with him, to explain, perhaps to tell him I was sorry and beg him to want me home. But, every time, the operator's voice informed me that the line was engaged, or that there was no reply. And I slid into an easy existence of long, solitary walks, shopping for groceries in the village shop and occasional short visits with my relatives. I renewed my acquaintance with my older cousin, Patrick Dolan, and was pleasantly surprised to find that he had become a well-spoken, quietly intelligent man who sometimes accompanied me on wind-battered strolls around the rocky headland which had become for me a haven.

Pat had always been aloof from the rough-and-tumble games Finn and I had indulged in. 'His nose is always stuck in some book or other,' Maggie would grumble, but her eyes glistened with pride as she spoke; then she would send Finn or me, complaining, to fetch in turf or bring water from the well, hushing us briskly so as not to disturb Pat's concentration. And he had rewarded her by going to university, to Dublin, then on to teaching. I wondered if she had been upset by his decision to go to England. Had she hoped he would come back to the village to guide and tutor the young minds there? Whatever, he was still her pride and joy, her first-born. Once I saw her reach out her hand to stroke his ruddy-blond head as he sat engrossed in a newspaper, then snatch it back as she caught my glance. Embarrassment rosying her cheeks and a deep sadness in her eyes that seemed born of long years of sadness. And despair? But I thought that was my imagination.

Until one day I called at the pub to find Maggie on her own in the bar. Without the offer of tea as

173

was the custom she rounded on me as I arrived.

'What's keeping you here, Ciara. For God's sake go home where you belong. That oul' woman up there'll drive you nuts.'

'Naomi?' I was amazed at her outburst. 'I like her, Aunt Maggie –'

'She's not all there, you know. Since the husband and son were drowned she's got even stranger.'

'But I thought her husband had left her and the baby died after it was born.'

'Huh, some baby. He was fourteen when Sam took him fishing in one of Finn's boats. They never came back, their bodies were washed up a few days later. Ach, she's more to be pitied than scorned, but she's not good company for you.'

I struggled to digest this piece of information while trying to get Maggie off the subject.

'Have Pat and Finn gone off for the day?' I asked, wondering if she needed any help.

'On business,' she muttered. 'The divil's business –' Then, slapping a tea-towel into the sink beneath the wooden counter, she reached across the bar and grasped my hand. Her fingers were cold as death, their grip clutching at my heart as I thought for a second she was ill.

'Ah Ciara,' she crooned, eyes watery, boring into mine. 'You shouldn't have come here. Go home. Go away before it's too late. They'll only drag you down into their own sickness –'

I felt frightened suddenly, as if I had never known this strange woman whose fear sat like a skin on her face, much as my own must have done.

'I know you know nothing. You're blinded by your own troubles. Things have changed here – Pat and Finn, they're not the wee boys you used to play with. They're men –'

Bitterness and heartache poured from her. The air

174

became full of demons and lost souls, screaming, fighting for entry to my brain. I couldn't take in all that she said, I couldn't believe. She was demented, crazed.

I stumbled back to Naomi's house in a daze, trying to make sense of Maggie's outpourings. She had talked of Mick, her husband, a faint shadow in my memory but more defined now. A brute of a man who, in good moods, would swing his diminutive wife clear off her feet and plant wet kisses on her tossed hair. But mostly sullen, his scowl would send us running for freedom, to tiptoe round the house for fear of attracting his attention. And yet Finn and Pat had revered him. After he died, I was about six at the time, the brothers tended his grave religiously, introducing its attention as part of our routine from then onwards.

It seemed now that Maggie blamed herself for their blind worship. When Mick flew into rages, blackening her eye or cracking a rib, she covered up. She protected them from their father's true character, vindicating him, excusing him. And, when he turned their heads with his stories of past exploits, of secret meetings and brave revenge she listened too, thinking to encourage their love for their father. He instilled in them the ideas of camaraderie and patriotism, ideals which lit fires in the hearts of himself and his friends and his steadfast belief in the 'cause'. Not once had she ever voiced her own feelings. Never had she told them of the long nights of terror while she waited for word of his survival, nor the bitterness of the long fight that had turned friends into enemies and brother against brother. And, so successfully did she cloud their view of reality that, when Mick died, Finn and Pat had mourned him as a hero and taken to heart his teachings and his ideology.

'I thought at least Pat had been saved. I thought he'd got out by going to college. But the damage was done.'

Maggie had shaken her head bitterly, cold tears dropping like needles on my hand. 'He's just as brainwashed as Finn. I can see steel in his eyes, his lovely grey eyes that were so soft and innocent and clear. There's shadows of hell in them now – but I love him, and Finn. They're still my boys, Ciara –'

What was she doing? I had shaken off her hand, horrified at the picture she was creating. Was she asking my forgiveness? Why?

As I reached the flagged stones in front of Naomi's front door I knew the answer. I knew what my cousins were and I knew why Maggie needed forgiveness. But I didn't know what to do about it. The wreckage of my neighbour's car seemed to float in the darkness of nearby bushes, Mark's face, chocolate-framed mouth reaching upwards for my kiss, and shadowy figures crouched, watching, planning, triumphant. No longer faceless. Now I could put colour and features to their murderous shadows. Oh, Pat and Finn hadn't planted the bomb. But they had helped. They were the flesh and blood of that spectre of evil which, until now, had presented no face for me to spit in. And they were my flesh and blood too. My own! Momentarily I wondered if Stewart would appreciate the sick joke. Then, like a blurred picture coming into focus, I saw it all. Stupidly, unknowingly, I was a part of it too. At least, Stewart, the police, could only see it that way. How could I explain? How could I inform?

I clamped down on the nausea which rose in my throat and went in search of Naomi. I needed her no-nonsense strength to weight my thoughts and put things in proportion. She could tell me the truth, if only about herself. She would know what I should do about the rest of it. What I could do. But the house was silent. I could hear no comforting click as she feverishly tapped out her hidden stories. No colourful figure draped across the sofa in the living room. From room to room I called her name until I reached the door of her private domain, a room I had never entered, bowing unquestioningly to her unspoken taboo. I had instinctively accepted this room as out of bounds and willingly allowed her the privacy. But now, after a quick knock, I went in, careless of Naomi's secrecy in my stricken search.

The room was even more untidy than the other parts of the house. Shelf upon shelf held books of all sizes, while every surface seemed layered with sheets of paper. Crumpled balls of paper lay forlornly around the base of an overflowing metal bin and the typewriter rose like a phoenix from the white mess surrounding it. A wide window, curtainless, shed wintry sunlight over another table, on which lay a pair of binoculars. I wondered momentarily if Naomi had taken up birdwatching while waiting for her thoughts to gel into whatever she might be writing. Casually I lifted the binoculars and peered through the window. They were powerful. Without adjustment I found myself looking straight into the back yard of Dolan's pub. I could even see Aunt Maggie stirring at the range, her shoulders bent and a towel held tightly to her lips. Sadness choked me for a moment, then was swallowed up in my realization that the binoculars were focused on that particular area. Still holding them I glanced at the pages strewn across the table. My own name glared out at me from the lines of typescript.

'Ciara had no qualms. Her husband had been wary of letting her carry out this mission, but she knew the rightness of her actions. The police were tied. They couldn't do what she could do. These men had murdered her son, they had to be destroyed –' I felt like Alice in her crazy dream of Wonderland. I seemed to be losing my grip on reality, thoughts cascaded through my brain

177

like rushing waterfalls, screaming madness as they flowed.

'So you've found my treasure.' Naomi's voice behind caused me to reel and stumble against the table, scattering the papers and dropping the binoculars in my distress. She rushed to catch the binoculars then turned to me, smiling, a strange, unfriendly smile.

'Now you know my secret. I've been using you as my main character. Just think, Ciara, when this is published you will be immortalized.'

'You've been writing about me?' I whispered, 'But I haven't come – I'm not going to – '

'You're not on a mission?' Naomi shrugged as she gathered pages together. 'Perhaps not, but then I write fiction. Of course, this time it will be based in fact. I've been watching the boyos down there. I have all the details of their activities, photographs, everything. They're busy little bees with their gun-running and hiding their friends on the run.'

'But – if you know all that why – ' I stammered, my brain seemed unable to give the rest of my body instructions anymore.

'Why haven't I told the police?' Naomi finished my sentence. 'Why should I? This is my book, my story – they're only characters. Just like you. Now it's almost finished I don't mind you knowing. They aren't important – what I write about them is. This is my baby, my family. Even when it leaves me it will still come home to me, like all the others.' She waved a hand around the shelves. I looked dazedly at one of the covers: 'Runaways, by Nancy Johnston'. But the photograph on the back was Naomi, a tailored, expertly made-up Naomi.

'I use a pen-name, of course. And none of these yokels would recognize the picture even if they did manage to read the book. I used Sam and the boy for that one, by the way.'

In answer to my dumbstruck, questioning silence, she laughed. A strange, bitter laugh.

'I only told you that yarn to keep you here, to make you feel sorry for me. You were beginning to feel sorry for that stupid husband of yours. Men! They're the cause of all misery. If I'd told you Sam was dead you would have started to panic, thinking you had to make up with Stewart, just in case.'

Then everything became a blur, an abstract painting of shapes and colours with voices in backgrounds. Words written, spoken, never stringing together in a full sentence. I know I ran, it seemed to have become a habit by then. Where I ran to or what I ran from I can't say. Disillusionment? Confusion? Hatred for a world that was alien to all I had ever believed and frustration in my powerlessness to understand.

I remember lights, bright, dazzling, holding my attention, rooting me. Then white lights above me and pain. Clean, understandable, physical pain.

Later, from listening, I put the pieces together. I had run into the path of a lorry, somewhere on the main road to the border. From my delirious rantings they pieced a part of my life together. Stewart came to collect me. But they couldn't sew my mind together as they had done with my body.

'Don't worry,' they said. 'Time will heal. Her memory will return when she recovers from the accident. Just give her time.'

But time can do nothing for divided loyalties, only spread them further apart. Now, I say nothing. One word might cause an avalanche and I would have no control. Who would trust me? Who can I trust? I'm not mad. Only afraid and silent. And safe.

BLACK SKY
AT NIGHT

Jeremy Cain

Jeremy Cain studied English and History at the University of East Anglia. He taught English as a foreign language in Sudan, and now works as a psychiatric nurse in Horsham. In his spare time, he is an amateur actor and a writer of mostly unfinished stories.

BLACK SKY
AT NIGHT

Well, I'm sitting at home in my living room and I just
fancy a nice cup of tea, so I call out to Dorothy to see if
she'd like one as well. And do you know who comes
round? Carol, that's my youngest girl. She comes into the
house and says,

'Dad, how are you, Dad?' And I say,

'Fine, I was just about to make a cup of tea. Would you
like one as well?' And she says,

'I'll make one for you. Don't worry, you have a sit
down and take it easy.' Then I say,

'I was just going to see if Dorothy would like one,' but
she says,

'Don't worry about Dorothy, Dad,' and goes into the
kitchen.

She's a lovely girl, my Carol, she'd do anything for
anybody she would. And Philip's there too, that's her
husband, but I didn't see him come in. And he says,

'All right, Dad, how are you managing?' Then I
say,

'How am I managing what?' because I don't know
exactly what he means.

'Oh,' he says, 'I just wondered how you've been getting
on.' So I say,

'Fine,' because I haven't got any cause for complaint or
anything.

Then Carol comes in with a cup of tea.

'Sit down, Dad,' she says. 'How have you been getting on?'

I'm not sure what they're all on about. So I ask her,

'Do you know where Dorothy's got to? 'Cause it's not like her to disappear when there's a cup of tea on the go.' Then Carol says,

'Mum's gone, Dad.' Well, I wonder where she's got to, because it's not like her to go out without saying anything. So I get up to see where she's got to. Then Carol says,

'Where are you going, Dad?' So I say,

'I'm going out to see where Dorothy's got to.' And she says,

'No, sit down, Dad.'

'Well,' I say, 'I wonder where she's got to, she didn't say she was going out.'

Then Carol comes over and puts her arm around me, 'cause she's good like that, my Carol. Then she says,

'Have a sit down Dad.' So I sit down, and she holds my hand and looks all sad. I don't know what the matter is.

Then she says, 'Dad, you know Mum died last night.' Well, I don't know what she's on about, because Dorothy was here just a few minutes ago. She must have gone down the shops or something.

Then Carol says, 'Dad, there's something we want to talk to you about,' and she's still holding my hand.

'What's the matter, Carol?' I say, 'What's up?'

Then she says, 'Dad, we think you ought to go into hospital for a while.'

I don't know, I'm absolutely flabbergasted. I mean what's all this about hospital? There's nothing wrong with me. I'm as fit as I've ever been. So I say,

'What do you mean, go into hospital? There's nothing wrong with me.' And she says,

184

'Don't be like that, Dad. Dr Elgin saw you and he said it would be best.' So of course I say,

'I'm not going into any hospital. I'm going to stay here in my own home,' because I don't trust doctors really. I mean I've never had much faith in them, and I don't like hospitals. I just never have done. So Carol says,

'Dad, it's just that we're worried about you, you haven't been yourself the last few days. Perhaps after a couple of days in hospital and you might be as right as rain again.' Then Philip comes over and says,

'Dad, we think it would be for your own good.' I hate it when he calls me 'Dad'. I'm sure he only does it to annoy me. So I say,

'What would happen to Dorothy? She'd be left here all by herself.' Then Carol says,

'The doctor's been to see you, and he says it would be best if you went in, and that's all there is to it.' I don't know. I haven't seen a doctor for a start, so I say,

'I don't want to go into hospital.' Then Carol starts getting all upset saying,

'Dad, don't start being like that.' So I say,

'Being like what? I'm not going into hospital and that's final.'

'Come on, Dad,' says Philip, 'you'll probably like it when you get there, and you won't want to come home.' Well, I'm not surprised that Philip wants me out of the way. He probably wants to make it more difficult for Carol to see me. Then Carol starts on me with her clever remarks.

'Dad, why are you so stubborn?'

'I'll tell you why I'm so stubborn, my girl,' I tell her, 'because I'm usually right, that's why.'

Then Philip starts huffing and panting, and Carol starts moaning. I mean she's a good girl, but when she

185

starts moaning, I tell you, you'd do anything to make her stop.

'Come on, Daaaaaad . . .' she says, in that nagging old voice of hers, 'it will only be for a few days.' That's a lie for a start, because once they get you into one of those hospitals, you can forget it, they'll never let you out.

'The doctor says you have to go!' she says. That's all I hear: 'Doctor, doctor, doctor, doctor,' as if he were some God or something. What do I care about what some doctor says?

'Come on,' says Philip, 'we're wasting our time.' Well, there's nothing new about that, I can tell you. Philip's spent his whole life wasting his time as far as I'm concerned.

'Well, you certainly can't stay here by yourself,' Carol says, 'what with you leaving the gas on, and wandering about the streets.' What a load of old rubbish. I've never left the gas on in my life, and I don't go wandering about the streets any more than anyone else does.

So I sit back in my chair, I fold my arms, I cross my legs, and I tell them in my 'no nonsense, I'm the boss' voice,

'I'm not going into any hospital, because I said so and that's final.'

'How long are we going to carry on messing about like this?' asks Philip.

'Will you give me a chance?' says Carol. 'He's my Dad, remember.' Then Philip makes this horrible sniffing noise, like he always does. I don't know why he can't buy himself a handkerchief.

'Dad, please don't be like this,' Carol says. 'You've got to go into hospital. There's nothing I can do to stop it.'

'Don't talk nonsense,' I tell her. 'I don't have to go anywhere I don't want to.'

Anyway, next thing I know, I've been dragged to my

186

feet, and Carol's virtually carrying me out of the doorway, shouting,

'If that's the way you want it . . .' and all sorts of rubbish like that, and I'm pleading with her to let me go. Then Philip opens the car door, and Carol shoves me inside like I was a piece of old baggage. Then Philip says,

'I'll get his things.' And Carol shouts,

'No, leave them, we'll get them later.' What a carry on, being dragged about and taken prisoner by your own family in your own home. I've never known anything like it. And Philip's driving like a maniac, and Carol's shouting and screaming at me, and no one will tell me what's going on.

Next thing I know, we're driving round the grounds of the old mental hospital over by where Maureen used to live.

'Why are we going in here?' I ask.

'We're just going to see some people,' says Carol. 'We won't be long.' So Philip parks the car, and Carol and Philip get out.

'Come on, Dad,' says Carol. But I tell them,

'Don't worry, I'll wait here for you,' 'cause to be honest I'm not keen on going round a mental hospital, even for a few minutes. There's something funny about those kind of places. But Carol raises her eyes to heaven like I was the biggest fool on the whole planet.

'Come on, Dad,' she says, 'let's have no more of your nonsense,' and with that she manhandles me out of the car, all pushing and shoving. Anyway off we go. So we go inside these big doors, and Carol holds on tight to one of my arms, then we go through another door, and Carol says,

'We're here now, Dad.'

So I look around the place, and there's all these funny old people wandering about, and I don't really like it.

'What do you mean "we're here now"?' I ask. Then Carol starts getting all annoyed and starts huffing.

'At the hospital,' she says. Then this big fat woman in a blue uniform comes up.

'We've brought Mr Martin,' says Carol.

'Oh hello,' says the fat woman. 'How are you, Mr Martin?' And she shakes my hand. Well I don't know quite what to say because, quite frankly I can't see that it's any of her business how I am, and I've got the feeling that something funny is going on. Then the big fat woman comes and puts her arm around me and says,

'I expect you're a bit nervous, but never mind, I'm sure you'll settle down quite soon.' I don't know about settling down quite soon, but I do know that I want to go home very soon.

'I think it's about time I was off, actually,' I tell them.

'Don't start that,' says Carol, 'after all the fuss we had getting you here.'

'Well,' says the fat woman, 'there's no reason to start thinking about going home yet. You've only just got here. Would you like a cup of tea?'

I have to say 'yes', because I don't want to appear awkward. Then Carol, Philip and I all sit down, and someone comes and brings us a cup of tea.

'Have you brought any property?' the fat woman asks. I don't know what property she's on about. The only property I've got is my house, and I could hardly bring that, could I?

'No,' says Carol, 'we'll bring that later. Actually we had a bit of difficulty getting him here.' Well I don't know what she's talking about but I have a funny feeling that she's talking about me here, but I think it's probably better to keep quiet. Then we finish off our tea and the fat woman says to me,

'Can you come with me, Mr Martin, I've got some

188

forms to fill in.' Well, I'm not too keen on filling in forms, but I don't like to be difficult so I start to go off with her, but Carol and Philip are still sitting there.

'Come on Carol,' I say, but Carol looks all sad and says,

'It's all right, Dad, we'll see you later, we have to go now.' Well, I don't know.

'Where are you going?' I ask.

'We have to go home,' says Carol, and she comes over and kisses me, and hugs me.

'Well,' I say, 'aren't you going to wait for me? I'll only be a few minutes.'

'No,' she smiles, 'We've got to go now,' and off they walk together.

'Hang on!' I shout, and off I go after them, but this big fat woman grabs me by the arms.

'Just a minute, Mr Martin,' she says, 'we've got some forms to fill in,' and she frog-marches me off into this small room.

'Sit down, Mr Martin,' she says, but I'm not keen at all. I can't believe that Carol and Philip have gone off without me.

'No thanks,' I say, 'I've got to be off now.'

'Mr Martin,' she says, 'you can't go anywhere. Sit down and help me fill in these forms.' I don't like to argue so I sit down.

'What's your name?' she asks.

'Mr Martin,' I reply.

'Christian name?'

'Peter,' I say, 'Peter Martin.'

'And where do you live?'

'40 Norwood Crescent, Perivale,' I tell her.

'And how old are you?' And do you know for a moment I can't think how old I am. Isn't that funny? It's just completely slipped out of my mind.

I don't want to look stupid so I say,

'Forty-six,' because that's more or less right. Anyway she looks at me like she doesn't believe me.

'When were you born?' she asks.

'The ninth of October, 1903,' I tell her.

'In that case,' she says, 'You're eighty-seven.' I've never heard anything more ridiculous in my whole life. Eighty-seven? I'm not eighty-seven, and that's for sure.

'Who's your next of kin?' she asks.

'That would be my wife, Dorothy Martin.' Then she asks me who my GP is. I haven't got a clue who my GP is because I haven't seen him for years, so I say that I haven't got one. 'Never mind,' she says, and she fills something in on one of her forms.

'Would you like to wait outside?' she asks. 'The doctor will see you shortly.' So I say, 'Thank you,' just to be polite, 'cause to be honest I'm not too keen on seeing a doctor, but I'm not feeling too sure about myself now, and I don't want to kick up a fuss.

So I get up and go outside. In a room opposite there are quite a few people sitting around so I go over to join them, but when I get there I see that they are watching telly. I don't really go in for watching telly much, because there's not a lot on that I like. It's usually a load of depressing rubbish, all about wars, or people just killing each other for the sake of it. Anyway, I decide not to stay, so I get up and go off in search of something better. Well, it takes very little time before I realize that I'm completely and utterly lost, and I just don't know which way to turn. What's more there was a lady who was here not long ago, and she seemed to know what was going on, but I can't quite remember where she was, and I'm not even sure what she looked like, but I'm fairly sure that I would recognize her again if I saw her. Mind you, with my memory for faces that's not all that likely come to think of it, but I'm sure she must be around here somewhere.

Anyway, next thing I know I'm outside the kitchen door. Well, whenever I have a crisis, I always think that the best thing to do is to make a nice cup of tea and think about things. So I go to open the door, and do you know what? It's stuck. This is odd, I've never known it to stick before, so I give it a good tug, and do you know what? I can't budge it at all.

'Mr Martin,' this voice says, 'what are you doing?'

'I was just trying to get into the kitchen,' I tell her.

'That's not the kitchen,' she says, 'that's the medicine room.' Well, I thought it was the kitchen. It looks just like the kitchen, mind you my eyesight is not that good.

'Where's the kitchen?' I ask her.

'You can't go in the kitchen,' she says, 'it's locked.' Now I really don't know what she's on about, because the kitchen has never been locked. In fact it hasn't even got a lock on the door.

'Anyway,' she says, 'the doctor's here to see you now.'

I'm really not sure about seeing this doctor. Usually they think there's nothing wrong with you, even if there is. They think you're just making it up to skive off work.

'I'm feeling a lot better now,' I tell her in the hope of getting out of it.

'Well, I think you should see him anyway,' she says. 'Come with me.'

Anyway, I follow her, and she takes me to this small room, with a table in the middle, two chairs and a bed along one wall. She then introduces me to this small man with a beard.

'This is Doctor Rogers,' she tells me.

'Good morning,' he says, and gives me a firm handshake. 'How are you? Sit down.'

'Fine, thanks,' I tell him.

'And what's been happening with you lately?' he asks.

191

'Well,' I tell him, 'I don't really know.'

'You don't really know?' Well, I'm not sure what to say.

'I seem all mixed up,' I tell him.

'Yes?' he says.

'I don't know what's going on.'

'I'm sure it must be quite confusing at first.' That makes me wonder if he's been playing tricks on me.

'Do you know where you are?' he asks. I don't know what he could mean by that.

'This is my house,' I tell him.

'Does it look like your house?' And do you know, looking around, it's not my house at all.

'No, it's not, is it?' I tell him. 'Where are we?'

'We're in hospital in Hanwell,' he says.

It does look a bit like a hospital, because there's no proper wallpaper or anything, but this is most odd because I thought I was at home just a minute ago. To be honest I feel a bit stupid now. I don't know what this bloke must think.

'Why am I in hospital?' I ask him.

'We want to do a few tests on you and find out generally how you're getting on.'

'I'm getting on fine,' I tell him. 'I can tell you that.'

'Yes,' he says, 'I'm glad you're feeling fine, but a few people are a bit worried because they think you're getting a bit forgetful, and I did notice when you came in that you'd forgotten where you were.' I can't argue with that, it took me completely by surprise.

'So,' he says, 'we'd like to run a few tests on you to find out what the cause of it all is, because sometimes it's something relatively simple that we can sort out quite easily.'

I'm not too sure on having tests done on me, but I'm

not sure that I can get out of this mess, now that I'm in it. The whole thing seems most odd.

'How did I get here?' I ask him.

'You'd have to ask sister that,' he says.

Then he tells me not to worry about it, but to strip down to my underpants. Then I have to stick my tongue out. Then he shines a light into my eyes, then he knocks my chest and my back in different places. Then he ties a black band round my arm and blows it up, and listens to my elbow with one of those listening things that doctors have, I'm not sure what they're called. Then he knocks my knees with a hammer, and all that kind of thing. He then sticks a needle in my arm and takes some of my blood. Then he tells me to get dressed again. And to be honest, I'm glad it's all over, because it's a lot of fuss really.

'Right, sit down, Mr Martin,' he says, and he takes out a pen and starts taking notes.

'Can you tell me what day it is?' he asks. Do you know what? I just can't think what day it is. It's gone just like that. It could be Monday or Tuesday, I don't know. So I say 'Tuesday', but it's a bit of a wild guess.

'Are you sure?' he asks.

'I'm not a hundred per cent sure really,' I tell him.

Then he writes something down in his notes.

'Was I right?' I ask, because I ought to know really.

'No, it's Thursday,' he says. I wasn't far out.

'Do you know what date it is?' he asks. But I can't think of that either. My mind's just gone a complete blank. It could be the fifteenth, so I say,

'The fifteenth,' but I can tell from his expression that I haven't done too well. 'The sixteenth?' I ask, but I'm guessing really.

'Never mind,' he says. 'I'm sure you must have had a bit of a shock coming in here.'

'That's right,' I tell him, 'I'm quite shocked really.'

'I'm sure you must be,' he says. 'Do you know what month it is?'

Well, that I should know, but for the life of me I can't think at all what it must be.

'Roughly,' he says, 'about what month is it?'

'September,' I say, but I think he can tell that I'm not too confident about it.

'That's good,' he says. 'Now can you tell me what year it is?' Now I feel a right Charlie, because that's the sort of information that everyone should know. I have a think about it, but I'm not sure at all. The trouble is I'm going to look a bit foolish saying that I don't even know what year it is.

'It doesn't matter if you don't know exactly,' he says.

I reckon it's about 1950, but I'm not sure.

'Is it 1953?' I ask.

'No, it's 1991,' he says. This comes as a bit of a surprise because I didn't realize we were that far up yet.

'Now, if I tell you something, will you try to remember it for me,' he asks.

'I should write it down if I were you,' I tell him, 'because I'm likely to forget,' but he doesn't think that's funny.

'Try,' he says. 'My name's Dr Rogers, and I live at 143, St John's Avenue, Ealing, London W5.'

'All right, I'll try,' I tell him, although it seems rather a lot.

'Dr Rogers, 148 . . .'

'143,' he corrects me.

'Dr Rogers, 143 St John's Road, Ealing,' I tell him.

'That's good,' he says. 'Now let's see how long you can remember that for.'

'Dr Rogers . . . 148 . . .' and now the name of the road's gone, and for the life of me I can't think. I thought it was too much to try to remember.

194

'No, it's gone,' I tell him.

'Never mind,' he says, 'it's not important.'

Then he tells me that he's finished and it was nice meeting me. I'm glad it was nice for him because it wasn't too nice for me.

'What do I do now?' I ask.

'Go outside, and one of the nurses will look after you,' he says. So I go out, and I'm in this sort of big long corridor, and there's a couple of old blokes walking up and down looking very serious. Opposite there's a large room, so I go in there because there seems to be something going on. And in the corner there's a television, with the volume up loud, and the sound blaring out, but to be honest I'm not that keen on television, because there's not a lot on that I like. I'm standing there minding my own business, and I hear this voice saying,

'Sit down, Mr Martin.' I look round to see who it is that's talking, but you know there is no one there.

'Mr Martin,' it says again, 'sit down!' This is most odd, finding there's someone talking to me who knows my name, when there doesn't seem to be anyone there.

'Are you talking to me?' I ask.

The next thing I know, this little lady comes up, grabs me by the arm, and pushes me down into a chair.

'Sit down,' she says.

'I don't want to sit down,' I tell her.

'You have to sit down,' she says.

'What do I have to sit down for?' I ask.

'Otherwise you might fall over.'

There seems to be some sort of logic here, but to be honest if we all spent all day sitting down, because we were afraid of falling over, the work would never get done. Anyway, I decide that she must have some reason for wanting me to sit down, perhaps something is going to happen or something. So probably the best thing is to sit down and wait and see.

Next thing this big fat woman comes and sits next to me.

'Mr Martin,' she says, 'how are you getting on?' You know, it's so embarrassing because this lady clearly knows who I am, and for the life of me I can't think of who she is. 'How are you settling in?' she asks.

'I'm not doing too badly,' I say. I don't like to ask her her name, just in case it turns out to be someone who I should know. I tell you I've got the most dreadful memory for faces.

'That's good,' she says. 'Your daughter Carol said she'd bring some things in for you later.' Ah, that means she must know Carol. That narrows it down a bit.

'Carol's good like that,' I tell her.

'She seems to be a very organized person.' And do you know what? I'm sure this lady is one of Carol's teachers from school. Dorothy used to know her from somewhere, and whenever we used to bump into her down the shops or anything, Dorothy would insist on spending the rest of the day talking to her about a load of old nonsense, right there in the middle of the street. They wouldn't think of arranging to go to one of their houses to gossip, where I wouldn't have to listen to it. No, whatever they were talking about would have to be discussed right there and then in the street for all to hear. But for the life of me I can't think of this blessed woman's name.

'Is Carol your only daughter?' she asks. So it must be someone who knows Carol, and not my other two. I'm sure it's this teacher, but for the life of me . . . Mrs Barton. I'm sure it's Mrs Barton. Mind you, I haven't got the confidence to call her Mrs Barton, because I could well be wrong.

'No,' I tell her, 'we've got another two, Susan and Julie, but Carol's the youngest.'

'What?' says this woman. 'Three daughters and no sons,' and she shakes her head and tuts loudly. Well, it's hardly my fault if we had no sons, is it? 'Does Carol live at home?' she asks. I'm sure this must be Mrs Barton. No one else I know would be quite this nosy.

'No, she's married now.'

'Oh,' she says, 'was that her husband who came with her?'

'I don't know,' I tell her. 'What did he look like?'

'He was a big tall man with black hair.'

'That sounds like him,' I tell her.

'Do they live nearby?' she asks.

'They live in Greenford,' I tell her.

'That's nice,' she says, although I can't think of anything nice about living in Greenford. 'It must be handy having one of your daughters living so close.'

'Not really,' I tell her. 'We don't see much of her. We probably see more of Susan, and she lives in Scotland. Carol comes round but she disappears almost as soon as she's arrived.'

'Why's that then?' she asks.

'Why's what then?' I ask her.

'If she doesn't want to see you, why does she come round. It doesn't make sense to come round and disappear straight away.'

'That's not because of Carol,' I tell her. 'I'm sure that if it was up to Carol, she'd probably spend most of the time with us. It's her husband, Philip.'

'Ah,' she says. 'The age-old problem with the in-laws.'

'It's nothing to do with that,' I tell her, 'it's just Philip, he's no good, and she should never have married him.'

'So he's not good enough for your daughter?'

'He's good for nothing,' I tell her. 'He's never got

a job, he drinks too much, and he smokes like a chimney.'

'And does Carol know what you think of him?' she asks.

'I imagine so,' I tell her, 'we've told her often enough. We even told her that if she married him, we wouldn't speak to her again.'

'Oh Mr Martin,' she says, 'it's not surprising she doesn't stay long with you. She probably feels embarrassed.'

'Embarrassed?' I tell her. 'She should feel ashamed.'

'Perhaps she does feel ashamed,' she says, 'but there are times when a girl wants to marry someone, but her parents don't agree, and what do you expect her to do? You can't not marry someone, just because your parents don't approve.'

'That's the only reason why she married him,' I tell her. 'All her other boyfriends were the same. You've never seen such a bunch of no-hopers, the lot of them.' Mind you, Philip wasn't half as bad as some of them.

'And I wonder if you weren't a little bit too protective of your youngest daughter?' Well, what a daft thing to say. Of course I was protective. When you see your favourite child going out with a bunch of yobbos. None of them were worthy of her. I just wanted to see her happy, that's all. 'Perhaps, if you care for your daughter, which you clearly do, you should forgive her for her mistakes, and try to make her feel close to you, not make her feel guilty or ashamed.'

'I'm sure she doesn't feel guilty or ashamed,' I tell her.

'She looked guilty and ashamed when I saw her, so if you care about her, you should try to make it up to her when you see her.' That's what Dorothy is always telling me to do. She says we should forgive and forget. I might be able to forgive, but I couldn't forget. I would remember every time I saw Carol upset.

'Do you think you could do that?' she asks me.

'I'll try to talk to her,' I tell her. I do hate it when other people come and nose their way into family business. Some people think that the whole world wants to listen to their advice.

'That's good,' she says. 'She'll be in later. Now I'll have to get off and do some work. I hope to see you later, Mr Martin.'

Anyway, next thing I know, this other lady comes up to me and asks me if I'd like to go to the toilet. I think she's a bit rude to ask something like that, so I say,

'No, thank you very much,' and off she goes. Then it's a bit embarrassing because I realize that I do want to go to the toilet, but I don't like to have to go and tell her that I've changed my mind, and I don't know where the toilets are, so I get up and go and have a look.

So I go out of the entrance to the room, and there's this big corridor, with a few rooms opposite. So I go over to one of the rooms, and open the door, but it's full of all shelves with blankets on.

'What are you doing in there, Mr Martin?' this woman shouts.

'I was just looking for the gents,' I tell her.

'The toilet's next door,' she says and takes me to this room, and you go in there, and I tell you, the stench, you've never smelt anything like it. It's indescribable, and I'm surprised I manage to go. Then I wash my hands.

'You must come down for dinner, Mr Martin,' the lady says. I hadn't thought about what to do about dinner. So I check in my pocket, and do you know what? I've come out without any money. I can see that this is going to be very embarrassing. I don't know how I came to forget to bring any money, because that's not like me at all. What if I have dinner then they expect me to pay for it, I don't know what I'd do except die of shame I suppose. I don't like to ask them if I'll have to pay for it in case they think that I'm mean. Anyway, I decide that it's better to go hungry than to be the laughing stock of the whole place, so I try to wander off in the hope that no one will notice.

'Come back, Mr Martin!' this voice booms at me. 'It's time for dinner.' Well, I'm stuck now. She comes up and grabs me by the arm. 'The dining room is this way,' she says.

It seems as if I haven't got any choice in the matter. Off she drags me to the other end of the hall, to this big room with lots of tables and chairs, and she plonks me down on a chair, at a table with three other blokes.

So, we're all sitting at the table waiting for something to happen and one of the men sitting opposite looks as if he's struggling with something, I don't know what.

'Can you help me?' he says. 'Please can you help me?'

I don't know what he's trying to do.

'What do you want me to help you with?' I ask him.

'Please can you help me?' he says. This is a bit of a surprise to me to be quite honest.

'What do you want to do?' I ask.

'I'm trying to get out, please help me,' he says.

So I get up to see if I can give a hand. I see that he looks as if he may be stuck under the table.

'Do you want to get out?' I ask him.

'Please can you help me?' Now he's just repeating himself isn't he. I decide that the best thing to do is to try to get him out and see if that makes him any happier. Anyway I grab hold of the back of his chair and try to pull it as hard as I can, but it's no good. It doesn't move at all.

'Can you try standing up?' I ask him. 'Then I can try pulling your chair out.'

'Please can you help me?' he says. I can see that I'm a bit stuck here, mind you, this bloke's not helping me much, is he.

'Mr Martin,' shouts this woman, 'what are you doing? Will you kindly leave the other patients alone, and stop interfering.' With that she grabs hold of both my arms and forces me down into my chair.

'I'm very sorry,' I tell her, 'but he was calling out for help, and I was only trying to see what I could do.'

'No you're not,' she says, 'you're interfering. Will you kindly mind your own business.'

Well, I can see that I've upset everyone now. This bloke's moaning at me to help him, this lady's all upset with me, and I haven't got any money for my dinner. But I'm not feeling that hungry anyway so I decide that the best thing to do is to sneak off when no one's looking. I have a good look round to see if anyone is watching me, and I can't see anyone, so I get up as if I'm just adjusting my trousers. Still no one seems to have noticed, so I walk round the back of my chair as if I'm looking for someone, then I start edging towards the door, but keeping a good look round just in case. I get halfway towards the door and still the earth hasn't opened up beneath me, so I carry on. I get to the door, take hold of the door handle, twist it, and the door opens quite easily. So I go through, and I'm just closing the door, and suddenly all hell breaks loose.

There's this great scream of 'Mr Martin!' and they all come running through the door at me. Then these two women grab me by the arms, and drag me back through the door.

'Where are you going, Mr Martin?' they shout.

'I don't feel particularly hungry,' I tell them, as they force me down into my chair.

'I don't want anything to eat, thank you,' I tell them.

'But Mr Martin, you have to eat.'

I can see that there's not a lot of point in arguing with these people, so I just have to sit there. And this man is still calling out,

'Please help me,' but I decide I'd better leave him alone because I think I've caused enough trouble for one day.

Next thing that happens is this woman comes and plonks four bowls of soup on the table. It's very watery and I don't know if I really want it. I'm not a great soup man really. I mean I try a bit now and again, just to be polite really, but I'm not that keen, so I decide to leave it.

'You gotta eat your soup,' I hear.

'Pardon?' I ask, and I look round to see who's talking to me, but I can't see anyone there. The man next to me is making a dreadful mess, spilling it all down his front, and making the most horrible slurping noise. Anyway I try not to look at him.

'Do you want to be fed?' says the voice. I have a look round to see who's talking, and do you know, there's still no one there.

'Are you talking to me?' I ask, but there's no reply, so I don't know what they're going on about.

'If you don't eat your soup, I'll have to feed you.' I start to wonder what's going on. I mean I've never been spoken to like that before. Imagine someone trying to feed me. I mean that's ridiculous, isn't it. I only hope they're messing about, but I can't imagine who's doing it.

'Eat your soup or I'll have to feed you,' says the voice.

'Well,' I tell her, 'I've tried it, but I don't really like it.'

'Please help me,' says the man sitting opposite. And do you know what, the man sitting next to me has spilt his soup all down his front and all over his trousers.

Anyway I've decided that I don't want to stay here any longer, so I get up and start to leave.

'Mr Martin,' says the voice, 'you haven't eaten your soup either.'

'I don't want it,' I say, and I start to leave.

'You should eat it, it's good for you.' And this lady comes up to me and stands in front of me.

'Where are you going?' she says, and she stands in my way so that I can't get out.

'I'm going home,' I tell her.

'No!' she says. 'Sit down and have something to eat.'

'But I don't want anything to eat,' I tell her.

'Well, have something otherwise you might feel hungry later.' I can see that I'm not going to win this argument, and I'm not going to get past her, so I decide to sit down, and she takes my bowl of soup away.

Next thing someone comes and plonks a plate in front of me. It doesn't look too appetizing. There's some potatoes, some funny green stuff, I'm not sure what, and two sausages.

'Eat your dinner, Mr Martin,' says the person. So I take a bit of mashed potato on my fork, and I try a bit of it, but it's not very nice. It's not that hot, and it's a bit lumpy. I don't think it's proper mashed potato like Dorothy makes. And then I think, what about Dorothy? She will have my dinner ready for me at home, and I won't be there. What will she think. I don't even know if they've told her that I'm here. She's probably worried about me. And the man next to me has got into an even worse mess. He's dropping mashed potato all over the place, and everything, and that puts me right off eating for a start, because I'm not used to eating and seeing that sort of mess going on.

'Aren't you going to eat your dinner, Mr Martin?' asks this voice.

'I tried some of it,' I say, 'but I'm not that keen. I'm not feeling that hungry.' I don't know why these people want me to eat this food anyway. After a couple of minutes I decide that I've had enough of sitting here anyway, I mean I don't know what they're trying to do to me or anything.

So I get up. No one seems to be watching, so I wander

203

off towards the door. I open it cautiously, and go through.

'Mr Martin!' this voice shouts.

'Leave him be,' says another girl's voice, 'he won't eat anyway.' So I wander down the long corridor. It's not very long before I realize that I'm completely lost. I seem to have got myself into a right mess here, because there isn't even anyone around to ask the way. The trouble is I have no idea where I am, and I haven't a clue about finding my way back home. Well, the best thing to do in these situations is to start walking in one direction, and keep going until you can find someone who can tell you the way, or tell you where you can get a bus or something. Then it suddenly occurs to me that I was speaking to a chap not long ago, and he seemed to know what was going on, so I go off in search of him.

So off I wander, but as you can imagine, I'm not feeling too sure of myself. I go through this door, and inside there is a large room with beds all over the place. Then I go through the room to see if there's a window I can see out of, because that might give me some idea of where I am. After a bit of looking around I see this window with the light streaming through. It's one of those old-fashioned windows, made up of all small panes of glass, and wooden frames. All I can see out is a big lawn with a big path going through. But it's nowhere that I know and that's for sure. Anyway, it occurs to me that one idea is to climb out of the window. At least that will get me out, then I can phone Dorothy, or Carol, or even phone for a taxi if it comes to that because I don't mind paying for it. Also the window isn't that high up, and it's quite a big one.

So anyway, I push the handle down, and push it open, but it will only go a small way then it sticks, so I give it a good push, but it still won't go any further. Well, I've always been a thin man. I've never been able to put any weight on however much I eat, so I decide that I really don't have much choice in the matter, so I think I'll try to climb out. So I get my leg up on the window sill, and I push myself up . . . and then all hell breaks loose.

'Mr Martin,' this voice screams at me, 'what do you think you're doing?' You can imagine, I feel a bit foolish being caught climbing out of the window.

'I was trying to get out,' I tell her.

'Come down here before you break a leg,' And this big fat woman comes over, and pulls me down.

'Do we have to keep an eye on you all the time?' she says. You can imagine, I'm not too keen on being spied upon, but I don't think I'll get far arguing with this woman. She then takes me out of the room, down the corridor, and into this large room.

'Stay there,' this woman says, 'and don't go wandering off.'

Next thing I feel this hand on my shoulder. I turn round, and do you know who it is? It's Carol. I'm so shocked to see her, I don't know what to say.

'Carol!' I say. 'What are you doing here?' She just puts her arm around me and gives me a big hug.

'I've brought some things in for you, Dad,' she says. 'How are you getting on, Dad?'

'I'm getting on fine!' I tell her, but then, I think that I'm not getting on fine at all. I just said that to be polite.

'Have you met any new friends, yet?' Well I don't know about meeting new friends. I can't think of anyone much that I've met lately.

'Not yet,' I tell her, because I'm not sure what else to say.

'How are you settling in then, Dad?' Then, I start to laugh.

'How am I settling in what, Carol?' Then Carol looks all lost and distant.

'Are you sure you're all right, Dad?'

'I like to think so,' I tell her in a joking manner, because I don't know what Carol's got to be so serious about.

'Have they shown you your bedroom yet?' she asks. Well, what would they want to do that for? Unless they've had it decorated or something behind my back.

'Oh yes!' I tell her. 'I've seen my bedroom. Lots of times.'

'And what do you think of it?' she asks. Well, she's got me there, to be quite honest because last time I saw my bedroom, it looked no different to any other time that I've seen it. I expect they've had something done to surprise me. But the trouble is I never notice anything. And although I tell them it's my eyesight, it isn't really. Even before I wore glasses, Dorothy could be wearing a new suit of clothes, have her hair dyed and cut, and I still wouldn't notice. It's just that I don't notice things like that. It's not my fault.

'I think it's very nice, thank you,' I tell her, and I try one of my crafty grins, in the hope she thinks I know what I'm talking about, because to be honest I don't

'What are the other people like?' she asks. I tell you, the kids sometimes ask you all these questions and expect you to know all the answers. And, to be honest, I didn't have the education that they had. Sometimes they just lose me completely. I don't know what they're on about.

'They're not too bad,' I tell her.

'That's good,' she says. 'I'm glad you don't mind it too much. Come and show me where your bedroom is. I've brought some things for you.' Fancy Carol wanting me to show her where my bedroom is.

'My bedroom's probably where it's always been,' I tell her. 'Unless someone's moved it.'

'Not that bedroom,' she says. 'Your bedroom here.' Now she's lost me because I've only ever had one bedroom in this house. 'Come on,' she says, 'let's see if one of the nurses can help us find it.' And she takes me by the hand, and takes me off down the corridor, until we meet this young girl.

'Do you know where Mr Martin's room is?' she asks.

'Has no one shown you where your room is yet, Mr Martin?' this girl says. 'Come on, I'll show you where it is.' And she takes us down this long corridor, and into this small room. There's this bed in there, and a wardrobe, but not much else.

'Thanks very much,' says Carol. The young girl then goes off and closes the door behind her. Carol puts this suitcase on the bed, and unzips it.

'I brought you some clothes in,' she says. 'Here's your shirts, and two pairs of pyjamas, and some trousers. And I got some new underwear for you because I thought you could do with some new stuff, and here's your dressing gown, because you might be needing that. I brought your toilet bag as well, and I bought a few extra things to go in it. There's a new flannel, and a new toothbrush, and some toothpaste . . . and I brought you a new towel . . .'

And do you know, the tears are running down poor Carol's face. I don't know what the matter can be, I've not seen Carol get upset for a long time. I hope she's not in trouble or anything like that.

'What's the matter, Carol?' I ask her. Then she turns round and puts both arms round me, and hugs me really tight.

'I'm so sorry, Dad,' she says, 'I'm so sorry.'

'Sorry for what, dear?' I ask her. 'Don't worry, everything will be all right.'

'I just hate having to do this to you. I hate having to leave you here.'

'What do you mean "leave me here"?' I ask her.

'I want to take you home, really I do,' she says, sobbing. 'It's just Philip . . . He says he won't stand for it.' I had a nasty feeling that it might be something to do with Philip.

'That Philip's not causing you problems is he?'

'No,' she says, shaking her head. 'It's not Philip I'm worried about, it's you.' Well, isn't that silly. You spend half your life worrying about your children, and then you find out they're worried about you as well.

'What would you want to worry about me for?' I ask her.

'Oh Dad, you don't understand, do you? You just don't know what's going on.' But the trouble is that I'm pretty sure I do know exactly what's going on. It's that husband of hers. She should never have married him. So I give her a kiss on the cheek.

'Don't worry, Carol, whatever happens, you know your old Dad will always be there to help you out.' Then Carol gives me a big squeeze again, and presses her face up against mine, so that I feel the warmth of her skin.

'I'll have to go now,' she says. 'Philip's waiting outside in the car. I didn't want him to come in.' She then takes a handkerchief out of her coat pocket, and dries her eyes and blows her nose. 'I'll be back to see you tomorrow. Now you take care of yourself, Dad,' she says.

'You take care of yourself too,' I tell her, 'and don't worry. Things always turn out right in the end.' Then she quickly grabs me, and gives me a kiss on the cheek, and she's off out of the door like a shot. So I hurry out of the door after her, but she's nowhere to be seen. It's a shame she had to rush off like that, just when we had started talking. It makes me feel quite sad to see her upset. There's a chair nearby, so I go and sit down.

You know how it is after a long hard day, you sit down

in a chair, and you start to feel quite tired . . . and your eyes start to feel heavy . . .

Next thing this young girl is waking me up.

'Mr Martin,' she says, 'Do you want to go to bed?' Well, you can imagine, I'm a bit shocked at being asked this.

'Come on,' she says, and she helps me up. I'm a little lost for words and I'm not sure what's going on, but I go along with her, because I don't know what else to do. She takes me into this small room with a bed in it.

'Take your clothes off,' she says.

'I'm a married man,' I tell her. Then she looks at me completely blankly, then she bursts out laughing.

'He's a married man,' she laughs. 'Take your clothes off, and put your pyjamas on, and go to bed,' she says. Then she walks out still laughing. 'He's a married man.'

It's very cold in the room, and the lightbulb is rather dim, and the walls are quite bare; through the window I can see it looks very dark outside, but I take my clothes off and put them into the locker next to the bed. Then I put my pyjamas on, and get into bed. The sheets are very cold and starchy, and I feel a bit lonely here, all by myself. I wish Dorothy was here.

A VIEW OF
ANATOLIA

Frances Watt

Frances Watt was born and educated in Edinburgh but has in the past lived and worked in both England and Wales. She now lives in rural Angus with her husband and two daughters.

She has been writing for several years and has had work, both fiction and non-fiction, published in a variety of publications.

A VIEW OF
ANATOLIA

Arabella arrived one wet Edinburgh afternoon in June while Scobie was teaching the dog to retrieve the socks it had hidden. When the doorbell rang he said over his shoulder, 'Put the kettle on now you're up,' and then returned to his applied behaviour modification. 'Sit. Sit Judith. Good girl.' He was crouched beside the dog on the floor at the end of the bed, one arm around its neck to hold it back, his balled socks in his other hand poised to throw. From the door, in the half-light seeping through the curtains, the white bony curve of his bare back looked almost frail. I could hear his voice behind me as I padded down the hall fastening my dressing gown. 'Stay now. Stay. Judith! Stay!' Only Scobie could have thought of calling that overbred, underdisciplined whippet *Judith*.

Some premonition made me glance at the hall mirror in passing and rake my fingers through my hair. There was half a chance it could be Scobie's mother at the door, making a last-ditch attempt to rescue 'her Bill' from the fleshpots of Marchmont. She'd come in late May, armoured with pacamac, rainmate and virtue. 'It's not right for a boy his age to live like this. You should be ashamed of yourself, corrupting the innocent.' The "innocent" had appeared naked behind me at that point, closed the door in her face and proceeded to grind his bottom against the back of it so that it creaked rhythmically. 'Why have you taken your clothes off?' I

213

hissed at him. 'What are you doing?' He grinned, increased the tempo, covered his mouth with one hand and emitted a series of tremolo groans towards the letterbox. I hadn't seen her since.

It was not Scobie's mother at the door this time. 'Hello,' said the girl in the velvet hairband, 'I'm Arabella.' Something in my expression must have suggested incomprehension, because she added, 'You did get Daddy's letter? It is all right, isn't it? I mean I know the lease isn't *actually* up till the end of September but since the others have gone already . . . Daddy thought reducing the rent would probably make it all right.' She gulped, watching me. 'I didn't mean to land myself on you, but you didn't write back to say no . . .' Her voice trailed away and she stood staring at me, eyes huge and worried, expression balanced between apology and apprehension.

I took a deep breath. 'Of course it's all right, come in,' I said, opening the door wider, stooping for one of the hand-stitched bags at her feet. 'I was working late last night. Still not properly functioning, I'm afraid. D'you want to put your things in the front bedroom? It's got the best views, sunrises one way, sunsets the other.' Thank God I painted over Marsha's mural last week, I prayed silently. And please let me stop talking so much. 'I'll put the kettle on, shall I? Would you like tea or coffee?'

'I don't remember a double bed in here . . .' Arabella said doubtfully.

'Oh, I forgot about that. Marsha had her . . . her little sister to stay for the last weekend of term. It's two singles pushed together; we can move one out again if it's in your way.'

Arabella turned back towards me from the window and smiled. 'This is such a beautiful room. When my brother was a student and I was small I used to visit him here. It always seemed to be Christmas – he'd take me to a

214

pantomime or something. I used to think this was a fairytale bedroom, for a princess to hang her hair down from.'

I paused in my strategic retreat at the door and looked at her properly for the first time. I hadn't noticed before just how young she was – eighteen? nineteen? Until then, through the haze of extreme shock, I'd only registered the status-markers; the 'Arabella', the 'Daddy' who would be reducing the rent, the litter of pigskins wrapped around her wordly goods; perhaps most of all the velvet Alice band. I hadn't moved much in circles where grown women wore Alice bands. I saw now that she was lovely. Not with that cheekboned, intimidating loveliness of so many beautiful women, but gently, self-deprecatingly heart-shifting. I smiled. It was difficult not to smile for Arabella. 'Tea,' I said, and backed out of the room.

Scobie didn't take it well. 'Don't call her "it". This is an aristocrat,' he protested. He was still naked, still crouched with socks.

'It's a bloody mongrel if it's been eating my mail. What else could have happened to Arabella's Daddy's letter?'

'Arabella's Daddy, eh?' said Scobie, looking interested. 'Are you going to be consorting with the enemy?'

'Don't give me that class warfare stuff,' I said, throwing his trousers at him. '"Daddy" is my land-lord, and "Daddy" is offering to reduce the rent till September. That makes him one of the comrades in my book. Now get dressed, do something about this mess and go as silently as you can while I take her tea.'

'Go?' said Scobie, looking hurt. 'Go where?'

'Back to the boxroom you give as your postal address.'

'Judith doesn't like it there,' Scobie complained. 'The woodworm keep her awake.'

'There's always your mother,' I suggested.

Scobie began to take me seriously. 'Are you throwing me out?'

'No, I'm not throwing you out. I'm just throwing you out.'

'That's all right then,' he said. He dropped his trousers on the floor again and began looking intent.

'Scobie, stop it. Scobie. Get off! I mean it!'

'My God, but you're beautiful when you're angry,' Scobie said in the voice he thinks sounds like Peter Sellers.

I breathed hard. 'If you don't get off me now, *now*, I am going to go abruptly into the foetal position.' There was an involuntary wince as Scobie worked out consequences.

'You mean you can resist me?' he asked.

'Easy.'

'So you're not going to suck my toes then?'

'Get Judith to do it. Sock-stealing is second cousin to foot fetishism.' I rolled out from under him while he pondered that. 'I'm supposed to be making tea,' I wailed. 'Will you get dressed! Oh, God, what state is the kitchen in?'

Despite my efforts Arabella met Scobie that day. She advanced in the direction of the kitchen saying, 'Can I do something to help?' Scobie was caught in flagrante, tiptoeing towards the front door with his shirt tail hanging out, his shoes in one hand and Judith's lead in the other. Judith was holding his socks and drooling.

'Arabella, this is Scobie,' I said, abandoning the shovelling gestures intended to speed him on his way. 'Scobie, Arabella. Scobie sculpts.'

Arabella looked momentarily and understandably startled. Then she sorted things out. 'Oh, I see,' she said, heliotrope eyes clearing to pleased complicity. 'You must be Elinor's fiancé?'

Scobie swithered briefly. I could see it in his face,

216

inverted snobbery battling with low cunning as he worked it out that *fiancés* might be allowed a latitude not open to those who generally described themselves as toy-boys. 'Yes,' he said as the pause was lengthening beyond expectancy and towards suspicion. 'Yes, I'm Elinor's fiancé.' He dropped his shoes to offer her his hand. As she shook it Arabella made a small, indecisive movement with her other hand, a smoothing back of hair already sleekly pinned under the velvet Alice band. I knew that Scobie saw the ring at the same time as I did because his eyes changed. That disbelieving glint made them exactly the same size and colour as the knob of diamond covering one entire joint of Arabella's third finger.

Over the summer Arabella and I slipped into an unexpectedly comfortable *modus vivendi*. I could not, absolutely could not, bring myself to address her by her full name. In the first few days I tied myself in knots trying to avoid calling her anything. When I discovered that Belle was acceptable it was a deliverance from acute embarrassment but also, somehow, an immediate intimacy. She called me Elinor always, but then everyone does.

I was truly grateful to have the rent reduced back to less than I'd been paying before Marsha and Libby swanned off to, respectively, Hong Kong and the EC secretariat. It meant I could give up my waitressing at Friday evening supper dances and Sunday family lunches, and concentrate on finishing my thesis for the end of September. Having Arabella around also cramped Scobie's style in a satisfactory fashion. 'You're not going off sex, are you?' he asked one day. 'They tell me older women do that sometimes.'

'Scobie, I'm four years older than you, not forty,' I said. 'Don't worry, I still lust after your flesh. I'm just relieved

217

to be getting some work done now I don't spend twelve hours a day in bed with you.' He looked unconvinced. In actual fact he had little to complain about since we had similar levels of libido as well as the same low sense of humour. It was simply the case that now the landlord's daughter was in residence I judged it politic for him to catch the last bus of an evening and take Judith back to their woodwormed boxroom in Stockbridge.

The arrangement over rent didn't include any provision for communal living, but unofficially, gradually, Arabella and I began to coincide over supper in the kitchen; it began to make sense to share a packet of cornflakes, to have a joint order for milk; I began, as Scobie saw it, to fraternize with the upper classes.

Arabella was a good listener. Over toast sometimes, occasionally midnight biscuits and cheese, she would fix those startling eyes on my face and I would talk. Mostly I told her about organizing the fruits of eighteen months' research into a convincing overview of the correlation between alcohol abuse and physical injury. By that stage I was no longer spending my Saturday nights wrestling coherence from bleeding drunks in Casualty. Instead I passed them wrestling conclusions from phenomena so apparently random that they made Scobie's lifestyle look well ordered. I can be boring on the subject even now, but Arabella listened with fascinated incredulity, as though to dispatches from another solar system.

At the time she was riding the crest of a full-scale tidal wave she described as 'Getting Things Organized for the Wedding'. As quid pro quo for my bulletins from the underbelly I heard, agog in my turn, accounts of shopping safaris conducted in the kind of retail establishment that generally ejected Scobie on sight. I was treated to reports of luncheons with godmothers at Gleneagles. I sat in on post mortems of balls held in a rural, lavishly financed hinterland beyond my ken. Arabella and I tacitly acknowledged the distance between us, sometimes enjoyed it, sometimes forgot it entirely.

'I do admire you, you know,' she said one morning over her coffee cup. She looked even younger without the velvet hairbands, her waist-length hair not sleek for once in the day but tousled like that of an infant seductress.

'I aim for an understated elegance,' I admitted when I'd stopped spluttering.

'Not that!' Arabella said.

'Thanks.'

'You know what I mean,' she said, blushing. I did indeed. I was wearing the Marks & Spencer dressing gown my Aunt Sybil had given me for my twenty-first birthday, with matching quilted slippers. Arabella was wearing oyster silk. 'I envy you what you've done with your life,' she said.

'I'm not that ancient,' I complained. 'You and Scobie seem to think I might be someone's grandmother. You'll have something to admire when I'm the youngest social sciences professor since records began.'

'That's what I mean,' said Arabella. 'You're so confident, you have ambitions. You know what you're going to do.'

'You know what you're going to do too.'

'No,' said Arabella. 'I know what's going to happen. That's different.'

I was too busy during that summer to socialize much – Scobie and his sex drive occupied all my spare time. He couldn't work then, hadn't worked for months, and as a direct result spent most of his waking hours trying to persuade me into bed.

Arabella on the other hand regularly brought people home, after New Town dinner parties or Range Rover-

219

borne picnics, before cocktails in the Caledonian. 'The Gang', she called them. Her use of the word disconcerted me. I was accustomed to 'gangs' of vomiting adolescents for whom 'socio-economic grouping' meant three initials and a slogan, spray-painted. I met most of Arabella's 'Gang', en masse and probably individually, over that July, August and September, but I never really sorted them out in my mind. As far as I could tell they all had the same expensive teeth, a curious unisex tendency to odd laughs, and what Scobie felt was a vulgar lack of respect for champagne. They were generally Sarahs and Hughs, Charlottes and Williams – this last much to Scobie's amusement since that was the name by which his mother, alone of all the world, still knew him. He would lie naked on my bed, oblivious to the effect on his bohemian image of keeping on his socks to thwart Judith, and listen to the echo of their distant, confident vowels. 'Hear that? That bray? That's William.' Scobie had developed what seemed to me an almost anthropological attitude towards the 'Gang', at once fascinated and patronizing. 'Wullie, they call him. He doesn't seem to mind being called Prick.'

I looked up from my desk. 'Why should he mind being called one, if you don't mind being one?'

'If that's your opinion,' Scobie said, 'why don't you come over here and let me practise my vocation in life?'

Despite himself Scobie liked Arabella. She was so entirely without guile it was impossible for anyone to dislike her, but in fact I began to suspect that Scobie and she had more in common with each other than either of them had with me. They were almost exactly the same age for a start, both with birthdays in December. That four-year difference seemed larger sometimes during those weeks than it ever had before, even after Scobie's mother's efforts to cast me as crib-robber. Now and then

I would find them tête-a-tête in the kitchen, talking about me. 'I think she's working too hard,' I heard Arabella say once.

'I keep telling her so,' Scobie said. 'But she doesn't take me seriously.'

'Who would?' I said, sailing in on them 'Let's face it, *mes enfants*, neither of you has the slightest idea of what real work is. Neither of you, to put it bluntly, knows much more about life itself than that you take one breath after the other.'

'What shall we do to her?' Scobie said, leaning back against the work surface.

'Oh, I leave that entirely up to you,' Arabella said and grinned into her coffee. She'd apparently accepted what Scobie liked to describe as our domestic arrangements, even in the absence of a ring to match the massive respectability of her own. Scobie had offered to provide one. 'Not my scene,' I said.

'Oh, good,' he said. 'Can you lend me ten quid anyway?'

I continued nevertheless, since it suited me, to pack him off towards the bus stop at eleven o'clock. There he occasionally supplemented his income with song and dance acts, appreciated mostly by the more comprehensively refreshed among his audience. Judith was by then a highly trained show-dog, though still no less crazed by the smell of feet.

Then in late August things changed. The Festival swung underway, Scobie was lent someone's studio for a month and began to work again, Arabella's fiancé's regiment came back from Germany – and Arabella began to talk in her sleep.

The first time it happened I was working late alone in my room and I heard someone speak in the distance. I'd passed Arabella on her way to bed hours before, clutching a tumbler of paracetamol and looking wan. 'Too much carousing,' I told her. 'This Oliver of yours is nothing more than a social butterfly.' She smiled palely. 'My head . . .' she said. 'Too much sun. We were at Portobello all afternoon listening to buskers.'

Now, in the quiet pool of light around my desk, I lifted my head from a catalogue of facial injuries – five self-discharged without medical intervention, forty-seven requiring sutures, fifteen with associated other injuries – and the distant sound came again. No, not talking. Someone was shouting somewhere.

Arabella's room was in darkness and apparently silent. 'Belle?' I said at the door. No answer. I was retreating, beginning to think the noise had percolated up from another flat, when there was a rustle as she turned against the sheets.

'Bosphorus,' she said.

'What?' I said. Silence. 'Are you awake, Belle?' There was no answer from the bed and no further movement. After a minute or so, satisfied that her breathing was regular again, I went back to my room and my gruesome statistics. I might have forgotten all about it if I hadn't had a headache myself the next morning.

'Can I borrow a couple of your bombers?' I asked.

Arabella looked uncomprehending. I was reminded again that we moved in different circles. 'Paracetamol,' I expanded.

'How can anyone have a headache on a morning like this?' she said, rummaging in her bedside-table drawer. I looked past her out of the window, and the corner of the Firth of Forth visible around the shoulder of the Castle Rock shimmered back at me unhelpfully. 'How late did you work last night?' Arabella added, in a fair imitation of Scobie at his bossiest.

222

'What does the Bosphorus mean to you, by the way?' I said.

'What?'

I turned round and caught her expression. The shining morning face had clouded over. 'You were rabbiting on about the Bosphorus in your sleep last night.'

'Oh,' she said. 'I've no idea. Must have been a dream, I suppose.' She sounded unconvinced.

'What's the matter?' I said. She'd sat down on the edge of the bed, looking puzzled and unsettled.

'I found this on my bedside table this morning,' she said, and she handed me a sheet from the square yellow pad that always sat there, beside the phone. I already knew her scrawl, a huge, rounded hand, quite unmistakable, quite unlike mine.

The chain is formed of gold, worked and pierced but even so, strong beyond my ability to bend it. The band on my wrist has chafed a rawness and before noon the eunuch changed it, replacing it over my other hand with a lining of leather below. While he worked at the fastening he showed in his mouth where his tongue has been removed. His speech is the grunting of an animal.

Out there, where two seas meet beyond the roofs and domes, the old woman says Mehmed had his last mistress drowned. With her, also sewn into a sack, died her daughters. The youngest was ten days old. Perhaps it was in this fashion that he earned the nickname they give him in the bazaar, the Conqueror. This should be added to the list of his victories; one Byzantine woman of almost seventeen summers, and three girl-children.

'This is wonderful, Belle!' I said, looking up from the

223

sheet. 'I didn't know you could do this sort of thing!'

'I can't,' Arabella said.

'But . . .'

'I don't remember writing it.'

'You don't remember . . .?' I said. I was, in the beginning, almost lost for words.

'I don't even remember dreaming,' Arabella said. 'I didn't see that' – she gestured towards the sheet still in my hand – 'till after I was dressed this morning. I went back to pick up my watch and it was there on top of the pad.'

I looked down at the sheet of yellow paper again. 'You didn't wake up in the middle of the night with an idea you had to get down?' It was something that happened to me regularly, though the brainwaves of the wee small hours seldom bore much examination in the cold light of day.

'I don't remember anything,' Arabella said. 'Except . . .'

'Except what?'

'When I picked it up,' she said, 'I thought I noticed a smell, then I thought maybe I just remembered it . . .'

I lifted the paper and sniffed, watching her face. 'It faded almost at once,' she said, 'but I seemed to recognize it. It was a mixture of things, with perfume in it, like roses, and some smell of English churches . . .'

'Incense?'

'Yes, that's right! It was incense . . . And something else. Dung.'

'Horses?' I said. I was beginning to lose track completely by then, unsure if the smell had been on the paper, or in the bedroom, or only in her head.

'No, not horses,' she said intently, thinking. 'Some animal I don't know.'

'How could you recognize it if . . . ?'

'I couldn't, could I?' Arabella said. She took the piece of paper out of my hand, crumpled it and threw it

224

towards the wastepaper basket in the corner. 'I must simply have half-wakened and written that down.' She laughed. 'I was probably thinking about some film or other. Bob Hope most likely, The Road to some-where . . .' She bent, picked up the crushed yellow paper from the carpet where it had landed and deposited it finally in the bin. 'Would you like some coffee?'

I remembered my headache and the two tablets I was still holding. 'No, thanks. I think I'll just take these and go back to bed for a couple of hours.'

I was already in bed when I thought of something. I padded through towards the kitchen, silent on bare feet, and found Arabella sitting at the table staring at her coffee cup. Then she looked up, the expression was gone, and I was quite sure that I couldn't really have seen fear on that open, perfectly oval face. 'Forgive my ignorance, but where exactly is the Bosphorus?' I asked.

'Haven't a clue,' she said. Then she took a look at her wristwatch and shot to her feet. 'Oh, heavens, I'm late,' she said. 'Oliver's taking me down for lunch with the aged grandparent, we have to be in Annan by half eleven.'

'The seventh Lord?' I asked, being by then quite well informed about Oliver's family tree.

'That's the one,' Arabella said.

When she'd gone I took my headache back to bed and lay there until finally I gave up on the paracetamol having any effect at all. Then on impulse I climbed out of bed, crawled below it and dug out my Collins New Age Encyclopedia from the box gathering drifts of dust and fluff underneath. The book still had the illuminated label inside the flyleaf. 'Presented to Elinor E. Sanderson. The Maisie Harkness Prize for General Excellence, June 1976.' I'd been a swot even then. No Bosphorus, but then I found, *Bosporus: – Strait connecting the Black Sea with the Sea of Marmara, and separating Asiatic and*

European Turkey. Istanbul stands on its W. shore.

I knelt there for a while looking at that with my head humming, then I went through to Arabella's bedroom. There was no crumpled yellow sheet in the wastepaper basket, nothing except a paper tissue with lipstick smudges on it. Arabella must have picked the note back out. I found, however, that I could remember most of what it had said. It's a talent that's frequently useful, occasionally a curse. I remembered particularly the line that had begun *Out there, where two seas meet . . .* Out there, in the Bosporus Strait, someone had had a woman and three small girls drowned in sacks.

Scobie was dismissive. 'Well, of course she's having nightmares. She's agreed to get hitched to that prat with the crewcut.' That was Oliver.

'But I think she really loves him,' I said. 'It can't be that.'

'Could you love him?'

'That's beside the point. She doesn't have my weakness for artistic types afflicted by satyriasis.'

'I'm glad you appreciate my strengths,' Scobie said, grabbing for the nearest handful of flesh. 'By the way, did I tell you that my head is wonderful?'

'It's not a bad little head,' I admitted, holding his hair back in a chignon with one hand, considering. 'A little over-hirsute to be appreciated by the likes of the seventh Lord perhaps.'

'Not my head,' said Scobie. 'My *head*. I'm beginning to think I might get it cast in fact. Can I interest you in a little practical patronage?'

'How much?' I said suspiciously.

'I don't know. Probably quite a lot.' Scobie grew serious for once. 'I've never worked like this before. It's as if I already knew what it was supposed to look like when I started – but I didn't.' Then he looked wolfish again. 'I'm probably possessed by the ghost of Henry Moore.'

'Oh, God,' I said. 'There must be an epidemic going around.'

The next time it happened it was my turn to be bright and cheerful. I'd just penned the last line of the conclusion, I still had three weeks to get it typed and I was disgustingly pleased with myself. 'Come on, Belle, the sun has got his hat on, and you've got a fitting for The Dress. I bring you probably the best coffee in Marchmont . . .' I turned back from drawing the curtains and saw her face.

'What's wrong?'

'Oh, nothing,' Arabella said. She squinted at me through puffy eyelids. 'I just feel terrible. Hormonal I suppose.' I'd never seen her waver from clear-skinned equanimity at any time over the last nine weeks. 'What time is it anyway?' She reached sideways for her watch and the sudden check of her hand in mid-movement caught my attention.

'What is it?'

'Nothing.' She looked sick. 'There's something written there again.'

In the end I read the note for her. 'You can't just throw it away unread!' I argued. 'It's fascinating stuff. If it is something out of your unconscious, you have to be interested in what's going on in there.'

'Spare me from professionals,' Arabella said, lying back against her pillow with one forearm held over her eyes. There was an echo of Scobie in that but when I glanced over the curve of her mouth seemed a lot more vulnerable. I looked doubtfully back at the writing in my hand. Perhaps it *would* be better ignored. But it was too late, the first line had already caught my eye.

The old woman can make sense of the eunuch's noises. She told me they have been here more than ten years, as servants and gaolers and custodians. Once he kept many women here. Is it the hard edge of war or all the daughters consigned to the seas that has dulled his appetites?

It seems the eunuch loved the last one very greatly. Her name was Irene. She was a Christian, and fair like me, the old woman says. So in the end not arrogance, nor impudence, nor being headstrong, nor having the temper of a camel brings me to this, but the look of my face.

The eunuch is ugly, being a Mamluk from beyond the Mediterranean, but amongst the Arabs was considered pleasing. Very often in the night, while half asleep, I dream that my face becomes the face of the eunuch. I lie and watch as he grows beautiful; as the chain slips from my wrist and fastens on his.

There was a silence when I'd finished reading that aloud. 'Irene . . .' I said at last. 'Do you know any Irenes?'

Arabella sat upright suddenly. 'No, I don't know any Irenes,' she shouted. 'I don't even know what the hell a Mamluk is!' Then she put her face down on her quilt-covered knees and began to weep, noisily, inelegantly, like a very small, despairing child. At first I tried putting a hand on her shoulders but she simply shook it off. In the end I shifted her box of tissues from the mantelpiece to the bed beside her, sat down in the basket chair at the long windows and waited, watching tree-tops swaying in the high, windy space between me and the square block of the university library.

'I'm sorry,' Arabella said at last. 'I wasn't shouting at you.' She sniffed hugely then blew her nose.

'Arabella,' I said, 'Are you . . . have you and Oliver . . .?'

228

I couldn't do it. I'd been cast in the role of village elder in that ménage only in the complete absence of competition. My real lack of nous was now thrust upon me. Until then I'd have claimed laissez-faire acceptance of all sexual mores, but I simply didn't know how to ask Arabella if she was a virgin or not. She was, in ways I had never stopped to consider, different from anyone else I had ever known.

'Look,' Arabella said. Her voice wavered and she stopped, blew her nose once more and began again. 'Look, this has nothing at all to do with me. It's not me in there.' She waved at the yellow sheet. 'Not in any way. Not symbolically, not subconsciously. *I didn't write it!*'

I took the page and stared at that large, distinctive handwriting, thinking hard. *I didn't write it.* This was tricky stuff. I sat down on the edge of the bed, trying to look neutral, receptive. 'Who do you think did write it?' I asked. Non-judgemental, facilitating, and totally misjudged.

Arabella stared back at me. 'Who . . .? I don't believe you. What happened to the iron rule? "Never case-work friends or family," you said. What does that make me?' She scrambled out of the far side of the bed and stood at bay, arms crossed across her body. She was barely decent in cream satin, that patrician length of hair tangled around her head like an irregular halo. She seemed hardly even adolescent; a defensive Lolita, armoured against all self-knowledge by that staggering, dangerous simplicity.

'I'm not trying to case-work anyone,' I said, meeting her eyes, but the lie somehow acquired a life of its own so that it echoed between us.

'You don't see anything, do you?' she said. 'You'd reduce everything to logic. You don't have any idea.' Then she turned and flung out of the room. In the distance I heard the lock of the bathroom door click home.

'How do you know the problem's sex?' Scobie wanted to know.

'That's not like you, William,' I said. The memory of Arabella's furious stare was still uncomfortably vivid and I was compensating by trying to irritate him. 'Don't tell me *you* acknowledge any other motive in life? How's the head by the way?'

Scobie smirked. 'Benny Visconti's seen it. He's arranging for it to be cast.'

I was impressed. 'Benny Visconti? The Visconti Gallery?'

Scobie looked both smug and guilty. 'He's offered me space in an exhibition. Someone else pulled out. He's going to call it the Scottish Internationals.'

'Scobie, you've never been further than Berwick-on-Tweed in your life,' I said. 'Is this you succumbing to grubby commercialism?'

Scobie stared down at his shoes and I noticed that they were new, and real leather, not the battered plimsolls he usually wore. He looked up and directly at me, without humour, without desire, almost without expression at all. 'I don't think I'm really clever enough to keep up with you all the time,' he said. It was not a compliment.

On the morning of the twenty-first of September in that year Arabella jumped to her death from her bedroom window.

That's not how it was reported, but then very little was reported at all. I suppose that may be why I feel the need to record this, however imperfectly. It might have been possible, from her name, her home address, to guess at the velvet Alice bands, to go on to envisage some Hooray Henrietta with an unhappy susceptibility to champagne and no head for heights. I felt sometimes that there might be almost no trace of the real Arabella left at all.

Pressure must have been discreetly exerted somewhere along the corridors of power because her death was very quickly, very smoothly tidied away. Death by Misadventure. I'm sceptical, by both nature and training, about accidents, but that verdict didn't seem to me to be rigorous enough even for the murky, inexact science of real life. Theories should take account of all known facts before projecting their shadows onward into the black hole of possibilities. I knew that the window of that room opened lengthways in half, but I also knew it had been bolted shut, and draughtproofing taped over the gap, for at least the previous eighteen months. Beyond the seal, behind a fat stone balustrade, there was a mere suggestion of balcony, barely a roost for the more anorexic pigeon. Was Arabella really lured out into thin morning drizzle by that grimy shelf? – I know it was drizzling when she died. At that precise moment I was walking across the Meadows with three copies of 'Alcohol and Violence in a Scottish Urban Environment' tucked under my arm.

However, I accept that I occupy no moral high ground when it comes to suppression of evidence. I destroyed the third and last sheet of writing on the yellow pad without showing it to anyone else. Before the police came looking for suicide notes I spirited it away – not just the top page but the whole block, in case they might grow curious about the huge, round, childish loops impressed on the sheets below. I burned it during the following night, as if burning coded treason from enemy intelligence. I still remember every word.

They tell me he rides against the Turkoman of the White Sheep in the East; his return is delayed by another two months.

231

In the mornings I am allowed to walk on the roof. The eunuch walks behind, holding the chain, limping badly from injuries received on his capture as a boy. The water of the straits is very beautiful in the hour when the haze is lifting and the city stirs. I look towards Anatolia and imagine what it is like to be free.

I find I cannot pray. I have forgotten what I might ever have wished to say to God. I go through the forms, since I do not want to distress the old woman and the eunuch. For the same reason I eat and drink well, play the eunuch's game of sticks, allow the woman to braid my hair. I am in good condition. But I am no ape, to perform at the end of a chain. I am no brood mare, dropping my foals to be discarded or retained according to market value. I accept that escape is impossible, but surely emperors may not go unarmed in any part of the day, even to the bed of their favourite? I am lately become impatient for the return of Mehmed, known as Fatih, the Conqueror. Inshallah.

My Collins New Age was unforthcoming on the subject of any Mehmed, except one I disqualified because of his second name, *Ali*. On the morning after Arabella was buried in the family mausoleum in Perthshire – *funeral private, no flowers please* – I walked down to the library. I think now I probably chose to go to the public rather than the university library because there was less chance of being recognized, no chance at all that the books I requested would excite remark. I was perhaps a little paranoid at the time.

I had to wade through several centuries of Turkish history. Even the most thorough general account devoted little more than two paragraphs to Mehmed II, an

232

Ottoman emperor who earned for himself the surname Fatih, the Conqueror, by his capture of Constantinople in 1453. There was nothing at all in those two paragraphs about a wife or concubine called Irene. I sat at a desk upstairs in the reference section, trying to decide whether to pursue the history of Mehmed Fatih into more obscure corners, and slowly, gradually, noticed the scent in my nostrils. It was a smell rising from the pages in front of me, but it was also everywhere in the very air – old paper, leather, cardboard, glue. I could have closed my eyes and been twelve again, acquiring 'general excellence' on my Saturday mornings. I might have been breathing in the complex, slightly sour memory of another life.

Oliver came to collect the last of Arabella's things in the week that the lease on the flat finally expired. I liked him more that day than I ever had before. 'It simply seems impossible,' he said, rubbing both hands hard over his crewcut, as if trying to roll back his scalp. 'I can't believe anything so random, so pointless has really happened.' I guessed that Oliver had not been party to the official re-working of the truth. 'I know about death,' he said. 'In the last show I saw so many people dead, so many people dying. It was always something one knew was there but couldn't afford to think about in relation to oneself. It was never anything to do with Belle.'

When I heard him say her name it overwhelmed me suddenly and I put my head down on the kitchen table between the coffee cups and roared aloud with sheer grief. Poor Oliver. I think he was embarrassed.

As he was leaving, finally, after making me more coffee and patting my shoulder rhythmically, silently, for more than half an hour, he said, 'I don't know what I shall do now. I just don't know what to do.' I stood at the open door and watched him disappear round the turn of the stairs, hurrying to hide his own tears. Then I went forward and leaned over the stair railing to watch his cropped head progress around and downwards for the three flights. It seemed to me that I must have conjured up demons from my own imagination; there was nothing ruthless or sinister or imperious about the Oliver who lived behind the professional soldier. He was as innocent as Belle herself had been.

In November an invitation came to a preview of the exhibition that was half Scobie's. It had been sent to the university, and I stood beside my pigeonhole for a long time, fingering its deckled edge and wondering how I could carry it off if I did go, how I could carry it off if I didn't. In the end I grew tired of reading bluff and double-bluff into his motives. He had invited me, therefore he wanted me to be there, therefore I would go. It was as simple as that.

The artistic in-crowd were a surprise to me. I'd expected less middle-class chic and more artistic licence. Then I realized that these people must be Medici not Michelangelo, that they would create pure, exhilarating forms only in their bank balances. I chose a suitable corner and headed towards it with my second glass of sparkling white. 'What d'you think?' Scobie said in my ear.

I spilled some wine. He was wearing a suit – a suit at least four sizes too big for him, but still a suit. 'You know me, Scobie,' I said. 'I'm one of the unwashed when it comes to art.'

He grinned. 'But then I'm one of the unwashed when it comes to education.'

'And when it comes to washing,' I pointed out.

'Have you seen my head, though?' Scobie said. 'They tell me it's "accessible".'

'You mean it's got an even number of eyes for once?'

'Something like that. You might like it.' He shuffled in a recognizably Scobie-ish fashion. 'I saw in the newspapers – about Belle. I'm sorry.'

'One of those things,' I said.

'Well,' said Scobie. 'I'm still sorry.'

'How's Judith?' I asked.

'She's fine,' Scobie said. 'Did you see the drawing of her?'

'The drawing? That charcoal one? That was Judith, was it?'

He grinned again. 'Yeah, well, maybe not to the unwashed.'

Just as the pause was growing uncomfortable, a very small, very bulky man with striking dimples came sweeping past. 'William!' he said, seizing Scobie's arm. Scobie avoided looking at me. 'Here you are!' the man rebuked. 'What are you doing *lurking* like this. Come and meet people.' He didn't even spare me a second glance. I was self-evidently not 'people' by any stretch of the artistic imagination. As they walked away from me I noticed that beneath the folds of loose trouser leg at his ankles Scobie was wearing no socks.

After that I felt I had earned an early departure – dues paid, humiliation by Benny Visconti duly performed – but as I was looking for somewhere to dump my glass I caught a back view of what could only be Scobie's bronze head. Even apart from the effect of the medium, the shape of the thing shouted power. It was bull-necked, crowned with tight, regular curls, and it looked from behind a lot more comprehensible than anything else I'd seen that evening. I put my glass down beside a corroded wire pyramid and began to thread my way towards it.

The face was unbelievably painful to look at. Large features, probably plain by classical standards, were settled and lined into an expression of such suffering, such understanding, such love, that it caught me by the throat. There seemed much more experience of life in that face than the Scobie I knew could possibly have defined. I checked the small brass label on the plinth. That confirmed that I knew nothing about anything. W. Scobie, it said, 1986. Underneath was the title of the piece. *The Mamluk.*

I stood for a few minutes looking at that face, thinking about the things I might ask, thinking about answers which would be either answers I didn't want to hear, or no answers at all. I looked at the Mamluk and thought about Arabella and Scobie and me, wondering which one of us it really was who had watched from a distance, from a safe, detached, leisurely captivity. Then I collected my coat from reception and walked out into the yellow Edinburgh night.

BLACK NOTES AND
WHITE NOTES

Gerry Fenge

After taking his degree at Newcastle University, Yorkshire-born Gerry Fenge lived for some years in Whitley Bay before going out to Africa in 1986.

For three years he and his wife taught in government schools in Zimbabwe, then for two years they worked at an international school in Kenya – where, amongst other students, they taught their two teenage children.

Now back in England, he is busy capitalizing on twenty years' writing experience. A novel, *Friend of the Rainmaker*, set in Zimbabwe, is getting its final polish – and other projects are maturing.

BLACK NOTES AND
WHITE NOTES

ONE

I know what did it. You can't go trying to work out what
music is, and what Africa is, and how they fit together,
and all the time you're playing late night gigs and
snatching junk snacks, so you end up crying with it all,
unseen tears that block your chest then drop like poison
into your guts – you can't do all that and get away with it.

So I was in hospital, and every day I didn't eat I got
thinner. And every day I crapped that terrible diarrhoea I
got thinner.

So there I was in the men's ward – I wasn't too bad at
this stage, I hadn't got round to chatting with death and
saying it's okay by me – but I was lying there when along
came two angels.

I saw them enter the ward, two pretty black girls, and
they stood among the cubicles and curtains, looking
round. Two orderlies got in the way, helping an old guy
with a wheelchair. A nurse walked in front straightening
her tunic. Then the way was clear and they saw I was
alone.

'Do you mind if we talk to you?'

I didn't mind. Half of Nairobi seemed like it was
walking through the ward that night, peeling off to this
bed and that bed.

Anyway being the only white guy in the place was

getting to me – everyone talking Swahili, except the odd Indian patient with his twenty visitors, and they'd be talking Gujerati. I mean, the Africans here do talk English, but for most it's not their best language.

And then you get the mamas, and mamas' sisters, and mamas' cousins all sitting on the windowseat with nothing better to do than stare at the muzungu – that means white guy – and they're all thinking, 'Hey, a muzungu being ill: I wonder if he'll put on a good display of being ill if we stare hard enough.'

So I didn't mind two angels talking to me, and when they asked about my illness I didn't say 'Being too visible' but answered 'Ulcerative colitis'.

I thought I'd better explain this, so I told them it's a sneaky illness that goes on holiday for two or three years at a time, then it comes back and hits you, bam, and the medicines don't work any more, and food doesn't work too good either, so you think you may as well check how a Kenyan hospital looks.

Now, I could still show interest at that stage, so I asked about them. They said they were Christians and they were visiting some crash victim in another ward ('Didn't you hear about it, that horrible Matatu crash?') Then for a moment I went into a sort of trance, reminding myself about the outside world. I pictured the matatus – homemade minibuses, like converted vans, rainbow-painted, passengers crammed through the back doors and driven like they were late for a fatal accident.

Well, the prettier girl, she sort of bent and looked at me. I think my trance caught her curiosity. 'And you,' she asked, 'what things do you do?'

I liked that, I liked her interest. 'I think about matatus,' I told her.

And I saw her smile. It was one of those horizontal ones, like it was painful to pull so wide, crammed with teeth and stretching from jaw to jaw. 'I mean what sort of work do you do?'

And I saw her eyes, deep brown, but bright, too bright, like she was too alive for her body.

So I forgot about the hospital and my drip feed and the visitors in the nearby cube praying for their relative as though God was deaf and not really concentrating. And I focused on her, and I thought maybe she wasn't just pretty, maybe she was even beautiful. 'I'm a musician,' I said. 'I play keyboards and sing in a band. Maybe you've heard of us – Black Notes And White Notes? We play hotels, nightclubs.'

Then – I don't know why I said it, it must have been those unnaturally bright eyes, those crazy eyes that could catch crazy words and live with them – but I told her 'I follow melodies. I chase the melodies you know, I don't play them. They just happen because I'm able to follow and find out what they are. And one of the guys, Mwangi, he's like my brother, he always gets what I'm doing. We both play keyboards, and he's black and I'm white, like the band's name. So the people listen to us swopping phrases and think we're really cute.'

And the other girl, the one who was only ordinary pretty, she stared like I was talking some sort of Swahili no one had heard before. But the really pretty one, the maybe beautiful one, she got it. She was like Mwangi, she knew what I was saying.

So I told them to sit on the bed, and I levered myself up to perch higher, because I was getting a good feeling from these girls. And I looked beyond my curtains at the Indian guy with the twenty saris round him, and the mad alcoholic guy with the three visitors all mugging God with prayer, and I felt I'd got the best deal.

That stuff about following melodies I really believe it, and right now I was picking up the music of these two

241

girls. I was there with the flow of it. 'You're Christians,' I said. 'How did you get into that?' Don't ask me why I said it. Normally I avoid scriptural salespeople, but right now the melody was saying ask them, so I asked.

So the maybe beautiful one, she started. Her eyes popped a bit, like she was working extra ideas into them. 'You're going to think I'm mad,' she said, and then her eyes didn't just pop, they exploded. A brightness flashed from them. 'Perhaps I was. Do you know what I did? One day at school I stopped talking. I wouldn't speak. I wouldn't move. They sent everyone to see me, but I didn't respond.'

And I could see those teeth of hers, flashing, flashing as she gave the story to me.

'I used to be so popular because I led the other girls in all sorts of trouble. But they couldn't follow me into this one. Do you know, my relatives had to come for me in a car and drive me home. But no one could get me to talk. They all decided I must be going mad.'

I could see her slender figure, animated with the story. She was a child woman, spiritually slim.

'But you know how it is? Once you have put yourself into a silence it is so hard to come out again. I felt as if there was no point. Do you know, it was a whole year before I could go back to school.'

And I saw the roundness of her chest and felt comforted to know she wasn't all slim.

'But now I had put myself in another world, and suddenly I'd know there was someone behind me. I would be walking along the street, and I'd turn and there was a warrior from the old days, dressed in feathers and cowhide and he'd be waving a panga at me, one of those sword things for cutting bushes. The city would go away and I'd be running, running over grass and past bushes, and he would chase after me waving the panga. Then at some point I'd black out. I might wake to find myself lying on the pavement or I might be in the road with a matatu pulling on its brakes to avoid me.'

She stopped for a moment, and I think by this stage I was already in love with her. I sat there on the hard hospital bed with the pillows propped against my back – and it seemed like she was the melody I'd always been chasing. I sat there in my brown hospital robe – and it seemed she could show me what was wrong with the universe. The world, I felt, was a beautiful woman chased by a madman waving a panga. I could follow the music of it. She was the suffering of creation.

Then she told me about becoming a Christian, but I didn't listen so close. I knew what it would do for her just like I can feel a routine tune beneath my fingers. It would keep the maniac at bay. It would stop her going mad. I knew that, but it wasn't the deepest music. It didn't tell me why the maniac was there.

Anyway, the other girl told her story next and it was very good, very Kenyan. Father had left home and mother had eight children and they had to be fed and schooled, so she was like a second parent earning money for them. It was a good story and she was a good girl, and the more I studied her the more she looked good too. But she didn't catch me with that note of tragedy. I didn't hear the music of the spheres with her, all bent out of shape, and sobbing, sobbing for what it was and what it might be. She'd set some other man on fire, but not me.

Visiting time was coming to a close. The malaria case in the next cubicle had got up carrying his drip feed bottle with him. He looked excellently dazed and a nurse came and asked what he was doing.

Then I did something weird. I took both girls by the hands and said I wanted to pray with them. Really, that's what I said. But you see, I've found I can get truly high

243

just murmuring nonsense – no words or anything. It works, honest it does. So I held them and mumbled the stuff and – I mean I'm a musician, so I could do it – I started singing it as well. It was jibberish I guess but it came out slow and gentle. And it did the job because I felt really close to them.

Well, the ordinary girl, she thought I was praying in tongues so she was just delighted. And the other one, my maybe beautiful one, what did she think with her crazy eyes and smile so wide it hurt? I think she sensed what was really going on.

That's when I think I hooked her. She realized I could fly just as crazy as she could, and I saw a kind of awe on her face. She never thought it would happen.

Then it was leaving time and a nurse was going to the guy in the opposite cubicle. She had her flute box with her, but it didn't have a flute, it had a pressure gauge. And her mini piccolo was really a thermometer.

So I got the girls to write down their names and contacts, and my crazy amazing one was Teresia Njeru. I liked that – Teresia. Then they were gone.

Well, they visited a few times after that, and once when Teresia came on her own our lips didn't say much but our eyes talked enough. Then there was a gap while they had some church business, and in that time I got discharged.

I wanted to call the girls, but I thought I'd get some strength back first. That didn't happen, though. I got worse and had to come back in.

So as I took the long slow dive towards the mortuary they couldn't visit me any more because they didn't know where I was. There came a time when the surgeon looked quiet and reckoned he'd have to attack me with his panga next day. I lay there. All that existed were my eyes and pain. Then I slid my look sideways, and there was Teresia.

TWO

My grandad left me some money in trust, but specified I mustn't do anything sensible with it – not buy a house or anything. I must use it for travelling the world, seeing places, seeing people. Only get sensible after that.

So I arrived in Kenya, but then I had to disappoint his ghost. I wanted to know more about the music this guy Mwangi was playing, and he wanted to know more about mine. So I got sensible enough to pay rent on a farmhouse near Thika.

And that's where I was two months after the operation, sitting in the garden, looking down the grass to the five-bar gate, the coffee bushes, and way beyond, the image of Mount Kenya. I looked, but not all of me looked. Some bits were missing.

Mount Kenya had clouds round its base but the rest jagged up into a blue sky. It was a mountain without a middle. You could recognize it by the stuff on top, the peaks, the faint glaciers, but something was missing.

Same with me. They'd removed my colon, and just so I couldn't forget, they'd given me an outlet in my abdomen. There it was, an inch or so to the side of my navel, and down a bit – my new bum.

Don't think I'd had a colostomy. That's the easy one for people who have something mild like cancer. But for those who want a truly major rearrangement there's a condition called Toxic Megacolon and if your ulcerative colitis really tries it can turn into that.

So my colon became huge and poisonous and therefore had to go, every inch of it, and a foot of ileum too, just in case that wanted to get mega as well.

I was left with a mouth in my belly. They call it that, a mouth, except they use the Greek word 'stoma' instead. And it's not a stoma made out of colon because that's all gone. It's a stoma made out of ileum, so they call it an ileostomy.

Africa was a place to be decolonized and I hadn't been left out. No one would notice, though, because I had equipment under my clothes to collect whatever needed collecting.

We musicians are credited with having senses of humour but at the time I saw nothing funny. Mwangi was different though. 'Hey John,' and he drummed his hands on the wickerwork table, 'you must go to the pathology lab and get back your colon. Witch doctors are always wanting these bones and things to summon up spirits. An item like your colon would be very fine, because it's half snake and half human. You might ask a fortune.'

I gave one of those African clicks at him which mean get lost.

I sat there on the wickerwork chair, under the avocado tree, beside the mango tree. I stared at the emasculated Mount Kenya, floating above its clouds, and I changed the topic. 'She's gone you say?'

That was the other thing that was missing, her.

Mwangi shrugged. He didn't like unpleasant truths so he drummed some more. (I must admit he could be irritating.) 'Yeah,' he said at last. 'I found Martha, that's the other one – she said there's no sign of her, not at work, not at home, not at the church, nowhere.'

He exhaled, tried to blow the topic away, and found he hadn't so he relented some more. 'Martha said she was worried that Teresia might have lost her faith and be ready to do crazy things.'

I stared ahead, a hollow man, gutless, disembowelled. I stared and remembered how she came to me before the operation. I stared till I lost all thought of Mwangi, Mount Kenya or anything . . .

I'd been in Intensive Care. I remember curtains beside

246

my bed and being wired to some pulse machine; oh and the nurses disliked me because I'd groan at night when they wanted their heads down.

That's all I remember, except I was a goner. I knew that because I'd lost the music. Therefore death seemed a good idea – because when you've nothing to lose you've no fear of losing it.

But then Teresia arrived. I felt her presence, I slid my eyes sideways, I saw her face.

She was looking at me, horrified and loving. Those eyes of hers, they weren't pushing out light any more, they were pushing out pity. I remember the pity sitting up in her face like there was too much of it to keep in one woman.

And her mouth which used to smile so wide it hurt – well, it was hurting still but I saw no smile.

'John, is it you?' Horror in her voice – as though her eyes were speaking, but richer like through a throat of tears. 'You mustn't leave me.'

Believe me, I was fading when she walked in – into that room where two or three bodies hovered so close to death they almost floated. But when she walked out everything was changed. She'd given me something to lose . . .

That was how long ago? A couple of months.

I glanced across at Mwangi. 'I bet I know what happened to her.'

'Uh?' He didn't fancy extending this topic.

'She'll have come while I was in theatre. I bet that was it. Or when they put me in the private ward.' I heard the thump of an avocado as it fell off the tree. Mwangi looked at it lazily like he wanted it to roll over to him, slice itself, and crawl up to his mouth.

'Yeah,' I continued. 'Some of the nurses were real sweethearts, but they must have sent the muggers and abusers to Intensive Care. They ignored you in a most

247

organized way. So I can imagine what happened. Teresia would say where was I. And they'd just answer "gone".'

Mwangi was still looking at the avocado. He couldn't work out why it wouldn't take the hint and slide over to him. 'Maybe if Shiro comes,' he muttered.

'Mm?' I didn't get the connection.

He flashed me his slack sideways smile, the smile that made hapless women think he was lovely, which he wasn't. 'A man like me is too important to pick up his own avocado. But Shiro – she needs an aim in her life.'

Shiro – my nurse, his cousin, our extra worker. 'You're a con man,' I said.

He scratched his head with amazement. So I looked at his horrible short hair. Why couldn't he grow that hair, get a Box or an Afro even? But every month he became a stubble head.

'John,' he oozed, 'I am one of life's givers. You needed a nurse, I gave you one.'

That much was true. I'd been kept fairly happy in hospital wondering how he'd cope with me all zonked and bumless when I got out.

But I forgot about the African extended family. A passenger like Mwangi would always find a Shiro somewhere amongst his cousins, someone who'd been abandoned by her husband and needed a way of supporting her kids.

'You're exploiting her,' I accused.

That hanging lower lip of his hung even more. 'Hey, I give her space to live in, I give her money, I let her kids wander round the back garden. All I ask is she nurses you. And does some more jobs.' He sat back as though distributing his largesse afresh.

I was enjoying this. 'Mwangi, why does she take so long cleaning your room? And why are you always there to help?'

248

He hadn't realized I'd noticed. 'Hey John, you're getting better.'

So I thought a bit about the types of largesse he distributed, then said, 'What about that blonde model you were dating?'

He stroked his horribly scalped head. 'I know. It would be easier to stick to just one woman.' He looked sorrowful. 'But they need me, John.'

Then I heard some noise along the garden. Two of Shiro's kids were passing the banana trees. Tall fronds, and from underneath came the sound of indignant chickens. Shiro's kids giggled. The chickens gossiped angrily.

I watched the kids head for the garden tap. They were fetching water, just like African kids have always fetched water all over the continent, all over the centuries. The only difference was they were fetching it in a muzungu's garden, well partly a muzungu's garden. Me and Mwangi shared, so it was a keyboard's garden, part black, part white.

'You know,' I drifted – I didn't say it, more like my voice drifted with the words – 'I think she's out in the wilds.'

Mwangi frowned. 'Shiro?'

'Teresia. Only the wilds are crazy enough for her.'

'Uh – you're imagining it.'

'No, you remember that bit in the New Testament – "My God, why have you forsaken me?" That's her, I can remember her eyes.'

'When did you become the local preacher, John? I know where her faith must have gone – you stole it.'

Then Shiro – I saw Shiro limping along to the vegetable garden, not limping, but heavy in the hips as though she really would limp if she could just decide which leg to favour. Poor Shiro, not yet out of her twenties, but I knew why her loins felt so heavy. And that parasite Mwangi (whom I loved like a brother) (and hated like a brother) – he was happy to make them heavier.

Africa, ah Africa, so much beauty, but what do the ordinary people know of it?

Well time passed and I got better and I played some gigs again. People in the audiences would remember me. 'The muzungu's back, you remember him, the white guy.'

But I knew I was incomplete. And the music was leading me nowhere, because it can only give you what you put into it.

And I'd go back to the farm and look at Mount Kenya, cloud sliced, floating high as though cut off from earth – an abode of gods, or maybe the land of unreachable dreams.

Like a good life for Shiro or a new gut for me.

Sometimes, though, the mountain wasn't even there. Just a sky full of cloud.

That's how it was when I found her again.

THREE

I had been driving my Datsun wagon and Moi Avenue was its usual crowded self. You could empty a petrol tank circling round Nairobi for a parking space. Anyway my eyes were flicking to the side of the road. Then they did a long gripping flick.

I saw her. She saw me and screamed. I stopped the car. She dropped her parcel of books. I waved to her. She bit her fingers and screamed again. I gesticulated. She ran to embrace me, or maybe the car.

Meanwhile they guy behind sounded his horn, so I

moved forward. But Teresia started running after me. This could have degenerated but the gods of high street meetings decided to send a Peugeot out of its parking diagonal.

So I drove in, switched off, and climbed out. However, Teresia, having alerted the whole of Moi Avenue to her enthusiasm, turned suddenly shy. She just stood there, looking at me.

I felt shy too. So I hesitated, vaguely conscious of shoppers and loafers gathering on the pavement. Then Teresia let out a howl. Don't ask me what sort of shyness enlists everyone to observe it, but she'd sent all her dignity away. She was going to howl and that was it.

So I went to her and she hurled herself round me. Her face pressed into my shoulder and her eyes set about giving me a soaking. Her torso and legs pressed against me. I really felt she'd be happiest if she could climb inside me and get all her crying done there.

Eyes lifted up. 'I thought you were dead,' she sobbed.

Meanwhile the watching humanity was enjoying the show. They ranged under the colonnade roofing of the pavement. They stepped out between parked cars. 'Hey, it's that guy from Black Notes And White Notes' – and I felt the voice spoke English for my benefit.

'But I wish I have a fan club i-like i-that man' – this one more struggling with the English.

Meanwhile the little robot in my trousers was starting to get irrelevant. Oh, I suppose a beautiful girl sobbing and holding a man long enough will press the button at some stage, but I felt my trousers bulge. No, I told it, this isn't the idea, we're meeting heart to heart. But the little moron didn't care and carried on transforming itself into a big moron.

And other things happened, like climbing into the car,

and everyone giving us a big cheer, and us waving back at them.

It was good, and we felt good, and soon we planned our holiday together. Here we were then, a couple of weeks later, heading up the Kenya coast.

Those days they still had a ferry at Kilifi, and soon as your car got to the queue you could see the difference. A woman walked up the road towards us, black breasts bobbing. You wouldn't see that in Mombasa.

Then she stopped and wrapped a kanga round them. A kanga is like a colourful tablecloth and women can tie it round the back of their neck then pass it over their chest, then tie it again over the thighs. That's all they need wear if they want.

Anyway Teresia was looking at me from the passenger seat. 'Happy?' she asked, following my gaze.

I felt sort of embarrassed. We'd talked about plenty since we met up, but not a word about chests or the irrelevance in my underpants. How could I think of intimacy in my condition? I was a belly-crapper, a gutless wonder.

I climbed out of the Datsun for distraction and looked about me. There was a double queue winding downhill, a line of cars next to a line of trucks. Drivers lolled against open doors or strolled down to the water.

Then Teresia joined me and trailed a finger along the bonnet. 'Good car,' she murmured.

I looked at the ice-cream vendors and cashew nut sellers walking from driver to driver, and I thought I could risk a reminiscence. 'You remember Moi Avenue?'

Maybe she thought at easy-going, breast-waggling Kilifi I might begin to unwind. 'More than you think.'

Oh no, the erection – so she'd noticed it. I gasped and walked away. I couldn't cope with such things. Not yet. But then I realized how bad Teresia must feel.

So I strolled back and we bought some cashews. Then the ferry finally got in, discharging buses, trucks, cars and swarms of pedestrians, not all of whom were wrapping kangas round their boobs. And we finally drove on to the ferry, crossed and headed north – up towards Malindi.

And if the spirit of freedom had not quite got to me, it seemed to have found Teresia – because when we arrived at the cottages she announced she was going to be my nurse.

We'd parked the car and the warden woman had crunched over the gravel with us to the cottage. And we'd checked the cutlery and kitchenware, we'd checked the shower and sink, we'd checked the single beds and – oh, all the colour outside, flowers and blossoms and trees cuddling the cottage. We'd checked it all and were just having a hot perspiring flop in the veranda armchairs.

And that's when she said it. 'Teach me to nurse your stoma.' And she gave me that vulnerable look which said she wanted to be brave so I must reassure her. It was a hesitation and an eagerness. Like she was aiming a question at me and begging for a nice answer.

I backed off though, because it's a sensitive thing to crap out of your navel (near enough) and you don't want to put people off.

But she was looking in such a clear, hopeful way.

I still resisted. I picked up a frangipani blossom from the veranda floor and twiddled it absent-mindedly. 'Hey look, you know what comes out of me.'

But she said she'd looked after her sister's babies and yes she did know what comes out.

Listen, I tell you there are lovely things in the world, but there's nothing lovelier than a beautiful woman who is willing to know every inch of you.

So I sorted myself out in the toilet then headed to the bedroom, and it was a relief to shrug off my shirt and

253

trousers. She left me with my pants, my pants didn't matter.

And I lay on the bed with the mosquito net above. It was twisted into a rope then knotted to keep it out of the way. Beside it the ceiling fan clanked and whirred.

Then she looked at my poor, ravaged belly. I had a seven-inch scar to one side of my navel, but the bad thing was on the other side. There was a beige cotton oblong there, but that was just the cover to make everything nice. Underneath was the pouch. This was about the size and shape of a hand – palm and fingers at full stretch.

But this wasn't the worst bit: that was underneath. I was scared about it, and so was she – but only a little. Chiefly she was eye-popping and curious. So I told her to peel back the adhesive round the pouch then lift it from the skin.

This has to be done gradually because little hairs will be stuck. And it's got to be done warily because there's no promise the stoma won't disgorge some of its stock.

So she had the tissues at the ready, and she covered what was underneath while she put the pouch in the waste carrier. Then she lifted the tissues and saw the horror of me.

I must have trusted her or I'd never have let her see it. The surgeon had made a spout – an inch long, maybe two – and it was floppy and red like some swollen tongue. This was the stoma, the mouth that let out what had to come out. It was made of guts – it was intestine itself – and of course it got into a mess.

I guess this sounds bad. And it was bad. And it should have put her off. But she just said, 'This is like changing nappies.' Then she got to work with warm water and cotton wool, dabbing and cleaning till all the yucky stuff was cleared away.

Then she got a razor and shifted the stubble round the

254

mad tongue, gave it a final clean and dried everything off. Next she wiped some protective film over the vulnerable bits of skin, put a new base plate on, attached a new pouch, put a new cover over the pouch and there I was – changed, clean and new.

'I'm a good nurse,' she announced. So I grinned: I liked the way she praised herself – as though testing the idea on the air.

I'd been looking at her as she did all this. She wasn't wearing much, you don't want to in that heat, only a kanga, so I saw lots of her dark flesh.

There was something about that flesh – warm, earthy, the colour of soil. Not parched soil though, it had the richness of fertility.

It beats me why people associate the colour black with bad things like death and so on. They're not thinking. She looked like she was grown from the soil, and she was, she'd eaten its fruits and cereals. But she was more shining, like life was glowing through her. I watched her and it seemed easy to believe the first humans emerged in Africa. They would.

And while the fan whirred and the curtains waved in its breeze, I looked at that flesh and realized what brought me to Africa in the first place. I wanted to see the old fossil places like Lake Turkana and Olduvai Gorge. I wanted to track everything back. I wanted to return to where we all came from and then maybe from there I could see how we went wrong.

And here was Teresia, a portion of the continent, Africa on two legs, moving, breathing – and she was nursing what was wrong in me. I felt almost dizzy. There was something here I could almost grasp, a solution to the mystery of it all.

I tried to explain this to her.

So she listened and gave me a strange look. I'd seen it

255

once before in hospital. 'Maybe you realize who I am then.'

I guess she really fancied herself. I guess she enjoyed imagining herself as some meaningful being. That's why she devoured my admiration.

'So what are you?' I asked.

She looked wistful then. 'We Africans, we have so much to give, so much – if only we are appreciated.'

I tried to follow this. 'How do you mean?'

She was never too precise on logic, but maybe she felt the topic had drifted a bit. So she came back to earth – well, close.

'I mean,' she said, 'I'm your nurse.' And she gave a mysterious smile like that was the most significant statement anyone could ever make.

FOUR

Not long into our stay she had a nightmare. It was that ancestor guy again, the one with the feathers and cowhide, the maniac with the panga. This time she was waiting at a stop for a matatu. It pulled up, the tout pointed inside where she could squeeze between the normal dozen sweaty bodies. But sitting there was this tribal psychopath. He just looked and waited for her to get on.

She wasn't sure about after that because she started screaming. But me, I leaped out of my single bed, crashed into the mosquito net, fumbled my way under it, and wondered where I was.

There was a light outside which let me see Teresia. Through her net I noticed her sheet thrown aside. We were still modest then, so this was the first time I saw directly between her legs. She was briefly horizontal, rigid, and in my confusion I thought the maniac must have got her. She looked like her crotch was sliced.

But then I got orientated and realized I was looking at beauty not terror. I was witnessing the portals of hope, the temple where life begins. Well, when you're only half awake you say things like that to yourself.

And then she sat up and I pushed her netting away and I wrapped the sheet round her. Then it was my turn to be the nurse. I soothed her and she calmed down and became my daughter. I held her like a frightened child and my heart was swelling to burst.

After that we gave up on sleep. It seemed a better idea to check the Indian Ocean before dawn.

It's a long walk to the beach at Malindi. I hear there's a lot of sand been deposited since the hotels and such were built, so it's a matter of leaving the stone walls then passing through bushes till you're with the sand creepers – not so easy in the dark – then over the dunes and on to the beach itself.

It stretches wide and white for as long as you could want. It's big like a huge outbreath, big like you swell your chest and give a long slow aah.

Even in the night we could see this, and the sky was majestic with stars. It's as though the blackness was pulled out and given edge with stars, stars and dust of stars.

So we walked to the water's rim, and all the time I was thinking – this is like music, I'll be playing some melody with major chords in it, the joyful ones, then somewhere there comes along a minor chord, one of the sad ones. And when I play the music it's fine.

But here, this was real life, and it seemed like a minor chord was approaching. And it left me – I don't know, not downhearted but serious.

Teresia was quiet too. She was just concentrating on the dark water with its deeps of swish and swill. She'd stand for a while to let her footprints fill with sea. Then she'd move on and leave gaps behind.

And I was busy asking the horizon a few questions, like did her loss of faith cause this fear? And is there a way of getting back to the benefits of faith – maybe through music, or love?

And I was so busy with these questions that I just fixated on the sky. It was getting a bit lighter, but the stars were still there, jumping at me, pretending to be still then leaping at my eyes. As day seeped closer, though, their leaps became more like waves of the hand. Farewell, they were saying.

I was so busy staring at all this that my mind sort of stopped and I saw the shape of a female.

I realized it was something about my eye sockets. So I closed each eye in turn and saw it was caused by the curve of the nose. It didn't block the vision, but sight went darker beyond it.

That gave the oval shape. So I stared at the pre-dawn sky and the sides of the oval came close to make a torso.

It was like I was seeing a goddess. Either side of me at the misty limits of vision I could sense her arms embracing. And the head was over, behind me, too sacred to be seen.

But the torso was in front of me and in the lightening sea it sent waves to be born. Wave after wave broke white from the loins of the goddess, rolling in like events from the womb of time.

Awed, I raised my arms and sang. I sang my heart like I'd sung once in hospital with some angels. I don't know what I sang because there were no words or tune that I knew. I just wanted my voice to go free and tell the sky how my heart was loaded.

258

And it seemed one of those misty arms pulled my head to look sideways, and there was Teresia — watching me like I had shown her something she needed. She was barefoot, wearing only her kanga, black and orange patterned. And as I looked she lifted her arms to the neck and let it drop. She walked towards me and the kanga was on the beach behind her. She walked to me naked as truth, black and beautiful in the Indian Ocean dawn.

And she shone like the glint of stars on sea. And she was curved like the full and circling sky. And she approached me like the sky overwhelms you when you tilt back your head.

She loved herself at that moment, I know that. She thought she was it. But so she was. And anyway she was moving into a role, and somehow I had sung that role for her. Yes, she loved herself but that love came out as a power, and she was aiming it at me. And it was right, it worked. I may have sensed a goddess over the ocean, but now I was seeing one and it was walking over the sand to me.

My clothes were gone — all apart from the empty pouch at my abdomen. And we were walking into the sea together, its warmth, its ripples, its waves climbing to our thighs.

No one was about, only curio sellers way down the beach, figures no bigger than my thumbnail, loitering where the rich hotels were. But we were alone and I could feel the flow of it and I knew we'd stay alone.

Teresia dived forward and in the clarifying light I saw her perfect back and buttocks arch into the water. There was a dip and swell of dark flesh — and it was like seeing the curve of deep space, the reality we glimpse as gravity.

Then she arced round so her breasts were towards me. And, speculative as I was, I saw those breasts as the ultimate proof of a good creation. There they were at her

259

heart, giving themselves out, full, and it was like seeing to the centre of deep space and finding that it is generosity and, ultimately, delight.

Gently I touched her.

Then we held each other, naked in the dawn, and the waves jostled and lifted us, surging us, giving us their curves and rhythm.

And I held her chest to mine and I was talking to her soul to soul. For the chest is what we tap when we say 'me'. And my me was pressed against her me.

And she lifted her knees, letting my hands and the water support her, so we could join where a man and woman need to join.

Listen, I'm not a person to tell you every detail of how it was, but I've got to tell you one thing. Some time back I read about a tribe who go so mad on initiation or betrothal or something that they actually flay the penis. They strip the top skin off. Don't ask me why. If I could solve that one for you maybe I could solve the riddle of Africa. But after some time the poor male is sent along to his woman, and he's got to make love to her. The idea is that her moistures will act as ointment.

I'm telling you this madness because of the saying that goes with it. These people say, 'In the vagina of a woman there is healing.'

That's what I want to tell you. I don't want to give you every detail, but I want to tell you that the sun was rising and the waves were buoying us up, and in Teresia there was healing.

There had been a hollowness in me like a womb, and Teresia was filling it. Just as I was sending my seed into her, she was sending her power into me.

I was complete.

And then we knew the curio sellers would come with the carved giraffes and figurines. And we knew that

260

tourists would wander from their beds and on to the beach. So we put our feet to the sand and walked from the waves.

I pulled on my trousers but Teresia was still in her dream of beauty. She walked naked up the beach, not even pausing to lift her kanga. The curio sellers stopped and smiled. They pretended to try and sell us stuff – 'Antelope, Bwana . . . See this bracelet' – but that isn't what they ran along for. They'd come to see the couple who made love in the sea.

Teresia walked on, walled invisibly round, like a painting in its frame. Two old whites, a man and a woman, passed nearby and the old man looked happy. His wife gave him an understanding smile, and Teresia walked on in her glory.

I loved her even more for it. Don't get me wrong, I'd no wish to share her, but that wasn't the point. If she wasn't divine right then she was giving a good enough imitation – as though from now on she'd belong somewhere beyond the world. It seemed her finest moment, and my heart sang for the joy of her.

She was naked all the way to our cottage. You can do that in Malindi. Then she turned and asked me for the kanga, and of course I'd brought it for her.

And she put it on and her beauty was hidden and I knew that was the end.

The minor chord was on its way.

FIVE

Even now, years later, I get emotional if I wake at dawn – because that's when she completed me and started to die. I didn't know it then. Maybe I should because I'm meant

261

to be the musician, but she got it clearer than I did. She cried that evening, told me she was afraid.

I didn't get this, but everything became plainer. I remember the car drive back, how she lolled and her mouth dropped. I pulled in at a garage, and she just looked at me. I knew she was trying to hold herself together, trying so hard.

So we'd drive some more, then I'd glance sideways and see her eyes wild, like an animal's. I don't know if this is some recognized illness, or whether her soul was simply falling apart as I watched, but I'd pull in again and I'd hold her and she'd be okay. Then we'd cover some more miles and she'd go blank again.

We got back and I asked Mwangi about it, and he said we should try some spirit healers. So I'd take her to some little room in a Nairobi township or out in the bush – but I couldn't live with the things they said.

One of them – this is the bit that spooked me – he pointed to my gut and said I'd sucked the life out of her and my only hope was to get what was missing and give it to her.

That didn't strike me as an option, so we tried other things. I wondered about Christianity. We found Martha, and she tried to turn the clock back for us, and for a while it worked. I could hardly believe it, because Teresia had gone into the wilderness where Christ had gone, and it seemed she could be no more helped than he could.

But she brightened, and I got too hopeful, and that's when it happened.

She was coming back from Martha's church when she caught the matatu.

Of course she caught it, she'd always been going to catch it. And of course it crashed, it had always been going to crash.

What made me desperate though was how badly the bodies were burnt. Some couldn't even be identified. So I kept telling myself she's still alive, she's still out there, I'll see her again.

I'd accepted different by the time we played the gig at the Safari Club. It was months from Malindi, the best part of a year, and I was playing like a zombie. She was dead and I was dead. True I was whole, but so were the rest of the living dead in the room.

It was a dinner dance for some private school, some international school out in the bush and they'd sold tickets to all the money people who can send their kids to such places, and the money people's cousins and acquaintances were there too. Hey if you squeezed that lot through a mangle you wouldn't get blood you'd get banknotes.

And the living dead were sitting at clusters of tables waiting for their buffet, but some other corpses were making speeches forever, or drawing raffles forever, and otherwise doing imitations of post-mortem eternity.

And sometimes we'd play tame music. No really tame, this was ectoplasm, this was simperings from the Beyond. Brushes for the drums, mild notes from the bass. It suited me. I stood there, quietly oozing crap into my ileostomy pouch, and equal crap from the keyboard.

But Mwangi's an impatient sort of guy and he wanted some action. 'Come on, man,' he murmured as some ghoul told all the mummies at table 12 to take some plates and line up for their embalming fluid. 'You gotta fly. Let's try "Beautiful Woman".'

But I shook my head. 'Beautiful Woman' was my Teresia song. It was – well, let me tell you how I shaped it. There were repeating chords – so it kept going from C major which is joyful, to E seven which is restless, to A minor which is sad, to G seven which wants to go home again.

263

You see how it works. It's always pulling us from sadness to joy to sadness again. To me it was life. It spoke about Teresia, about Africa, about my messed-up guts. It spoke the mystery of it all.

Now I wouldn't call Mwangi a romantic but he went for that song. 'Come on,' he growled. But I refused. I couldn't do 'Beautiful Woman', not that night, maybe not any night.

So time slouched along and by one a.m. the cadavers were dancing and chatting. My fingers were plodding over the keyboard, my throat was bleating and I got to thinking of Teresia again.

It started coming to me in pictures. I didn't need to will it. My hands and voice were doing the activity, and that left the rest of me passive. I just received the pictures one by one.

I saw her that first time in hospital, her crazy eyes and smile so wide it hurt. I saw her last visit, the pity in her face giving me reason to live. I saw her on Moi Avenue as she dropped her parcel of books and screamed. I saw her at Malindi, nursing my ravaged abdomen. I saw her on the beach before dawn, letting her kanga fall. I saw her in the car, her mouth lolling.

I saw all these things and my heart became full with the sadness of them. Yes, my poor dead heart was feeling something. And my poor dead fingers were playing something. And my poor dead throat was singing something.

Mwangi noticed. He might be a pain but he's quicker on to new music than anyone I know. He was looking across at me, urging me, willing me. I think even the dancers sensed something, because one or two snapped into some real strong movements.

But I wasn't looking at them. I was looking over them. I was looking to the back of the room like I'd once looked

264

over the sea. And just like I saw a figure then, so I saw a figure this time. It was the eye corners did it, the way they make curves at the nose. But I saw it. I saw a torso rising up.

My heart was full. My fingers were leaping. My throat was soaring. Way behind the dancers and drinkers, I saw the torso become detailed, till it had arms and legs. And it was walking towards me. And its face was Teresia's

Through the tops of the dancers she floated to me, and her body glowed under the wisps of angel stuff.

Teresia was approaching. I felt her proximity.

And I felt her pass into me.

Everybody else felt it.

Because at that moment we'd arrived at a G seven chord and I held it. I held it and held it. Mwangi knew something was happening and he was with me. And when Mwangi was with me the rest of the guys followed.

I don't know how long I held that G seven. And my fingers were jumping all over the keyboard with it, and my throat, I was soaring, screaming like I was singing to the sea. But I wasn't. I was singing to Teresia, through Teresia, with Teresia. She was inside me and she was my song.

And of course we were straight into 'Beautiful Woman' and – okay, people know that song now – but I've never sung it like that. It flew, it arced, it lifted all the world's pains with it and it held them in hands of love and it moulded them into something complete.

And I didn't realize the effect till I saw Mwangi's face running with tears. He was singing, playing, he was there with me. And then I realized the wetness of my own face, and I saw the dancers had stopped. They were crying too.

But I've got to tell you, I wasn't looking at corpses any more. Their eyes were pressing out real, living tears.

And then the force in me surged. It was like Teresia

265

poured her every last bit of craziness into me. And I could do anything with the keyboard, and I sang wordless glories, and Mwangi had never heard music like it but he kept up because he can keep up with anything, and the guys did all they could.

I don't know, it was like a revelation. I looked out and I didn't see the ballroom any more, I saw the night sky, shining with stars but warm, till it was the glow of her dark flesh, the glow of Africa.

And I saw the slash of the primal wound, with blood coming from it, and I realized it was Teresia's vagina, and she was saying that was my first initiation. I had to be slashed – like a woman's loins are slashed.

And I was still singing, crazy with song, while the dark healed and grew and rose till it became Teresia's breasts. And she was saying there was my second initiation, when her love came out to heal me.

And the notes rushed and scattered, till I saw those breasts become her eyes and the wound became her lips. But all was changed. They were part of her face now, lovely and clear as it could ever be.

And she was saying everything is transmuted. This is your third initiation. This is when all you have learned is lifted to the level of your mind so you can see it, hear it, sing it.

And there was no more maniac with a panga. At worst there was a nurse with an injection. My abdomen had been broken and healed, my heart had been broken and healed, and now at last my ignorance was broken and healed.

The universe is like a song that goes from C major to E seven to A minor to G seven. The universe is about being broken time and again so everything can be healed again.

No, this isn't madness. It's true for me. I wouldn't rub out my agonies in hospital. I wouldn't rub out my ileostomy. I learned from these things, they built me. And if I could learn, even me, then maybe the universe can learn as well. And maybe the nurse with the injection is really a schoolteacher with a stick of chalk.

There are times I wonder just what is possible – like could he sometimes be a musician with a keyboard?

Oh I don't know, maybe you've heard all this before. And maybe Teresia was just a girl I fancied. And maybe I was just a rocker with more urge to speak than sense to speak with . . .

But I needn't tell you any more. You can look back at the newspapers for the impact of our gig. And people know the tale from then on. Yes, I've had love affairs because I'm a complete man and that's what a complete man must do, he must hold a physical woman. So I do, and I'm grateful. And I love them for giving themselves and they love me for my gratitude.

But they know and you know that all my songs are for one woman. You've asked me who it was. Now I've told you.

TROPICAL FEVER

Josephine Chia Over

Josephine Chia Over is a Singaporean Straits Chinese who came to England on marrying her English husband in 1985. She holds a Bachelor of Arts degree with Honours in Philosophy from the University of Singapore. Upon graduation, she embarked on a career in hotels as Convention Organizer and worked her way up to Public Relations Manager. In this country, she holds the same position in her husband's company.

Since her arrival in the UK, she has completed the British Wheel of Yoga Teachers' Diploma and now teaches yoga once a week to the mentally handicapped. Josephine has had short stories published in Singaporean magazines and she has just written a Singaporean cook book and finished writing her first novel.

TROPICAL FEVER

He sat on the bench, watching, as the cotton-white swan glided along the mirror-smooth surface of the lake. The bird half-raised its wings and stretched its elegant neck in an air of narcissistic confidence in its own beauty. In the same sort of self-love indulged by a young girl who's sure she's pretty or that of a youthful colt, proud of its fitness. Edward Aster smiled, bemused.

It was unusual for the lake to be so deserted; usually it was dappled with the colourful sails of windsurfers from the windsurfing school on the far side of the lake. He could always tell beginners from the more advanced, the way they fell into the water more often or the way they got themselves stuck in a part of the lake where the wind died on them.

The warm sun was kind to his old bones though the slight chill in the air warned him that summer was coming to an end. Youngsters could never understand how hard the English winters were on elderly folk like him.

'If only the sun never stopped shining,' he said, *sotto voce*, shifting slightly to make sure of the warmth reaching all of him.

He closed his eyes, enjoying the heat on his face. Singapore. The thought of that little island no larger than the Isle of Man made him sigh. He had a vague sense that he had been happy there. Forty years slid away as if they had never been. He was forty-three again. The burning

271

tropical sun bore down on him. It was so real that he could even feel the gritty sand on his back as the surf gently ebbed and flowed over his legs. Just at that moment, someone came and stood astride him. The glare was blocked off momentarily and all he saw was a dark, curvaceous shape.

'Ed-ward! I've been looking for you-*lah*.'

The voice was light and cheerful, speaking English with such a delightful accent, using the Malay tag-word as she often did when she wanted her statement to sound less of an imperative.

'Chempaka? Is that you, *sayang*?' Even his voice had regained its timbre of youth.

His hesitancy became a certainty when she stretched herself full-length on him. He gasped with pleasure when her flesh touched his for she was completely naked. She had always been so uninhibited, so sensual.

Those thoughts amazed Edward. There seemed to be two of him, one totally absorbed in the joy of reunion while another hovered like a ghost from the future, observing, questioning.

'Oh, *sayang*.' He whispered the endearment he had learnt from her, pulling her head towards him, his hands gripping her luscious, black hair. His heart thudded uncontrollably at her nearness, her soft breath brushing his face. Between them, there had always been fierce passion, wild and unquenchable.

So why had it stopped? An alarming thought tugged at his memory but try as he might, he could not recall the cause of the heavy anxiety that had entered his breast.

'Ed-ward!' This time the voice that penetrated his consciousness was strident, adamant, and certainly very English. 'Let me go!'

He was confused, unsure of what was happening. Like in a film of a dream sequence, he seemed to float between dimensions until a firm shaking of his shoulders brought him back to Mrs Baxter's hawk-like face, so near that he could smell the gin fumes. His heart was still beating wildly, like a bird thrashing in a bid to free itself from a trap.

'What's the meaning of this? Clutching me to you as if I'm your floosie!'

If he had not been so perplexed, he would have told her that he could never regard her as anyone's floosie, let alone his.

'I've been looking everywhere for you!' She was irritated. 'Lunch is ready, lunch is ready!'

She had that patronizing habit of repeating herself as if she were talking to the deaf and senile.

'Everyone's waiting for you. Are you coming?'

He would have if she had not wrenched him back to dull reality. So, despite his annoyance, he laughed at her inadvertent pun.

'Have I missed a joke, Edward?' she bristled.

'Sorry, Mrs B., something I remembered.'

She stomped away with impatience. He followed her undulating hips, incongruously wide in one so thin. They crossed the immaculate lawn towards the red-tiled Victorian manor house which had been reduced to a residential home. Barry's wife had selected it.

'Weyfold's just right for you, Dad. You'll be happy there,' his daughter-in-law had assured him. 'You'll have your own suite of rooms where you can do what you like. And we're just down in the village. We can come and visit you often.'

At first he felt like he was some kind of useless rubbish which nobody wanted. But then the more compassionate part of him analysed the situation and realized that it was indeed for the best. Barry always seemed cross with him for no apparent reason nor was he getting on well with

273

his wife. Their constant bickering had proved to be embarrassing and awkward for him too. Strangely, it was Stella who earned his sympathy. Somehow his son never seemed like his, always whimpering like a spoilt mummy's-boy. The idea of posterity hingeing on one so unlikeable was not a pleasant prospect.

In the dining room, with its high ceiling and ornate plaster mantelpiece, lunch had already begun amidst the sound of meal-time chatter.

'Ah, there you are!' one or two exclaimed, noticing his entrance. 'Mrs B. is really on the warpath today. Where've you been?'

'Fell asleep on the bench by the lake,' he said with feigned good cheer. 'When you get to be my age . . .'

'I've been worried about you,' grey-haired Ethel greeted him when he sat down at his usual table. 'Penny and George have gone down to their daughter's for the weekend.'

Ethel was referring to the couple who usually shared their table. To be frank, he had not even noticed their absence, so absorbed was he in his own thoughts.

On his plate, two slices of roast with pink centres and congealed gravy, over-baked potatoes and mushy peas sat unappetizingly; almost daring him to an afternoon of indigestion and Rennies.

Once she had ensnared a willing ear, Ethel let loose her woes of the day. Edward let her talk, making appropriate noises at intervals in an act of listening though his mind was preoccupied. He felt disturbed. Not willing to admit to senility, he was yet unable to explain his morning's experience. Had he really fallen asleep and daydreamed? It was not unusual for him to drop off unexpectedly but the whole thing had been so real! Chempaka had been so tangible! Why had she been blocked from his memory till now? He who had loved her with all his soul? And why

274

did the thought of her cause him to wince with pain? Why could he remember some bits of his past and not the rest? Why was she not here with him?

'Are you all right, Ed?' Ethel sounded concerned.

'A bit of indigestion, that's all. The food here is not fit for human consumption, is it?' he said, purely for conversation.

Ethel agreed, then proceeded to cite a litany of the shortcomings of Weyfold Manor. His life with Martha had taught him how to withdraw himself from a woman's wagging tongue without her knowledge.

Martha. She had been his wife and they had a son together. But how was it that he could not recall his life with her? Not that he particularly wanted to for though he couldn't remember any details, he had the *sense* that theirs had not been a happy marriage. He only knew that she had been bored and fed up with Singapore, hated its heat and people, and did not understand his work out there. So she had left him and returned to England with Barry, who had been eleven then, and eventually she had married her MP.

Edward prodded his peas abstractedly; he was still puzzling over whether he had been dreaming or had walked through another dimension. He had read of people reliving their past lives but had always considered them either eccentric or mad. Besides, his was not a past life regression as such, after all what he recalled was something from his present lifetime. Or was it? Had it all happened to him or was he making it all up? What was happening to his brain, for God's sake?

'Ethel. What's the word for that mental disorder when someone remembers events and circumstances which have not happened?'

'Loony?' she laughed, then said seriously, 'Paramnesia.

Why? Are you trying to find a word that would increase your score?'

'Not a bad one, is it? Needs too many "a"s though; the "m" and "p" have got fairly high points. Hmmm, too many letters.' He went along with her assumption that he was thinking of Scrabble.

'The people here are so unfriendly,' Ethel then said. 'I don't know what I'd do without you . . .'

She touched his arm briefly. Since he moved into the rooms next door but one to hers, she had attached herself to him. On rainy days, with the wind howling outside, it was pleasant enough to sit together, playing at Rummy-Cub or Scrabble. But her incessant chattering wore a bit thin sometimes and he was glad to escape to the lake. Dependent on a walking-frame, Ethel never joined him for his long walks over terrain she had difficulty in coping with.

I don't know what I'd do without you . . . I don't know what I'd do without you. I don't know what I'd do without you . . .

The words hammered at his brain until he found himself slipping, slipping again to that nebulous world where time seemed to have no meaning. Ethel's reedy voice was replaced by Chempaka's, full of vigour and laughter.

'I don't know what I'd do without you, my *sayang*.'

'That will never happen,' he said, looking into her sloe-eyes which looked back with unabashed longing.

It seemed a crime that one so young and beautiful as she, who could have the choice of men, should fall in love with him.

'I'm twenty years older than you,' he reiterated so that she could get things into perspective. 'When I'm sixty, you won't even be forty!'

Why he should want to discourage her, he did not

know; perhaps it was from a sense of chivalry. He wouldn't like to think that he was taking advantage of her naivety.

'*Sudah-lah*!' When exasperated, she would revert to Malay. '*Asam di-atas gunong/Garam di-dalam laut/ Kalau ada jodoh, jumpa juga dalam periok.*' A proverb she cited again and again: Tamarind on the mountain/ Salt in the sea/If it's destined, must meet eventually in the cooking-pot (in a dish called *asam-pedas*).

She had explained to him her people's strong belief in destiny or *jodoh*. 'You're my soul-mate, Ed-ward. We are meant to be. In soul-terms, we're compatible. In the spiritual world, there's no concept of time nor age, so you're neither younger nor older. Stop looking through your physical eyes only. Look beyond the body for we exist on so many different planes. Can't you see how wonderful we are together despite our many differences in age, race and creed?'

It was impossible for him to look beyond her body. Standing no taller than five feet four, she glowed with health. Firm of flesh, her burnished skin appeared to have the sun shining out from every pore. Everything about her was delicate, her wrists were so small that he could circle each with his thumb and fore-finger. Her breasts, though not large, were pert and proud. When he saw them for the first time, he was surprised because her nipples were like buttons and they would harden and be more erect when she became aroused or cold. In jest, he had called the phenomenon her Nipple-Scale. Her face, oval in shape, had a complexion as soft as the yellow petals of the flower she was named after.

'Chempaka,' he said, his heart full with love for her. He reached out a hand to trace her smooth cheek.

'Not here, Edward, everyone will start gossiping. I

didn't know you feel that way about me!' Ethel's voice was breathless with joy.

Edward stared with horror, at first uncomprehending, and then realized that his finger was touching Ethel's dry and crêpy cheek. He withdrew his finger as if stung.

'Oh, Ethel, I'm sorry.'

'I'm not,' she said with a new twinkle in her rheumy eyes. 'Shall we have coffee in my lounge?'

'There's . . . there's something I've to attend to in the village. Can I get you anything from there? Papers? Thornton chocolates? Should be back for tea. Perhaps this evening you can get your own back at Scrabble . . .'

His words were rushed, his sentences clipped.

Edward was troubled. What's going on, he asked himself as he toddled along the earth-packed shortcut to the village, his arthritic hip forcing him to slow down. I must be going mad!

Twice that day, he had lapsed into the past, living it as if it were the present. Or was it a past of his own construction? The second time, it was Ethel's words which had triggered it off because she echoed Chempaka's. Was his mind playing tricks on him? Was this what they called senility? Why hadn't he thought of Chempaka until now? When and why did he come back to England? Why couldn't he remember the intervening years? He must ask Barry. Perhaps he could enlighten him.

How the condition of his hip made him feel his age! And yet, inside himself, he felt youthful and spritely. He wondered whether reality was something physical or mental. When he arrived at the village, he went in search of his son. He could have telephoned but needed the walk to clear the cloudiness in his mind. He was still no nearer to clarity when he found Barry on the village green playing cricket. How his son could lend justice to such a game was beyond him. He had grown large and ungainly, his beer-gut spilling over his white trousers; it reminded him of the orang-utan, jungle-man, of the Malayan forests.

On the outskirts of the cricket ground, the locals were lazing in the sun, half-watching the game and half-engaged in their conversations and pursuits, pint glasses in their hands. Some of the children were playing catch, yelling, screaming; weaving themselves around the adults strewn on the grass like litter. Fringing the green were the delightful cottages which had won Weyfold the Most Beautiful Village in Surrey award that year.

'Dad! What are you doing here?' Stella startled him with her abruptness. Dressed in a summery dress in canary-yellow, which went well with her blonde hair, she looked fresh-faced and quite attractive. Edward suddenly realized that his son's marital problems were of a sexual nature. 'Are you all right? You look worried.'

'I want to speak to Barry.'

'Don't ever mention that . . . that . . . woman's name in my house, Dad. She ruined your career and our lives.' Barry's face was puce with rage.

'I don't remember anything of that sort . . .' Edward said uncertainly. There were so many gaps in his memory which made it difficult to piece things together. The teacup he held was rattling in its saucer.

'You were in line to be governor of Singapore! And you chucked it all up for some . . . some . . . *native* girl . . . who's half your age.' He pronounced the word as if it was leprous. 'Mum was so distraught and shamed by the whole affair that she had to leave the country.'

Despite what Barry was claiming, he knew that Martha had long ago been disillusioned with the East, that much he could remember. His liaison with

Chempaka was probably the excuse she needed to leave.

'She's not a figment of my imagination, then?' There was such joy in his rhetorical question that Barry glared at him.

'You simply went *gaga*, Dad. As if you'd had a tropical fever. You lost your job, shacked up with her in an *attap*-hut and swanned around nude on Changi beach!'

Edward could not help but smile at the idyllic picture Barry was painting. A sexual fantasy for most red-blooded males. Any man would give his right arm to make it a reality! He couldn't have been that *gaga* then! Was Barry using anger to mask his jealousy because one whom he considered to be a doddering old fool could have such a colourful past?

'No need to get so uptight, Barry. That's all water under the bridge now.' Stella tried to diffuse the situation.

'What do you know? I had to grow up fatherless while my mentally unstable parent made himself the laughing stock of the Colony! I could have had the right opportunities if he had become governor; then my life would have been different. Don't you think I went through enough trauma because of him? And now he's trying to dredge up his sordid affair to twist the knife in me.'

He paced the room while he raved, like a tiger cooped up for too long. He was so incensed that his saliva escaped him when he spoke. At first Edward simply saw a selfish brat who could not think beyond the 'I' mode. Then it dawned on him that perhaps his son was carrying a deeper hurt, a sense of rejection and neglect because of what he had done. *If* that was what he had done. It was annoying that his mind did not hold enough information for him to sort out fact from fabrication. There were too many blank pages in his memory-files. Perhaps he was senile after all!

280

'If my behaviour in the past has caused you any grief, I am sorry,' he said, edging himself out of the armchair more suited for a large person like Barry. From his son's attitude, he knew he'd not get further enlightenment on the subject. In a way, he could not blame Barry because he had been too young to make judgements himself; his mother had probably constructed and sustained her version of the incident throughout the years.

They stood, Barry and he, facing each other. They had not hugged for years. Martha had forbidden it since Barry was ten. She said that men should not exhibit such cissy behaviour. The emotional chasm between them made Edward sad. Had he been remiss in failing to show Barry love? Was it entirely of his own making or had other actors in the play contributed to the division too?

Yet whatever the real truth, he felt it was time to start afresh. So he moved forward to take Barry into his arms. But Barry just turned and walked out of the room.

'I'll give you a ride to the Manor,' Stella said gently.

In her car, Stella tried to make excuses for her husband. 'He always gets into a bad mood when he's lost a game, don't take it personally.'

'You're a sweet girl, Stella. I'm beginning to feel my age, you know. What happened this morning is rather unsettling, suddenly I'm remembering things that I didn't even know had happened to me.'

'I understood from Barry that you had lapses in memory when you were brought home in '54. Apparently some kind of tropical disease had taken hold of you and you had wandered into the Embassy feverish and delirious, bare-chested and wrapped only in a sarong. Fortunately your good friend Alistair was still out there, he put you in hospital and then contacted Martha. Martha was already married to Hugh Priestley by this time. Hugh was rather good about it and arranged for you to come back to England. It was he who found you a nursing home. When Barry and I got married, we thought it might be nicer for you to live with us. I'm sorry that didn't work out.'

'You don't know anything else? About Chempaka, I mean.'

'Barry refuses to talk about her. All I know is what you heard him tell you just now.'

The wheels of the car crunched the loose gravel of the Manor's circular drive. She stopped at the front porch with its hanging baskets of mixed coloured fuchsias and geraniums.

'I'm sorry I can't be of more help . . .'

'You've been wonderful. Will you let an old man kiss you?' He reached out and gave her an affectionate peck. 'She was beautiful, my Chempaka. And you are too.'

He wakes up with the distinct feeling that he is alone. The waves are crashing on to the sand underneath the house and the wind is lifting the *attap*-leaves, bringing in a cool rush of breeze to his skin. For a moment, he feels an incredible sense of loss, as if Chempaka has been taken away from him.

'Chempaka? Chempaka?' His voice has a tinge of panic as he walks barefoot on the floorboards in search of her. She's in neither the living room nor kitchen.

But he sees the steamer bubbling away over the clay stove and he is relieved. He recalls that she likes to meet the fishing boats when they come in so that she can get him his breakfast. Quickly, he slings a sarong round his hips, tying it in the way she had shown him.

Outside, the first few strips of blood-orange are beginning to light up the horizon. Edward walks near the water-edge, enjoying the feel of the cool water, smiling at the relativity of things, what is cool here would be

282

considered warm in England. In the distance, he can see the sampans, lying half in and half out of the sea. There is a cluster of people around each boat, housewives and fishmongers, Chempaka amongst them dressed in her *sarong-kebaya*, bargaining with the burnt-brown fishermen for their night's catch. Many of the fishmongers have come to buy fish for their stalls in the big wet-markets like Tekka and Lau Pasat, where the English do not go. The European community prefer to go to Cold Storage, a supermarket in Orchard Road where everything is sanitized and clean. 'Where we're not likely to catch anything!' as Martha had said.

'*Sepuloh sen? Eh, man boleh*! Ten cents? How can!'

'*Berapa*? How much?'

Edward smiles at the animated bargaining that is going on. A shopping ritual which the locals love and indulge in with as much fervour as negotiating for better deals from the colonial government.

'*Selamat pagi*. Good morning,' he says in Malay, wrinkling his nose slightly at the strong smell of fish.

The men return his greeting while some women snigger at his odd accent. They are slightly wary of him, the *orang-puteh*. These simple folk who only know the white men in their smart colonial suits and hats, placing themselves a cut above the local people, find it strange to see one bare-bodied and dressed like themselves.

'Ed-ward!' Chempaka smiles at him, making her dimples appear.

Not wanting to breach social conventions by kissing her in public, he merely brushes her hand with his. Suspicions still surround a mixed relationship like theirs because of the tainted affairs between bawdy sailors and dance-hall girls.

'*Laki saya* – my husband,' she says proudly.

With her information, the crowd relax, his whole

status suddenly changes. He is no longer an outsider but an honourable man who makes an honest woman out of a local girl.

They come away with a basket filled with two mackerels which she plans to salt, then steam for their breakfast; half a *kati* of *ikan-bilis*, those tiny fish sweeter than whitebait which she wants to fry for their *nasi-lemak*; and skate wings, which she intends to rub with spices and wrap up in *pandan*-leaves to be baked over hot coals. Even the thought of the latter makes Edward's mouth water, for the fragrance of that dish being cooked would make anyone hungry.

Away from the others, they hold hands, hers small and soft in his. Next to hers, his fingers feel like pork sausages and his hand like that of an ape. Chempaka skips as she walks, making the salt-spray fly into his face.

'Look!' she cries out.

As they watch, the great ball of smouldering orange slips from the line where sea meets sky and fires the whole of the east coast with its brightness. Its ascent into the sky is swift, unlike any sunrise he has ever seen.

From Chempaka's reaction, one would think that she has not seen the phenomenon either. To Edward, that's one of her most engaging ways, her *joie de vivre*. Through her subtle influence, he has come to shed his very English manner of understating everything and holding his emotions always in check.

Meeting her was the best thing that had happened to him. He was visiting a colleague of his in Alexandra Hospital and she was a nurse there. It was his good luck that she should fall in love with him too.

'Have a good fling if you can manage it discreetly. Why do you have to marry her?' Alistair had admonished him. 'You've got your whole career at stake. You've been working hard for this, don't let the affair jeopardize it.

No one's going to see your point. You've still got a wife and son here, for Chrissake!'

'You're mad, Edward! When the romance is gone, you'll regret sacrificing so much!' another said.

They could not understand. They called her names. Forgot that though she may be *native*, she had a mind too. And more, a heart. So big and warm that he could not see how he could have lived without her for so long.

But above all, she had taught him freedom; freedom from the straitjackets of bureaucracy and politics and meaningless social norms. And best of all, freedom from himself. He did not realize till he knew her how much his own attitudes and fears had shackled him to a life of doing things from obligation rather than desire. So he left. Not just his wife and son, but a total way of life.

'How dare you disgrace me by shacking up with this . . . this . . . tart?' Martha had railed at him despite the fact that he was leaving with only the shirt on his back and some favourite books. How easily she had shifted all blame to him, forgetting her own contribution to the marriage breakdown, her lack of warmth. The pregnancy had changed her, she shunned his advances. If ever he managed to make love to her, he was made to feel dirty, as though she was bestowing a gift to the undeserved. For the sake of Barry and his career, he had tolerated it, had fled to the bathroom whenever there was an overwhelming need for physical release. But the masquerade was over, he was going to lead a real life.

Martha cried on the shoulders of all the colony wives, made herself out to be a martyr. So apt her name. Colony wives who laughed at the small breasts of the *native women* in case their husbands judged them desirable; made fun of their funny noses and eyes. They supported her, not so much from friendship as from the fear that lurked within their breasts, that their own husbands might stray from them.

From being nearly a governor, he became a simple sampan-repairer, providing a service the local fisherfolk badly needed. Every minute, every second he is by the sea, working on the boats, walking on the sandy beach or sitting on the back steps of their house-on-stilts, Edward's heart is filled with so much joy that he feels like shouting it to the world. Through Chempaka, he has come to understand that true happiness comes from simple pleasures. The structured world of Eton, Cambridge and the Foreign Office seems like a bad dream. Blake was right, it's better to be like an innocent child, ruled not by Urizen but the creative impulse. Chempaka is that embodiment.

'I love you,' he says, stopping to take her in his arms in this private part of their beach. In doing so, he lets go of the basket of fish. An incoming wave tips the basket over and the dead fishes float about as if being given a new lease of life.

'*Alamak*!' Chempaka exclaims, freeing herself from him and dashing about to pick up the fish.

He laughs, glad to hear its ring in his own voice, smothered so long by other people's expectations of him: his parents, teachers, superiors, Martha. Chempaka joins in his laughter, the sound of their outburst resonating through the trees, startling the birds out of their nests in the palm trees.

'The water in your steamer will be dried up soon if we don't hurry,' he reminds her.

'*Ya juga*!' she gasps, and then rushes towards their home, swinging the basket in her hand.

He follows closely on her heels, feeling proud of the sylph-like figure of the girl running before him.

If life held no meaning for him before, the total

opposite is true now. His life is full. He is vibrant, pulsating with its sheer energy. Sometimes he even forgets he is close to middle age. As far as he's concerned, he is in paradise, clichéed as that may seem.

'Let's see who can swim out furthest underwater, without drawing breath,' Chempaka challenges him.

He can sense that she is in a playful mood. But the sky is broodingly grey, telling him that a storm is imminent. As it is November, in the season of monsoons, the winds and undercurrents are stronger. They are already quite far out at sea, their house, amongst the trees, almost indistinct. Though the waves never rise to the heights of those in Brighton or the Solent, Chempaka is nonetheless sometimes hidden from him in the swell.

'No, I think we'd better swim back,' he says. 'It's going to rain soon.'

'Co-ward,' she says, splitting the syllables as she does with his name.

Before he can say anything else, he sees her feet momentarily in the air as she duck-dives. Slightly exasperated but not unduly worried as he knows she is an excellent swimmer, he follows suit. The water is warm compared to that of the English sea though Chempaka can never understand what he means. Unlike the water off the coast of Pulau Tioman, which is so clear and blue that people have glass-bottomed boats to admire the corals beneath, the water here is somewhat murky, the visibility poor. In a few minutes, he loses sight of Chempaka. In another few, feeling the tightness in his chest, he decides to surface.

'Chempaka?'

She's nowhere about and an absurd feeling of dread clasps his heart. Then a dark head bobs up nearly thirty feet away, her long hair streaming like black seaweed, arms waving in triumph, and his relief is great. Just at that moment, a motor-launch appears and to Edward's horror, goes straight for Chempaka.

'Look out!!!' His voice is lost in the wind and the roar of the engine. 'Chempaka! Chempaka!'

The sound of the motor reverberates in Edward's ears as a sickening feeling comes over him.

'No! No! No!' he cries in utter despair, cold sweat enveloping him.

But suddenly he realized that he was not in the sea, he was back on the bench by the lake at Weyfold.

Oh, my God! It has happened again, he thought to himself, I've taken myself back to the tropics. And the culprit that had triggered off his strange mind-travels this time was the chugging of the outboard, being used to rescue windsurfers who found themselves stranded on the far borders of the lake.

Edward was distressed. Was Chempaka dead? The thought was too much to bear. Too agitated to sit still, he got up and walked slowly along the shore of the lake, passing underneath the weeping willows. He wondered if he was going insane or regaining his lost memory. Was the information that was filtering through now correct? Had Chempaka died that way? Was that why his brain had gone into a sort of freeze to spare him the pain? Was that the cause of his delirium when he had wandered into the Embassy where Alistair had found him? How would he ever know the truth? Perhaps he could try to contact Alistair.

If only he had remembered Chempaka earlier in life. Up until now, he had never thought he had been loved, neither by Martha nor Barry. To learn that he was the object of such consuming love as Chempaka had for him was a wonderful revelation. Perhaps it was not too late to go to Singapore to discover the truth. Unless of course she had been killed in that accident. What if she had spent all these years withering into old age, wondering why he had deserted her? Waiting for him in their *attap*-house? For God's sake, what was the damn truth? Was there some kind of malevolent deity who was flirting with his senses?

'Ed-ward! Ed-ward!' Mrs B. was out looking for him again. Oh, bother! He'd probably be told off for being absent at tea. He was in no mood to eat, so he got up from the bench and walked in the opposite direction to the voice.

'Where are you, Ed-ward?' she sounded impatient.

He stood underneath the long, flowing strands of the willow so that he was hidden from her. He could see her peering here and there, her hand above her eyes to shield them from the glare of the sun. Her stance struck a familiar chord in the deep recesses of his brain and, in a breath, he crossed over to that other time in Singapore.

He is peeping through the long blades of the half-reclining palm trees, watching with mirth as Chempaka looks this way and that for him.

'Ed-ward! Where are you-*lah*?'

The sand is hot under his bare feet and he wants her to find him soon so he pretends to cough. She pounces on him.

'Caught you!' she says with the glee of a child.

'Fancy a swim?' he asks.

'Race you!' she says in reply.

They both flick off their sarongs and race into the sea, laughing with sheer joy.

Mrs Baxter saw Edward Aster come out from behind the willow tree. He was running towards the lake as if he were a young man. All the time he was laughing, as though crazed. Before she could call him again, he had plunged straight into the icy waters of the lake. Knowing that he could no longer swim with his arthritic hip, she began to scream.

LIFE BEGINS
AT 40

Chuck Anderson

Chuck Anderson is creative director of a Soho advertising and marketing consultancy. He has worked in advertising for twenty-five years, mostly in London but also in Hamburg and New York.

He has published two 'insider' guide-books, *Passport to Soho* and *Passport to Covent Garden*. *Save the Jubilee Hall!*, a book he has written about the community struggle to preserve a local recreation centre and street market in the Piazza of Covent Garden, will be published in October.

LIFE BEGINS
AT 40

The flat brown paper parcel had been posted in Rotterdam two days ago, with a colourful commemorative stamp. It was about the size of a magazine, but felt soft and lumpy. Not paper, but fabric. More than a headscarf, less than a blouse.

There was no other identification. She turned the homely envelope over in her hands several times, prolonging the pleasure of surprise, forestalling the inevitable disappointment.

April didn't know anyone in Holland. She walked back down the hall to the bedroom. Tim was knotting his tie before the mirror, as usual admiring himself just a little too much.

'I thought you were in Germany last weekend,' she teased.

When she thought about it later, his reaction was false, though only a wife, or a lover, could have seen it. It was something about the timing. Too deliberate, perhaps. He continued to gaze into the mirror, but he was no longer looking at himself. The eyes were elsewhere. And then he didn't answer the question.

'What have you got there?' he asked.

He smiled a bit too brightly, as if he were chatting her up. And the voice was a trifle tense. But she realized that only later. Now she felt only that she was teasing and he wasn't playing the game.

'A birthday present from a secret admirer,' she trilled.

He took it from her and turned it over, as she had, more than once before giving it back.

'I was in Germany.' His voice was normal now. Something about the parcel had relieved his anxiety.

'You could have got someone to send it,' she mused.

He turned and took her in his arms and kissed her nose.

'I gave you a gold watch last night. Plus dinner, a long-stemmed rose and a better than average screw. Remember?'

'You didn't send it? Cross your heart?'

'No. Cross my heart.'

'Then who – '

A sudden thought squeezed her heart and choked off the sentence. What if it were from someone in the past? One of those nutcases – Jack, or Robert, or Cosmo? She placed the parcel, now freighted with emotion, as casually as she could on the dressing-table and turned away to comb her hair. But somehow her tiny fear had sparked across the gap between them. Tim picked the parcel up and held it out to her again, just as casually. Stupidly, she realized, she had put it on top of his cufflinks.

'There's one way to find out,' he smiled. God, how handsome he looked and how much she loved him.

'It is from you,' she insisted.

'No. Promise. And I'm not leaving until I find out who your secret admirer is.'

She was being silly. There was nothing to worry about. She loved Tim and that was her life now. Her fingers tore open the parcel.

It was a dark blue T-shirt. On the front in white letters it read 'Life begins at 40'. The 40 was writ large and defiantly, like the number on an American football player's jersey.

'It's marvellous,' she squealed, and threw her arms around him.

He slipped away. 'Nothing to do with me.'

'Honestly?'

'There's a card.' He picked a neat white card off the floor, glanced at it and handed it to her with an eyebrow raised. A small knot rose in her throat.

'From your secret admirer,' it read. There was no signature, and the handwriting was not familiar.

'Well, then,' said Tim, 'there's a surprise.'

If anything it looked like a girl's handwriting. 'Sharon,' she exclaimed. 'Or Jane.' But she knew it was in neither hand.

'Jane? You haven't seen her in years.'

'No, but it's just her style. It's from some bitchy woman.'

'But you would say that, wouldn't you, darling?' Tim kissed her forehead. 'Anyway, I'm not surprised you have admirers.' He was teasing now. 'Keeps me on my toes.' He kissed her again. 'That's my baby,' he said. And then he left.

Forty wasn't too old to have a baby. But time was running out. She would have to make her decision soon.

When she got to the ward that evening her patients burst into a chorus of 'Happy Birthday' and she burst into tears. There was a shower of small presents and the nurses produced an apple tart from M&S with forty tiny candles wavering bravely around the edge. The mystery of the T-shirt was the talk of the ward. When she showed it to Sharon the round eyes in her friendly black face widened, her hand flew to her mouth and she giggled. 'You can give me one in a couple of years. I'll let you know when.'

'You didn't send it?' asked April, but she already knew Sharon was incapable of any deception, however innocent.

Her favourite old duck, Mrs Briody, beckoned her close to her pillow with a bony, brown-flaked hand. 'Maybe it was one of your old lovers,' she whispered.

'Maybe it was one of yours, Mrs B.,' she answered, and the old lady chortled until April had to pat her back and give her a sip of water to stop her wheezing.

Later, in her office, the girls made the same suggestion. 'I only ever had three,' wailed April. 'And none of them knows my address. I made bloody sure of that.'

In the wee small hours when they were alone, Sharon presented her own special gift. When she saw the gay pink and blue wrapping paper showing a stork carrying a baby in a nappy, April said, 'It's not my first birthday, Sharon.'

'It is if life begins at forty,' she laughed. 'Open it.'

Inside was a tiny oval picture frame. It was made of solid silver.

April hugged her. 'It's lovely.'

'It's for the baby,' said Sharon.

Tears welled up in April's eyes again and Sharon folded her large black hands like gloves over her friend's thin pale hands. 'You've got to get started now, ducks.'

'It's Tim,' moaned April. 'You know he's infertile.'

'What did the gynaecologist say? About donor insemination?'

'My tubes are patent. I could have it done tomorrow. And a baby in nine months.'

'So, I'll take your duty tomorrow.'

April shook her head. 'I want Tim's baby.'

Sharon sighed with the wisdom of ages. 'That don't matter. He wants your baby. That's what matters.'

'I can't,' April mumbled. Then she stood up and dried her eyes with a tissue and walked out the door. An instant later she poked her head back around the frame with a sad smile. 'I'm a one-man woman,' she said.

The next morning the one-man woman decided to take some things to the dry cleaners and found the small crumpled handkerchief with the faint scent and the smear of eye make-up in Tim's jacket pocket. It was the kind of thing a bitch like Jane would have done. Stuff it in his pocket so the wife would find it. Too bloody corny.

There had to be a sensible explanation. A sudden gust of wind, a woman with grit in her eye. Tim had lots of female colleagues and clients.

She didn't go to the dry cleaners but sat down and had a coffee and a cigarette instead, as if she were taking a break on the ward. She rummaged through her file boxes and found Jane's phone number in an old address book. She thought a long time before dialling it, and finally convinced herself that it didn't matter because Jane would have moved long ago anyway. After two rings, a little girl answered the phone and went to fetch Mummy.

Jane hadn't sent the parcel either. 'How exciting,' she said. 'I suppose you've been through your old address book?'

Jane's address book would have been more interesting. Once, when they were flatmates, while they worked their way through a bottle of Martini, Jane had counted up her lovers. She reckoned she'd had forty-three, as far as she could remember. That was when she was twenty-seven. April was shocked, and had wondered if she herself were normal.

Now Jane wasn't counting lovers anymore, but she had two babies. With Tim, April's score had crept to four, and she had no babies.

'I bet it's Jack-the-lad,' said Jane. 'That's the crazy kind of thing he used to do. Following you back to London, and standing in the street throwing pebbles up at your window.'

'That was fifteen years ago,' said April. 'And he finally got the message.'

'What about Robert? He kept coming back like a song.'

This was why she had called Jane. The past was real to Jane too, and now she completed the trilogy, 'And there's always Cosmo. Did he ever surface again?'

'No, never.'

April had married Cosmo. And when he had pushed her out for another piece of skirt, just like the others, she had slammed a steel gate on that part of her life. Jane had fancied him. Well, Jane had fancied all of April's pitiful trawl, but Cosmo she had actually known first. And when she was twenty-seven the men Jane fancied she generally got. April had seen the procession tramp through the flat.

'Did Cosmo ever make love to you?' April heard herself saying. In the little silence that followed she made two amazing discoveries. It was the first time she had said his name aloud for years. And she had not been embarrassed to ask the question. It had just popped out. What did it matter now, anyway?

Jane laughed the way she did when she was twenty-seven. 'You wouldn't expect me to remember, would you? But I would have wanted you to think I did.'

The next day she went down to visit and was shocked once more. Jane, the gamine, was fat and looked more fifty than forty. Once she had embellished their flat with artistic disorder: purple knickers on the door handles, make-up between the sofa cushions, wet magazines in the bath, the stale aroma of ciggies stubbed out on saucers, and when she freaked out April would have to cuddle her and coax her, red-eyed and nailbitten, out of the decorative fireplace. Now her home was a tip of children's toys, dirty washing and empty food cartons,

298

and the sour smell of damp towels rose up in the bathroom. Jane, no longer radiant, was blissfully, piggishly content.

But of all the men who passed through her parade, why had she chosen Harold? Jane answered the unspoken question. 'Harold is a bore,' she said. 'Grousing all day at the office, talking back to the telly at night, or playing prop forward at the bar in the rugby club. But then who needs a challenge at our time of life? Romance is behind us, thank God. Nappies are not for drying tears on.'

She broke off to stop her eldest from stuffing the remains of a very dingy teddy bear down her youngest's throat.

'Harold is comfortable,' she said, settling down to her cigarette and coffee again. 'We don't have any great expectations of each other. Besides, when it came to your actual crunch, he was the only one that wanted the goods on offer.'

Now her eyes scoured April through the smoke with the old venom. 'You're still like a rail,' she said, which was vintage Janespeak for 'you have no tits'. 'How is that ever so dishy, rich and sophisticated American you live with?' she added, which translated as 'how on earth did someone like you ever bring it off?'

'I finally got him to marry me,' April replied. It was not possible to say it without sounding smug.

'Bravo for you,' said Jane joylessly. 'You always were the forever girl, weren't you.' She paused, and April knew what was coming next. 'With all of them.'

'There were only three,' she said, annoyed to discover her eyes were examining the stained carpet as she said it, just like in the old days.

'Four,' corrected Jane. 'Don't forget Tim.' She laughed throatily. In a few years it would be a husky cackle. 'Or send him round to me if he's a discard. With his pockets full of dollar travellers' cheques.'

April had stepped into Jane's house in a bright and cheery mood and given her a great big hug. When she emerged from the voluptuous chaos she was downcast and envious, just as she had always been with Jane. But they hugged each other warmly again, because they both remembered how it had been in the late '70s. In her handbag, written on the back of a 10p-off voucher for a bottle of Oil of Ulay, was a phone number for Jack in Australia, only three or four years old.

'I bet you don't dare,' Jane had said. And then giggled, 'but I want a word-for-word report.'

In the middle of the ward a bouquet of red and white carnations raised a silent scream against the muddy walls. 'Get them out of here,' April hissed to the student nurse as soon as she came in.

'But they liven it up so.'

'Red and white means death.' Didn't they learn anything in nursing school these days? April swept down, plumped up Mrs Jennings' pillow and tidied the evil flowers away into her office.

These days domestic telephone bills showed itemized calls so April used the phone in the Senior Registrar's office. Sally was on switchboard and they both reckoned the NHS owed her a thing or two. Sally promised not to listen.

A woman's voice answered. Broad Australian rising above a cacophony of kids shouting against a background of TV sports coverage. 'Who is it?' she demanded.

'I'm calling from England. My name is Mrs Moseley.' That much was true. 'We're trying to trace a Mr Jack Glennon. It's a legal matter.'

'Jacko, it's for you,' she heard. 'Proper English lady. Your great-uncle's died and left you his butterfly

300

collection.' A bright lady. She would be listening hard in the background.

Suddenly he was there. 'Jack Glennon speaking.'

He sounded old. A scratched recording of himself. A crude picture of a lonely girl in a white shift standing on the end of a jetty flashed before her eyes. Like April then she had long, straight hair which hung down her back. But it was blonde. Behind her she could not see, but surely felt, the presence of the dark man who lurked with his hands in his pockets, looking at her. It was the print by Munch that had hung on the wall of her tiny bedroom, which she used to stare at during those long conversations when she had tried to find a way to persuade Jack simply to go away, he wasn't wanted anymore. He had become a pest and a nuisance. It was called *The Lonely Ones* and he had hated it. She wondered where it was now.

'It's April,' she said.

'So it is.' A little silence, then, 'Oh, God Almighty!'

'I don't want to bother you. But there's something I have to know.'

'Yes?'

'Do you know where I live?'

'No.'

'You didn't get someone to send something to me recently?'

A pause. Then, 'I think I understand. Something to do with this time of year – early April.' Now it was her turn to pause, and he filled the gap. 'The third or fourth, wasn't it? That's why they named you April. You must be – good God, you're probably forty!'

A great weight fell from her shoulders. 'Thanks, you've answered my question. I just wanted to be sure.'

'Why did you call me?'

'Just a birthday greeting.'

'It's your bloody birthday, not mine. Somebody sent you a present and you thought it might be me. I'm right, aren't I? So, how do you know it wasn't me?'

'What was it you sent?'

'Ah – well, I would have sent you a present if I knew where you lived.'

'I shan't bother you again. Sorry.'

'Don't go. Where do you live? What's your phone number?'

'Hush! Your wife is going to get the wrong idea.'

'Call me on *my* birthday!'

'I've forgotten when it is,' she said, and that was true.

'Do you remember what you said about feelings that last forever?'

'I suppose that's why I called,' she said quietly. 'To find out if they change.'

'Are you married?' It was the old Jack, jealous, suspicious, and neurotic. Now the woman was shouting in the background and a baby wailed. She must have it on her shoulder.

April giggled. 'Are you?'

There was a crash. She hoped it wasn't the baby.

'April, for Christ's sake, I still love you. Get me out of here!'

'Ta-ra,' she said musically.

She rang off laughing and danced through the rest of her shift. Mrs Briody sensed it right away. 'You're in a good mood, dear,' she said. 'Did your young man send you another gift?'

That was just before Mrs Peabody gave a genteel little cry and let slip her feeble purchase on the world in the bed at the end of the ward. Afterwards, April took the vase of red and white carnations from her office and tossed them in the bin. She forgot all about the parcel until the next day when she returned from her appointment at the

302

infertility clinic. This time it was an arty card she found, not, it had to be admitted, by accident, but after a careful sifting through Tim's desk drawers.

On the front was a black-and-white etching by Picasso, the one where a gaunt couple are sitting at a table with a large bottle of wine, some glasses and an empty bowl in the foreground. The man wears a kind of derby and his arm is cast negligently over the woman's shoulder. Perhaps he is a travelling clown. Both of his bony hands with their impossibly elongated fingers press into the woman's flesh beneath her thin dress. She is thin, too, but her breasts hang full and fruity.

Something tore in April's gut. She had been here before. A romantic Monet impression, a silly elephant cartoon, she could have coped with. But this was oh so witty and sophisticated. On the back was the caption, *Le Repas Frugal*. And inside was written, in a clear and confident female hand, 'Thanks for the dinner invitation'.

Ever so clever and understated. It meant nothing but what it said, and everything that was unsaid. Picasso's man and woman know each other so well in this embrace that their faces, sharp and intelligent, turn away from each other. Was it before or after? Had the dinner yet, so to speak, been consummated?

She was being perfectly outrageous. It was an ordinary business lunch. Well, dinner. And a thank you note just a little over the top. But why did he keep it? Why not? It was amusing. Probably he had meant to show it to her. But why didn't she sign it? Not even an initial. The knot tightened again in April's stomach, and she put the card back where she found it. There was no envelope in evidence.

Locating Robert was simply a matter of looking him up in the Medical Register. She rang the hospital. He wouldn't be there at night. But he was.

'I have a simple question to ask you,' she said. 'There's nothing more to it. I just want to know if you sent me something recently.'

Robert was never one to be caught off balance, even by a risen ghost. 'Meet me for lunch tomorrow and I'll tell you,' he said.

Suddenly she had no defences. 'I can't,' she parried. 'I'm on an early.'

'Dinner then. Remember *Otello's*?'

Tim was going to be away that night. 'It closed years ago,' she said weakly.

'The place on the corner then. *Il Siciliano*, was it? Seven-thirty. Must fly. The pubs have closed and the broken heads are coming in.'

When she arrived at the restaurant Robert was already there, at a corner table, with some flowers. The face still had its youthful intensity, but the hair was thin and he wore bifocals. The owner of the restaurant, an older replica of the man they used to know, greeted her like a long lost friend. But then he did that to everyone, and Robert had probably prompted him.

They talked mostly about his family, just as they always had. His eldest was in medical school now, would you believe, the other two were punks and he and Esther were very worried about them. Just as they always had been. Finally, when the bottle of Chianti was two-thirds gone, the conversation got round to her.

'If you don't mind my asking,' he ventured, 'why did it go wrong so abruptly with us?'

'You mean the first time or the second time?'

'The first time, I left you.'

'Because you were married.'

'I mean the second time, when you left me.'

'Because you were still married.'

'You knew that.'

304

'To the same woman, the same children, the same house even. Do you still live in it?'

'We moved to Blackheath when I became a consultant.'

'I left you because someone wanted to marry me.'

'Just like that?'

'I loved him.'

'The way you loved me?'

'A different way.'

'Forever?'

'Is there any other way?'

He offered her wine but she put her hand over her glass. He shrugged and poured the remainder into his own glass.

'I wanted to marry you,' he said.

'So you said,' she laughed. 'Both times.'

He ordered another bottle of wine, and raised his glass to her.

'I hope you and Cosmo are very happy together. It must be, what – ten years?'

'Twelve, or it would have been. But it only lasted a year.'

Robert snorted.

'And then I married Tim,' she concluded.

'A nice British name at least.'

'He's American. Cosmo was – is British.'

'For a one-man woman, a "forever" girl, you've certainly been around the course.'

'While you have stayed happily married to the same woman, with only a few dozen broken-hearted nurses on the side.'

He smiled. 'Irresistible, I suppose. Even you rang me up after a dozen years.'

'I wanted to find something out.'

'If I still loved you?' He leaned forward and took both

her hands. His were warm and strong, but they were a stranger's hands. 'The answer is yes. And the marriage is over. Has been for years. I mean it.'

'Did you send me that present?'

He let go of her hands and looked away. 'A way of getting in touch?' he mumbled.

'That's not an answer,' she said.

'What are you really looking for, April? Perhaps we could find an answer again.'

'I don't know,' she said. 'It's just something that's nagging me. But it has nothing to do with you.'

'So why did you call me?'

'I'm sorry about that.' She wiped a tear from the corner of her eye and folded the handkerchief neatly into her handbag. 'I shouldn't have come.'

He took out his Filofax. 'What's your telephone number?'

'Sorry,' she said. 'Wrong number. Will you let me pay for the meal?'

He didn't answer, but looked stonily over her shoulder. She left as the second bottle of wine arrived at the table.

'Goodbye, forever,' he called after her, but it didn't hurt at all. It was just a relief to be out of a stuffy restaurant and into the cool spring air. She was home in plenty of time to get Tim's call, but it didn't come.

Mrs Briody's ticker collapsed just after four a.m. on her next shift. April flew to her bed, almost knocking the auxiliary nurse into the next bed. 'Ring the crash team,' she shouted and leapt on the old lady's chest, pumping strongly, rhythmically, as she had been taught all those years before in nursing school. She had raised more than a dozen people from the dead this way. But this time there was no response. When the crash team burst into the ward three minutes later the houseman had to pull her off. 'Use the defibrillator,' she pleaded, but the doctor, a girl not much more than half her age, shook her head. She led her, crying, into her office and told the auxiliary to give her a cup of tea.

The next day, before starting her shift, she was summoned by Matron. 'You're my best ward sister,' she said, 'so I'm surprised you could have been so unprofessional.'

'She was a very special person,' said April.

'She was an NFR.' Matron spoke in the old language they shared, hospital parlance for Not For Resuscitation, which had been used until patients and their visitors began to wise up to the acronyms written on their bed charts. 'Her quality of life wasn't worth putting the old dear through the pain.'

'I know,' said April. 'It just suddenly seemed that the most important thing on earth was to keep this very special person alive.'

'It's hard not to get involved,' said Matron. 'But when it comes to the end you have to recognize it. There comes a time when you really do have to let go.'

April nodded. 'It won't happen again.' But something inside her still urged 'No. Some things are forever.'

The Picasso card was still there in Tim's desk, in the compartment next to some of her own love letters. She looked at it to feel the pain again. And then she saw his passport. It was filled with stamped entries, many from foreign cities, and, as a resident alien, one blue square or triangle for every time he left or entered Britian. And there was her name. A stamp for April 1st. Tim had returned from Germany not on the Monday, her birthday, but on the previous Friday. April fool! He had spent the weekend somewhere in Britain. The pain welled up in her chest and she doubled over gagging. She didn't deserve this. Not for a fourth time.

She didn't have to look up Cosmo's number. It was in her head; it was the number of her 'former matrimonial home'. Once, years ago, when she was feeling low she had dialled it after drinking most of a bottle of wine. She had heard Cosmo's crisp voice on an Ansafone message, blurted something out, and felt better for it, and righteous.

Now, unfortified by wine, as soon as she dialled she hoped it would be the Ansafone again. But there was only the dead tone of a disconnected line. So he had finally left the 'former matrimonial home'. It must have taken a powerful woman to dig him out of there. Or maybe, she suddenly thought, he was dead.

It was her day off. She had not been up to the West End for some time, and she decided to go shopping. Once she got to Oxford Circus it was only a few stops away but they had changed the routes of the tube lines. Dreamlike, the station was actually now on a different line. There were new shops and buildings, too, so as she walked the familiar streets April felt she was moving in a trance.

As in a dream, the *leylandii* they had planted behind the front garden wall now towered above the first storey. The house was the wrong colour, too. Someone else lived there now. But she could not find the courage to ring the bell and find out for sure. She walked by, her legs moving in the treacle of dream slow-motion. The pub on the corner had been tarted up in gold and maroon. She went past it to the little shopping parade, and looked in all the windows. There was a fishmonger now, and a video rental shop had wedged itself into the tiny place where she used to bring her shoes to the shoemaker. She could have carried on around the block back to the tube station, but instead went back down the street for a second look.

Coming around the corner, she ran into Cosmo.

Almost literally. He stopped and smiled, and he looked exactly the same.

'It had to happen some day,' he said. 'You look great. How are you?'

'I tried to call you, but your phone was dead.'

'071?'

Of course. The London codes had changed. 'How stupid of me. Things don't stand still. Everything's different now.'

He smiled again. 'Look, I've spent years rehearsing what I would say when I ran into you. But it's all flown out of my head. Come and have a drink.'

'I just wanted to ask you – did you send me a birthday present?'

'Not in the past twelve years or so. I don't even know where you live, remember? But I always think of you on your birthday, and it's just as I always told you. When you're forty you're going to be a real cracker.'

They went into the pub and she had a Bloody Mary for old times' sake, but she might have been in a new country. Nothing was the same as it had been, she recognized nobody, and no one knew her.

Cosmo was different, too. No one had been more evasive, more anxious to procrastinate. Now he plunged right in. 'I want to say I'm sorry. I was wrong and I was rotten to you.'

'I don't want to remember,' she said.

'I've never been able to forget. But I paid for it. It took me years to get over you. It's so unreal now. Talking to someone who's been dead all this time.'

'Am I different?'

'Yes. And so am I. Everything changes.'

He was right, she thought. You have to let go.

'Did you ever get him to marry you?' he asked. 'Old whatsisname.'

'Yes. And you remember his name.'

'I honestly don't. Mental block. Good-looking weedy sort of Yank. A philosopher trying to escape from a family fortune.'

'Tim. He never escaped.'

'Still together?'

She nodded.

'Good. I'm glad you're happy,' he said, looking at his glass. Then he fastened his faraway blue eyes directly on hers. 'So did you get that little boy you wanted? Luke, you were going to call him.'

Now she shook her head, and her eyes brimmed with tears. He touched her shoulder. 'I'm sorry about that, too,' he said. 'But you always said you didn't want a child.'

'Because you didn't want one.'

'And I believed you. Until it was too late.'

'Would you want it now?' she asked.

'Not now,' he said. 'You can't give back a dozen years. But I want it then, if that makes any sense.'

'Yes,' she said. 'And I forgive you.'

'You were hard on me, too. Just going away, leaving no address.'

'You were going to thrash him.'

'Yes, I would have. Beat my own guilt out of him. Did you ring me once upon a time? On the Ansafone?'

She said nothing.

'A crazy drunken lady's voice – just sobbing. The only thing I could make out was "you've ruined my life".'

'Could have been anybody.'

'Was it you?'

'Maybe.'

'If you'd told me where you were I would have come for you then. But now, I couldn't come.'

She had not touched her drink. Now she took a sip. 'Did you have children?'

He shook his head.

'Are you married?'

'Worse. A relationship with a lady who lives in France. We see each other most weekends.'

'Is she married?'

'Not now.'

'Why is that worse?'

'Too permanent. There's nothing to rebel against.'

They went back to the matrimonial home then and all that had changed, too. There was nothing she remembered except some Waterford glassware which had been a wedding present, and a certain cupboard in the kitchen.

'Do you remember the day I moved in?' she said. 'My kitten took one look at you and hid in that cupboard for two days. And then she ran away.'

'Smart kitten,' he said. 'I'd forgotten that. Do you remember that photo album?'

'I couldn't look at them,' she said.

'I burned it,' he said. 'But only a couple of years ago. Because there was a page that you wrote on in the front, which said "Promise me never ever to throw this away, because I will love you forever". Remember? One of those nights when you came here to decide finally between Tim and me, and I made you a spag bol, and we drank lots of wine, and wound up in bed crying together? I kept it for years before I burned it.' He took her hands now. 'Ten years is long enough to mourn, don't you think? They even let you off for manslaughter after ten years. Or womanslaughter.'

She remembered. She cried again now and so did he, and he took her in his arms, they kissed, and because it was so sad the rest was inevitable.

She remembered the bed, too, and how she had curled

311

her body up against his, playing spoons, every night for almost a year. Now they lay together, and their bodies were still taut and lean. He kissed her all over and she kissed him all over, and they clung to each other again. But it was no good. He couldn't get it up and neither could she. He pulled her to his chest and stroked her hair.

'I think I can say I'm usually better than this,' he said.

'I remember.'

'It's not you. It's just that I have one hell of a guilty conscience. And it squats in my groin.'

'I remember that, too.'

'You should see me in the morning. It rises to salute the dawn.'

When she was getting dressed he said, still lying in the bed, 'The last time you were in this bed, and you were going off to Tim, do you know what I made you do?'

'Something awful, I should imagine.'

'I asked you to leave your knickers behind. And I kept them under my pillow for weeks.'

'That must have cramped your love life.'

'I didn't have any after you left. Not for a long, long time.'

'What happened to Susie?'

'I told you that was over.'

'I didn't believe you.'

'I used to fantasize about you in your nurse's uniform.'

'Did we ever make love that way?'

'Never.'

'It's just a work outfit to me. Something to change out of as soon as I can. Funny what lovers never say to each other.'

When she kissed him goodbye she left her knickers behind again, saying, 'These French girls, they say, are very broad-minded', and tucked her tights into her handbag, walking bare-legged and bare-assed down the street through the fresh spring evening to the Underground, and through Waterloo Station, and from the train back to her own home with that free, swinging confident stride that you get when you have a special secret that no one else can guess at.

Tim was waiting for her, tired and moody, and relieved when she didn't press him to make love. The next morning he made the tea and, just for the hell of it, she put on her 'Life Begins at 40' T-shirt. When she came down he was reading a letter. The opened envelope on the kitchen table was addressed to her, and it had a Dutch stamp.

She lunged to snatch the letter from him, but he danced out of reach and put the table between them.

'Good thing you've got your T-shirt on,' he said, with a strange wide grin. 'The secret admirer stands revealed. Shall I read it to you?'

'If it gives you pleasure,' she managed. Heart pounding, she turned to pour the tea, and found herself filling the sugar bowl. Tim didn't notice.

'Dear April,' he read. 'I hope you enjoyed the gift of our "Life Begins at 40" T-shirt on the occasion of your recent birthday. It's yours to keep in any case, because you are one of the opinion-leading professionals we are trying to reach. We hope you would like to order a supply of these thoughtful and amusing T-shirts for your friends who may soon be nearing the magic age. Just £8.95 each, or five for £39.95, using the order form enclosed. Also available, "Sweet Sixteen", "Over 21", and "Still 39".'

'Ha bloody ha,' said April to the world at large, drying the sugar bowl.

He came over and put his arm around her. 'It's all right, darling. I love you.'

April had the experience to know that philandering men with trusting partners get careless. They find it hard not to drop the name of their beloved into an innocent conversation. For an extra frisson of sexual power, perhaps? Or prudently, on the grounds that if the name were never mentioned it might leave a black hole of suspicion? The name is inflected with a certain tremor, inaudible to all except the afflicted, and perhaps neighbourhood dogs and cats.

'I have a confession to make,' he intoned. 'One of the girls at the office told me about the T-shirt company, so I had them send you one.'

'You lied so plausibly you fooled me completely.'

'That's a bit strong. Economical with the truth, perhaps. I didn't actually send it myself.'

'Which girl?'

'I think her name is Alison.'

'That your new secretary?'

'No. Alison Blake. In PR.'

'How old is she?'

'Oh, twenty-five or so I should think.'

'What a little stinker.'

April was on a night shift, ending at eight a.m. but she went off early, getting Sharon to cover, and drove to London. At seven she was standing outside the former matrimonial home, bare-legged, in her uniform. The spare key was where it had always been, and she let herself in.

Cosmo woke up as she came into the bedroom. 'I've come for my knickers,' she said. She never had a chance to take her clothes off. He was up into her hard and good and sure, and it lasted a long, satisfying time.

Level with her eyes, a jolly banner tacked above the headboard read *Je t'aime*. She thought that the woman who shared that view wouldn't mind, just once. 'I love you,' he said then, and she answered, 'You see, every now and then, fantasies can come true, if you want them enough.'

314

When it was over he lay contentedly like a little boy without a wrinkle on his face. 'Go back to sleep,' she said.

He opened his eyes. 'Give me your number.'

'Don't call me. I'll call you. Maybe. But probably not.'

'Nothing lasts forever,' he sighed.

'I love you forever,' she said. 'You know it, don't you?'

'I know it now,' he said, and she left.

She missed her next period and went to her GP. When the test came back positive, she waited until Tim was away on a short trip and late in the afternoon rang his office and asked to speak to Alison Blake.

That night Tim said, 'I have to go to Germany again on Thursday.' Then he noticed that there was no ashtray, no crumpled packet of fags, no burning snout. 'You've stopped smoking.'

'I'm going to have Luke.'

'You've decided to have donor insemination?'

'It's in there. I'm full blown, four-star pregnant.'

His pretty mouth sagged. 'Darling, that's wonderful. But –'

'You sound slightly less than delighted.'

'I thought you'd gone off the idea.'

'We talked it all through. You were okay about having a baby that wasn't yours. I came round to the idea eventually.'

'I thought we had to go together.'

'Darling, I don't want to hurt your feelings, but in this case you were definitely fifth wheel on the wagon. Will you be away for the weekend?'

'Maybe. I'm not sure.'

'Better talk it over with Alison.'

'I beg your pardon?'

'She knows. I've played my trump card and she's spitting.'

'What do you mean?'

315

'I'll give you six weeks to get rid of her. Until I've had a scan to confirm our baby is alive.'

He sat down hard. 'Who told you about Alison?'

'In the meantime you can sleep in the spare room. And if you must screw her, please use a condom. We have to think about Luke now, and God knows what twenty-five-year-olds do for kicks these days.'

The first time she had given her husband his freedom and hoped he would come round. He hadn't. Not soon enough. This time she would fight because Luke should have a father. And if impending fatherhood didn't make Tim see the light, she might introduce Luke to his real father one day. And whatever, there was Luke inside her. For a one-woman man, suddenly there seemed to be plenty of options.

Tim was stunned. He slumped in the kitchen chair staring at her like a tomcat nailed to a fencepost. He would either erupt in a temper now, which would be tedious, or make some idle remark, which would be a good sign.

'What's that form you're filling in?' he asked eventually.

'I'm ordering a dozen "Life Begins at 40" T-shirts.'

'A dozen?'

'For distribution to the needy,' April replied with her gentlest smile.

316

MAGS AND JIZZY

Sarah Goldsmith

Sarah Goldsmith was born at the beginning of the Second World War, and discovered the excitement and power of fiction during the long noisy nights of the bombing, creating dramatic adventure stories inside her head when she couldn't sleep.

Writing remained a secret ambition until her tutor at the London School of Economics advised her to take up teaching as this would leave her plenty of time to write. The scheme misfired as the school was in an area of London of growing social unrest. Eventually, she found herself the deputy head of a large comprehensive school with a cupboard full of uncompleted fiction.

She now runs a successful antique business, and has found more time to write in the last two years.

MAGS AND JIZZY

It was a good day for a journey, one of those quiet autumn days when it's easy to travel further than you intended. Then, as I neared the house, the light changed, as though someone, somewhere, had opened a great door, and I knew I was close to the sea. The books turned out to be disappointing, mostly early history with the past tidied safely inside leather and buckram. He'd only had one other major interest. 'A scholar rather than a gentleman, if you ask me, Miss,' said the porter tartly, as he brought the catalogue. 'The London trade's all over it in there, like flies on meat,' and he nodded at the tables holding the discreetly listed 'specialist items'. The piles of children's books, when I found them, were just the leftovers of childhood, his name on every flyleaf. I wondered if anyone alive had still called him Davey.

When I left I was still thinking of the child, who'd kept his books as carefully as later he cherished his collection of pornography. I imagined him slipping out with me down the stone steps, drifting through the leaves at my side. I was touched by a grief I couldn't explain and couldn't shake off. Now I know it was a warning, for ahead of me was my past, waiting, alive and painful in the comfortable snug of the Moon and Oyster, 'Accommodation Available'.

On the way through the village in the morning the place had looked appealing, hanging baskets bright with flowers, and an old dog sleeping in the doorway. Across the road the Blackwater was barred with light, and small boats swung in the tide. But by evening, tired from the viewing and troubled by the intangible presence of the child, I wasn't so sure; a pub's always a pub, especially after dark. However, I'd booked a room; I'd made a commitment. I had supper by the log fire and set to work tidying the catalogue for next day's sale. I hoped I'd be in bed before the two men arguing loudly in the corner actually came to blows.

The pale youth listening open-mouthed behind the bar didn't look capable of dealing with trouble. The three-legged cat, who'd arrived with the steak and kidney, obviously didn't think so, and jumped into my lap. I hadn't the heart to abandon it, and sank back in the red plush chair wishing I was somewhere else. I spread my newspaper in front of us, watching the men in a brewery mirror.

Suddenly the smaller, bald man lurched towards the other, arm swung back to punch. The lad only had time to gape wider, when he was swept aside by a thin woman in a voluminous overall who barely reached his shoulder. She had a snapping vitality that drained the aggression from the combatants in seconds. The small dark eyes, brilliant in the narrow white face, assessed the scene in one comprehensive sweep. Her voice had the cutting edge of South London and the easy authority that comes from subduing many rowdy Saturday nights. Anger barely gave colour to her cheeks.

'Out!' she said. 'Both of you. Out! Mike, go home to your poor wife, and behave yourself when you get there. You'll not get served in here again if I hear you haven't!' She turned on the aggressor, 'And you, Ossie, walk round the quay and cool down.' She put a hand on his arm, adding more gently, 'You can pop into the kitchen later, if you like.'

320

If either man considered arguing, the ferocity with which she skewered a thin strand of mousy hair back into the knot on top of her head encouraged instant compliance, and they were both in motion towards different doors as I let the newspaper fall and said, 'Mags. It's Mags.'

The small figure, scanning the other self-consciously well-behaved drinkers in the snug before leaving, looked across at me, frowned and then smiled; a wide generous smile more warming than the fire. 'Well I never. After all this time, Miss. You, of all people.' She lifted the flap of the bar counter and came to sit opposite me. The cat changed laps.

'You were designed to be a landlady,' I said, and laughed. 'It's lovely to see you again, Mags.'

'You're not still teaching?' she asked, stroking the tabby fur. 'No, not wearing a suit like that.'

'I have a bookshop,' I said. 'Old books, a lot of children's stuff.' I saw Mags looking at me. 'It's peaceful,' I said.

'You're wasted on books,' she said, simply. 'Are you married? Not to that long blond chap that used to come for you, I bet.'

'Not to him at all.' I shook my head. 'Two others though, and nobody now. What about you?' As I said it, I knew the answer. She'd never been pretty, never had a sense of fashion or style; but Mags was solid gold, and there are enough people in the world needing kindness and strength close to them to see she'd always have a queue for her kitchen, and no doubt for her bed too.

'I lost Ted a year ago,' she said, and I felt myself suddenly shut out of her world. Then she smiled at me, 'Are you the Kate O'Meagher who's staying here tonight? I didn't recognize the name when I saw it in the book, of course. You were Miss Callan then.' I nodded.

321

'Give me ten minutes with the silly devil who picked the quarrel,' she said. 'He'll be back in a tick; widowed last month and not managing too well.' She stood, looking tired, smoothing her skirt. The cat climbed round her neck, hanging like a tippet. 'I'll make us some tea when he's off home. Elvis there will tell you when the coast's clear, and show you the way. He ought to be able to manage that,' she said disparagingly. 'Mrs O'Meagher,' she added quietly. 'After all this time.'

'You called me Kate once,' I said. 'I'm still Kate.'

I watched her go. I'd last seen her in the late sixties when I was fresh from university and still new to teaching; learning by doing. Mags was fourteen, and she'd never had to learn anything; she'd been born knowing and understanding. I worked it out. She must be nearly forty now. She'd never been a day younger than that. Eight years between us now; then it had been a lifetime. I wondered if I'd caught up with her yet.

On the first day of that autumn term, I found I'd been rewarded for surviving a year with the worst class the school had on offer. I'd been promoted to a group of girls nearly at the end of their compulsory education, already hardened against all attempts to educate them. Most of their energy was consumed by the care of their backcombed and lacquered hair, piled on top of their heads in elaborate structures called beehives.

A colleague ran her eye down my list, 'You're lucky,' she said, 'you've got Mags.' I looked puzzled. 'Thin mousy girl. Leave everything to her. She ought to be on the staff really.' Then she pointed to a name written in ink at the bottom of the typed column, in the neat handwriting of the elderly head. 'The gods haven't smiled on you entirely,' she said; 'you've got Jizzy too. I suppose that's fair.' The bell rang before I could discover more.

In the classroom my new charges and I eyed each other warily. I was expected to teach them everything except a few practical subjects. 'I'm Miss Callan,' I said, and called the register. They were bored already. Neither M. Roper nor J. McPherson were present. I tried to interest them in electing a form captain.

'We always have Mags,' said the owner of the biggest beehive flatly.

I talked of proposing, seconding, and secret ballots. Someone proposed Mags Roper. Someone seconded her. Nobody else stood. 'But she isn't here,' I said. They said her mum had had another one. 'She'll be back soon,' they assured me comfortably.

Mags and Jizzy turned up together on the following Monday, halfway through the morning. A murmur of approval ran round the class while I was busy at my desk. I turned and looked into the oldest eyes I'd ever seen, set in the pale face of a weary teenager who was leaning against the back of my chair. Her hair was lank, not a vestige of the uniform backcombing; a tattered cabbage white in my crowd of painted ladies. 'Hello Miss,' she said. 'You look like you could do with a cuppa. I'll just nip to the kitchen for you, shall I?' I made a faint protest about staff who were teaching not sending girls to make tea. 'Never mind that,' she said kindly; 'you can't teach us nothing with a headache. I'll bring you a aspirin'; and she'd gone. The class relaxed, clucking approvingly. Ten minutes later Mags was back, with one hand round a cup. 'I found Jizzy too, Miss,' she said, 'in the cloakroom. She didn't like to come in as she didn't know you. I told her to come in after break.'

Before I could investigate further, the bell rang and my charges swept Mags off into the playground. Why they liked this thin, plain girl so much, what appealed to them in someone so unadorned, I didn't know. Their happiness

323

lay in lipstick, combs, and nail polish; and the best you could say of Mags was that she was clean and neat. All her clothes had been bought for her to grow into, but she'd failed to live up to their expectations. Her father, someone told me later, was a small-time criminal of the honourable old-fashioned kind, no violence, no mess; and no prosecutions either. The class were neutral about his criminal activities but generally hostile to his genius for procreation. It wasn't glamour from her dad that made her so attractive to them.

In the staffroom, I told my friend Mags had turned up, and the J. McPherson from the bottom of the register had been sighted and was joining me next lesson. 'You're in for a treat,' she said sardonically. 'Good luck.'

After break came Religion, a subject pretty equally beyond all of us except a quiet Muslim who stayed, looking baffled, and two Seventh Day Adventists who contemptuously left us to our amateur efforts. As the class got out their Bibles I ran my eye round the room. The slight, dowdy form of Mags was in the seat of honour, by the radiator. And we seemed to have been joined by something very exotic indeed.

In the back row sat a girl with a startling face. At first glance she looked like an exquisite eighteenth-century French doll. Her skin was pale, with a delicate rose blush spreading across the high cheekbones; the texture was flawless, the colours blended with astonishing artistry. The lovely painted face was framed by shining black curls, but the whole effect was unreal; like a picture on porcelain, not powder and paint on living flesh. I wondered if she could speak without cracking the mask. As I moved closer, I saw that each long, carefully blackened eyelash was paired with a neighbouring lash, at the tip, to make a delicate lace edging to the pansy brown eyes. The lids were a subtle mixture of blues and mauves. Her lips were beautifully shaped, moist and brilliant. The class had become unnaturally silent.

The rules about wearing make-up were the stuff of life to pupils and staff, and the removing of nail polish and lipstick the primary educational aim of the remote head. I didn't know much in those days, but even I saw that this was something other than the terminal statement of defiance it seemed. The painted ivory head and neck vanished into the collar of a blue school shirt. The hands coming out of the cuffs were unadorned and brown. Inside their frilling of lashes, the eyes were nervous.

'Hello, Jizzy,' I said.

The mask moved slightly round eyes and mouth. 'Hello, Miss,' she whispered. 'Sorry I'm late.'

I never discovered her background. She claimed the mother she'd never seen was English; and her father, who appeared intermittently, was certainly from Martinique. She lived with someone she called Gran, who was a St Lucian. Those were the days before large-scale immigration into South London, and the handful of black girls in the school, straightened their hair and tried for frumpy respectability. They were quietly, unapproachably, miserable. Jizzy seemed to be secure and happy behind her mask.

The school was collectively baffled by her, and she was sheltered by a human conspiracy, as elephants are said to support weaker members of their tribe. Colleagues would tell girls sitting next to her to remove their lipstick, and the order would be carried out – with a routine dragging of feet; neither side referring to Jizzy's thickly painted face. Senior staff would send her on interminable counting trips to the stock cupboard to hide her from visiting dignitaries; and the day of education welfare officers and psychiatrists had not yet dawned. The only person not part of this community of wilful blindness was the head.

She was elderly and in the straight-backed tradition of female education. She gave me her first acknowledgement of my existence early that term – a slight frosty smile. She'd never approached the room where I'd battled with the unruly class of my first year, but now she occasionally looked in through the corridor window. Then she'd send her deputy to complain. We all resented this except Mags, who said her auntie had been like that. 'They get spiteful towards the end. You can't blame them,' she said philosophically.

When a good deal of anticipatory sharpening up was going on before an inspection, a mass confiscation of cosmetics was ordered from on high, and met with near rebellion. The goods demanded were expensive and represented many hours at Saturday jobs. The head made her first personal appearance inside my door just after the order had been relayed, and derision rumbled towards her across the room. She was caught, old and helpless, in their scorn, saliva quivering in the corners of her lips, and her small eyes hot and venomous. I was a knot of disgust and pity. Mags put up her hand. 'Please Miss, I've got a message for you from my Dad.' She slid out of her seat and took the head's arm, and the unlikely pair left the room. The deputy, a tall elegant woman who would have looked more at home shopping in Harrods, leant towards me. 'What a remarkable girl she is,' she said quietly.

The storm about the mask broke a week later, when the inspector took everyone by surprise by growing tired of girls and going to inspect the stock cupboard.

The deputy came to see me in the staffroom. 'We've got to do something about Jizzy,' she said. 'The inspector noticed her.' How could he not? An orchid blooming among the exercise books, pens, and blotting paper could not have looked more bizarre than Jizzy; as she counted and stacked and tried not to hear the rustle of mice.

'The head says she must be made to take it off.' There was silence.

'I've never seen her without it,' I said. 'No one has. It takes her two hours every morning.' I tried to make it sound like some kind of achievement.

'I realize that's why she's late every day. And the lateness is another thing we can't ignore.' She paused. 'She'll put it straight back on again, of course; they all do. But the head feels she's getting away with it. We're not even trying to make her conform.'

'She isn't like the others,' I said. 'They paint to be pretty and grown up, and attract the boys. Jizzy does it because that's her face. She works harder than a lot of them, she's polite, she wears school uniform. She doesn't wear nail varnish,' I added.

'If she painted her nails as well she'd not be in before lunch,' she said crossly. She sighed, and looked out of the window at the crowds in the playground. 'Every time I see her I wonder what's going on underneath. When I was a child I had a book of watercolours of Japanese women. They had extraordinarily serene painted faces; as though they didn't feel anything. I spoiled the book, trying to wash off the masks to see what they were really like.'

'Taking it off would be like making her undress in public. We can't be so cruel.'

The head's representative sighed and showed me her orders, written in the tiny unmistakable handwriting; clear, unequivocal. 'I'll write to her grandmother first,' I said.

Before the letter was posted the head took action. She chose the afternoon assembly for Remembrance Day, with the whole school present. 'Jezebel McPherson,' she said from the platform, 'you will go and get that stuff off

327

your face. Miss Callan, go with her and make sure she does it.' My class gasped, there were giggles from the first years at 'Jezebel', in common humanity never used. Jizzy crept out, the rigidity of the mask allowing for no expression. Stiff with anger, I walked after her.

The cloakroom was narrow, long and cold. There were shallow stone sinks, green brass taps – cold water only, one grubby roller towel, and a few warped squares of rock-hard soap. I sat on the edge of one of the sinks, waiting until I stopped trembling. The concrete floor had a drain down the middle, like a slaughter house. When I looked up at Jizzy two tears were making their way across the flower-like cheeks. 'If you like,' she said unsteadily, 'I could run home. Gran wouldn't mind.'

I searched my handbag and found a clean handkerchief. 'We could use this,' I said. I handed it to her. She ran it under a tap, and dabbed her face. Where the icy water had touched her skin there was a slight blush visible under the mask, but that was all. She peered into the stained mirror and then looked back at me. We both knew it wouldn't do. To our enormous relief, there was a rustling outside in the corridor, and Mags came in.

She was carrying a bulging school bag. By the set of her shoulders I realized she was very angry indeed. 'I've been to the classroom,' she said. 'The girls said I could take what we wanted.' On the floor she spread some shapeless fabric, her offering for the afternoon's needlework lesson. On this she tipped all the cosmetics my class considered essential to survive a school day. Jizzy examined them with interest.

While she chose what she needed, Mags collected the staff kettle from the tea cupboard, and a clean white enamel bowl. We sat Jizzy in a chair, put someone else's needlework over her hair and round her neck, and to the muffled sound of war-like hymns, we stripped Jizzy's face

328

to the skin. Mags, not normally a chatterer, kept up a steady flow of conversation.

After we'd patted her skin dry, I combed out the shining black curls and stood back to look. Jizzy painted was exquisite, and disturbing. Jizzy unpainted was something simpler, something more alarming. She was beautiful. Her flawless skin was the colour of dark honey, the hollows of her cheeks had bluish shadows and an apricot's fine bloom covered everything. Her dark lips were beautifully shaped, and her lashes, without the corseting of the thick mascara, softly fringed her almond eyes. Both her lashes and brows had tawny lights in them, and the slanting shading on her eyelids had a subtlety not even her skill with brush and colour could match.

Mags, pushing a lank piece of her own hair back behind her slide, and stuffing both her hands under the apron (also courtesy of the tea cupboard), looked at Jizzy with admiration and said, 'You're really pretty, Jiz. You don't need another face. Why'd you do it?'

Jizzy looked down at her hands. 'When I was little I wouldn't go out. Then I put on my face and it was all right.'

'You look better without it,' said Mags.

Jizzy stared up at us, then pointed at the dirty tissues on the floor. 'That's me,' she said. 'That's me inside.'

'You don't seem to mind us looking at you now,' said Mags.

'You're different,' said Jizzy flatly. I hoped it was a compliment.

The singing started again, loudly. The final hymn. 'What are we going to do?' asked Mags. The brown eyes looked anxiously at her, then at me.

'We're too late to go back in there, thank God,' I said. 'It's form rooms for the last hour.'

'I can't,' said Jizzy, panic rising in her voice. 'I can't go out. Not without . . .' And she looked at where her face lay in ruins. Tears began to slide down her cheeks again. 'I can't even go home now.' Her voice was thin with fear.

'There's no one outside now,' said Mags 'We could go to the classroom while they're still in the hall.' She looked across at me. 'That big cupboard in the back . . .' I nodded. 'You take her,' she said. 'I'll clean up in here.'

It wasn't far to the classroom, through the large tiled corridors, but it was a nightmare for Jizzy. She clung to me, her face buried in my shoulder, shivering like a terrified animal. Her fingers tore my clothes where she clutched me. In the classroom she bolted into the book cupboard and closed the door.

The girls clattered back almost at once, chittering with collective indignation. 'Fancy calling her Jezebel like that. In front of everyone! How would she like it?' 'Doesn't she think she's got feelings?' 'Why didn't she pick on me? I wouldn't have cared.' 'Just like her to pick on poor Jiz. She can't help it, can she, Miss?' 'Miss, wasn't fair, was it, Miss?' 'Miss, don't you think it was unfair?'

'I think it was unfair and unkind.' There was a sudden silence. No teacher ever criticized another, let alone the head. 'The headmistress isn't very well, and she isn't being as kind as she would usually be.' The silence became incredulous. 'Jizzy's sorting some books for me now.' I pointed to the back of the room. 'It's easy to criticize other people. But can you do better? I'm going to read to you, and Jizzy will sit in her seat in the back row. Can you be kinder than the head's been, and not turn round?' Mags slipped back into the room and sat down.

'Did she take it off?' someone asked.

'Yes.' I said.

'What's she like, Miss, without it?' asked someone else.

'Beautiful,' I said.

330

Mags sat, straight-backed, facing the front. Silent. The eyes slid along to look at her. One by one they straightened in their seats. Backs rigid. 'I'll read to you,' I said. I'd already read them part of Paul Gallico's 'The Snow Goose'. This story had somehow pierced their lacquered shells, and touched their hearts. I knew they were looking forward to the rest of it. I started reading. Jizzy slipped into her seat. It was the most attentive audience I'd ever had. The love story of the misshapen man and the young girl, and their love for the injured bird, filled the room. I finished the story seconds before the bell rang. They'd managed to pass each other handkerchiefs without so much as a small glance behind them. I was close to weeping myself, what with one thing and another. Somebody gave me a nearly clean tissue and I used it gratefully.

They stood up and filed out, eyes forward. Jizzy had her head buried in her arms.

Mags sat still by the radiator. She looked across at me. 'Do you have a scarf, Miss?' she asked. I didn't. I walked over to Jizzy. 'It's dark outside now. Could you walk home?' She shook her head without raising it from the desk.

The door opened quietly. The tall figure of the deputy came quietly into the room. She dropped her silk scarf on the desk in front of me, and left. We made Jizzy a headdress a terrorist could have worn with confidence. We showed her in a tiny mirror from someone's desk. Mags said she'd walk home with her, and I watched them heading for the stairs, Mags with a firm grip on Jizzy's arm.

The boy lifted the wooden counter, grinning and beckoning me into the area behind the bar. In the cheerfully cluttered kitchen the old dog slept by the Aga,

331

his chin on a cardboard box, and Mags was smiling at me across a large brown teapot.

'It's a bit off the beaten track for a Clapham girl,' she said, pouring tea into huge cups. 'It's all sailors and Cockneys round the Blackwater. My dad said it should have been Kent if I'd wanted the country. He remembered the hop picking.' Mags hadn't put on weight with the years. She looked well, wiry and strong, inside the large apron. 'You know you're a bit responsible? Do you remember that book you read us, about the marshes and the wild goose? I loved that. We all did. Well, after I met Ted he had the chance of this pub, although he wanted Battersea really; South London was all we knew. But I came in here and looked out the windows, and I could see that book. Daft, I suppose.'

'I was thinking about that, outside,' I said, taking the tea and sitting at the table. 'Do you remember Jizzy?'

Mags looked at me, her face crinkling with laughter. 'Remember her! I should think I might! Whose boy do you think that is, minding my bar? That's her Elvis. I told her not to call him that, look at all the trouble she had with her name. You'd think she'd know better.'

'What happened to her?' I asked, casually.

'You didn't stay to find out, did you, Kate?' said Mags drily. 'A year of us wouldn't have been too much, would it?'

'I always thought you realized,' I said. I stared into the dark liquid in my cup. 'I was pregnant. Do you remember what that meant if you weren't married? I wouldn't marry him. It couldn't have been worse than the marriages I made later, but it seemed a matter of principle then. Now, I don't know. I'd have had the baby.' I heard my voice as though it belonged to someone else, someone upset. Mags sat down opposite me.

'It was one of those backstreet affairs. I couldn't have

332

children after that.' I drank some of the tea. 'I was ill for a long time. I didn't want to teach any more. It had gone somehow, with the baby.'

'A pity,' Mags briefly touched my hand with hers. She still looked tired. 'You warmed that place up a bit, and it bloody needed it. Women pretending to be God, and knowing less about life than we did. Not that it's better now. All "see the social worker, why don't you", and teachers not knowing whether to be mates with the parents or the kids.' She sighed. 'Still, we survived. Children do.'

'Do you have any of your own, Mags?' I asked. I couldn't imagine she didn't.

'Two girls,' she said. 'One's at college and the other's nursing. But it seemed like a regular tribe here most of the time; my brothers took after Dad, if you know what I mean, but without his luck. Their wives couldn't cope, having them inside so much, so their kids were here a lot of the time. And Elvis of course. He was born here.'

I thought of when I'd last seen Jizzy. I'd negotiated an uneasy compromise with the deputy. Every two or three weeks, usually on a Friday afternoon, Mags helped Jizzy take off her make-up. I was the official witness. Then Mags and I would return to the classroom leaving Jizzy to 'clean up', which meant repainting enough to get her home.

My last Friday at the school was several weeks before the end of the summer term. Both girls were part of the resentful rump who had birthdays too late to be Easter leavers, and were therefore sentenced to a final term's education. They tried to kill time graciously, but were less prepared to work than ever. I read to them a lot. They slept and dreamed, and waited for the day of deliverance.

I'd felt extremely ill all day, sick with the pregnancy, sick with fear. The abortion was arranged for the next morning. I was exhausted by the scenes following my refusal to accept the dutiful offer of marriage. The very seed of myself seemed threatened by the existence of that child, poor little thing. I knew I didn't have the courage to be an unmarried mother, and I knew if I kept the baby I'd have to take the man. I was quite sure I didn't want the man.

I sat, that afternoon, on the edge of the sink, while the girls worked. I felt suddenly dizzy, great clouds of darkness in my head. I was falling, then someone held me and I heard Mags's urgent instructions, 'Make her some tea, Jiz. Unless she gets worse, she won't want another teacher. Say she sent you, if anyone asks. Lean on me, Kate, you're all right.' I held Mags's arm as though it was all that stood between me and drowning. I remember the warmth of the early summer sun. Neither of us spoke. The tea helped; the world stopped spinning. 'Go home,' said Mags. 'Go on, Miss, go home. I'll tell them you had a migraine coming, and went off while you still could. Can you get home all right?' I never returned to the school.

In her warm, safe kitchen, I told Mags of the time that followed: hospital; then back with my parents. Then marriage, divorce; marriage, and divorce. Somewhere along the way I'd become a bookseller; a quiet business in a tiny shop, in a sidestreet in Cambridge.

'It's funny you mentioning Jizzy.' Mags looked at me thoughtfully. 'I've had no word for a long time. Then last week my sister met her boy off the train at King's Cross. She rang me to say guess who she saw at the station. She recognized the face. Well, you wouldn't forget it, would you? I've been wondering if I should go up; have a look myself.' She paused, inviting me to say something.

'But Mags, seeing someone at a station . . . it's hopeless, you can't just go on the off-chance. She could have been going anywhere.'

Mags was scornful. 'Liz didn't say exactly, but Jizzy's a

regular there, of course.' She looked at me, then exploded, 'My God you must have learnt something in all these years. What else do you think the girl could do with a face like that, and nothing else to go with it? Who'd have given her an ordinary job? If she was lucky and tough, she'd be in Shepherd Market by now, her own flat and a nice little nest-egg for when she's past it. Unlucky, and it would be King's Cross and a nasty pimp. Anyway, I've got to find her. I've got some lost property of hers. He treasures his birth certificate like it was made of gold, he's a right to see her.'

Small noises came from the cardboard box on the floor. Mags collected a dish from the dresser, knelt by the rustling box and took off the lid. The tiny hedgehog inside rolled into a tight ball, leaves from his bedding stuck in his spines. As he smelt the food he uncurled trustingly and began a noisy assault on it. She put the lid back on the box.

'He's a road accident,' she said, looking up at me. 'I'll look after him for the winter and he'll be off in the spring. Like Jiz. That's how I came by Elvis.' She bent over the old dog, stroking him. 'Things were bad, after you left. They got a replacement, a friend of the headmistress. She scrubbed Jizzy's face in the hall. You wouldn't have thought she had it in her, but Jiz put up a fight, it took four teachers to hold her. It'd be a lesson to all of us, the old bitch said. The headmistress came to watch. She looked like she enjoyed it.' Mags sighed. 'She died just after. Perhaps she wouldn't have done it if she'd been right.'

I sat appalled, my hand frozen to the cup. I'd learnt to live with the fact of my abortion. Responsibility for the harming of another child was unbearable.

Mags glanced up at me, and then back at the dog, gently pulling his soft golden ears. 'Jizzy never came

335

back. She never went home either. We all looked for her, but she'd gone. She kept in touch with me, Christmas cards and such. I don't know how she found out I'd married Ted, but one night she turned up here. Just before her time. She looked really poorly, or her body did. That face of hers had a life of its own. Thin as a rake, except where Elvis was lying. She didn't look fit for anything. Ted didn't want her to stay, but what could we do? Elvis was born here a week later.

'Poor little bugger. I never thought he'd live, he was that weak. She didn't know the first thing about looking after him, she could have been holding a doll. I told Ted we'd sort something out when the weather got better; find somewhere for her. But the first warm day she was off. I went upstairs because Elvis was crying, and there was a note, saying she'd be back in a day or two. I'm still waiting.'

'What does Elvis know about his parents?' I asked.

'Not much. His dad must have been white, I suppose,' said Mags, pulling herself up from the floor. 'She never said, but Elvis looks white. He's a good lad, but not a lot up top. He doesn't have his mum's looks, for which I'm grateful, but he's as kind-hearted as she was, and as soft. He worshipped my Ted.'

Mags had been widowed a year. Ted had died in a sailing accident in a friend's dinghy. She shrank as she spoke of it, as though the lamp of her life flickered. She needed to be busy, she said. Elvis was talking of getting engaged to a local girl, and she was asking about his family. 'If you go up there, will you look?' she asked. 'All he knows is his mum was a friend of mine. And I've said she was nice looking and a bit shy. When you come to think of it I don't know a lot else. Ted used to bring him books from the library about Mauritius, but Elvis never seemed interested. He'd go off with Ted birdwatching on

336

the marsh for hours, but he never seemed to take to reading.'

We settled comfortably round the table. It was a good evening. At some point, before I went to bed, I realized I'd committed myself to looking for Jizzy.

I had a few words with Elvis before I left next morning. Mags had told him I'd been his mother's teacher. He asked me what she was like. I looked at Mags. 'Beautiful,' I said. 'The most beautiful girl I've ever seen.' 'Beautiful,' he tried the word, looking out at the wind driving the tide across the Blackwater. 'Like out there?' he said, grinning. I nodded. He had his mother's eyes.

King's Cross was worse than I'd imagined. I hadn't been there for a long time and I knew there'd be beggars and prostitutes, male and female. But the station and the area round it was part of a city I'd never seen, or never noticed. It was the new London, risen from the ashes of the old bad London the Victorian philanthropists believed they'd crushed for ever. But it was only playing dead, and now it's risen again with dreadful energy, mocking our affluence as it did theirs. We never defeat the dark.

Thin youngsters lolled everywhere waiting for trade; pathetic and servile to their strutting young masters. There was no one remotely like Jizzy, and I felt painfully relieved. I wondered what on earth I'd have done if I'd found her. I rang Mags that night and told her it was hopeless. She sounded unconvinced.

Winter set in early. I was busy in the shop and I thought I'd let the matter slip from my mind. I went to London several times, but made no detours to King's Cross. Then, one night in December, I found myself staring at a pathetic bundle of rags huddled in a shop doorway. I'd found Jizzy.

She was searching for something she'd mislaid in her

layers of clothes. Strings of black greasy hair trickled from under a khaki knitted hat. A collection of bags lay next to her on the pavement.

I'd been to a reception at a hotel in Russell Square, and instead of getting a taxi for Liverpool Street and the train home, I'd told myself I wanted to walk off the noise and the pressure of people. It was a freezing night, the commuters had gone from the station, and the hawkers of goods and bodies were warming up for the evening trade. I was making a last circuit of the side streets, wondering why I was doing it, when I saw her.

When she looked up her eyes were unfocussed, like a baby's. I bent down and said gently, 'Jizzy, Mags is looking for you.' The mask had become grotesque, as though something feral was dressed up as human. White streaks barred her cheeks, and patches of random colour splotched eyelids and mouth. But the eyes, lying in the nests of lines, were still the gentle nervous eyes of the child I'd known. Her glance slid across me.

'Jizzy,' I said, urgently, 'Jizzy, I've been looking for you.' I thought suddenly – why should she recognize me, after so long? On the streets people survive by hiding: inside the layers of clothes, inside the thin bodies, inside their spirits; deep inside – so far in and so deep that nothing can touch them – hide the people they once were. I crouched down and put out my hand, willing her to know me. She leaned away but looked up. 'Jizzy,' I said. She frowned, then her mouth gaped in a nearly toothless smile. 'Miss,' she said. 'Miss. What're you doing here?'

She didn't wait for an answer, bundling her possessions hurriedly together. I put out a hand to stop her, and withdrew it as speedily as she pulled away from me. Beneath the layers of cloth, her arm was like a stick.

She coughed, not looking at me. 'I'll give you money so you can stay somewhere tonight,' I said, opening my bag

and hunting for my wallet. She took no notice. 'Mags wants to see you. Can we see you tomorrow?' She was turning to go. I was losing her. 'Would you like some new make-up?' I said softly. 'If you meet me here tomorrow I'll bring you some.' She stopped, her back to me. 'Tomorrow, Jizzy?' Without lifting her eyes from the pavement she nodded and shambled away.

I didn't telephone until I was home in Cambridge. I poured myself a drink and went downstairs to the shop phone. I felt better with the books round me. Mags took the news of Jizzy's present condition philosophically. 'I didn't fancy dealing with a pimp,' she said. 'It'll be easier this way. We'll just collect her.'

'Are you sure you want to take her back with you?' I asked. 'She looked perfectly dreadful.'

'You'd not look too hot yourself, Kate, sleeping rough,' said Mags sharply. 'I'm not frightened of dirt. You can clean dirt.'

'I think she's ill,' I said, 'There was no flesh on her.'

'Then we'll not waste time thinking about it,' she said. 'Where shall I meet you?'

There was no point in arguing. I had help in the shop, so I had the time. I told Mags if she drove down in the morning I'd buy her lunch and take her to a cinema before we went to meet Jizzy. That would give her a break before the long drive back to the marshes.

Mags brought down the pub's van, and negotiated a parking place for it in the arches behind the station. She had dressed for London in a brilliant red coat that engulfed her in its folds. She was carrying a large carpet bag. We took our time eating, and went to see the film I'd chosen. I didn't take in anything that happened on the screen, but Mags enjoyed herself enormously.

At dusk we went to the sidestreet. Jizzy wasn't there. The air was heavy with the smell of fried onions, poor meat and grease. It was too cold to stand for long, so we kept walking.

Mags had to deal with a pimp after all. We'd been to get cups of coffee from the station, and as we returned we saw a young man with a shaven head and boots, requisitioning the doorway for his two girls. They stood behind him, too bored to watch him kicking the bundle of rags off his patch. Rings in his ears and nose glinted in the street lamp as he turned towards us. Mags, with her small head and the thin bun loosely secured on top, looked like a fierce animal peering out of a burrow. He was no match for her. Her sheer force of will drove him off; his turn for abuse easily outweighed by hers. The girls smiled discreetly at his discomfiture. He grabbed their arms and marched them away. Mags knelt on the pavement.

'I've been looking for you, Jiz. You left something with me, remember? Well, I done my best by him, but it's time you came home.' Her voice was a soft comforting murmur. Jizzy seemed dazed, not quite conscious. Forgetting the best coat, Mags hauled Jizzy to her feet, keeping her upright with a firm grip.

'We'll get something hot in her before we go,' said Mags. 'Can you take my holdall, Kate?'

We made a curious trio as we headed into the warmth of the station. 'The ladies,' said Mags. 'We'll wash what we can reach.' We cleaned her up as well as we could. From the bag Mags took a coat and a pair of shoes. She stripped off the outer layers of Jizzy's clothing, throwing it, and her old shoes, into a plastic bag which she ruthlessly forced on the sour-faced attendant. She washed Jizzy's hands and face. Jizzy was upright, but her eyes were only half open; she didn't seem aware of what was being done to her. Mags produced a biscuit tin labelled 'Property of Sea Scouts', full of sticks of theatrical make-up. We used them freely on the bony

340

little face. 'Better not look under there,' said Mags, pulling the wool hat more firmly over the coils of black hair. 'And I don't want to think about what's underneath. But she'll do for the trip.'

Mags propelled Jizzy, shuffling in her new shoes, into the café, and I collected three cups of coffee and three plates of fish and chips. Jizzy stretched out a hand to pick up a chip; deftly Mags moved a fork into it. Nobody spoke. Jizzy ate little, gazing at her face in the mirror by the table. Whether it was the food, or warmth, or our company, Jizzy was fading; perhaps into sleep, but it looked as though life, having beached her at our feet, felt it had done with her.

When Mags came back from collecting the van, I offered to go with her. 'Well, I hoped you'd do that,' she said. 'I can manage, but I'd like the company. I can get you back to Cambridge tomorrow. Ossie'll be pleased to have something to do. Once I've cleaned her up, our doctor can look at her.'

In the back of the van, Mags improvised a bed – also courtesy of the Sea Scouts. We made her as comfortable as we could, and set off. I felt so tired, I had to struggle to keep my eyes open. Mags drove mostly in silence, only saying, as we turned down the road to the pub, 'I don't think I'll tell Elvis yet. It might be a bit of a shock.'

'After she's had a bath, perhaps,' I said. 'Can we get her in without him seeing her?'

'He'll still be in the bar,' she said. 'It's just on closing time. We'll manage.'

We did, just. We half carried her through the back door, and upstairs. The pub sounded busy. Mags ran the bath, and sent me downstairs to make tea. I heard her saying, 'I know you're tired, but you're not getting between my sheets with King's Cross all over you. And those clothes could walk to the dustbin on their own.'

341

When I went back upstairs with the tray, Jizzy was in bed, a towel round her newly washed hair. She ought to have looked better, cleaned up, but she didn't. She looked old and ill, and she was covered in sores. When I handed her tea, she made no effort to take the mug.

Mags persuaded me to go to bed myself, while she tidied up. She must have got to sleep in the small hours, but she was up before me – giving Ossie breakfast in the kitchen before our journey to Cambridge. 'Thanks for everything,' she said as I left. 'I'll have a word with the doctor today. She's no flesh on her, and she isn't what you might call awake, even when she's not asleep. I won't tell Elvis yet. I'll wait till she's a bit more with us.'

I rang the pub next day, and then every few days, for news. The doctor said she needed rest, she'd been seriously weakened by malnutrition and untreated chest infections. He said her heart wasn't strong, and that he was concerned by her lack of awareness. He said she was a big responsibility; and I think he was more concerned for Mags than he was for this outsider she'd casually adopted. Elvis had been told that Mags had brought an old friend to stay, someone who'd been ill. He hadn't made the connection between 'Jiz', old and ill, and the beautiful 'Jezebel' of his treasured birth certificate.

I drove over to them a fortnight after the rescue. The doctor was talking about tests in hospital, but said the shock of moving her might do more harm than good. Mags wanted to know what I thought. Jizzy was propped up in bed, and I thought if I moved a pillow she'd slip over and never move again. Despite the food, the warmth and care, she had shrunk. The skin was pulling back from her bones and, although the sores were healing, she looked dreadful. Her hands were cold when I touched them. Her eyes were half open, staring out of the window at the rocking masts. When I moved in front of the window,

342

they stared at me. She'd known me on the pavement, but she didn't know me now.

'I did her face for her, the first few days,' said Mags. 'But I don't think she notices now. I just rub some cream on. She likes that.' She produced a pot from her apron pocket and began smoothing it across the grey-brown skin. Jizzy's mouth moved slightly. Her eyes closed.

Later that afternoon Mags and I went for a walk, to discuss what should be done. The tide was coming in fast. The rigging rang sharply against the masts in the frosty air; so we walked to the music of bells. Geese flew heavily overhead, calling to each other. The air smelt of the river and the sea. I watched a white feather picked up by the water and whirled away. 'If I hadn't had that abortion, if I'd stayed until the end of term, if she hadn't run away,' I said. 'When I see her I want to think about her now, but that's what I think about.'

Mags took my arm. 'When you fall down a flight of stairs,' she said, 'there isn't one stair that's responsible. It's all of them. You can't say it was your fault, you going like that, you were just another step.' Mags screwed up her eyes and looked up at more geese heading inland. 'Somebody's responsible though,' she went on. 'Fate, Destiny; whoever arranged for a girl with those looks growing up where she did. She couldn't look after herself, and there was no one to protect her. That so-called gran of hers was nothing of the kind, and her dad vanished soon after she did. She was too soft; that's why she was only happy inside that mask, in her little shell. My mum thought she was pretending to be white, but it wasn't that. It wasn't colour.' I felt Mags propelling me back to the pub. 'You get through life the best you can,' she said. 'Fighters do best . . . Shall I let them take her to the hospital?'

Jizzy saved everyone the trouble of deciding. Two days

later she died. 'She'd become so quiet you'd hardly notice the difference,' said Mags.

I went to stay for the funeral. The coffin had been brought to the house for the night, and Mags had made her sitting room look lovely for it, with berried holly and Christmas roses. 'It's the only Christmas I can give her,' she said. 'Poor Jiz.'

The coffin was open. In death it was the bones of her face you noticed, balanced, elegant, beautiful. 'What about Elvis?' I asked. 'I told him,' said Mags, blowing her nose. 'I said he could see her tonight. He didn't make a fuss. I said we were waiting for her to get better before we told him, but she never came round properly. He's got some flowers to give her.'

Mags touched one of the cold hands. 'It's all right, Jiz. Your boy's coming to say goodbye, but I'll not let him see you looking wrong.' From her apron pocket she pulled a little pile of jars and boxes and, between us, we painted Jizzy's face. When we'd finished, I saw her as the child I'd known, and the woman she could have become. Elvis came in with a bunch of red roses and laid them on his mother's hands. Looking at his face, I could see he thought she was as beautiful as he had imagined her.

'Goodbye, Mum,' he said. 'I wish I'd known you.'

I put a single white Christmas rose in her hair. I couldn't speak.

'Godspeed, Jiz,' said Mags. 'You're safe from everybody now.' She reached into her pocket and took out a long white feather from a wild goose. She tucked it carefully into the scarlet roses.